D1236803

BOOKS BY RICHARD FRANCIS

Swansong   1986

The Whispering Gallery   1984

The Enormous Dwarf   1982

Daggerman   1980

Blackpool Vanishes   1979

Swansong

Swansong

Richard Francis

ATHENEUM   NEW YORK

1986

This novel is a work of fiction. Any references to historical events; to real people, living or dead; or to real locales are intended only to give the fiction a setting in historical reality. Other names, characters, and incidents either are the product of the author's imagination or are used fictitiously, and their resemblance, if any, to real-life counterparts is entirely coincidental.

Library of Congress Cataloging-in-Publication Data

Francis, Richard H., ———
    Swansong.

    I. Title.
PR6056.R277S93   1986   823'.914   86-47661
ISBN 0-689-11843-0

For Jo, William and Helen

And that your eyes come to the surface
from the deep wherein they were sunken

Ezra Pound

The Sooterkin

'Was this the face that launched
a thousand ships . . . ?'

CHAPTER ONE

David

The country was a wash of pale colours: pale yellow, pale green, pale blue of the foliage on the horizon. Or perhaps it was just his deteriorating sight – he hadn't been to the optician since Lorna died, nor to the doctor, nor to the dentist. He didn't know why. At first he'd thought it was simply because he was sick of such people and places, saturated with ill-health. Then he wondered if he hadn't developed a subconscious sense that there was something wrong with attempting to take care of himself now that she was beyond care. At his worst moments – which had begun, strangely, almost a year after his bereavement – he suspected that he just wanted to make sure that he would die himself as soon as possible. Hardly rational – you didn't die of toothache, the common cold, the only symptoms he'd experienced – but he was hardly in a rational mood during those times. He would walk around the graveyard, noting that *Anne Margaret Lacey b. June 7th 1826 Departed this life 19th July 1857* while *John Scott Lacey b. November 11th 1821* joined his *beloved Spouse* on *14th April 1905*. The poignancy of that vast interval of years, and then the sudden juxtaposition again, being buried in the same grave, side by side with a being from another life, another century, another world, would bring automatic burning tears behind his lenses, and the gravestones, plots, the houses, trees, fields beyond, would retreat even further into paleness, a landscape glimpsed underwater.

He wasn't in such a state today, but of course it had been a damp morning, like so many this summer, and the air itself, even though it was not actually raining, seemed continuously to have a film of water implicit in it, like a reading lens in distance spectacles. He was surrounded by the indistinct delicacy of the countryside. Something fast traversed a field to his left, a rabbit presumably. Then came a sudden putrid smell from the ditch by the hedge, where the exit water from the Maxwells' septic tank discreetly trickled in. It was a relief to be getting back towards the village after the loneliness of his walk. He had tried hard to find, over the last few months, the sort of consolations you were supposed to experience in the countryside, but had become less and less convinced of their availability. The countryside was just a place where people weren't, much like his life as a whole. He had a yearning for some northern industrial town, a hodge-podge of ugly buildings, thin busy people. It occurred to him that this image was based on the paintings of Lowry rather than on his own memories of being a curate in Oldham in the mid-1950s. Memories were a cheat: you simply remembered remembering. Already he was reliant on photographs to bring back Lorna, photographs that at the time had seemed so unconvincing.

But as his past grew more inaccessible, so did his very existence. He had a fading picture of himself.

He climbed over the stile and on to the verge of the main road. A freighter rushed by, churning up the air. In the past, as chairman of the village preservation society, he had made a fuss about them: now he couldn't think why. That rabbit had rushed over its field in just the same way, it hadn't stopped to admire the view. Only people like himself admired views, when they had nothing better to do with their time.

Anyway, there was the Cricketers, a hundred yards down on the right. Of course his dog-collar severely restricted intake. There were times when he envied Catholics, with their jollier, more generous traditions. Father Sweeney could drink himself legless and the community just thought he was one of the boys. It was to do, of course, with the mystical status of the priestly function in the Father's church. What the latter's congregation wanted was for him to behave like a human being. But an Anglican priest was a human being to start with; so people expected him to be a saint. And saints drank the occasional dry sherry, interspersed with many cups of tea.

Nevertheless he could have a couple of pints without eyebrows being raised. Concentrate on them, don't think of the third and fourth and fifth pints he wouldn't be having, and that pleasant state of warm muddle in which he could have gone back to the vicarage to drowse the afternoon away.

A group of farmers stood at one end of the bar, coarse and rich. He had come to dislike the breed more and more over the years, particularly as he realized the extent to which their income was made up of public money. It was as though they were on the dole, but receiving ten times as much as everybody else. Not a Christian attitude really; certainly not a pastoral one. He should sympathize with their difficulties in getting to the Kingdom of Heaven. They murmured 'Hello vicar' as he came in and looked sheepish. Then Gerry, a stocky one of about thirty, who was halfway through the process of turning from muscular to fat, so that at present he was of uncertain consistency, like a cheap mattress, began talking loudly about the recent birth of his daughter. No doubt it was for his vicar's benefit: an assertion of family commitment, a reminder of the forthcoming christening. His natural priorities immediately intervened and the account became a catalogue of boozing, a champagne breakfast to celebrate the birth which went on till late at night.

David turned to his own pint. At that moment the landlord's wife, Jean, came in from the vaults. She was plump and attractive, the perfect backdrop to his glass of beer. David had had a number of sexually cynical thoughts recently, quite independently of his grief, or rather in apparent contradiction of it. Sometimes he would have a heady sense of being fancy-free once more; though where his fancy could take a vicar in the middle of the Shropshire countryside was a question that didn't bear going into.

Jean leaned forward, resting her bosom confidentially on the bar.

'Have you heard the one about the man on his honeymoon, vicar?' she asked.

He took a sip of his beer to conceal his sudden interest. There was an undeniable intimacy about being on the receiving end of a risqué joke from a woman, particularly as even men rarely confided such things to him. Also, jokes made sex seem a simple thing, independent of particular people: men and women at large, not vicar so and so, not his dead wife.

'. . . Fished all the time, so he asked him, "Excuse me, I hope you don't mind, but here you are on your honeymoon and you're fishing all the time." '

She was leaning far over now, her breasts squeezing across the bar towards him like two round, tentative, interested animals.

'. . . "No, she's got a lovely face." '

'. . . "What about her figure then?" '

'. . . "She's got a perfect figure. Absolutely superb." '

Jean stepped back a moment, cupped her hands under her bosum and hoisted it up an inch, downturning her mouth and giving him a wide-eyed piquant look as she did so. Then she settled forward into intimacy once more.

'. . . "No, she doesn't smell. She wears the most beautiful, expensive perfume." '

'. . . "Then why on earth are you spending your honeymoon fishing all the time?" '

Suddenly, a voice from the heavens, definitive, even booming: 'Because she's got worms.'

David shuddered, shook, he could actually feel himself go pale. In front of him Jean's mouth dwindled in disappointment, opened up again to give a somewhat pragmatic laugh – landlady to the core – at the joke which had been wrested from her, then shrank in alarm as she realized David's state. He leaned forward to support himself on the bar; she leaned forward to attend to him. Even through his distress he noted how strange it was to approach each other with fixed feet, like a form of courtly vegetable intercourse.

'Oh David,' she said, 'I didn't mean – they're not that kind of . . .' Suddenly, seeing the opportunity of transferring blame, she looked up and beyond him: 'That was brilliant, that was.'

'Very average,' the aerial voice agreed. A hand came down and struck David on the back. 'How you doing, rev?' the voice continued.

David collected himself, turned, looked up. The speaker was only Terry Sutton, six foot two, be-blazered, cravated, brylcreemed, a fugitive from the early 50s, except that he was only thirty. It was as though he'd grown up in the opposite direction from everybody else: that was, of course, intrinsic to the effect of independence, of being his own man, qualities vital to the success of an insurance salesman.

'I'm fine,' he replied.

'You look a bit rough.' To Jean: 'Get the man another drink.'

Jean looked for a moment as if she wanted to explain, then thought better of it and poured the drink.

'I've got one already,' David said.

'Now you've got two,' Terry replied. Then he turned to Jean as she passed David's glass over: 'What about me?'

'You said get the man another drink. You didn't say anything about you.'

'Come on. You want to sell it, don't you?' Perhaps by an association of ideas he turned to David: 'Heard anything about the whatsit yet?'

'The what?'

'You know. Your . . . good lady's policy.'

'Oh. No.'

'Don't worry, the bastards will have to pay up. Sorry vic, but I know the sort of sods they are. I've sent enough memos to paper the wall.'

Lorna had had a small life-insurance policy. After her death there was some problem over its validity, since she hadn't declared, on her application form, that she'd had rheumatic fever when she was a teenager. It hadn't even crossed her mind, she was a forgetful person. Or rather, she had her own priorities. But since she'd died of heart

13

trouble, which could have been a long-distance consequence of the illness, the company had demurred about paying up the full amount of the cover. And while it demurred, it paid nothing. David didn't care. The whole business had come to seem like selling a corpse.

'Oh well,' he said philosophically.

'No, no,' Terry replied sharply, as if he'd been offered some sort of counter-argument. 'It's been, how long's it been? Nearly eighteen months.'

David put his glass on the counter abruptly.

'I suppose it has.'

'You're looking a bit rough, padre.'

Vicars weren't supposed to mourn; at least, not for eighteen months. Their loved ones went to heaven, what was there to mourn for? It would be an admission of failure.

'Bugs are having a field day.' Terry went on. 'It's the rotten summer. You see it in my line, of course, especially. Clients dropping like flies. Your line too, come to think of it, padre. You send them on their way and I shell out to the ones they leave behind.'

'I *am* a bit under the weather,' David agreed.

'Tell you what,' Terry Sutton said, leaning down towards him, 'I've got some of the old duty-free at home. Spanish brandy. Très medicinal.'

The upshot was that David had his boozy lunch-time after all. It lasted, in fact, until the early evening. During that time he made various confidences; spurred on perhaps not just by the brandy but also by the fact that he could say nothing directly to the likes of Terry Sutton about what was on his mind. What could one say, in any case, about a vacuum? He told him instead, to his later embarrassment and regret, about what had happened to him one night last February.

·

CHAPTER TWO

David

It was snowing. David sat in his study until late, working on his village history. Lorna had suggested the project, telling him she didn't want him sitting around all day worrying about her illness. She thought it would be a way of putting down roots, since at that time they had only been in the village for a couple of years. Even then David had suspected she wanted to feel he was settled in Saxton before she died. Nevertheless he had taken some persuading, since he feared becoming a bore, the hazard of his profession. Characteristically she had made the point that just because other vicars had written tiresome monographs on their own parishes, that didn't have to pre-empt what he chose to write about his.

He worked with the curtains open. Lorna hadn't liked that, claiming to fear invisible eyes in the darkness outside. Resuming his old habit, now that she had gone, had been one of his few small triumphs of post-bereavement practicality. Being reminded of the world beyond his study diminished his tendency to restlessness, and tonight he particularly enjoyed glancing up and seeing the light from his room catch the nearest flakes, establishing a territory that lay between inside and out. In a warmer climate he would have loved balconies and verandahs.

He was working this evening on the history of the most important of the local families, the Hartleys of Saxton. The line had become indistinct through a tendency towards daughters in recent times, but as you tracked back it became easier to identify. The Hartleys came into focus, perhaps because they were dead.

His gas fire in its tiled surround hissed enjoyably. Large snowflakes came out of the dark beyond the window, bloomed suddenly. The moment of pleasure dwindled away as abruptly as it had come. He'd developed a puritanical sense that he wasn't entitled to such moments; he had lost the touchstone of enjoyment. Lorna was dead too but *she* wouldn't come into focus. Sometimes he felt panic-stricken as he tried to summon her into his mind and she wouldn't appear. Of course, the more he panicked, the more elusive she became.

It was ridiculous, tinkering with long-ago Hartleys when what he wanted to do was remember his wife. Surely it could only be a matter of concentrating?

He sat and concentrated, then and there, feeling a little furtive, as if he were doing something not quite right, like conducting a seance.

Where to begin?

Her first heart attack, that was what came immediately to mind. That was important, a turning-point. It changed her. As losing your virginity was supposed to do in the old days. Losing your health-virginity. But perhaps he didn't want a moment when she changed, no, of course not, he wanted a moment when she simply *was*. When she was herself.

But she had seemed acutely herself when she had had her first heart attack. Even as she changed. You didn't change from one person into a different one. You moved on from one part of your own nature to another, you went round a kind of corner in yourself. He had seen her do it as her body bent, twisted, shuddered under the attack.

She was more acute, watchful, febrile, from then on, treading some boundary line of pain or exhaustion. Previously she had gone in for grand, rather sloppy gestures, frequently misunderstood: she was considered dotty by many of the parishioners. She had once thanked a WI speaker on flower-arranging or some similarly appalling subject for her 'extremely boring talk' and then, when she realized what she'd done, collapsed into roars of laughter that were so contagious that even the speaker, before going home to cry her eyes out, had joined in. But after the attack Lorna became tactful, concerned. She didn't like David worrying, even though she obviously worried herself. She

16

was both sharper and more gentle than she had ever been. He sat and remembered. He couldn't remember.

That is, he remembered *how* she was, but he couldn't remember *what* she was. He remembered the impact she had on his world; he couldn't remember the world she was in herself.

Try to visualize something else about her, there was so much . . . The experience was exactly like that of forgetting a word that is on the tip of your tongue. You forget it because you know you are going to forget it, and for no other reason. The missing word leaves its exact shape in your mind, but none of the others you have to hand fits its space. It was as though, while he shared his life with Lorna, she had a particular height and width, and from them he made certain assumptions about her corresponding depth. But when she died he had to step out of the continuum and see her side-on, when he discovered that she was in fact paper-thin, photograph-thin, the next thing to invisible. They'd had a honeymoon, holidays, meals together, love-making, prayer, but it was as though he'd done these things with someone he now hardly knew; or perhaps that he'd been someone else when he'd done them. As if all the incidents had been very vividly recounted to him, rather than experienced. As if Lorna had simply *told* her life.

He walked over to his sideboard and poured himself a scotch. The cool liquid hit the exposed nerve of one of his upper back teeth and he nearly jumped in the air; then the alcohol seeped through, warming and anaesthetizing. He sipped gingerly from then on, however, making the whisky take a roundabout route across his mouth. The snow continued to flutter down silently, a thick creamy stratum forming against the bottom of the french window. He carried the remainder of the drink over to his desk and resumed work. How ironic that it was possible – or that it at least *felt* possible – to bring back some long-ago Hartley with whom he had no connection whatsoever, while he wasn't able, as historian, vicar, or husband, to breathe life back into his dead wife. Perhaps that was the whole point.

17

You could make Hartleys come alive because you yourself weren't part of the picture.

He worked until late; until the early hours. He had consumed a number of whiskies in the process and suddenly his eyes were blurred, his head fuzzy, even his body numb. It was time for bed.

He awoke abruptly, after perhaps an hour of dreamless sleep. All the effects of alcohol had worn off, his tooth was screaming. It was strange to be visited by such extrovert agony while the house and the landscape around were completely silent, while he was silent himself. He fumbled at the clock. Nearly three. Why was pain so much sharper at night? He remembered the long hours of Lorna's angina. Then it occurred to him that he was trying to make a cheap comparison, using her suffering to put his petty toothache in its place, and he experienced a pang quite independent of the sensation in his upper jaw. His head, and his emotions, were beginning to whirl. It was stupid just lying here. He got up to take some paracetamols.

He didn't bother to turn on the lights. It was as though you only turned on lights for effect. If Lorna had woken up and heard movements in the darkness she would have been afraid, if only for a second. The landing-light had been a signal, a beacon, informing her that there was nothing to worry about.

He walked down his creaking stairs. One half of his mind seemed to have devoted itself to experiencing the torments of his tooth, the other taking no interest in it whatsoever but simply carrying on as usual with his moment by moment impressions as if nothing untoward were happening. He passed the open door of his study, noticing the smell of whisky and the room's diminishing warmth.

At the end of the hallway was the door to the dining-room, through which he had to walk to reach the kitchen. It was as he put his hand on the knob of the dining-room door that he began to experience a sense of evil.

In the darkness it came through as forcibly, with as much substance and detail, as a visual image. He felt as if he had taken a crucial step too far. The coldness of the brass doorknob, the suddenly oppressive blackness all round, the sickly threads of whisky in the air, combined to give him the impression that his surroundings were organic and malevolent, and that he was enmeshed in them. The possibility of not opening the door, of simply turning and going back to his bedroom, didn't even arise. Even at this moment, however, he was aware that his fear was being handled by a mere section of his brain, like his toothache, leaving the remainder free to monitor the flow of experience. While his hand at the door shook, therefore, this part of his intellect noted that the hand was shaking, and thought how absurdly he was behaving. He opened the door.

The dining-room was just itself. He could see, dimly, the sideboard, the table, the unnecessary chairs.

He could see, dimly.

The room was being illuminated by thin cracks of light around the kitchen door. Oh my god, he thought, this time with all of his mind, his throat constricting, heart pounding. Then the same element disentangled itself once again. He had had a glass of water, to compensate for the whisky, last thing. He must have left the light on.

Then: a lurch back. The light around the door was not that yellow of an electric bulb, but white, pure, unearthly white. How boring, said the independent sector of his brain, making its last stand, terror is such an undifferentiating emotion. It takes no account of big or little but gasps at jack-in-the-boxes. People shivered at the thought of Dracula while Jews were murdered in their millions during the last war.

David walked across the dining-room as though it were rational territory, as though he were no more than an unimportant vicar in an ordinary room. The scheme of things wouldn't warp and twist itself merely for his benefit. But as he opened the kitchen door that outpost of confidence collapsed and he remembered that he was all he knew of the world and therefore willy-nilly centre of the stage. You couldn't stand indefinitely in the wings of yourself, looking on.

It filled the kitchen, bulk without mass. White, glowing, tapering towards the top, alive but unmoving, horribly silent. He cried out, turned, and ran.

CHAPTER THREE

Terry

It had seemed a good idea at the time. Have a heart to heart with the vicar in your nice little country cottage and then the local squire, who just happens to be your landlord, and who just happens to run a shooting syndicate, just happens to walk in. Hard to think of a better way of establishing your credentials. Hello Frankie, you know the rev, don't you? Oh yes, Terry, the god-botherer and myself are well acquainted. Everything spick and span, the brassware gleaming, a small summer fire going in the grate, carpet vacuumed, furniture plumped out, a bowl of fruit on the polished oak trestle. Terry liked things neat and tidy in any case, but he had spent his whole morning putting a warm shine on the rainy afternoon. Perfect. Except for his fatal error: the vicar.

Terry had just slipped into the pub for a lunch-time pint, a fair reward for all the effort he'd put into housework, and who should be there but the vicar, thin, glum, toothy, leaning over the bar so that he could point his spectacles down Jean's cleavage while he pretended to listen to one of her jokes from yesteryear. So of course Terry decides to improvise.

It didn't seem such a good idea now. Any minute Frankie would draw his Range Rover up on to the grass verge and clump in in his green wellies. Afternoon, miserable day, rub the old hands together, bring up the racing results, and gloop his local padre is barfing all down his front. Thanks a bundle for the hospitality, Terry.

'. . . hospitality, Terry.'

'You're welcome, vic. Fancy a cup of coffee?'

'I think just a little bra-uk-endy,' David replied. 'I seem to have a bit of hiccups.'

'A coffee might do the trick. Strongish.'

'I understand brandy good for settling the stomach.'

'Très medicinal,' Terry agreed sadly, pouring him another glass. 'Frankie Rutherford will be here any minute, said he'd call in,' he added in a warning tone.

'Really?' David replied without interest. He took another swig. 'This is a strong concoction hump. Tween you and me, more used to beer.'

'You should have said, I've got –'

'Yes, ghosts, you see.'

'Ghosts?'

'Here I am, a vicar, saw a ghost.' David's eyes, magnified, moist, rolled towards Terry. Even dressed in spectacles those eyes looked naked. Press the wrong button and you got such bloody awful claptrap.

Terry walked over to the window and looked out. The rain was teeming down. Ghosts, Jesus.

'Course I went down again,' David continued. 'Nothing there. Lay awake the rest of the night wondering what on earth. On earth, that's the point. The only supernatural. Eesh.'

Terry span back. No, disaster hadn't quite struck yet. David was taking deep breaths and staring at the carpet, fortifying himself against its pull. Terry knew that phase, dragging air in in the hopes it would dilute the booze. He turned back to the window. Sodding it down. Terry hated late afternoon, rain or shine. That was one of the points about joining the syndicate, being buried deep in some wood or field, your mind on the people you're with and the shooting, instead of moping around the cottage thinking you should be getting on with some work, lunch-time opening out of sight in one direction, evening opening below the horizon in the other, the sunshine, the rain, the day, winding slowly, depressingly, downwards.

Today was going to be different, with Frankie calling in, and the prospect of things to come. And here Terry was, trapped with a drunken vicar.

'Transubstant-tia-tion.' Intent on not slurring, David failed to slur when he needed to, like an over-the-limit driver thinking it was clever to go too slowly. 'That's all the mysticism I need. So I thought, what in the name of heaven?' Uncertainly, groping for his lost point: 'In the name of heaven.' He stopped, thought for a moment, rubbed at himself irritably. Then inspiration returned. 'The following morning I understood the whole thing.'

'What was it then, padre?'

'It was my tooth.'

'Your tooth?'

'What I'd seen. Ghost of my tooth.'

Omigawd. It was going to be the full works, green men, pink elephants, hairy things in his clothes, birds pecking his eyes, a whole zoo-full would be let out in front of Frankie, the cast-list of delirium tremens. Haunted by his bloody tooth.

'It was an upper tooth, see.' David opened his mouth. Terry made out a grey tongue, back molars agleam with fillings. He'd had his share to drink too, of course, and he was glad when the mouth closed again. 'Growing down from the root. That's what I saw, see. Big white thing, tapering up. My tooth was giving me gyp, in pain, ick, prodjeck the whole works outwards, imagine something evil in the kitchen.'

'I see.'

Terry was aware, suddenly, of a silence in amongst the crackling of the fire, the maundering of the vicar, the crunch of the rain against his leaded windows, as if, after all, there was something haunting about David's story.

'Also been snowing,' David continued. 'You know how shnow sines. The white light. And been working. Doing my history. Thinking about the past. Research on the Hartleys, matter fact, figures from the past. Take my point.'

There was a pause. David rubbed his hand over his face in an odd impersonal way, as you might rub your hand over a piece of furniture, or as an animal might wipe its face with

22

its paw. 'Perhaps my wife, you know, gone. Personal history too, in other words. Inpinge. My own ghost, so to speak.'

Bang.

Terry nearly jumped out of his skin, what the sh- bang, just for a moment he'd thought the vicar had . . . something, anyway, other than just drink, really seen a ghost, perhaps conjured one up, bang, bang.

'That'll be Frankie Rutherford,' Terry said.

'Oh yes. A Hartley, you know. In's much anyone is, so to say.'

Don't I know it, thought Terry sadly. The local aristocrat, welcome to my small rented cottage. *Your* cottage, rather. You know the vicar, don't you? No, no, that person on the settee with his eyes revolving. Answers to the name of drunken blob. Look, Frankie, can I join your shooting syndicate? I'm only an insurance salesman, but I'm good at getting the local dignitaries paralytic.

'Bucketing down,' explained Frankie, when Terry opened the door. 'Every time I step out of the bleeding ancestral pile, great lumps of water land on my head.'

He was small and plump, with a smooth pink face like a peeled shrimp. But the quilted sleeveless jerkin, the endless damp jumpers, one over the other, all different sizes, the ancient baggy trousers, sure enough the green wellies, displayed a total absence of style that Terry couldn't even attempt to imitate. You had to be born outside – above – the rat race altogether.

'Come in,' Terry said.

Frankie came in, dripping a trail. He smelled like horse manure. It was like inviting the scenery itself into the cottage.

'You know the vicar,' Terry said. The vicar rose to his feet, managed to stumble while standing still, sat down again.

'Well I'm damned,' said Frankie, 'the church and insurance both. Only need my quack and I'm all set for a coronary.'

'A connary's no joke,' David said sharply.

23

'Only a joke, reverend,' Frankie explained, unconcerned.

'Would you like a drink, Frankie?' Terry asked.

'Thank you, no. Steaming cuppa would be just the job.' Wonderful. He didn't want a drink. Of course not, it would spoil the show. The things the lower classes get up to.

'I'll go and put the kettle on.'

'Good lad,' said Frankie.

Terry left the kitchen door ajar. He filled the kettle with water, went over to the stove, lit a match, for some reason placed it to the far side of the gas ring. A circle of blue teeth promptly appeared, biting his hand. Christ, thinking so much about the goddam vicar, didn't notice how far gone I was myself.

He couldn't remember, on the spur of the moment, how to get his hand out of the way. He stood there, watching it cook. Suddenly, pain to the very marrow, a huge waaaaaaaaaaaaaa inside his head, only the mouth, remembering Frankie, syndicate, outside world, remaining clamped. He whipped his hand away. Impossible to keep it bottled up, a blister was forming before his eyes. He allowed himself a tiny whimper, ooh, umhum, just a teeny little groan, I'm entitled to that. Then he lurched to the sink and ran his hand under cold water.

'Topping up the kettle,' he called out unnecessarily above the rushing water. There was no response.

He returned to the cooker, put the kettle on the flame, and then went to the doorway and listened.

'Don't suppose you had a bob on Baskerville's Pup, reverend?' Frankie was saying. 'The two-thirty at Cirencester.'

There was no reply.

'Saw it coming a mile off,' Frankie explained. 'Good as money in the bank.'

Still nothing.

'Wondering what to make of that giant thermometer effort in the graveyard, vicar. Bit of an eyesore, between you and me. Bloody great billboard. Still, good cause, I gather. Recording donations. The old tower falling down, or so I understand. Something falling down, that I *do* know. Something always falling down, same with my bloody roof.'

More silence. Terry thought he detected a snore. He got the teapot down.

Suddenly Frankie was in the kitchen behind him.

'Pally's passed out,' Frankie explained. 'Never seen that before, vicar drunk as a lord. Ha, that's not bad, is it? Drunk as a lord.'

'It's since his wife died,' Terry explained. 'He's not been himself. He's been hitting the bottle very hard.'

'That right? Been widowed myself, but I managed to see the silver lining. Course I've lost the occasional animal from time to time. Horse or dog. Never binge, funnily enough, usually go for a walk, something of that kind.'

'He was boozing in the pub at lunch-time. I thought he'd be better off here.'

'Quite right, good lad. That's a nasty burn you've got on your hand.'

Terry was pouring boiling water into the pot. 'I fell asleep while I was smoking a fag.'

'Nasty. Don't smoke myself.'

What *do* you do? wondered Terry in despair. Surely aristocrats were *supposed* to be decadent.

'Anyway, I was wondering, you don't fancy joining a syndicate, do you, lad? Shooting. It'd cost you a few hundred a year, of course. But we've just got a vacancy.'

'Oh. That sounds interesting, to tell you the truth.'

'You *can* shoot, I suppose?'

'Oh yes,' said Terry, not necessarily lying. He didn't know whether he could shoot or not, never having tried.

'Big feller, aren't you?' Frankie suggested approvingly, as if Terry were so much livestock.

25

CHAPTER FOUR
David

Frankie offered to run David home, but his jeep-thing wouldn't start.

'Never mind,' David said. He stepped out of the vehicle and spoke into the open doorspace. 'I'll make my own way.'

'Bloody roof one week,' Frankie was muttering. David shut the door and stepped back onto the sludgy verge.

'I'd run you home myself,' Terry said. Then his eyes were inevitably drawn towards Frankie's small moon behind the puckering windscreen.

'No,' said David. 'It's only a couple of hundred yards into the village. Bit the worse for wear. It'll sober me up.' He paused for a moment. 'Been letting things get on top of me. You give Frankie a hand.'

'Funny about it conking out, isn't it?' Terry said, barely able to restrain his glee. 'Those things set you back the best part of ten thousand quid. He must be rolling in it.'

'He's a Hartley of Saxton. Hasn't got the name. All been girls in recent years.'

'Well, *he*'s a bloke.'

'Plethora of women,' David insisted. Long words seemed more accessible than short ones at the moment.

'I know my way round an engine,' Terry said.

'I'm sure you do. Yes. Many thanks. Off I go.'

'All the best, vic, we'll do it again sometime.'

'Yes,' David agreed brightly. Never, he added by way of a codicil, as he headed towards the blur. To have got so drunk; to have told him about the ghost. Even as he thought about it, that part of his jaw began to glow. He hadn't had toothache proper since the night in February, but every now and then he experienced a sort of decadent warmth. He thought suddenly, luridly, of hanged bodies

26

being decomposed in lime. Why on earth had the authorities indulged in such redundant cruelty? The condemned man had had to sit in his cell knowing that in a few hours or minutes, at a specific time that approached without mercy, he would be killed. Why add the information that he would then be rendered down brusquely, as if the powers-that-be didn't merely loathe what he'd done, but hated every detail of his body. To look at your own hand and know that in a few hours the flesh would be falling off the bone.

Lorna had been cremated. But of course that was different, dying from the inside rather than having death forced upon you. You didn't have the indignation, the sense of assault. She had simply developed a watchful engulfing sadness, as if being herself wasn't, after all, what she had expected it to be. One always knew one would die in the end; but when you became acquainted with your death it still seemed to contradict so much of the life that had gone on before. You didn't fear, like the condemned man, what would happen, you feared that nothing had ever happened.

He was now in the village. The dark cloud and rain made it seem dreary and much later in the evening than it was. His church tower looked like a greyer shaft of rain. Certainly the thermometer in the graveyard was an eyesore, as Frankie had said. The whole image of rising temperature was surely alien to the spirit of village Christianity. In any case, the pound marker had been stuck in the mid 1700s for some considerable time. Probably he ought to do more about it, milk a few farmers, prod Frankie Rutherford himself, but he wasn't able to put his heart into the work of patching together a rotting building. He spent enough time salvaging the past, one way or another. What he needed to be convinced of was the viability of the present. Nobody supplied you with a thermometer for that purpose. Warg. He belched and was nearly sick.

Arriving at the vicarage didn't improve matters. He went into his study and sat in an armchair, but the room began spinning and he stood up again. He felt irritated at the inconvenience. Even being on his feet and moving gently

27

around gave him slight vertigo, although a different one from the spinning variety. He became conscious of squares and rectangles – desk top, window frames, doorway – and they seemed to float towards him in insistent cubism. It was so boring – he couldn't sit down, he couldn't stand up, he was too tired to go for yet another walk, it was too early to go to bed.

He went into the kitchen and made himself a sandwich: two rectangles of cheese laid with drunken neatness between two squares of sliced bread. If you can't beat them, join them. He bit his way through in large semi-circles, but the sandwich still seemed to be angular in his mouth and slightly uncomfortable to swallow. Nevertheless it made him feel better, as if, having taken on ballast, he was less vulnerable to every whim and eddy of his surroundings.

He returned to his study. It felt damp and cool so he lit the gas fire and went over to sit at his desk. The rain was still beating hard against the french windows. He looked across his mushy lawn: between the big sycamores beyond you could see a section of road winding away up the hill. As he watched, Frankie Rutherford's jeep puttered past, leaving blue smoke in its wake. David took the cue and turned back to the record, on his desk, of some of Frankie's more interesting ancestors.

He had obtained it for the weekend from Shrewsbury Library, by benefit of clergy. It was *A History of Saxton*, written by a mid-eighteenth-century minister, the Reverend Richard Lloyd, though it hadn't been published during Lloyd's lifetime, indeed not until the nineteenth century, and it had never been reissued since, so the work inevitably was classified as Reference Only. But David hated working in libraries. He had gone in late yesterday afternoon, Friday, and had managed to persuade a timid young librarian that no one was likely to want to consult the text on the Saturday morning – indeed, on any other morning, or afternoon, in all probability. He promised he would return it first thing on Monday, emphasized that he was engaged in local research, ensured that his dog-collar was much in evidence, and slipped it into his briefcase. She hadn't said yes but lacked the nerve to object.

The Hartleys, one of the principal families of this region, live peaceably in their seat, are mindful of their obligation to the deity above as to their neighbours below, and discharge the responsibilities, as they accept the blessings, of the position which has been bestowed on them. All in all they are mild quiet people, who combine solidarity of understanding, agreeableness of demeanour, and benevolence of heart; excepting the younger son, Thomas, second child of Sir Francis Hartley and Margaret his late wife. This Thomas being a harum-scarum young fellow, much given over to idleness, his father

David turned over.

For a moment he thought a triangular patch of print was missing about halfway down the next page, and then he realized that a piece of torn-off paper had been inserted in the book – probably somebody had used it to keep his place.

He took it out and inspected it. On the obverse side, neatly typed, were two meaningless words: PREMO BULGE. Suddenly he remembered the offensive Frankie bellowing on about Baskerville's Pup in the two-thirty. Perhaps someone had placed a bet on Premo Bulge.

With the pernicketty exactness of lingering booze David placed the scrap of paper back in the book and read around it. The Rev. Lloyd catalogued young Thomas's debaucheries with gusto (it wasn't surprising that he hadn't endeavoured to publish the work during his lifetime). Tom had deflowered a village-full of virgins; obtained two hundred pounds, by false pretences, from Mr Jones, Sir Francis's steward, and squandered it by gambling in London; then romped off to the Welsh countryside and, having established himself with his friends in the town of Brecon, formed a club called the Terrors and, sure enough, terrorized everyone within sight.

It occurred to David that they must have been rather like

a chapter of hell's angels: bullying passersby, damaging taverns, making drunken nuisances of themselves. They held meetings in a room in the church tower, despite the pleadings of the vicar and churchwardens, indulging in adolescent satanism and on one notorious occasion systematically having sex with a girl they'd picked up locally. Whether this counted as group rape (or "ravishment" as the Rev. Lloyd put it) was a moot point, because they claimed she had voluntarily joined their organization. *Droit des seigneurs*, no doubt. They seemed to be able to get away with anything; indeed, the good Reverend was puzzled as to why they'd finally found it necessary to run off to sea. Run off they had, though. Thomas took a commission to sail to Farquhar Island in the farthest corner of the South Atlantic, where a fort was to be built, and any Spanish or French settlers were to be persuaded to leave. He had never returned, much to his chronicler's satisfaction, and nothing was known about his fate.

It occurred to David that he had noticed a Thomas in the Hartley collection owned by Frankie Rutherford, which he'd received rather grudging permission to photocopy some weeks ago. He hadn't got round to reading through the material yet: it was still stacked, unsorted, on top of his filing-cabinet. He riffled through it now, and shortly came across the remembered document. It was a single sheet, obviously the latter part of a letter to an unknown addressee, and was signed simply Thos: H.

We apples float, says the horse-turd, and sure this horse-turd, for such he is in truth, floats also and bobbes constantly at me. My troubles, if they could lie a little, would I have no doubt, settle, but this man will never cease to stir and agitate against me, preventing my peace with those I have offended, and destroying my credit, so I cannot patch my affairs together. Therefore I must go, leaving my businesse, and certain persons with whom, alas for them, I have had dealings, both undone together. This large fellow does not offer slander but sad truths about me; nevertheless

Justitia sine temperantia crudelitas est, as our good doctor would doubtless remind us, and to my knowledge I have done the gut-bag no harm on his own account. On whose account he thus pursues me I know not, nor what species of Mortal he may be. You may have heard tell of certain Dutch women, that on cold winter's nights they will draw up their skirts to warm their legs by the little pot-bellied stoves they favour in those parts, and tis said, in a few moments there is much rolling of the eyes and panting of the breath, and shortly tally-ho and taran-ta-la, they are heaving in the most exquisite Extasy, and all without a man being ever present in the room. These women bud out as tho with child in the natural course, only not so large, and finally drop a strange thing they call a *Sooterkin*, neither man nor beast, but a little like a Rat, having an unbreech'd woman for a mother, and to call Papa merely a Dutch stove. This Fat Man may be some such Sooterkin fully grown, whose origin is naught but heat. But whether a Dutch *Uncle*, or merely some Bastard of the human sort, he has chas'd me to the water's edge, and I must embark.

Surely this was the same Thomas? And yet, of course, it was also a different one. The letter gave a glimpse of the inner man – oppressed, resigned, practical, wryly humorous, well educated, frightened – which added a whole dimension to the Rev. Lloyd's itinerary of a rake's career. For a moment Thos: H. stepped out of the shadows, although behind him the shadows remained, in which stood the strange bulky figure he'd called the gut-bag. The latter could have been the father of some violated girl; a hatchet man employed by Mr Jones; an envoy of Sir Francis. Perhaps Thomas had finally solved the mystery; or at least escaped from it, in whatever future had awaited him on Farquhar Island. At the time of writing his letter, though, Thos: H. had been as much in the dark about the gut-bag as David was to be two centuries later, and this was no doubt the reason why David had a sudden, acute sense of the past

31

coming alive, if only for an instant. Perhaps an instant was all that counted: you lived your life in instants.

David was beginning to feel dry, his head was beating, he was developing an uncomfortable light sweat. He needed to wash the booze out of his system.

He went into the kitchen, poured himself a glass of water, and opened the fridge door to get some ice. His eye caught a four-pack of beer he'd bought the day before and forgotten all about. For a moment he was tempted; then he told himself not to be silly; then he picked out one of the cans, poured his water away, and replaced it with beer.

It was delicious, cool, bitter, thirst-quenching. He became drunk again immediately. Oh lord, he thought, as surfaces began to shift once more: how boring. He went to bed, held on valiantly while it span beneath him, and then suddenly fell asleep.

He awoke with equal abruptness in the early hours, frightened.

CHAPTER FIVE
David

The house was quiet, even the rain had stopped, just the occasional low swish of the trees. But he was shaking, restless with fear. He felt his jaw: nothing. He would go down, along the hall, through the dining-room, into the kitchen. If it was there, large, white, tapering, it wouldn't be his tooth but something from outside his body. Yes, he thought busily, if ghosts exist, they are all that exists. Everything else comes to you through your senses, and all experiences must therefore take place within your nervous system, your brain, your soul. But a ghost would be genuinely out there, beyond the mechanism of contact, making its presence felt by sheer overriding authority. Like God. He had come across bizarre religious sects, of course, but had never personally entertained the idea that there might be an evil god. That God might be evil. Alive, evil, and living in his kitchen. He heard himself giving a nervous laugh. That beer had been the straw that breaks the camel's back. He was still drunk.

He left his bedroom, taking his glass with him. Some water was necessary. A good excuse. If one went to *look* for a ghost in a sense the point was already conceded. He was going to his kitchen for a glass of water.

He walked to the top of the stairs. They were more visible than they ought to be. Perhaps drink sharpens the sight, like carrots, he thought, and laughed again internally. The stairs in faint procession condensed from an undue paleness in the well. Halfway down he stopped, rested his hand on the banister, leaned over, looked.

A thin shaft of light came from beneath his study door.

As before, a part of his brain remained uninvaded by the shock of fear, remarked that the light was yellow, not white, forced the tide back. He had left his desk light on.

David drifted down the obligingly creakless stairs, taking pleasure in the thought that his house was after all untouched, walked equally silently along the hall, silently opened his study door, and stood silently looking in. His desk light was on, sure enough, and beside it, leaning over, was a preoccupied silent figure. He wasn't God but he was enormous.

David stood and watched. The man was tall and even more fat, wearing a smart lightweight suit. He was bending from the darkness of the room into the light upon the desk, and David could make out his absorbed small eyes, a large mole on his cheek, a reflected circle of light glowing on his forehead. He appeared to be reading *A History of Saxton*. He didn't look up.

Not being noticed by the fat man was almost as unnerving as encountering him in the first place. Perhaps it's *me* who isn't here, David thought, and suddenly wanted to laugh again. Then he realized he was shaking all over, almost out loud.

He pulled the door to with wobbly hand, turned, walked through chilly water back down his hall. The front door was ahead of him. No, the unbolting would be too loud, take too long. He turned instead to the staircase and suddenly he didn't care how much noise he made, he rushed up it two steps at a time, and into his bedroom.

Bed, chair, table, wardrobe, Lorna's picture: there was no room here for the fat man.

When David woke up the following morning the incident hadn't happened. The fat man was a phenomenon of drink, of a disturbed night, of a difficult period in his life. David had told Terry yesterday about the ghost of his tooth; that must have predisposed him to another visitation. Then he had drunkenly ruminated on the story of Thomas Hartley, as recounted by the Rev. Lloyd, and revealed by the letter fragment. He had indulged in lots of overheated imagery about people looming out of the shadows of the past; and he had speculated about Thos: H's gut-bag. Thank god for the broad light of day.

Meanwhile it was Sunday, the big day of the week. He got out of bed, dressed, and went downstairs. As he passed his study, en route to the kitchen to make a cup of coffee, he opened the door and glanced in. Yes, all was in order, there was no sign of intrusion. His reading-light was off.

Just to be completely sure, he stepped into the room. Damp sunlight streamed through the french windows, there was no atmosphere of another presence. The windows were locked and they didn't seem to have been tampered with. He approached his desk. Again, everything was in its place. *A History of Saxton* was shut, as he'd left it. He picked it up and turned to the section he'd been looking at last night.

The scrap of paper was missing.

He checked his desk of course, his other papers, even the wastepaper basket, but it was nowhere to be seen; in any case he knew perfectly well that he'd put it back exactly where he'd found it.

'Did your friend get in touch?' the librarian asked as he approached her desk first thing on Monday morning. She glanced rather furtively around her to make sure nobody else was listening.

'My friend?'

'A man was looking for the book on Saturday. It put me in a very awkward position. I told him you'd taken it for the weekend for your research. The vicar of Saxton, I said. Oh yes, he said, I'm collaborating with him as a matter of fact. *I* was just relieved he didn't make a fuss.'

'He was a . . . ?'

'A large man, yes.' She blushed faintly.

'Yes, he got in touch.'

'I was worried.'

'I'm sorry to have put you to all this trouble.'

David was having rather more success in bringing history to life than he'd ever wanted – at least as far as the Hartley family were concerned. Thos: H's gut-bag had emanated from the past like a genie out of a bottle, visible enough to be seen by a young lady in Shrewsbury Library. *The* fat man. The Fat Man.

CHAPTER SIX
Terry

Terry was putting cream on his toes on Wednesday morning when the postman came. He suffered from athlete's foot verging on leprosy. The letter was from his ex, Ange.

Darling Terry, she began. That was a lie for a start. You couldn't have it both ways. You couldn't tell someone that going to bed with them made you want to throw up and then call them darling. Well, Ange could. I thought I ought to write to let you know of our change of address next month. We're buying a sweet little . . .

Mansion, of course. Sweet little mansion. Sweet little Georgian mansion, in all probability. Something for Ange to 'do up'. Something for her to make into a 'proper home'.

He put the letter to one side and carried on with his foot. The crevice in question was between his big toe and the next, whatever that one was called, his index toe. The maddening thing was that the medication seemed to make it itch more. Perhaps he was allergic to the blasted cream. He rubbed it in viciously until blood started to seep through. Giving up, he sprinkled talc on the resulting mess, and pulled on his sock.

What made Ange's rise up the social ladder so unfair was that she had been a secretary of the most basic kind when he married her. Perhaps he hadn't understood how basic. He'd been so full of enthusiasm, after his London disaster, so sure that he'd fallen on his feet at last. Really, it had been a matter of pulling something out of nothing. He'd told Tom Rutherford that he'd had enough of the big city and fancied a spell in the countryside. Tom, to Terry's amazement, since Tom lived with him in Battersea and worked for a crooked waste disposal operation called Renwick's, had originated in what he called an 'ancestral pile' in north Shropshire. Also his father, Frankie Rutherford, had a cottage for rent in the nearby village of Saxton. Within a matter of weeks, Terry was installed in the cottage and using what you might call street wisdom, Downing Street wisdom even, had got himself a job as a life policy rep in the local branch of a big insurance company. Ange was a secretary in the branch office. His cottage could just do with a wife; so could his white collar job. They were married in months. Ange had 'loved' the cottage; she thought it was 'sweet'; she was determined to 'make it into a proper home'.

This meant frilly toilet roll cosies, kidney-shaped cocktail cabinets, endless plastic and nylon rubbish. When Terry inspected Ange closely, he realized she was made of the same sort of materials. Certainly her hair looked nylon having been dyed and permed in a state of exhaustion, and her dress sense was strictly mail order catalogue. But she was pretty all the same and Terry was attracted to her.

Ange didn't reciprocate. She wasn't basic in *that* way, no

such luck. She 'put up with it'. Once she was so obviously lying on her back and thinking of England that he couldn't perform. He would never forget the bitter look her eyes gave his unsuccessful member. 'It's not a fat lot of use,' she said, 'and my god it's certainly not an ornament'. Ange adored ornaments.

She twisted the knife by having an affair. As far as Terry understood, the 'affair' side of life was just the part that didn't interest her. Also it was as sordid as possible. In the back of the other bloke's car, in laybys. Terry wondered glumly what she saw in him. Perhaps his *was* ornamental. Terry pictured frills, ribbons.

Everybody seemed to know about it. Of course. When Terry walked into the Cricketers he got the feeling that people had just stopped talking about him. He had begun to get in with the farmers; now they seemed *too* friendly.

And then Terry found out that the bastard who was screwing Ange was some kind of millionaire, and she moved with one step, although jump was perhaps a better word, into the economic stratosphere. Good riddance. She took all her nicknacks out of the cottage and he began the long task of replacing them with nice objects. He bought a silver mustard pot. He liked to be surrounded by quality things. He had always tried to extract style out of whatever he did. Dressing well, for a start.

Just as he was flipping his cravat, the phone rang, and ruined it. You had to catch your cravat on the hop.

'Glorious day,' said Frankie.

'Yes, it is indeed,' said Terry, cravat dangling.

'One thing I like to do on a lovely morning,' Frankie went on, 'is kill things.'

Today, of all days! His monthly receipts had to be recorded and they were hovering round the disaster area. Too many visits to the Cricketers, perhaps, but he always regarded that as time well spent – in the long run, anyway. Any of the farmers would know who to turn to when the time came to take out life-insurance. In the meantime he'd planned a busy day touting for trade and catching up on his rounds, followed by a long evening going over the accounts.

On the other hand, he'd been waiting to hear from Frankie for a while. In fact, he'd been wondering if Frankie had thought better of letting him into the syndicate in the first place.

'Will the other members be coming?' Terry asked.

'No, just the two of us.'

'Oh.'

'I thought I could show you the ropes.'

It was, then, going to be a test. A sort of probation.

'All right,' said Terry. Look on it as an investment, he told himself.

Frankie once more had on his quilted sleeveless coat, decayed jumpers, shapeless trousers. Terry felt conscious of the newness of his hacking jacket and cap. His wellies glowed in the sun. They started off with a roar.

'The old banger still seems a bit sluggish,' said Frankie, gnome-like behind the large steering wheel.

'This is a heavy-duty vehicle,' Terry reminded him. Having tinkered with it previously he felt he had a stake in it.

Soon they were slewing along mud paths into Frankie's woodland. It was idyllic, you had a pleasant sense that members of the public weren't allowed in. Virgin territory. Between the trees there were glimpses of fields of stubble.

'You've not started burning off, then,' Terry remarked.

'Burning off? Good god man, what are you talking about?'

'No, no,' Terry assured him quickly, 'I mean the stubble. Over there.' He pointed through the trees.

'For Christ's sake, you don't start playing with fire within miles of this woodland. This woodland is priceless. Goes up in smoke, it would be five hundred years before you could get it back.'

'I realize that,' Terry said, 'I just thought . . . Fire-breaks.'

'Firebreaks my arse,' Frankie said testily, and they jerked on in silence.

It was deep wood when they stopped. Terry took his shotgun out of its cover. Like his jacket and boots it seemed new and raw compared to Frankie's battered weapon.

'That's a nice gun,' Frankie said obligingly, and the dislike Terry had begun to feel since the fire-break business promptly dissipated. 'This old bugger shoots round a corner. Got used to it now, though. Aim at something else entirely and likely as not I'll hit the little bleeder between the eyes.'

'What little bleeder is it going to be?' Terry asked. 'Wood pigeon?'

'Heavens no. Give them a chance, it's still summer. We're just going to bag a few crow.'

'Crow? That sounds a bit –'

'Just making way for the game later. The crows have gone berserk this year. I always have a notion that wet weather makes them randy. They're a pest if you let them get out of control.'

'Yes, I suppose they are.' Humbly: 'They're a big bird, of course.'

'They're not so big when they're sitting on the top of a tree,' Frankie said. 'Like that one up there.'

He pointed. Sure enough, one sat obligingly up a tree, perhaps sixty yards away. It did look big as a matter of fact, big and feathery, as if loosely knitted. Terry raised his gun to his shoulder.

'Where's my effing cartridges?' complained Frankie, groping in the Range Rover.

Terry fired.

Three things happened. The right side of his head exploded. His shoulder was shattered. The crow fell off the tree.

Terry staggered, dizzy and in pain.

'A new gun takes a bit of getting used to,' Frankie said sympathetically. 'Perhaps you haven't been shooting for a while.'

Terry's vision was halved as an apple might be halved,

only with a ragged edge. Hearing ditto. Feeling as well, except that he still had some sensation in his left leg, which, like the right, shook as if it were working loose. All the deprived areas had an opaque numbness, with an insidious vibration or hiss involved in it, the afterwaves of that enormous noise.

But from his still receptive left side came the little bastard's accusation: Terry was lying, he had never shot before. The injustice of it made Terry frantic. What was worse was that Frankie was right, he *had* never shot before. But surely in the name of heaven he'd been vindicated by bagging his first bird immediately?

'I killed the crow,' he stumbled out.

'They always fly away, they're not daft, you know,' Frankie said unpleasantly, still loading his gun.

'This one didn't fly, it fell. I'll just go and fetch it.'

'Oh no, for heaven's sake. We never retrieve crows. I would have brought my dog, else.'

Perhaps that conceded Terry's point. You couldn't not retrieve a non-existent crow. Frankie's tone didn't indicate a change of heart, however.

'We'll wait here a few minutes, see if anything comes back,' Frankie went on.

'Mine won't come back,' Terry insisted. 'It's meeting its maker.' The numbness in his right side had become less widespread and sharper: a whistle in his ear, a twitch in the corner of his eye, a pain around the collarbone.

A few minutes passed. Terry and Frankie stood motionless side by side, Terry very aware of his height, which seemed a kind of silent insult to small squat Frankie, or at least a form of showing off. He felt taller than usual in fact, while beneath Frankie's battered clothes you sensed the sleek dumpiness of another species altogether, perhaps related to frogs. There was the occasional wash of stray wind in the leaves; the odd scuttering of an animal possibly, or just something falling through foliage; a pleasant oily smell from the Range Rover engine seeped into the atmosphere. Then a crow appeared, flying tiredly in and settling on the top of a big tree to the right.

'There we are,' whispered Frankie, nodding at it. He spoke as if it proved his point. Certainly the crow was big and sloppy-looking, much like its predecessor, but then what crow wouldn't be?

Terry raised his shotgun. The sod was something, god knew what, dressed up to look like his dead crow just to shaft him with Frankie. I'll get the little bastard, he thought, hoping his anger would insulate him from the pain of firing.

The explosion hit him on both sides this time – raw on the already damaged right, a dull concussion on the left where Frankie had fired simultaneously. Nevertheless he kept his focus, felt along the gun, probed through the air until he reached the point where the crow disintegrated.

'Got it,' said Frankie, fatly satisfied.

What can I say? Terry wondered desperately. There were white things, like space invaders, moving over the right side of his vision, and he felt as if he'd gone deaf in both ears, although inexplicably he could hear everything that was going on, as though the deafness were in a different dimension, so different in fact that it seemed to muffle his power of speech as well. Tell Frankie that I can feel things with pellets, just as you can feel that you're feeling something with the end of a stick? Very likely. But it was true. He'd actually experienced a sensation of impact; and felt Frankie's shot wandering off amongst the greenery, unsatisfied. Who would have believed it, he was born to shoot? Nobody would have believed it, particularly Frankie.

'Let's take a bit of a stroll,' Frankie suggested, thoroughly pleased with himself now. 'The local crows are probably becoming wise to us.'

As they walked, Frankie asked about the vicar.

'Seemed a bit the worse for wear at your place the other week.'

'He was completely gone,' agreed Terry. 'He seems to have fallen apart.'

'It's that bally thermometer gets me. It's the worst eyesore in the village.'

'It's all in a good cause, of course. Raising money for the church.'

'Churches are *supposed* to be falling apart.' Frankie became irritable again. 'They're not supposed to have giant thermometers stuck outside them.'

'I suppose not. But it's –'

'Shut up!' ordered Frankie in a whisper. 'Sorry, but there's a couple of the buggers up there.'

Sure enough, two crows sat side by side on a faraway branch, as though waiting for a bus to roll up.

'We'd better shoot from here,' Frankie continued. 'There's no cover if we get any nearer.' A largish clearing lay between them and the quarry, which were perhaps eighty yards away. 'One each,' Frankie suggested, raising his shotgun. At that second, as though intuitively, the left hand bird lazily rose and flapped heavily out of range. 'Shit on it,' said Frankie, 'the bastard cottoned on to us.' He lowered his gun. 'That one's yours,' he suggested.

This was the test. Terry sighted the bird, squeezed. As if the penny had finally dropped the bird rose a fraction before he fired; through the ringing of yet another explosion he sensed his pellets peppering the branch.

'Not too bad at all,' said Frankie. 'Missed him by a whisker. You're shaping up nicely.'

Terry had, quite clearly, passed his test. He was exactly as not too bad at all as he was expected to be. Long live the aristocracy, he thought bitterly, as the thunder, bells, the terrible pain, the contradictory numbness, continued.

CHAPTER SEVEN

Terry

Gerald Flowers looked out of his rainy window.

'We received two telephone calls from clients who were waiting in,' he said finally.

'Oh dear,' said Terry. There was a long pause. 'Of

course, I have a lot of clients who *didn't* phone you,' he added.

'Not as many as some of your colleagues,' Flowers said. 'Where are your monthly figures, incidentally?'

'They'll be in tomorrow.'

'They are supposed to be done by today.'

'That's what I mean. "Done by today". So they'll be in by tomorrow.'

'You believe in stretching a point, Mr Sutton.'

'I wasn't skiving off, sir. Useful contacts.'

Flowers finally ceased his auditing of the rain, and turned to face him, with pale fat eyes in his eroded face. 'Oh. So something came of all your shooting, did it? You bagged a customer?'

'In the long term,' said Terry. 'You've got to work on it.'

'I know all about working, Mr Sutton. The question is, do you?'

'Yes sir.'

'I hope so. Perhaps you'll bring in your monthly accounts first thing tomorrow morning to prove the point?'

'Yes sir. Obviously.'

'The point does need proving, Sutton. Otherwise I shall be compelled to review your career with us.'

'I understand, sir.'

'I hope you do, Mr Sutton.' And Flowers turned back to review the career of the rain. Terry left the office.

In the outer office Nicola, Ange's replacement, was still sitting at her desk.

'I thought you would have gone by now,' said Terry. He felt suddenly as if he had come out of Flowers' office naked. He touched his cravat. Of course not, everything was in place. He brushed invisible dandruff off the shoulder of his blazer.

'I thought I'd better stay here in case I was needed,' Nicola said. 'To pick up the pieces. Mr Flowers was hopping mad. Didn't you get the push?'

'Come on,' said Terry.

'I felt sure he would fire you.'

'It would take more than Flowers to fire me. To tell you

43

the truth, Nicola, I've been fired by the highest in the land.'

'Good for you.'

'Why don't you come out with me,' Terry suggested, 'and I'll tell you all about it?' It suddenly struck him that he hadn't been out with a girl since Ange left him. Strike while the iron was hot. You only had to stride out of the lion's den intact, and you started *off* with the track record of the lion. He thought of Flowers' thin face, gooseberry eyes. Not much of a lion perhaps, but that was beside the point. When you were at school and some character had an old battle-scarred conker, a fighty-eighter, say, you only had to come along and smash it with your brand new untried one and that became a fifty-niner. Not that Terry's conkers were exactly untried: he was a man of the world, divorced. But shiny and uncracked they were, if you put to one side for a moment a nasty case of athlete's foot.

'Tonight, you mean?' Nicola said, rather cautiously. You would almost think she was stalling for time. But of course: the whole point was that he *was* a man of the world; she was just a kid. Terry surveyed her carefully. Her hair was shorn upwards and flounced out a bit at the back, so that it resembled what they used to call a duck's arse. Now it was called punk. She had four earrings in her left ear. She was only eighteen, much younger than Ange had been, and was playing at being a semi-dropout. In actual fact here she was, a secretary, and she came from a very middle-class family. Upper middle class, if the truth be known. Terry happened to know her father was a pal of Flowers. She was a nice kid, and she probably found the prospect of a night out with a divorced man slightly alarming. Especially one who had just had an up and downer with the boss: a divorced man, living in proximity to the edge.

'Of course tonight,' Terry said. 'Seize the day.' Oh god, he suddenly thought, I've got to do my accounts for Flowers by first thing tomorrow. 'Or tomorrow,' he added. 'What about tomorrow night?'

'I can't come tomorrow night,' Nicola said. 'I'm going out. To a concert in Shrewsbury.'

'A concert?'

'Yes. Premo Bulge.'

'Oh,' said Terry. 'Not really my style. A bit raw. A bit gimmicky.'

'Sorry,' said Nicola.

'I've got a lot on myself this evening, on second thoughts,' said Terry. 'I've got myself a bit booked up. Tell you what, let's just have a quick drink now, on the way out.'

'I'd better not. I've got to catch my bus. I'll be late as it is. My mum will wonder what's happened to me.'

'You're a big girl now,' Terry suggested. 'Anyway, I can run you home. It's only a mile or two, isn't it?'

'I suppose so,' said Nicola, still sounding doubtful. One step at a time, that was the way when you were dealing with a kid like her. There was a streak of pink in her hair, but she was a girl guide at heart. Terry knew the type.

'Miserable weather,' he said, as they stepped out on the streets of Market Hanking. The rain was pouring down. They made a quick dash to his car. 'It was a lovely morning, though,' he said, letting her in.

'You should know,' she replied.

He automatically set off in the direction of Saxton.

'I live the other way,' she said.

'Oh yes.' Stupidly he'd been thinking of taking her into the Cricketers for a drink. That would have given the farmers something to think about. Now he stopped, turned round, and drove towards the northern outskirts of Market Hanking. He pulled up outside the White Hart.

'It's got a nice garden, leading to the canal.'

'I don't think it's quite the right weather for the garden,' Nicola said, almost pertly.

'I suppose not,' Terry said. 'But,' improvising, 'it's very pleasant inside.'

Terry had never had a drink inside before, and it was a bit dark and dank in the lounge bar. Also surprisingly crowded considering the time of day – full of working men, farm labourers and the like. At one table, though, an elderly man was sitting alone. He was leaning forwards, with his head resting on his hands, dozing.

45

'Anyone sitting here?' Terry asked him. There was no reply. 'Obviously had a heavy day,' he told Nicola. 'Sit here and I'll get you a drink. What would you like, a half of shandy?'

'A Bacardi and coke,' she replied to his surprise. Why not? She was trying to prove she was a big girl too.

When Terry returned with the drinks, Nicola said in a whisper: 'Terry, I think he's dead.' She nodded towards the old man.

'Give him a chance,' said Terry. 'He's just having forty winks. I'll take a bet that you've never seen a dead body in your life.'

'Yes, I have. Well no, not *seen* exactly.'

'There you are then. Take it from one who knows.' He took a sip of his drink. Nicola looked nervously towards the sleeping man. 'Oh yes,' Terry went on. 'I was going to tell you about being fired. And I *mean* fired. Big-time firing. I've been fired by the Prime Minister.'

When Mrs Cheeseman came into power, she used her new broom on 10 Downing Street as well as on the economy as a whole. In the aftermath of the massacre, Terry managed to get employment as a kitchen assistant.

'She paid rubbish, of course,' he said. 'But I thought the experience would be useful. A good jumping-off point.'

'But didn't you have to have qualifications?' Nicola asked. 'I mean, you're not a caterer. You're an insurance salesman.'

'I am now, that's the whole point. But she paid bottom rate, so she couldn't get fully qualified staff. And I've always been a good cook. Anyway, I'd had experience of the licensed trade.'

In a sense, that previous experience of the licensed trade had been the greatest success of his career. As a barman at the Castle Inn he'd been left in charge two nights a week. He encouraged singsongs, hired local entertainers, finally arranged to make a record, starring himself and the regulars. A Night at the Castle. Of course it wasn't modern rubbish like Premo Bulge, but classic rock and roll, ballads, pub favourites. Trade increased to such an extent that the manager got promotion to a bigger pub. Terry was so incensed with the injustice of it that he resigned on the spot, forgetting that he had a thousand copies of the record to sell, and only one market to sell it to. He still had them, in crates, at the back of the garage.

But then he got his job in Downing Street.

'Did you live in?' Nicola asked.

'Oh no,' Terry said. 'I lived in Battersea, as a matter of fact. Between the power station and the dog's home. All the best people live there.'

Nicola looked impressed. A lamb to the slaughter, poor kid, Terry thought. At least my touch hasn't deserted me.

'In fact,' Terry went on, 'my digs in Battersea led to my undoing.'

It wasn't so much his digs, of course, but who was sharing them: Tom Rutherford. Tom was a likeable young ruffian in the waste disposal business, ostensibly anyway. In point of fact he seemed to spend a great deal of his time disposing of stuff that had fallen off lorries, which was waste of a kind, perhaps. Terry was helping with the Downing Street order at the time, and he confided to Tom the difficulty of keeping within the cost limits set by the Prime Minister. Tom offered to help.

Everything worked perfectly well until one day when the kitchen staff, ironically with the exception of Terry himself, went down with salmonella. There was an investigation, of course, and it was discovered that one of their main suppliers was Renwick's, Tom's waste disposal firm. What made the whole episode even more frustrating was that it turned out that the salmonella had nothing to do with Tom's supplies. It was caused by a Chinese takeaway meal the kitchen staff had eaten to celebrate somebody's birthday. Terry was exempt because he didn't like prawns. Nevertheless, if you were going to be fired, you might as well be fired by the Prime Minister. Or at least by her underling.

'Of course,' said Terry, 'as soon as I left she upped the

kitchen allowance. They can probably afford pet food now, instead of garbage.'

The landlord came up to the table, and took their glasses.

'Will you have another?' Terry asked Nicola. She hesitated.

'Oh my god!' the landlord suddenly shouted. 'Jesus Christ,' he said to the room at large. 'Rupert's dead. Dead as a doornail.' He tapped Rupert's prone head, as if to prove the point.

'I think I'd like to go home now,' said Nicola, in a husky voice.

Terry drove her home. He tried for a little cuddle after he'd parked by her garden gate, but nothing doing. She wasn't in the mood. The house looked nice, modern and very substantial.

That's my luck, Terry thought as he drove off, trying to chat a girl up with a dead body sitting at the same table. Just before he reached Saxton he pulled into the carpark of the Cricketers. He needed a quick pint to cheer himself up.

CHAPTER EIGHT

Terry

The phone rang not long after seven the following morning.

'It's only me,' said Frankie.

God, thought Terry, public school and all that. Up with the lark. Cold showers, probably. Meanwhile *he* could feel last night's beer sluicing about inside him.

'Hello, Frankie.'

'Wondered if you fancied taking another pot at our feathered friends?'

Oh no. Terry remembered that he hadn't done his figures for last month. One thing had led to another during the evening; one pint to another. It was just as well Frankie had woken him up in good time. He gave himself a shake. What on earth was the man on about? They'd only been out yesterday.

'I'm afraid not, Frankie. Pressure of work.'

There was a pause. 'That's a pity,' Frankie said, somewhat shortly. 'In fact, it's more than a pity, it's a nuisance. A bloody nuisance.'

'I'm sorry,' Terry said. It was a shame to think of all the goodwill he'd engendered yesterday being dissipated, but there was nothing that could be done about it. He remembered the way Flowers had counted the rain.

'The point is, Terry, I'm getting the other members of the syndicate round. I took it that you'd welcome the opportunity of being introduced to them.' He sounded distinctly testy; surprisingly like Flowers.

'Hang on a minute,' Terry said. He placed his hand over the phone's mouthpiece, as though Frankie might overhear his thoughts. If only he didn't have so much beer inside him. The point was that Flowers would raise hell if he didn't deliver his monthly accounts first thing this morning. On the other hand Frankie would raise hell if he didn't turn up for the morning's shoot. All that time and energy he'd spent in trying to get a foot in the door would have gone to waste. Big businessmen were at this moment giving up their breakfasts to meet him. People who could have eaten Flowers *for* breakfast. It seemed madness to throw over an opportunity like that, just for the sake of a tinpot area manager who could only think in terms of one month at a time.

'All right,' Terry agreed. 'But just till lunch-time.'

'You're a good lad,' Frankie said. 'Knew I could rely on you.'

Terry pulled up on the gravelled parking area outside Frankie's mansion. Frankie was there, standing beside his Range Rover, but there was no one else around.

'Glad you could come, Terry,' he said welcomingly. He was in his usual get-up but strangely, considering that it was an overcast morning with a chilly breeze, all the various layers of his sleeves were rolled up. Terry got out of his car.

'The others not here yet?' he asked.

'Oh, none of them could make it,' Frankie said casually. 'They've all got business interests, you know, lots of irons in the fire. They're not able to arrange things to suit themselves, not like you.' He winked. 'You've got a nice little number, by the sound of it. Fixing your own timetable, knocking on people's doors when it takes your fancy. Ideal. Fits in nicely with shooting, that's for sure. If you can't shoot first thing in the morning, you might as well not shoot at all, that's my philosophy. I've never been a great one for going out in the afternoon. You all right, lad?'

Terry was staring at him open-mouthed. No, not at him. He was staring at Flowers, who in turn was staring bleakly out of his office window. Terry felt a sudden yearning to be in that unpleasant office with him. It was like a feeling he'd had on a day-trip from school as a child, when by lunchtime he was miserably homesick and almost panicked at the thought of all the miles, twenty or thirty of them, that lay between him and his mother. Now it was Flowers who was inaccessible: only six miles or so, but it was another world, a world in which Terry was sitting on the client's side of the desk, going through his accounts, and Flowers was grumbling and looking out of his window, and Nicola was at her desk in the outer office, and everything would go on as normal. Another world.

'. . . all right, lad?'

Frankie came back into focus. There was no point in crying over a spilt career. 'Yes, I'm fine,' Terry said. 'Had a bit too much at the Cricketers last night.'

'Not to worry,' Frankie said. 'Nothing like a spot of fresh air for getting rid of a hangover.'

Terry walked round to his boot, fetched out his gun, and followed Frankie to the Range Rover.

'By the way,' Frankie said, 'I've been having a bit of a problem. You know that business with the carburettor you sorted out the other day? It seems to have clogged up again.'

Terry spent an hour cleaning Frankie's carburettor. He

didn't know much about engines, as a matter of fact, but he'd always believed in being practical and using his common sense. He memorized the position of every nut, bolt, cap, bit, piece he took off, and hoped for the best. Frankie passed the tools.

'It must be handy, being able to find your way around an engine,' Frankie said admiringly.

They didn't set off for the woods until gone ten. After yesterday's rain the cart-tracks were more slippery than ever so that you felt it was impossible to commit yourself to the seat, you had to use your weight to counterbalance the skids and slides as you might on a yacht.

Suddenly they slewed round a semi-circle and were stuck, in the very middle of a gateway that had been pulped up by cattle. The wheels span in the mud.

'Put it into neutral and then let it very gently into second, so it doesn't bite too hard,' Terry said. There was an insurance company booklet called 'Become a Safer Driver', designed to cut down accident claims.

Frankie let the clutch out so rapidly that the vehicle jerked briefly forward, and stalled. It wouldn't start again.

Terry, standing in mud up to his ankles, cleaned the carburettor once more. It took rather less than an hour this time, he was getting used to it.

'You must have dirt in your petrol tank,' he told Frankie, who had remained in the driver's seat.

Frankie leaned towards him out of the window. 'I'm glad of your company, that's for sure,' he said.

There was a hose that needed fastening on the other side of the engine. Terry stepped round and suddenly he was arse over tip in a welter of cowflop, mud, thick puddle. He lay there, looking up at the grey sky. It was almost a relief, he couldn't fall any further, he'd finally got to the bottom of this sodding morning.

There was a squelching sound and then Frankie's round pink face appeared in the sky. 'Rustic pursuits, I'm afraid,' he said.

'There's not much rustic about mending an engine,'

Terry said bitterly. Some water, surprisingly cold, had begun to trickle up one sleeve.

By the time the car was going again, it was gone eleven, no longer worth shooting crows, especially as the mud on Terry's shoulders and back had hardened into a thick crust. They drove back to the mansion.

'You'd better have a shower, clean yourself up,' Frankie said.

'Thank you,' Terry replied.

The bathroom was draughty, with peeling wallpaper.

'Tell you what,' Frankie said, 'I could do with one myself.'

Terry surveyed him. No oil, no mud: he hadn't done anything to get himself dirty this morning, and his skin had its habitual pink, freshly peeled quality, despite a scattering of blackheads on his nose and the grubby old clothing. 'Share and share alike, eh?' Frankie continued.

Oh no. Boys together in the pavilion. Leaping about under the shower. Public school fun and games. There was no escape, he couldn't leave in this state. Damnation.

Terry took his clothes off with his back determinedly towards Frankie. He folded each garment carefully, however soiled it was, and placed it neatly on the pile in his corner. He could hear Frankie undoing himself behind him, and panting slightly with the exertion. Finally naked, Terry still faced away, unpleasantly aware of the existence of his own bottom, pimpling now with exposure. Frankie's panting seemed louder, interspersed with little preoccupied flips and smackings of the mouth.

Suddenly Terry was struck by an amazingly obvious thought. Queerness. A feature of the aristocracy. And he was facing the possibility bum-first! Oh god, all the implications. He'd put his job on the line for someone who just wanted to use him, he'd put up with the frustration of the crow-shoot, the unreliable car, the cowflops, the suggestion of a joint shower, the whole works, for a decadent aristrocrat who wanted to exploit him! He'd been a lamb to the slaughter.

He had to turn round, face the music. He felt a strange

unwillingness to do so, however, despite his vulnerability. He couldn't stand the thought of bringing matters to a head. As he turned, his eyes slid back the way they had come, unable to bear the prospect. Finally, though, he looked.

Frankie was in the act of pulling off a pair of baggy, almost knee-length, underpants. His vest stretched tight over a plump pot. Below it, the descending pants revealed a tuft of pubic hair, ginger like the balding head. Then:

Then nothing.

For a second Terry felt relief, elation even. No erection. Nothing to erect.

Then the horror of it struck home. Some terrible accident. The lives these people led. Vicious public school games, hunting, military service, perhaps duels.

Frankie hadn't noticed his gaze, he was still absorbed in undressing. His arms were thin and white compared with the tubby body. They grasped the vest, and pulled it up over his head. Shock upon shock.

As though by way of compensation for the lack down below were a pair of large, almost muscular breasts, topped by big, raw-looking nipples.

'Oh no,' cried Terry, unable to stop himself.

Frankie's head emerged from his vest and he stared back, quizzical, searching. 'There's no need to gawp,' he said.

They stood facing each other in silence, body to body. Terry wondered how a woman's anatomy could suddenly seem a catalogue of disasters.

'Don't tell me you didn't know?' Frankie's question was sarcastic, contemptuous even. 'If so, you must be the only person in the whole of Saxton.'

Suddenly the vicar's drunken babbling came back into Terry's mind: *all been girls in recent years, a plethora of women.* He thought of the farmers in the Cricketers, their dry amused reaction to the news that he'd been invited to join the syndicate. How they must have been laughing up their sleeves.

'Do you want me to spell it out?' Frankie was at his most

imperious now, speaking with icy hatred. 'All right, I will. I am a male homosexual trapped in a woman's body.'

'You bastard!' Terry suddenly shouted. He would have run, but he had to get dressed first.

CHAPTER NINE

Premo

A real pig. I'm unwashed and somewhat high for a start. Raggedy underpants; born-again string vest. A pair of jeans that were once a pair of jeans but are now a model of a pair of jeans fashioned out of a sort of hard resin, composed of sweat, grease, food, even urine. (They are so tight round the groin that no matter how prolonged my farewell shake, the apparently empty member always emits a few final drops when the hatches are battened down, and these slide with horrible persistence and determination down my legs.) My jeans are quite realistic except that nobody has got round to colouring them in yet. They're not blue, nor black, nor white, nor anything else, just the colour things are when they haven't got a colour at all, you can't even tell whether they are dark or light, stained or faded. Above the jeans is a tee-shirt and unlike them it is a definite colour indeed, fluorescent lime-green. On it is stamped a message: PISS OFF.

On top of all this is a rather old-fashioned cotton dress, a bit 1940s, square shouldered, waisted, coming to mid-calf. It's done in downward stripes, which are said to have an attractively slimming effect. It's a sort of pale coffee-colour, and the stripes are pink, although as usual a certain amount of variegation has taken place since manufacture. The dress's button-up front is left fetchingly open, so that glimpses of PISS OFF can be had, as reticent and brazen as the more usual glimpses of cleavage.

The whole effect is topped off by podgy, unshaven cheeks, and shoulder-length hair that is somewhat contradicted by a bald patch on top. My bald batch doesn't shine. My eyes come in black bags.

So I look the part. But nevertheless it is a part. Premo is not, in the end, a pig at all, he is – however sincerely – simply piggish. I have developed a pig tendency on purpose, as you might compress a spring to hoard energy. Then one day, PYOING, the moment of release. The pig will have wings.

The curtain goes up. There are all the hoppers, standing in rows, guys sprinkled in amongst them. It's a dance hall, so there aren't any seats but thank god there are too many of them to dance. It's impossible to make out faces, only smiles. Row after row of whitish caterpillars. The audience have to smile because they don't know what else to do with Premo. I'm not big enough on the scene to cheer. You get fame by being banned from the Beeb but it isn't exactly the sort of fame you get from being *on* the Beeb. They've come out of curiosity, and now they smile and clap to indicate that their money has started to be spent, that this is what they're paying for. The hoppers are alert, even suspicious.

Premo unclears his throat. A clotted effect is called for, a voice with an oily edge, like the oil round a frying egg. A high-cholesterol, animal fat, heart attack voice. Pig music. Nothing subtle, a simple ballad, a song that tells a story. The group starts up, pyow, bong bong:

> Sat in my pukey sitting room
> Looked at the pictures tacked on the walls
> First of my mummy then of my dad
> My dad's the one without any balls.

The hoppers shift about worriedly. They peer round to see what the other hoppers are doing. The other hoppers are shifting about worriedly. Time to add a new ingredient to the mixture and, lo and behold! on trot the popsies.

They are popsies to the exact degree that I am a pig. There are three of them, all (apparently) blonde. They have pony-tails. They wear pink dresses with flounces. White tights and white high-heeled shoes. They come wiggling on in step, like one of those cute pre-rock groups, the Beverley Sisters perhaps. They assemble in a line behind Cinderella Bulge in his stained old skivvy's shift, and do the reprise in sweet chorus:

His dad's the one without any balls.

It's enough to win the audience over. The whole room vibrates, flutters, becomes animated. The experience is sufficiently complex, the money is well-spent. I can slump, relaxed, into the next verse:

Sat in my speeding motorcar
My girl beside me crooned a sweet hum
Lips were like petals [repeat it leeringly] *lips*
    were like petals, eyes full of dewdrops
Wanted to bite her round little bum.

The popsies cutely agree:

He wanted to bite my [wiggle wiggle] round little bum.

It isn't only tasteless, it's stupid. It's perfect. The audience laugh but they shift nervously also. They're thinking: yes, we came here for crap, and we're getting our money's worth.

Sat in a dingy public house
Poured beer inside me, jar after jar
Wanted a pee, the bog full of wankers
They said come in, let's drink at your bar.

The popsies, charm itself:

They said come in, let's dwink at your bar.

The 'w' in 'dwink' is so clear that although I've got my back to them, I can feel the popsies' pouted lips whizz through the air, like so many blown kisses. The strain of singing pig has deposited a residue in my throat, now it is possible not to clear it *par excellence*, so my voice, now low, lugubrious, husky, actually bubbles:

Lay in an upmarket funeral parlour
Well-scrubbed and shaved, hair neat and trim
Arms crossed on chest, along came the manager
Smiled as he said, it's time to stuff him.

And to conclude, Premo in disharmony with the popsies,
a chunk of meat in a lavender-scented handbag:

Smiled as he said, it's time to stuff him.

Roing dlum bing.

Ra ra from the fans. Who knows *what* they feel? A good
time well had? A song that lived up to expectations? Or
relief that it's over, that they haven't got to put up with it
any more?
Either way, I can't lose. On to the next.

At last they are *all* over. Now a local group comes on. God
knows what they are going to do, express the spirit of
Shrewsbury in song, perhaps. Give a musical rendition of
what it's like to be young and mediocre.
Tired as always. Throat aching with misuse. Also suffering from the hots. I follow the popsies over to the dressing-
rooms. They share the one next door. They giggle amongst
themselves, as if they've done something naughty and are
proud of it, ignoring me, the source of whatever naughti-
ness there might have been. There's no justice, but for
heaven's sake, how can there be justice in a world in which
one makes a living by singing pig?
Once, only once, did Premo try it on with a popsy.
Flushed, hot, rancid after a performance, like tonight, I
happened to come across one in a corridor by herself.
(Who knows what had happened to the other two?) The
one in question was the one on my left (on the audience's
right), a bit hefty, with a slightly pear-shaped figure and
indeed a slightly pear-shaped face. It seemed the most
natural thing in the world, a dim corridor, the residual
charge of being on stage, she and I. A pig and a popsy.
After a session like tonight, I said, I'm just ready to roger a
parrot. Granted that was somewhat indirect, but even the

most primitive creatures undertake a courtship ritual, walking up and down as if they are thinking about somebody else entirely, but making sure meanwhile that they are looking their best. She didn't seem to take it in. That of course is the trouble with indirect approaches. You, for example, I explained, having concluded my mating dance. You would do nicely.

Of course it was somewhat squalid, she being my employee, but that just proves my point, squalor *is* the most natural thing in the world. To my amazement she muttered something about a boyfriend. A popsy, involved in the process of singing pig, with a *boyfriend*? It didn't make sense. I tried to get her to explain. Where, who, was this person? Somewhere and someone else, apparently. I said, here you are, with a little rice pudding between your legs, and there is this so-called boyfriend, *somewhere else*. It doesn't tie up, I said: pig-singing concerns itself with the here and now. The immediate bliss of the wallow. The surrender to warm mud. Sunshine on thick pink skin. Munching your way through god-knows-what, through *everything*. 'Auld Lang Syne' is a different musical tradition altogether. Given that I'd spent the whole evening singing horribly, my eloquence was remarkable. But it cut no ice.

She gave me a cold look up and down, as much as to say, *you pig*, and rushed off. I've never tried anything with the other popsies. They seem to have coalesced into a conspiracy against me. They are always in a huddle, giggling. They look at me with that contemptuous admiration women have for men who've made a pass which they've rejected. So I sit in my dressing-room, pondering on my hots.

There is actually one of those mirrors surrounded by light bulbs, so that a flat shadowless illumination is shed on Premo's unprepossessing mug. The bags under my eyes are still black. I fantasize about hoppers. They cluster around the stage door, pretending to want my autograph. I let them in, and lead them to my dressing-room, making them queue outside in an orderly fashion. I'll give you my autograph one at a time, I say sternly. In comes the first one. I recline on my couch and watch her undress. She deals from the top of the deck, as always, and seizes up when it comes to the lower half. Hurry up, I say gently, to nudge her on, there's others waiting, you know. She blushes. Yes, mohican haircut, weird make-up, load of junk through the earhole, she still blushes, a woman to the core. I know what the trouble is, of course. Tits are fine, tits are aesthetic, women are pleased with their tits. But the other end is a bit of a poser. Non-aesthetic, nitty-gritty, functional. That's the source of all that famed womanly modesty, from Eve on. Deep down women have a sneaking suspicion that they have something to be modest *about*. They're wrong. Part One may be beautiful. Part Two is true. The two things are not the same; if you learn nothing else from singing pig you learn that. Truth isn't smooth and spherical. Truth is pink, crinkled, hairy.

Having got to what you might call the moral, there's a knock on my door. My heart leaps! Can it be? No, of course it can't be, that's the other thing you learn from singing pig. Pig might get them where they live, but it also stops them wanting to live there altogether. They up, and move house. Pig turns them off at the very second it turns them on. Off the groupie-material trots, and goes to bed with an estate agent or insurance man. They put pig, Premo, behind them. There is no queue of lascivious parrots at my door. All there is is Steg.

CHAPTER TEN

Premo

Steg drifts in, snowed. His legs are bendy and pliable. They don't quite reach the ground. His eyes are watering into his beard. He looks wistfully down at me. Then he bellows.

'One day I'm going to die,' he roars. His eyes suddenly gleam madly. He plucks his beard. He looks every inch the mad Irish bugger that he is. This man is my manager. Dear god. You know, my equivalent of the bullet-headed businessman with a briefcase tucked under his arm. One of those thin fat cats who grease the world of pop. Premo has a pig manager. What authenticity!

Steg is not, by any stretch of the imagination, a fat cat. But he *is* thin. Tall and thin. He looms. Even standing still, his legs don't reach the ground. But then, praise be, his battery goes flat. With that agonizing delicacy of a lunar module making its final descent, his feet search out the floor. He droops. His eyes fade. His voice becomes wingeing and dependent. 'I'm going to die some day, Premo,' he tells me.

So much for moments of illumination, induced by drugs. 'How original,' I reply.

His battery is even flatter. A little boy voice comes out of the hairy gorilla face. 'An nen,' it says, 'I'm gon er liv wid God up dere.' He has just about enough juice to turn his head in the direction of the ceiling. 'High up in space,' he explains, 'where you don feel de rain.' His head lowers slowly back to face me again. 'Where you don feel de rain, Premo.'

'Is it raining again?' I ask tiredly. 'I wouldn't have thought it would concern you, Steg, being so high.'

Steg tries to take this in, and fails. His eyes are totally juiceless for a moment. Then he finds what he's looking for and gets a tiny charge. His eyes have that dim glow you get in bulbs when there is almost no electricity, and only the filament glows. Steg has found his thread again.

'What tears me up, Premo,' he says mournfully, 'it's not just the weather.'

'What isn't just the weather?'

'The rain, Premo.'

'For god's sake, do me a favour, Steg.'

'People rain too, that's what I keep thinking.'

'Is that what you call thinking?'

'No Premo, you got to listen.' Steg catches hold of my arm. 'I've been talking to the sod. The sod who runs the building.'

My heart sinks. When Steg talks to anyone, disaster is on

the menu. Somehow misunderstandings arise. One thing leads to another. He's much better off just mumbling to himself.

'Mr Musgrove,' I say.

'That's right, Premo,' he agrees, quite animated. He lets go of my arm and clutches my shoulder. 'Mr Musgrove.' He says it as if, by a huge effort, he has succeeded in saying the sort of thing you hear other people say. He says it as you may say 'Vienna Convention'. 'I've been talking to Mr Musgrove.'

'And what did you and Mr Musgrove have to say to each other?'

'It was just after your session, Premo. Everything was wound up. *I* was wound up. The hoppers wetting themselves and that. I said, I said to Mr Musgrove, did that get *through* to you, Mr Musgrove? I said, did that ring your bell?'

'Shit's creek,' says I. Already the truth begins to dawn.

'Do you know what he said, Premo? Do you know what Mr Musgrove said?'

'No, I don't know what Mr Musgrove said. Why don't you tell me?'

'He said, those little maniacs have broke two windows at the back, and if you don't cough up for them, I'll have to keep the fucking deposit. That's what he said.'

'And? And?'

Steg's eyes are watering again. No, no, they're not. He's crying. This gets worse and worse.

'All I wanted,' he sobs. 'I just wanted him to give a little, Premo. And all he can talk about is fucking taking. Right after your act, that's the point. I said, thank you very much, Mr Musgrove, I said. I said, I'm going to crush your head for you. Oh Premo.' He shakes his head a little, so that tears actually fly around the room, catching the light from my dressing-table light-bulbs.

'You didn't, did you?' I ask wearily.

'Didn't I what, Premo? Premo, you know me better than that. You don't say didn't to me. I'm not a didn't kind of guy.'

61

'Didn't crush his fucking head for him, that's what
didn't. Please?'

'Oh Premo, what is it that makes people rain?'

'Look Steg, go and have a lie down. You've got your
weather forecast mixed. Snowing's *your* problem.'

Steg doesn't move. He stands in the middle of my
dressing-room, swaying like a tree about to fall, but back
he drifts each time, sway and back, sway much farther than
anyone else can without falling, then magically back, then
sway to the other side, almost to the floor, and then back
again, crying quietly meanwhile into his beard at the
question of what it is makes people rain. I close the door on
him and scuttle down seedy corridors, looking for Mr
Musgrove.

He is lying in a small hallway by the stage door. In fact
EXIT is written above his head in big red letters as if it's the
title of the picture. He is groaning, but he doesn't look too
bad. He looks as you expect a dance hall manager to look
when he's had his head thumped in.

'Have you had an accident, Mr Musgrove?' I ask, helping him to his feet.

'You've got a bloody nerve,' he says. 'I'm going to call
the bleeding police.'

'It's always a shock when you have a fall,' I say, giving
him thirty pounds.

'That man of yours is a maniac,' Mr Musgrove says,
rubbing his head. 'All the time he was hitting me, he kept
saying, you got to learn to give yourself, Mr Musgrove.'

'His heart's in the right place,' I say. 'You look as if you
could do with a nice cup of tea.'

Mr Musgrove shambles off, muttering to himself. Leaving Premo standing by the stage door. Beyond it lies my
heart's desire, a restless queue of parrots, timid and randy
by turns, no, not by turns, simultaneously. I cock a waxy
ear. Do I hear chanting? Premo, Premo, we want Premo!
Premo Bulge OK! Give it us, Premo! No, I don't. Perhaps
they're chanting quietly, overcome with emotion.

I press down the bar and push the door open, to let in the
blank Shrewsbury night.

*

She stands there in the rain. She is medium height, medium build, medium face, medium legs. She is wearing medium clothes, C & A with a whisper of drop-out. She has a faint streak of pink in her medium brown hair. She is my first hopper. She is . . . the one. Her features are so ordinary that you can't even remember what she looks like while you're looking at her, with the rain falling past her face.

I commit her to memory.

CHAPTER ELEVEN

Nicola

Once, when she was quite young, Nicola Gilmour had gone in a rowing boat on a boating lake. She hated anything like that, but her father always wanted her to *do* things. He had gone over to pay the woman who owned the boats and before Nicola knew what was going on she found herself in a heavy wooden rowing boat, being pushed out on to the water. The oars were so big she could hardly handle them.

'Go on, Nicola!' her father shouted from the edge of the lake. 'Don't go catching any crabs!' He pretended to laugh, as he so often did.

Nicola splashed the oars about for a little while as best she could. She sensed the other children in their boats were laughing at her. She sensed the people on the lakeside were laughing at her. Worst of all, she sensed that her father *wasn't* laughing at her. He was showing his teeth in what looked like a laugh but underneath she knew he was hot and irritated. If you look at somebody's teeth for long enough when he's drawn his lips back you get to realize that teeth are a sort of bone, and then you imagine the way they fit into the bone of the jaw, and from there you move outward to the rest of the skull, and then, however well-fleshed the person is, you see him as a skeleton. As she watched her father standing on the lakeside, pretending to laugh,

Nicola saw *him* as a standing skeleton, even though he was quite a fleshy man. Muscular, he always said. Every morning, while he was brushing his hair, he would say admiringly to his reflection in the hall mirror, 'Lucky girls.' Nicola would think to herself: 'Doesn't he realize *I'm* a girl?'

Nicola stopped trying to row, out of sheer embarrassment. She was more or less in the middle of the boating pool now anyway. The sun was hot and the wood of the boat had a nice smell. She realized that now she was just drifting everybody had lost interest in her, except her father, who was waving at her from the side, doing pushing movements with his hands. He couldn't bear to see her drift.

She lay down in the boat and pretended to sunbathe. Now she couldn't see anything but the blue sky and the gently rocking sides of the boat. Even the shouting of the other children had grown dim. Every now and then came a sudden, mysterious gargle of water, but otherwise all was peaceful. She felt she was in a cocoon of warmth. Periodically across the blue of the sky she detected the faint film of a water breeze which could no longer reach her. She lay like that for a long time. Once she heard an ant-like voice calling 'Nicola', but she didn't care. No doubt her father was still at the lake edge, doing his pushing movements.

After some time she heard his voice calling 'Nicola' again. No, it wasn't so much that she heard as that she remembered. He had been calling but she had not been listening. And there was another voice interwoven with his, a fat woman's voice calling, 'Number eleven come *in*. Number eleven come *in*.' Suddenly in a panic Nicola sat up.

The boat woman's face was red with rage, a red splodge on the top of her body. Nicola's father was pushing and pushing with his hands. In their boats the other children were laughing. A big boy, a teenager, paddled past in his canoe and said: 'What you going to do? Hi-jack your rowing boat?' Nicola picked up her lumbering oars and began to row.

It was horrible. She could hardly make them reach the water, they seemed to want to go up, not down. And when she did get one in, it came up again with a shallow pool of water on the flat blade, like a spoonful of soup. The sun felt unbearably hot and she was sweating. She felt a sudden extra pulse of warmth in her pants and realized she'd wet herself a little with shock. She rowed and rowed but the boat didn't move. She kept thinking to herself, I ought to be able to say, I give in, and walk off, but of course she couldn't, she was all alone on a boat in the middle of a lake. She also thought: this is silly, this is unimportant, this is only being stuck on a boating-lake, much worse things are happening to people all over the world. Unfortunately this way of thinking didn't help. However trivial it was to be stuck in the middle of a boating-lake, she was still stuck in the middle of a boating-lake. Her father was calling and pushing, the boat-lady's face had become a frenzied tomato. Nicola almost burst out laughing, but burst into tears instead.

But of course crying didn't help, as her father would have been the first to point out. Where was her mother? Afterwards she couldn't remember. Going round the shops probably. Or perhaps she was there, but Nicola just didn't notice. Tears, like water wind, were obscuring her eyes. She couldn't row. She had no choice but row. She didn't want to arrive at the shore. She had no choice but head for it, with unbearable slowness.

Nicola's experience on the boating-lake formed itself afterwards into a dream, but this was some time later, when she had found out about her dead sister.

She found out by chance. It was one of those things. In fact, there were all sorts of words for it. Her mother let the cat out of the bag. The skeleton out of the cupboard. The baby out with the bathwater.

The baby had slipped out by mistake, one day when Nicola was 'just moping'. When her father was there Nicola's mother would defend her against the charge of lacking get up and go. When he was at work, though, she became almost as bad, going on at her to stop moping and *do* things. She would use her father as a threat. 'What he'll have to say when he comes home and finds you've just been lying about all day, I've no idea.' Nicola would think to herself: well, he won't know, if you don't tell him. They lived in a big modern house and Nicola's mother did housework with a passion.

It was a miscarriage in words. Nicola's mother said: 'Sometimes I think if there'd been the two of you.'

Then her mouth locked tight, as if it had hit a full-stop. After the horse had bolted.

Nicola said nothing but looked back at her mother, and her sister was in her mother's eyes, her sister for a moment came to the surface in her mother's face, a dead baby's face, with its eyes shut. Her mother shut her eyes, but the baby had escaped. From now on she was always beside Nicola, a dead baby, her size.

Some weeks later, Nicola asked about the baby. Her mother was unsurprised, tired. Nicola realized she'd always been tired beneath her busy exterior. It must be tiring giving birth to a dead baby, you were built to produce life, there would be a terrible strain involved in doing it the other way round.

'You were twins,' her mother said. 'It was full term, not a miscarriage. You were born alive and she was born dead, that's all.'

Nicola tried to cope with this in her mind. She had never realized she'd had a sister. But her sister had been dead from the beginning. Nicola had shared her mother's womb with a dead baby. Perhaps she'd always realized she didn't have a sister. Perhaps this was the reason why she found it so difficult to *do* things.

It was after this that she had her dream about the boating-lake.

It wasn't the boating-lake, it was a sea. A cold sea, there were ice-floes in it and grey tumbling cloud above. The waves were grey and large. Every now and then she was hit by flurries of hard snow that stung her eyes. She was in her heavy rowing boat, rowing and rowing. She wasn't trying to get anywhere, she was trying to get away from something. Whatever it was, was pulling her back. She couldn't quite make it out through the driving weather, but she visualized it as a long dark tunnel in the water, a tunnel that sucked at her, a whirlpool.

The picture in the dream faded, and she was left with the emotion. Straining, straining, to go in one direction, and being pulled back and back. Everything bone cold. The sense of a frozen whirlpool. These emotions remained in her waking life.

Nevertheless, Nicola did quite well at school, not because she was good but so that people wouldn't notice her. She talked with the other girls about clothes, imaginary boyfriends, period pains, pop-records, what they were going to do when they left school. They all went through a phase of deciding they were doomed, and would scuttle up to each other and say 'The Bomb' in sepulchral voices, raising their eyebrows and shaking their heads in despair.

When she was fifteen she went with her mother and father, and her dead sister, on holiday to Wales.

CHAPTER TWELVE

Nicola

Her father had lost his driving licence for a year after being breathalysed, so they went by train. Her mother didn't drive. They sat in the waiting-room of Shrewsbury Station. Her father was ashamed of not driving them.

'I suppose,' he said, for the benefit of the other people in the waiting-room, 'being done on the breathalyser is a sign that there's life in the old dog yet.'

Her mother was ashamed that he'd been breathalysed, and made an effort to change the subject. 'Look,' she said, pointing to a poster that said "Have a Happy Holiday in Wales Go by Train", 'that's a good omen. That's where *we*'re going.' The poster was not a photograph but a painting, and showed a fairy-tale landscape of dramatic hills, lush valleys, castles and picturesque cottages. Nicola had never been to Wales before, and wasn't convinced.

Her father was ashamed that they were going to Wales, and not somewhere on the continent. 'Oh well, it's only a trial holiday,' he said, although they knew already. 'See whether it's worth investing in a cottage down there.' They were going to South Wales, near the border: somewhere that would be within easy week-ending distance if they did decide to buy a cottage.

They had to get a taxi at Brecon railway station. It took a country road which wound up a slope on one side of a green, sheep-spotted valley. On the other side rose the tall, barer curves of the Brecon Beacons. The taxi turned off up a muddy lane, with trees on either side, and stopped outside a square whitewashed cottage. The garden was full of old fruit trees.

It turned out that a Welsh boy of about Nicola's age lived in the next cottage down the lane. He came along with the key to the out-houses and asked Nicola if she'd like to go for a walk with him the next day. This had never happened to her before, and although she and the girls at school talked about boys a great deal, she'd always secretly regarded them as figments of the imagination. Not as real, for example, as her dead sister. Her heart thumped. The boy was called Gareth Evans. He was small and dark, and he talked very quickly. She loved the slight sing-song of his accent, it made him sound as if he was joking about everything.

Her mother wasn't too keen about her going off with a 'stranger'.

'I should think you'd be pleased,' Nicola said. 'You're always on at me for mooning around.'

'That's right,' said her father. 'Go off and enjoy yourself for a few hours. Your mother and I can amuse ourselves for a while without your help, can't we, my love?' He looked at her mother with his hot irritable smile, perhaps sneering.

The walk took them down into the valley, across the warm fields, and up the first slopes of the Beacons on the other side. They lay on the short brown grass, looking down at the intricacy of the patchwork farms below. The river glinted amongst the green. It was a blue and white day, with small scudding clouds and bright sunshine. It was cooler on the hill, though warm near the grass. Some insect cried weeble loudly nearby. After they had been lying there for some minutes it began to snow.

'I can't believe it,' Nicola said. 'It's the middle of the summer.'

'Oh, we get some funny weather in these parts, boy-o.'

'Boy-o?'

'Girl-o.'

The flurry stopped as abruptly as it had started, leaving just the odd white dot on the baked grass. The white dots vanished as you watched. The insect, which had been angrily silent, began to call out again. When Gareth had said girl-o, it was like hearing the word girl for the first time, as if Nicola had at last been told what she was. They began to kiss and fondle each other. Gareth put his hands inside her blouse, undid her brassière, caressed her breasts.

For once in her life Nicola was determined not to drift. She placed a hand at the top of his trousers, and began to undo his zip.

'No,' Gareth said, 'I don't think that's a good idea.'

The words, in his delicate intonation, came out like a wavy line:

$$N^{o-}_{o\ I\ \underset{don't}{}\ \overset{think}{}\ \underset{that's}{}\ \underset{a\ good\ id-}{}\ ea.}$$

It made her laugh. She let go of his zip, but kept her fingers pressed against his bumpy groin.

'Why isn't it a good idea?' she asked.

'Someone might see.'

'But there isn't anybody for hundreds of miles,' Nicola said. 'Look.' There was simply the great sweep of sky, the bright hills, blotched here and there with the shadow of clouds, and the darker green of the meadows below. 'There's only sheep.'

'We wouldn't want to shock the sheep.'

'The sheep would need binoculars,' she said. 'Anyway, you've undone *me*.'

'Oh, but that's different.'

'What's different about it?'

'They're not so big. Easier to put away if someone turns up.'

'You've got a nerve,' she said, and began undoing his zip again. Suddenly she felt nervous. She'd only seen pictures. She wasn't quite sure whether she knew what to expect or not.

She didn't.

'It's like a little man,' she said, giggling. She only said that to flatter him. It wasn't like a little man, it was a bald baby with an irate face, it was a foetus. It was her sister. She'd expected it to be threatening, off-putting, but it was sweet, protruding from his trousers with its purple face like something newly born and awaiting its first breath. She stroked it gently.

'Don't,' Gareth said in a whisper.

'Don't worry,' she whispered back. 'No one's going to come.' She kissed it, and then lay with her face pressed up close to it, while she fondled it again.

'Don't, don't, don't,' Gareth whispered.

'It's sweet,' she whispered back.

'Please,' he said, quite loudly. Then fluid pulsed from its mouth, as when someone dies, and the sisterkin curled round on herself once more.

Gareth lay silent, head down, on the grass, while Nicola wiped herself off with her handkerchief as well as she could. He didn't move or speak. Eventually she left him there and headed back towards the cottage. He never spoke to her again.

The Gilmours didn't buy their country cottage. Nicola's mother thought Wales was a bit 'common'; her father agreed, and was also worried about the Welsh extremists who set fire to English people's country cottages.

At school, everything was as before. Nicola didn't mention Gareth, but was happy enough to talk about imaginary boys, and the Bomb. Her dead sister was particularly strong on the Bomb.

CHAPTER THIRTEEN

Nicola

When Nicola left school the other girls melted away. She had never been very close to them in any case – her sister had always been in-between, so that Nicola had had to project her voice over the interval like a ventriloquist. After school her sister grew nearer and nearer, until Nicola felt that she was completely intertwined with her. Everything else was beyond: other girls, getting a job, boys, clothes, music, periods, even food. The doctor prescribed eating as if it were medicine, and that's how it seemed. Her mother and father pushed biscuits, sausage, apple at her, but they didn't realize her sister was in the way.

Eventually her father pulled strings and got her a job with an insurance company.

'It's about time you got off your backside,' he said. 'There's a big wide world out there.'

Fancy, thought Nicola sullenly, the big wide world is an insurance company. Who would have believed it? She didn't refuse to go, she never refused anything. I shall just stay sitting here, she thought, on my proverbial backside. She liked the idea of having a proverbial backside. Her father gave her a grin, more tentative and worried than usual. He didn't look like a skeleton this time, he looked like a little boy. She felt sorry for him. She thought to herself: if only my sister wasn't in the way, I'd do something *for* him. He looked lonely. He did nothing with his life but pull the knobs and levers of the big wide world. He kissed her goodbye as he set off for work. His kiss didn't reach her.

'Have a good day, darling,' he said. He bent his arms, clasped his hands, and shook them, as much as to say, *do* things. She didn't reply. She hadn't felt his kiss because her lips were so cold. She was very close to her sister. She listened to him drive off, his car tyres crunching the gravel. Somewhere in front of her her breakfast sat on its proverbial backside, congealing. Beyond stood her mother, peering down at her. She was standing in exactly the place where her father had stood to say have a good day, darling, as if now he was in the big wide world, she was his domestic representative. Indeed, she was wearing a checked housecoat and looked every inch the executive housewife.

'Why don't you just *try* it?' she asked, pointing to the breakfast, the job, the big wide world. Nicola and her sister remained as they were.

Suddenly the lean, elegant, tight face split, like the skin of a snake. The trim executive housewife's body fell open, and out stepped a mother Nicola recognized, a dead mother, the mother of her sister.

'I've lost one baby already,' her mother said. 'Now I'm losing the other.' Her eyes were open and dead, like a fish's. Her face was grey. Nicola realized her mother was in her boat with her, a passenger.

'Mummy,' Nicola said. She began to row fast, not caring how much she splashed, intent on getting away from her dead sister. She gobbled her breakfast, ran for her bus, apologized to her new boss for being late on her first day. At lunch-time she went out and bought some clothes. Not executive clothes like her parents', nor drop-out, but something in-between, clothes that kept her at a moderate distance from the hole, a distance she could sustain by hard rowing. Clothes which showed she was trying to *do* things.

She had no friends, but she was friendly. The only male in the office was Terry Sutton.

'I'm sure we'll find we've got a lot in common,' he told her. Certainly there were similarities, Nicola detected them from the very start. Terry found it difficult to do things also, but unlike her he was proud of it. He didn't even try to row, he just let himself fall overboard and waited for someone to pull him back in. He was a clown.

Needless to say he eventually got round to trying to take

her out. It was impossible to tell him the truth of course, that she needed someone who could take the other oar, so she lied. She told him that she was going to a Premo Bulge concert in Shrewsbury the next night. There were posters advertising it all over Market Hanking. Even as she told the lie, she felt her boat begin to pull her in the wrong direction. Telling a lie was *not* doing something. They went out for a drink instead, and a dead body sat at their table.

The next day Nicola went to Shrewsbury before going into work. The concert, luckily, wasn't quite sold out, so she managed to buy the ticket she'd lied about the evening before.

When she eventually got to her office, Mr Flowers was furious.

'Is there some public holiday I don't know about?' he shouted. His eyes slid from her to the window, as if he wanted to check up on the holiday weather. It was grey, but not raining at the moment. 'First Terry, then you!'

'Terry?' she asked.

'He's not turned up a-bloody-gain,' Mr Flowers told the window. 'There's something fishy about our Terry. I've been looking for his file all morning.'

'I'll get it,' Nicola said.

'And I'll be wanting you to get 10 Downing Street on the line.'

'Downing Street? I don't think I'll be able to get through.'

'Yes, Downing Street. The kitchen department. You must be able to get through. How are their suppliers going to find out how many teabags they want, for god's sake? Or caviare, or whatever muck they eat?'

Nicola was deliberately obtuse. She felt that by being late herself she'd made things worse for Terry.

'But we're not in the teabag business,' she said.

'I don't need any cheek from you, either,' Mr Flowers glumly informed the window. 'What I propose to do is check up on young Terry Sutton's references.'

*

73

Nicola went to the Premo Bulge concert. She hadn't intended to. She'd thought that buying a ticket would amount to buying back the lie. But it had only made matters worse for Terry. I must keep my nose clean, she thought to herself. I must keep my proverbial nose clean.

The hall was crowded. You just stood in rows, shoulder to shoulder, getting an occasional glimpse of the sweating form of Premo on stage. He was disgusting. For most of the time, though, Nicola found her view blocked by a huge man who seemed old enough to be her father. He was wearing a tropical-style lightweight suit, and was talking business with another middle-aged man who stood beside him. Nicola caught occasional references, in amongst the general bedlam, to waste disposal. A Bulge concert seemed a funny place to talk business, but if you *were* going to, waste disposal was perhaps the most appropriate business to talk about.

By the time the concert was over, Nicola's head was spinning. Perhaps that was the source of her sensation of drift. She couldn't shake off the thought that she had to prove her good faith to Terry. She had refused to go out with him; he had lost his job. Although the two things weren't connected, they worried her. Deep down she thought what a change it was to worry about somebody other than her sister.

Suddenly she realized what she could do. She could *prove* she'd really gone to a Premo Bulge concert. She could go backstage, and ask for Premo's autograph.

CHAPTER FOURTEEN

Premo

All I can remember about her is not remembering what she looked like, and it was only yesterday. There wasn't anything else not to remember. Nothing happened. It was raining. All that happened was she asked for my autograph. She seemed a bit old to ask for an autograph, although she wasn't old. My heart thumped. I said: 'You make such a change after Mr Musgrove.'

'Who's Mr Musgrove?' she asked.

'Just a man who was lying in the corridor with his head bleeding,' I said.

'Thank you very much,' she said.

'Would you care to come in,' I said. 'Out of the rain?'

'No thanks,' she said.

'We've cleared him away.'

'I only want your autograph.'

'I'm sure I could give you my autograph better in my dressing-room.'

'Just on my programme,' she said, handing it to me.

'For a couple of minutes, that's all.'

'I've got a bus to catch,' she said. I signed her programme. She went. Another unsharded hopper. No, not another, she was the only one. *The* one. Just as well, when I thought about it: Steg was still in my dressing-room, not falling over.

Another session in front of Shropshire's young farmers draws to its close. It's a hot close evening, not raining outside, but dripping. The occasional warm drop down the almighty trouser leg. The young farmers moo, it could be worse.

> Nice sunny day, turn to a chick
> Give her a once over, undo her zip
> And she rains wow zonk pling pling
> And she rains.

My eyeballs swivel in their bags to glimpse the popsies over my shoulder. They're doing little twiddling movements with their fingers, to indicate falling rain. Not bad, given that they only had today to work it out. Their twiddles are not in time of course, but there again, nor is rain. They croon:

And she rains

Anything *they* can do. I mime the action of putting *some*thing up. The young farmers almost get it.

> Put my umbrella up, it's still bloody pissing
> Why don't you open your door, girl, let me in
> And she rains pling pling
> And she rains.

And the popsies:

> Oh yes she does, she rains
> Oh yes she does.

Good god, where did they get that from? Studying the classics? A crash-course at the conservatoire? *And* they remember to twiddle.

> Trousers are wringing, my Y-fronts are wet
> T-shirt is soaked, it's all over my shoes you git!
> And she rains, ping a ling pling ping a ling pling.

A tapping sound behind. I turn round to look. This time the popsies are doing a little dance! So this is what they get up to when they're not being rogered by me. They have plenty of time, god knows. Their white high heels chime more or less together on the bare and grotty stage, so many white mice operating as a corps de ballet, a shoe fetishist's wet dream.

And she rains

And she rains.

They still remember to twiddle their fingers.

Premo finishes at last. Luckily the artistic breakthrough on the part of the popsies was not sustained, so that for most of the act I've been able to scrutinize the audience without being distracted. What do I mean, luckily? That is hardly pig-thinking. Premo isn't the lucky type. She isn't there. I have inspected all the parrots and there isn't one whose face I can't remember. Just so much Shrewsbury youth: merely a quantity of hoppers.

Suddenly I can't be bothered to follow the popsies over to the dressing-room. They are squeaking and gibbering more than usual, elated with their prowess. They cast little giggling glances back at me, as much as to say, that showed *him*. They are obviously under the impression that their adornments to the raining song will have put my nose out of joint. God knows why. Or maybe they are just sharing their experience of not going to bed with me. Either way, who wants to follow them as they snicker their way along the corridor? And like as not, my dressing-room will be invaded. I will be forced to indulge in the cut-and-thrust of a discussion with Steg; I'll be pestered by Mr Musgrove, with his head and windows. I feel like some fresh air. Me, Premo. Don't tell the parrots.

What parrots? The parrots will be climbing aboard their buses, and going home. Insurance reps and salesmen will be rogering the parrots.

I walk towards the EXIT. At least Mr Musgrove isn't bleeding in the corridor. I press the bar down and push open the door. Outside there is the Shrewsbury night, in which I can dissipate my aromas.

Outside is my hopper. I remember her so well. She is the one I don't remember. There are a few drops of golden rain, falling past her face. No, they are pale freckles on her skin.

'I came to see you,' she says.

'You weren't at the . . .' I reply.

'No,' she says, 'I came to see *you*. In your dressing-room.'

I lead her to my dressing-room. Steg is drifting down the corridor towards us. He looks impressed at the sight of Premo Bulge with a hopper in tow. He grasps her by the shoulder.

'There's something I want to ask yous,' he says.

'Leave her alone, Steg,' say I.

'Sure, it's just a small item of information.' He fixes her with watery eye and hairy beard, and speaks in a low confidential tone. 'D' yous happen to have a warm receptacle?' he asks. Then, snorting to himself, without waiting for an answer, he floats off.

'Take no notice of him,' I tell my hopper. 'He's merely a psychopath.'

I lock the door of my dressing-room. She stands in the middle of the room and quietly, deliberately, takes off all her clothes. She is lean, with round, goose-pimply breasts, and a little scrub of brown pubic hair at the base of her stomach. She is beautiful, and true.

I, Premo, feel embarrassed at the thought of taking off my clothes under the gaze of my dressing-table lights. Under the gaze of my hopper. I pull my dress off first (obviously), to reveal the full horror of my tee-shirt and my model of a pair of jeans. I feel like making excuses. I'm completely clean under the layer of dirt. Pigs are very hygienic animals. At the same time, of course, she has come to me *as I am*. It is all very difficult. But I still feel ashamed.

To hide my awkwardness, I ask: 'Are there any more at home like you?' I hope it makes it sound as if this is a routine situation for me. Just another hopper.

'No,' she replies, 'only me.'

CHAPTER FIFTEEN

Mrs Cheeseman

'Premo Bulge?' the Prime Minister asked.

Her Secretary of State for Defence winced at the question. The overhead fluorescent tubing explored his countenance with unkind rigour.

'It's very bright in here,' he said, taking off half-moon spectacles. She thought of all those tank-drivers, SAS men, commandos with knives clamped between their teeth, who were in Raymond Durrant's charge. Heavens. But of course the whole point of installing the new lighting in the first place had been to enable her to confront her colleagues as they were.

'I decided it was about time I was able to see what people were getting up to at the bottom of the table,' she said.

Raymond laughed worriedly, obviously wondering if she was serious. She was always serious.

There had been the inevitable fuss when she ordered the removal of the Cabinet Room chandeliers and their replacement by neon tubes. Not from the Cabinet of course: they weren't consulted. But the Downing Street civil servants had been agitated. They presented the usual arguments: tradition, convention, propriety. She'd been sorely tempted to remind the ones who broached the matter with her directly, of the second word of their job description. She'd thought better of it, however – being overtly abrasive could sometimes savour of defensiveness – and confided in them instead, making the point that she wanted to bring some of the government's dustier specimens blinking into the light.

Not that anyone could say that Raymond was dusty. Fragile was the word that sprang to mind. He had small delicate features. Under her new lighting the parts of his nose around each nostril were coral-pink and almost translucent. He had a thin, nervous mouth, small teeth. He was undersized, finely-made, intricate. Some of the newspapers had claimed that in appointing him to his present post Mrs Cheeseman was displaying a sense of humour.

That wasn't the case at all. What had happened had been a misunderstanding on her part. Mistakes were made from time to time but she usually managed to work them invisibly into the fabric of her career. Not by trying to cover them up – defensiveness again – but by making use of them, building on them, coping with the changing perspectives of life in a practical and productive manner. Thus she managed to remain consistent.

The mistake, in the case of Raymond Durrant, had been to imagine that he was some sort of intellectual. This had arisen as a result of a couple of meetings she'd had with him during his time as a junior minister in the Defence Department. Several of the things he'd said had given her the impression he was a bright spark, and contrary to certain press allegations she liked to have a few bright sparks around her. She had, for example, two academic economists on her personal staff. She felt that it would do no harm at all to have an intellectual in charge of the armed services: the service chiefs themselves could supply the brawn, goodness only knew. Unfortunately it had turned out that Raymond had had an academic of his own, and it was from *him* that the interesting ideas had emanated.

Nevertheless she was stuck with Raymond for the time being at least, and she would make the best of it. Making the best of things was exactly what she was best at: indeed for her, producing a silk purse from a sow's ear wasn't just a proverb, it was a mystical principle. Her vision of herself was precisely as the catalyst which triggered off that strange alchemy.

In fact Raymond was an asset in two respects. The first was that he had the virtue which you might predict: he made an excellent errand-boy. The second was that his very failings could be used, and she had already begun to put into effect a line of action which would do just that.

For the moment, however, it was his role as errand-boy which was to be the subject of their Cabinet Room meeting.

'Yes, Premo Bulge,' Raymond finally agreed. 'That was his name.'

'I thought for a moment I was hearing things,' Mrs Cheeseman said.

'He's one of those pop singers,' Raymond explained. He pinked nervously. 'He didn't know anything about it of course. It's just that I arranged for the rendezvous to take place at one of this Bulge person's concerts.'

'Good heavens!'

'Plenty of background noise, that was the idea. There's nothing more conspicuous than some park bench.'

'Raymond, I do believe you've got your head screwed on after all!'

'Thank you, Prime Minister.'

'Did you make contact in person?'

'Oh no,' Raymond said, flurried once more. He paled visibly. 'Did you expect –?'

'I had no particular expectations, Raymond. It was very much your pigeon.'

His anxiety lessened marginally. He approached the top of the table and began to seat himself in the place next to hers.

'I don't think Martin would like you taking his chair,' she said warningly.

Raymond stopped in mid-sit, nonplussed. He straightened up, put his spectacles on again, and peered around the room, as if expecting Martin to spring out at him suddenly from behind a piece of furniture.

'No, Raymond,' she said with strained patience, 'Martin isn't here. It's just you and me. But it's the principle of the thing. The rules of the game.'

'It seems a bit unnecessary to meet here in that case,' Raymond said, or rather muttered, as he walked down the Cabinet table to his own place, number five on the left-hand side, making him ninth in the hierarchy overall. 'I count from the left,' she'd joked at their first meeting. 'That means I'm always going in the Right Direction.' The Right Direction had been their slogan at the landslide election that brought them in.

'We're meeting here, Raymond,' she said as he took his place, 'because this room is a hundred percent secure, and this is a matter which requires one hundred percent security. That is why I asked if you'd seen him in person. I must say, I did have hopes that you would.'

'How could I?' Raymond replied, still in a sort of raised mutter. 'I'm a well-known public figure.'

'You'll have to speak up. We're not nose to nose, you know.'

'I'm a well-known public figure,' he repeated with due embarrassment. 'I would have been recognized. That's why I used a go-between. He was very reliable.' He paused. 'One hundred percent,' he concluded, with his little tentative smile.

'And your go-between, he wasn't . . . ?'

'No, no. He was Defence Department staff. Not the secret services.'

'Thank God. This is a matter which must never, *never* get any further. Let me tell you again: neither you nor your go-between must ever speak of this arrangement to anyone. Even to each other. Even to me. Except of course when I have further errands for you to run.'

'We don't even know what the arrangement *is*,' Raymond said, almost sulkily.

'That, Raymond, is the whole point.'

'It's not *us* you've got to fear.'

'What do you mean by that?'

'Well, I don't understand why you wanted me to find this Fat Man for you. He's an anarchist. He's a Trot. He's not the sort –'

'He's a contract terrorist. This is a business arrangement. And in any case the whole point is that he should not be identified with the government. Don't worry your head about it, Raymond, he's perfectly reliable. Let's leave him to be the man of action, *we* can worry about ideology.'

Mrs Cheeseman was fully aware of the irony of the distinction. Here she was, the most active Prime Minister of modern times, and all she actually did was *say* things. Politics, history itself, was simply a matter of words. When people were beheaded in the old days it was to stop them expressing their point of view. To change everything all you had to do was word it differently. That was all Joseph Harper, her adviser on political economics, had done on that terrible afternoon when a routine conversation had left her career, and therefore the future of the nation at large in chaos. The future was only words. Joseph's words had brought a whole historical cycle to an end, terminated a movement in economics, politics, society. They had quite literally sent her deaf.

CHAPTER SIXTEEN

Joseph

Joseph Harper had been a professor at Harvard when he received his summons from Kathleen Cheeseman. At that time of course it was only early days – she had just been elected head of the Tory party, but Labour were firmly ensconsed in power, and a general election was a couple of years away. The offer, then, was simply of a consultancy: planning on the Right Direction election strategy had already begun, and his services were required as a political economist. The emphasis was on the political: Joseph wasn't in any sense a theoretical economist. Indeed, the theoretical side of Tory monetarism was being worked out by a colleague of his, a Yorkshireman called Ian Priestley, who also had an American chair – at Washington, in Ian's case. Ian formulated the economic principles; Joseph attempted to evolve a political programme out of them. Luckily the two of them were appointed to Mrs Cheeseman's staff at the same time.

Joseph was able to cluster his teaching and spend three days a fortnight in London, travelling by Concorde along with filmstars, pop-singers, businessmen. His fees and expenses were paid for by Conservative Central Office. He loved commuting: Boston was red, London was blue. Any political appositeness in the coloration was coincidental – these were, quite literally, the colours of Joseph's experiences, just as he always saw Tuesdays as yellow, Wednesdays as green, Thursdays as brown, and so forth. His sensibility, developed by the discipline of political economics, discovered surfaces, sometimes substances, in dimensions which to ordinary people were simply transparent. Although of course anybody not colour-blind could pick out the basic blueness of British vegetation from the plane, a blue which seemed to seep into the air itself, hover in the chilly streets, accrue upon the faces of the buildings – of the passersby, even. Meanwhile, the New England leaves turned vivid red in the fall, and behind the temporary-looking wooden houses of the Boston suburbs, where Harvard was situated, one could intuit the Indian past. New England, apart from being new, was also vertiginously old.

Nevertheless, there *was* a political contrast, equally exhilarating. His economic beliefs were the same in both locations, but in England they fitted into Kathleen Cheeseman's new Toryism with the smooth exactness of gear cogs in an expensive car; in America, with its much less categorical way of dealing with fiscal issues, and the far more blurred ideological identities of the major political parties, he was considered simply as an important landmark on the academic scene. He could switch from the concentration of energy, that Concorde-like penetration consequent on *parti pris*, on the one hand, or rather, on the one side of the Atlantic, to academic neutrality and judiciousness on the other. In England he had an elegant estranged wife, prim and proper, cold as charity, and two sons at public school; in America he had a live-in girl-friend, earthy, spontaneous, sloppy, voluptuous. Laurette she was called; his English wife's name was Emma. Similarly in America he was known as Joe; while at Conservative Central Office Kathleen Cheeseman and all the rest insisted on calling him Joseph, as if losing half his name meant he would go around half-dressed. Kathleen herself had not, of course, been able to avoid being known as Kathie or even as Kath by the popular press since her election to the leadership.

Joe and Laurette lived in the Boston suburb of Somerville. They had the ground floor of a rather grand house in a tree-lined street; most of the surrounding township was dingy and even rough. Another contrast; again it appealed. A turbid solution could precipitate its middle-class crystal at the most unexpected points. Keynesianism, like Marxism, was a monolithic structure crudely evoking vast forces; it had no respect for the detailed, the intricate, the local. It required huge accumulations of capital, artificially manufactured, divorced from value or work, just as Marxism did; in Marxism they would act as the stimuli of revolution; in Keynesianism they would sweep through society like a series of tidal waves, washing frantic consumers along with them. Neither system respected the delicate balance of forces to be discovered in a place like Somerville. But if you gave people sound money to play with, however limited the amounts, there was no limit to the ingenuity of the structures they could make with them: dynamic businesses, luxurious residences. Robert Lester, the Shadow Industry spokesman, had talked to Joseph once about the little shops you sometimes saw under railway bridges, just a counter, a few cubic feet of space. Usually they sold sex-aids nowadays, or perhaps magazines. Robert foresaw the day when a fortune could be founded on such minimal premises, given monetarism as a *point d'appui*. Many of his colleagues thought Robert was mentally ill, with his gaunt rapt gaze. Joseph, though, had a certain amount of time for raptness.

Laurette took the big phone call when it came two years later. They were entertaining an American couple called the Millers at the time. Bud Miller was an archaeologist from Mississippi, a dark brooding sort of individual. Mississippi struck Joe as in some ways a tropical equivalent of Yorkshire, and, used as he was to dealing with Ian Priestley, he was on familiar territory with Bud. Denise, Bud's wife, was very different, a brittle intense New Yorker who talked, cleverly, nineteen to the dozen. Like Laurette she was one of those eternal students who seem to be part of the very fabric of American academic life. The four of them had been out on the town, celebrating (for Joe's benefit) Kathleen Cheeseman's triumph in the British election; they had ended up in the swimming pool of Adams House, one of the Harvard halls of residence – quite literally in it, skinny-dipping. Now they were back at Joe and Laurette's apartment, finishing the evening as they had begun, with highballs.

Bud and Denise were bickering on a settee at the far side

of the L-shaped lounge. Laurette, glass in hand, came over and flopped beside Joe.

'Oh Jeez,' she said in a low voice, 'that was a *night*mare.'

'What was?'

'The poo-ol, that's what. Just hanging on to the edge like a stranded damn whale.' To his surprise, as she was such a physical person, Laurette had turned out to be unable to swim.

'Well, why did you agree to go when Denise suggested it?'

'I don't know. I was so full of goddam booze I had an idea I'd swim by sheer willpower. The thing of it was, I was a lamb to the slaughter for that bastard.' She nodded across the room at Bud. 'He was goosing me all the goddam time I was in the water.'

'I thought he was teaching you to swim.'

'Swim, my sweet ass. I think Denise set the whole thing up. Perhaps she gets a kick out of seeing him do his archaeology on another poor bitch.'

As Joe laughed the phone rang. Laurette took it.

'It's for you,' she said quietly across the room to him. Something in her tone made Bud and Denise stop squabbling.

'Who is it?' Joe asked, his voice uneven. He suddenly knew who it was.

'It's the British Prime Minister,' Laurette said.

He could feel the eyes of the others looking up at him as he walked over to the phone. Harvard suddenly seemed very provincial.

Mrs Cheeseman was offering him a job as one of her personal economics advisers – the post he'd held before, except that now, crucially, she was not Leader of the Opposition but Prime Minister, and of course it would need to be full-time.

'How much?' he asked, still conscious that the Americans were gazing at him, as it were from their burrows.

'You don't take long to get down to brass tacks,' the Prime Minister said.

'For an economist it's the crucial question.'

'You'd be on the rate of a permanent Under-Secretary. About twenty-five thousand.'

'It's not enough.'

'It's more than enough.'

'It's not enough.'

There was a pause. The silence failed to become ominous. Joe wasn't a politician and so he wasn't as susceptible to Mrs Cheeseman's bullying as most of her colleagues. This was truly a transatlantic call.

'But it was you who proposed a four percent pay award in the public sector.'

'But *they*'ll take it. That means they're worth it. I won't take it, which means I'm worth more. I *know* I'm worth more because I'm getting more at the moment. If you add together my academic salary and various consultancy fees, much more. You should know the second law of monetarism: if you pay peanuts, you get monkeys.'

He felt intoxicated, confident, American, grateful to the highballs of the evening, to the recklessness of skinny-dipping, for giving him an edge on Mrs Cheeseman. She replied with that weary amusement of a strong woman dealing with a man she has to admire.

'And what is the first law of monetarism, then?'

'Most people are monkeys.'

'We'll pay you from Tory funds,' she said resignedly. 'Fifty thousand. Ian Priestley insisted on the same amount.'

CHAPTER SEVENTEEN

Laurette

So OK the pool. So someone suggests the pool. So OK. In the destructive element immerse. Laurette remembered Prof. Duckett, spittle round his lips, quoting Conrad in the Lit 601 course. The old faker even said it in a kind of Polish accent, Eastern European anyway, or German or something. In zer desktructive element.

'I'll go and get my things,' Laurette said.

'Come *on*,' said Denise. 'What things? We're four grown-ups going for a dip in a swimming-pool at night, we know all about the little accessories we got to do a tinkle from.'

Impossible to argue. Denise was just being mature. OK, OK, maturity was a fake, nobody ever got mature enough not to devote a large part of their attention to the tinkle area. But if you started arguing it would just look as if you were papering over some sort of hang-up. And who could say you weren't? Straightaway it had crossed her mind, shit, here I am getting all this prestige from screwing Joseph Harper, charming English big-deal economics professor, with his cute English half-timbered Toryism, and his big beard and his serious eyes and all, and now Bud and Denise are going to discover that Joseph's little accessory is indeed on the little side, a kinda cute itsy-bitsy timid withdrawn little prick full of charming English reserve. I mean, what kinda attitude is that to take? For one, it implies all that sort of possession and identification crap, like as if my, Laurette's, own identity is attached to a certain modest accessory, like as if you could measure *my* inner depths by placing a ruler alongside Joseph's external not-very prominence. Surely in this day and age a woman doesn't need to be assessed on an inch-by-inch basis by the length to which she is screwed? Sisters, rise up, even if your men don't. Or at least, don't very. For two, if you can't judge a woman by the length of a man's prick, surely to god you can't judge a man by it either? Hang on here, though, this is a dangerous area to move into, this is one of the traps of certain kinds of feminism, where sexlessness rears its ugly lack-of head. You can't characterize a woman by a man's maleness, but you got no choice but to characterize a *man* by a man's maleness, without denying the God within, the life-force, the whole bundle of energies that strives for connection, not that Max Weber argument that Joe talks about, converting religious drives into a capitalist success-ethic, only of course Joe thinks that's bingo, believing it gives like sanction and sacrament to mercenary transactions. Jeez that's significant, a kinda economic alternative to satisfactory give and take in some other area, be it religious or tinkle, take your pick, but it's significant that Joe holds the views he does given the equipment he's not particularly got. So you got to look a prick in the face and say that's part of *you*, man, Man, you got to nail your flag to that mast, we're all beasts of the field. But still this size business savours of fascist garbage, the measuring of Jewish bottoms or Negro lips or whatever else those racist madmen want to turn their attention to. Joe's maleness is not definable in terms of the *size* of his tool, it's an indefinable essence, it suffuses the being, like sex suffuses society, culture, literature, despite fakers like Professor Duckett with spittle round their lips.

But on the other hand the unveiling by the pool. It had an elemental implication, it sounded like a nineteenth-century French painting, or some totem or taboo in Freud, or a classic of pornographic literature. You can't hang a little placard on poor Joseph's tool saying this may be small but it's a regular powerhouse. In any case it wouldn't be true. In any case maybe I don't *want* it to be true. Maybe it suits me just the way it is, or isn't. Maybe it is exactly all I can cope with. And *that*'s what I don't want unveiled by the pool.

The pool was cavernous in the dim evening, you could imagine some goddam dark and slimy thing moving beneath its smooth skin, some mutated left-over from dinosaur days, like that monster in Scotland, a creature from the depths of the psyche rising to the surface like Moby Dick. Yes, you could analyse it just like the scenery in Melville or Fenimore Cooper or Edgar Allan Poe, the paraphernalia of the conscious mind all round the edge, diving boards with ladders so you kinda climbed away from the destructive element before you dropped towards it neat and curvy, grace in the face of danger, or lack of face, big hooks on the walls for fishing people, fishing *people*, jeez, that caught the back-to-frontness, the mirror reversal as you plopped down into the regions of the subconscious, for fishing people *out* of the destructive element, cork life-savers for the same purpose, and in the middle of it all the inscrutable, smooth, subtly shifting surface of the pool waiting to gobble you up without even opening its lips. Laurette had found something horrible in a pool once, hadn't swum in a pool since.

Joe was frisky enough, as he had been all evening, no fears of what might lie beneath the surface, pool- or short-wise. In fact his shorts were off so fast it was like a conjurer doing a trick, and he sort of strutted round waiting for the others to finish undressing, with his tiddly little moby dick doing like bellyflops from side to side with each movement of his legs, and his big bearded bespectacled head looking quite pleased and proud of the effect like it was some sort of good conduct or long service medal that the fisher king or sacred mushroom or life force had stuck on the front of his groin.

Laurette watched Denise take a peek, a whole bunch of peeks in quick succession, as she knew she would, as any woman would, quick peeks like their eyeballs couldn't accommodate too much prick at any one time, not like men who go fixed and starey in the face or rather the body of bare women, as if *their* eyes have arrived at an oasis at last and can't stop drinking. Fear not Denise, those well mascara-ed, pencil-lined, green-shadowed eyes of yours can cope and to spare, especially holy cow, a sudden interior yawp like the sound effects at a high school party as Bud's shorts come off in turn and his variation on the prehistoric theme, in major key, in massive chords, became apparent and Laurette understood the strategic necessity of the quick peek. That thing could hypnotize you like a goddam snake. Oh Denise, if you have limbered up on such a piece of equipment your eyes can take Joseph's willy in their stride, like a bird a worm.

But still Denise was taking quick flurried glances at Joe's target area, no disapproval, no smirk visible, just short appraisals, tick tick, some process of evaluation going on inside, tick tick some minus grade being assigned shit I've been through all that, it's not *my* prick, and anyway it's all beside the point.

Into the pool. So, OK, the pool.

Dark yet transparent the pool, your tapering legs wobbling and floating off, jeez they feel like that to swim with too, talk about dead legs, it's like swimming with no legs at all. Isn't that one of the pieces of wisdom your parents handed down to you when they weren't busy screwing you up? You never forget how to ride a bicycle, or how to swim, or how to you-know-what, thanks mom thanks pop, I just did. Forget how to swim, that is. I know I swam like a fish in the amniotic fluid, swam in dark swamps far far back when time hadn't started yet and only geology reigned, but since then I been born, I evolved. You lose your fins as you go on, like an angel her wings when she's thrown out of paradise. So one arm up over round, thin wing, shit, nothing happens, it's not that the water won't hold you, it's the opposite, the water feels like glue, a thick medium your thin wing can't gain purchase on. You're like a butterfly on fly paper. So she hangs there, flailing, while Joseph swims about with a kinda prissy English breaststroke contradicting his big furry sealion's head and spectacles, fish eyes, round and gleaming in the dim light. That was one of the nice things about Englishmen she always thought, they were so bad at *doing* everything, not like efficient crude American males with their hard finite cleanshaven faces and their high school training in football and press-ups. Englishmen thought that *doing* things was not cricket, and since they never seemed to actually *play* cricket either, at least not in her company, they developed a sort of ornate marginal charm while the American world blasted past with all the tact and sensitivity of a freight train. Once, in her sophomore year, she had been in the university library doing some work at a paper she had to give to her section and opposite her sat this cute little English academic, reading Swinburne or some goddam English thing. He had a sweet little suit on and a tie and all, and neat hair, and he looked sort of delightfully weird compared with all the

American late sixties weirdos, he looked like a little refuge of order, manners, reserve, in a world of ranting ghouls, like as if he was the one outpost of civilization left. And then he did a burp. Just like that. Halfway through some attenuated piece of Swinburne, some etiolated, tricky, delicately-charged English homosexual lyricism and – burp. But it wasn't like a brutal American male eructation, it wasn't some aggressive, armpit-scratching, easily-earned gaseous ejaculation, yankee-style, it was a burp that belonged in the context of European civilization like: The Human Burp meets the Court of Versailles. She actually caught a sweet perfumy scent that had drifted across the still dank mouldy air of the library, a whiff of aftershave perhaps, but it could have been the afterwash of the burp, as if the Englishman didn't come from a world where nature was red in tooth and claw but from a serene, bejewelled, artificial landscape, where *every*thing in the garden came up roses.

But of course in her naivety she hadn't thought of the bedward implications of all this. *That* wasn't cricket either. Still there was Joseph calmly swimming round in his little circles, he was *game*, you couldn't take that away from him. And he was going better than *she* was, she was not swimming at all, not even sinking, just stuck here between two worlds, like some ugly incompetent lungfish gasping on the shore. And then Bud, with long proprietorial strokes, as if he and the destructive element had some kind of understanding between them, swam up and joined her.

'You OK?' he asked.

'Sure,' she replied.

'You just don't seem to have much forward momentum.'

'Not a lot.'

'Being at the deep end and all.'

'This pool is nothing *but* deep end.'

The pool sure enough was six feet all the way along. She'd noticed that from the markings on the side at just about mid-point in her trajectory from the edge to the surface, when it was exactly too goddam late to turn back.

'I'll help you to the rail, if you like.'

He took hold of the top of her arm, and began to propel her railwards, his body close, cool, strongly heaving the water, lying side-on so he could speak to her, so that (*maybe* so that, certainly *effectively* so that) down below a long cool eel-like thing could brush against her thigh, and suddenly a sense of cool fishy life blindly pressing at her through the water, a sense that the cavernous pool hall was a great box enclosing her like a lobster in a pot, a sense of the past both primeval and personal rising up towards her from hidden depths, combined to make her panic, shake, almost scream, the scream stuck in her throat, only the sudden thought of Denise's lofty dismissal of anything that savoured of tinkle anxiety keeping it in; Denise who didn't even fill her prissy clothes, but strangely filled an area on the diving board where she was standing as if carved, as if the dank savagery of this place were profoundly favourable to some principle of feminine roundness that had resided deep within her, so that she had unexpectedly thrust herself into the air, like some pulpy fungus in a dim damp woodland glade. Only Denise's sudden complacent femininity prevented Laurette from screaming, so that she suddenly realized you don't go about raving from terror and repulsion for one reason only, only one thing holds you back, prevents you from howling like a wolf at those blind, unexpectedly plump breasts with their blank pink eyes leering down at you, at the blind long water-snake probing up at you from below, only one thing prevents you from yelling your pain at the sheer claustrophobia of the body, and that was good old all-American, small-town, gingham-befrocked, corn-fed, puritanical embarrassment. It was embarrassment made the world go round or anyway stopped society blowing apart at the seams, a thin sneaky pressure of embarrassment, pressing gently outwards from some hollowness in your very soul, equalizing the pressure of intrusive physicality, procuring a locked interface between you and the molesting world so there was no room even to scream, all you did was play your part, fulfil your role, chat about this and that with Bud while you clutched the rail with *your* hand, and *he* clutched your *mons veneri* with his, and while a certain cold dark blind tenuous thing flickered and slithered round your thighs, and while in the distance Joseph swam badly in small cheerful circles and Denise dove plumb in the centre of his circles to the merriment of both concerned, and while in your mind it was all coming back, the sunny southern spring, the weather-beaten planks of the little pier that stuck into the lake, the lazy smell of dogwood, the boy saying 'Princess, princess,' because pop called her princess, trying to persuade her to have a dip, and she, the princess, resisting, because princesses and thirteen-year-old girls were supposed to resist, saying the water will be chilly, but sunlight everywhere, thick as corn, as butter, as yolk of egg, and finally the argument not holding up, and the princess, the thirteen-year-old girl agreeing, not remembering what happened to pubescent girls, to princesses, when they strayed too near the water, not remembering then but remembering ever since, remembering up to the present when it was all happening again, a pool, Bud's southern accent, but now not southern spring but Massachusetts fall, not sunlight but dimness, as if this was a reflection, a transparency of the original experience, perhaps everything always has to happen twice, the wheel to come full circle.

CHAPTER EIGHTEEN

Joseph

Joseph Harper was walking across Hampstead Heath. He needed some fresh air, having spent a difficult morning at Conservative Central Office presenting unemployment projections to the party chairman.

The figures had been worrying. In several crucial sectors of the economy the redundancy rate showed signs of declining, and in two it looked as if employment was set to increase. Ian Priestley took a lofty attitude to the statistics:

his model was working perfectly and that was what he had been employed to produce. It was Joseph's responsibility to relate the model to actuality, and this was becoming increasingly difficult to do. How ironic if, after all they had done, the job situation should bottom out prematurely and the good old slack machinery of British industry should start to whirr and clank once more before the economic springs had been tightened sufficiently to force it into a new, dynamic mode of operation.

Sir Arthur Burton, the party chairman, like so many people even in the top political echelons, found it difficult to accustom himself to the monetarist perspective. This morning Joseph had tried to make things clearer by using the analogy of slimming. A person goes on a diet, loses a few pounds, puts up with a lot of aggravation and suffering, and then, before achieving the sort of weight which would make him athletic and vigorous again, begins to munch once more. Of course society at large didn't have a sufficiently focused identity for terms like willpower and motivation, the vocabulary of dieting, to be relevant. Starving – in terms of investment capital – would be nearer the mark.

Joseph could quite understand how Sir Arthur found it difficult to cope with a certain topsy-turveydom in the monetarist approach. The point, of course, was that monetarism was a revolution. The reorganization of the nation's economy was inevitably bound up with new ways of thinking, new modes of behaviour. The problem Sir Arthur had to face was that the traditional political vocabulary had to be used to describe what amounted to a mirror-reversal of traditional reality. In public he had to 'deplore' any rise in unemployment and claim that everything possible was being done to halt it. He had to 'regret' the necessity for a rise in interest rates. Since he was not a charlatan he was baffled when he heard Joseph, in private, deplore a fall in *un*employment, and discuss ways of forcing financial institutions to raise their interest rates even further. Naturally any normal person would feel uneasy at having to utter the sort of double-speak which Sir Arthur's political position forced on him: unhappily we (i.e. five million, ultimately, of *you*) will have to endure some years (i.e. permanent) austerity, in order to ensure a brighter future for all (i.e. of the rest of us). This sort of speaking with forked tongue sounded immoral, of course it did. But in the end the state had as much right to respond to economic imperatives by laying off twenty percent of its workforce as an individual company had. The problem arose because the necessity could not be baldly expressed. The government had sold 'realism', even 'austerity', as indications of its integrity; what it could not do was sell unemployment as a deliberate policy aim. It was necessary to bemoan it as a natural disaster, a socio-economic act of God. Therefore Sir Arthur had to wring his hands in public, and at some deep, private, intellectual level which he didn't possess, endeavour to reconcile rhetoric and reality.

His unease had communicated itself to Joseph. No, no, that wasn't quite true. During their discussions Joseph had become uneasy but the cause of his unease was different from Sir Arthur's. It didn't emanate from the communication gap that lay between government policy and the ordinary voter; nor, for that matter, from the possibility of diminishing levels of unemployment. No, it was something other, something he couldn't quite put his finger on, a certain intangible something that merely seemed to flit around the identifiable problems, brushing against them in passing. A glimpse, a momentary sensation, an intuition of disturbance: nothing he could formulate.

Denise was out when he arrived back at the flat. She was probably at some extramural course or attending a meeting of do-gooders. She didn't share Laurette's reckless compulsion to search out the good life, whatever that was (and Laurette herself probably had less idea than anybody, except that it was some state of emotional, possibly even sexual, anarchy in which, paradoxically, no one must get hurt), but Denise was an earnest liberal in her own quiet way. She didn't disapprove of his involvement with a right-wing administration, she just didn't notice it. The terms of British politics were simply foreign to her. She would be critical about general issues, never of him. And she was a marvellous housekeeper: tidy, tasteful, even elegant. A far remove from Laurette's slobbiness.

Today, though, Denise must have been in a hurry. She'd cut herself a slice of bread and left a scattering of crumbs upon their gleaming working-surface. Those crumbs somehow made the whole kitchen seem empty and forlorn: they were the raw edge of their domestic life. Laurette's comprehensive chaos, by contrast, had not suggested anything larger than itself: or at least nothing except the exuberant movements of the living woman. At the other extreme Emma, his English wife, still undivorced at Kathleen Cheeseman's personal behest, was the quintessence of frigid Englishness. Denise lay exactly between these opposites, a mid-Atlantic synthesis. Her identity was less clear than either, but she was deep.

Nevertheless, as he looked at Denise's crumbs he couldn't help thinking, rather wistfully, of Laurette. He'd received a letter from her the other day. She and Bud were now in Chicago.

Bud screws around as much as ever. So what? It's an expression of the needs of the inner man, or the outer man, anyway. No, that sounds like I'm sore. We all have to find ourselves, and Bud seems to have been broken into little pieces and concealed inside a whole bunch of different ladies. There's something beautiful about it if you look at it right. I mean, the sheer *number* of human beings with whom he's made intimate contact. It's a kind of community coalescing together around the sex act, like Bud's at one with a much bigger chunk of humanity than most of us ever get tied up with. You can look on seminal fluid as a kind of biological glue; and it's *salty*, like the blood that flows through all our veins.

Gee, Joe, you wouldn't believe how icy it gets in Chicago this time of the year.

As he reread Laurette's letter in the empty flat Joseph felt a sharp nostalgia for American vigour and openness:

97

for the red instead of the blue. The nearest he could get to expressing, or perhaps combating, this feeling was to go for a walk upon Hampstead Heath.

The weather was icy here too, in fact the heath was covered by a thin layer of snow. He thought of Bud screwing his way through the chilly wastes of Chicago; then he remembered skinny-dipping in the pool of Adams House. Yes, perhaps the vocabulary of Laurette's letter did mean something: they had been like a tribal group. Or, alternatively, an experimental mini-utopia: New England was both old and new. They had remained a foursome during his last month in America, while he wound up his affairs. Then they had had to break up.

Maybe that was the wrong way of looking at it: *breaking up*. It implied waste, and nothing had been wasted. Two new couples had been formed, that was the result – a process of parturition, like some bulging amoeba finally dividing. And each couple had some of the salt of the other, even though each constituted a new entity in itself. It was a process of synthesis. Nothing had been broken, nobody had been damaged.

Joseph was acutely aware that this was not his vocabulary. This was the vocabulary of an Hegelian mystic, celebrating the economy of the dialectical process. Such terms did not reflect the economy of reality, because reality *was* wasteful. There had to be five million unemployed. There could be no such thing as an economic economics. Nature *itself* was wasteful.

The heath, under a winter sky, did not seem wasteful, it had an austere, efficient economy in every contour. All of it, like a great white bloom, was unfolded into aesthetic use. But that was the point of course, the heath wasn't a natural landscape – the whole environment had been acted on, organized, by man. It represented a human manipulation of ecology. It –

Suddenly, strangely, Joseph, too, was looking on the bright side. Not in Hegelian terms, indeed, but in that other manner that was just as sweeping. What now seemed to be swept up was the intimate detail, the very ecology, of life itself. Crossing the bare common, in snow puddles, at twilight, under a clouded sky, without having in his thoughts any occurrence of special good fortune, he found himself enjoying a perfect exhilaration, became glad to the brink of fear. Or rather, *from* the brink of fear, because what he experienced was the earlier disturbance, his sense of unease, of subterranean shiftings, fully manifested, like a snake sloughing its skin. But what appeared was not a snake, it was nothing specific, indeed the whole manifestation was of the end of specificity, it was like seeing the world from a new angle of vision, bathed in light from another sun, or in radiance when, as now, the sun was not shining. It was like listening to the music of the spheres.

Slushy and cold as his environment was, Joseph had a sense of not being apart from the landscape, indeed of being invaded by it, of being a component in a unifying system. You could call it what you liked – Laurette, that voluble American, would have words for it: God pantheism, zen.

In the economic domain, its name was Keynesianism.

CHAPTER NINETEEN

Mrs Cheeseman

Kathleen Cheeseman sat in her Downing Street office at her tidy, indeed empty, desk, under the severe illumination of neon. Joseph Harper lounged in a Parker Knoll opposite. The room had been full of antiques when she'd first come to power, but she felt that they provided the wrong sort of atmosphere, apart from being uncomfortable. She'd had them put in store as a signal that, in every sense of the phrase, she meant business. The chandeliers had gone too; the same fate would befall the even more elaborate ones in the Cabinet Room, but she was biding her time for that until next summer's recess.

Joseph relaxed deeply into his chair, as if he'd been

softened like cooking chocolate. He was actually a big-chested narrow-hipped busy-looking man, with a grey academic beard and thick spectacles that came out at you like headlights out of fog; the lassitude was a pose. It emphasized the fact that they had an informal relationship which lay completely outside the political hierarchy. She'd told him once that he was a sort of Prime Ministerial valet. 'You mean,' he'd replied, 'that I have access to you in a state of ideological undress.' She didn't even resent the suggestiveness of the remark, although in normal circumstances she kept that frame of reference firmly at bay: there was no mileage for her in sexual imagery, except of a housekeeping variety which emphasized not female passivity in the courtship cycle, but womanly control over the domestic environment. But Joseph provided input, he was her ideas man: it wasn't entirely unnatural that he should resort to masculine imagery.

Despite the affectations of certain continental leaders, it was footling to pretend that an individual at the summit of national power could devote the requisite time and energy to the task of being an intellectual. Operating the machinery of power was a full-time task, not something you played at after a long session in your study. That machinery, however, was fuelled by words, and in the economic sphere many of those words were provided by Joseph Harper. However much Joseph lolled, he always had a carefully argued brief propped between the rakish legs, and he would go through it word by word, glossing if necessary. He was a man with a talent for the specific; and therein lay his whole commitment to monetarism.

Until this afternoon.

At first she'd hardly noticed. Joseph seemed to be speaking more quietly than usual, and one of the neon tubes began hissing. She had a bit of a headache also, which savoured of female nonsense and was not like her. His remarks, as they penetrated her mind in rather fragmentary form, perhaps seemed on the vague side, but she set this down as a series of opening generalizations. The hissing looped in and out of his comments. *Thought that monetarism would provide saturated solution in which wealth would crystallize by means of removal of extraneous elements from the economy. The discarding of insufficiently productive sectors would stiffen the fluid. Now realized this was an inadequate model because it didn't provide any sort of repository for the unwanted material.* The neon hiss had intensified into a sort of hum, a hum moreover which seemed to hit the exact note of her headache. *Nothing in the material world ever ceases to exist entirely . . .* That rang a bell, was it Newton, somebody like that? *. . . any case economics had to be coextensive with the continuum of reality, otherwise sort of game. A system whereby waste becomes surplus provides solution . . .* The humming was intense now. What sort of solution? Was he referring to the aforementioned fluid which needed stiffening? Or did he mean the answer? Or both? *. . . brings the discarded material back into the arena. In a sense monetarism does that anyway but refuses to admit . . . supporting five million unemployed exactly like spending a fortune on TVA . . .* The initials boomed through the hum, like foghorns through seamist, like Joseph's spectacles through fog. What did they mean? She knew and didn't know. They meant something outrageous. They meant the Tennessee Valley Authority. She had that kind of memory. What she couldn't remember was what the Tennessee Valley Authority meant, except that it meant something outrageous. The initials had come through that cloud of neon like the knell of doom. How could neon be sharp and vague at the same time? The humming blurred all outlines; the light was piercing. Pure neon bored through her head from ear to ear. Through blinding illumination she could still see Joseph's pink mouth opening and closing. It had lost its male charm and now seemed like some pulsing, glutinous creature caught in a web of beard. His voice was tiny, inaudible, and yet she could hear what he was saying. No, not hear, see. The neon brought out every movement, nuance, of that mouth as it chopped the academic sentences into words, the neon was so harsh, intense, that she could actually lipread by it. Words arrived in her head, writing like insects against the loud shining. *Keynesian system prints money to provide the leverage of surplus spending power. We print money to provide dole for the unemployed. By dropping the real level of production in the economy in order to raise the productivity rate what we have really done is to ensure that the present level of money in the economy is in fact a surplus. Which is another way of saying that we are manufacturing paper money. Indices show a decrease in the inflation rate but we are still operating by means of the diminished inflation we have left. We are, then, utilizing the Keynesian system but at half cock.*

The Keynesian system. Joseph's mouth rippled along the phrase and disgorged it into the room like some pink, terrible baby.

Kathleen Cheeseman spent a week in a small private hospital while her ears were scraped and small spherical hearing aids, called 'pearls', were inserted. Her inner ears had waxed up, the consultant explained, and the pressure from the accumulation had been the cause of her headache. Some damage had resulted, and her hearing was impaired, but not gravely. Her press officer informed the nation that she was undergoing treatment for eye trouble. Then, when she left the hospital, she could demonstrate to the world her rapid and complete recovery; and nobody would pay any attention to her ears. The hospital staff had been asked to sign the Official Secrets Act.

When the pearls were in place, the Prime Minister asked to see Joseph Harper. He came in clutching flowers and grapes, but he made no recantation. He leaned forwards at her from the bedside chair, not lolling this time.

'I realize I've talked myself out of a job,' he said. 'Never mind, you've still got Ian Priestley.'

'Ian doesn't do the politics, you know that.'

'You'll manage.'

'There's no question of your going.'

'I would have thought, all things considered, there's no question of my staying.'

'Everyone knows that you have been the driving force

behind my economic policy. If word gets out that you've changed your mind, the "Right Direction" will become a laughing stock.'

'You could sack me because of my irregular personal life.'

'Since you're not a member of the government, your private life's your own affair.'

'You didn't seem to think that when you asked me not to let Emma have a divorce.'

'It's always best to keep a low profile, that's my whole point.'

They remained silent for a while.

'I don't see how I can continue to work for you,' Joseph finally said. 'I can't pursue one economic policy while I believe in another.'

'You know the saying. Politics is the art of the possible. Let's review the possibilities.'

'There aren't any possibilities, only impossibilities.'

'Let's review the impossibilities then, and perhaps a course of action will emerge. It's impossible for you to go, number one. You won't stay on if the administration remains monetarist, number two. I can't change course, number three.'

Again they were silent.

'There is always an alternative,' Mrs Cheeseman said. The alternative hovered in the air, not quite formulated. Joseph's spectacles looked opaque through *her* dark glasses, as if he'd deliberately shut them down. The Prime Minister sensed that he knew what the alternative was, but wasn't saying. Didn't dare to say. Couldn't accept it himself. It was on the tip of her mind. But she wouldn't ask.

'I'll modify my policies within a year,' she said finally. 'I'll make some major concession in your direction if you agree to stay on. You can spend the interval developing your ideas. In the meantime I'd be grateful if you could keep quiet about all this.'

'All right,' Joseph said.

She took off her dark glasses and gave him a long look. 'I don't like to be let down,' she said.

'I won't let you down,' he replied quietly, and left.

Her hearing aids felt oppressive, much bigger than they actually were, as if somebody had pushed a stubby finger deep into each of her ears. She became aware of a faint hiss, and looked up at the fluorescent tube on the ceiling. Surely not. They couldn't all do that. And even if they did, she wouldn't be beaten. She wasn't that sort of woman. She would still order the removal of the Cabinet Room chandeliers next summer, and their replacement by neon.

She leaned back against her pillow, breathless with heat, invaded by hearing aids, conscious of buzzing, more oppressed by external factors than at any time she could remember. However, the more pressure, the more resistance, that was Newton too, irresistible force, immovable object. Anyway, the buzzing wasn't coming from the fluorescent tube, but from the hospital as a whole, it was just the sound institutions made as they ticked over, the humming of the very machinery of civilization. Her ears had been silting up for years, before reaching an acute stage at the horrible consultation with Joseph last week, and she'd simply forgotten what the world sounded like.

What was it Joseph had had in his mind this afternoon? What idea lurked, unspoken, behind his spectacles? What else would you spend money on in the Keynesian system besides the sort of public philanthropy that her public would be the first to reject? She had looked up the TVA during her time in hospital; discreetly of course. If she had broached the problem directly with one of the civil servants who scurried back and forth between her bed and 10 Downing Street, suspicions might have been aroused, rumours set in motion. So she had simply requested the appropriate volume of *Encyclopaedia Britannica* and looked it up for herself. Of course. The Tennessee Valley Authority had been one of the major public projects of the New Deal, part of Roosevelt's Keynesian strategy for ending the Great Depression. Dig a huge hole in the ground to pour money in; but pour water in as well so that it wouldn't be too obvious. It was not a policy she could pursue, even if she wanted to. It would certainly be too obvious now.

In any case, that wasn't what Joseph had in mind. She was positive that he knew of a way out of the impasse. What on earth was it? She almost knew herself. There had to be something, she *always* fought back.

Then she had it. In a flash.

She always fought back. That was the clue. That was her cue indeed.

CHAPTER TWENTY

Horace

Horace Bentley was sure the Prime Minister was up to something. The signs were familiar. Her hair burned even more intensely than usual beneath the neon tubing that had somehow materialized during the summer recess, but her face below it was remote, abstracted, vague even. The dark glasses which she'd worn since her eye treatment last spring only emphasized the fact that, whatever the Right Direction was, at the moment it was taking her away from the matters in hand. She let the meeting meander on, producing inharmonious decisions. Weak ministers had their moment of glory; garrulous ones talked themselves out.

Horace was well aware that those terms, weak, garrulous, could apply, no doubt in the minds of some of his colleagues did apply, to him. So be it. Weakness was intrinsic to his department, Art and Culture; and his garrulity was, he hoped, flighted with wit. But it could give him no satisfaction to test the ambivalence of those qualities, cheek by jowl with other putative mice, in an arena where, mentally at least, the cat was away. His lips were sealed; he doodled; the afternoon wore on.

And then suddenly she was back.

It oughtn't to have come as such a surprise: cat was

indeed the word. His mother had owned one during his rather intermittent childhood, a Siamese, and he had often watched it on the lawn. It would sit, glazed, statuesque, firm of outline, as if its energy were exactly equal to the task of etching its silhouette on to the consciousness of any onlooker, beetle, the young Horace, some discreetly distant bird, and no more: and then! a passing leaf was mutilated, savagery had been drawn magically from the very air. Horace, now, was the passing leaf.

Redundant to emote at the injustice of it: what had any leaf done to deserve its fate? The claws grasped at what was available when the cat's eyes came into focus, as those eyes behind dark spectacles so effectively had, despite recent surgery, possibly perceiving Horace offering a whispered joke to the bulbous Andrew Carstairs beside him.

'We have got to save money,' she said harshly, 'it's the old story.'

What a point to surface at, the old story! Where had she been meanwhile, perusing new stories? If so, could one assume that the story had in reality changed? Or to put it another way, that the old story was a story indeed?

No time to speculate, as the passing leaf, betrayed by nondescript and invisible breezes, encounters a merciless paw.

'It's the non-essentials we should lean on, I'm afraid we have no other choice, Horace.'

Possibilities crowded through the head of the passing, indeed the trembling, leaf. Justifications of art streamed by as lifetimes should in the case of drowning men. Horace discarded them at once, he wasn't a politician for nothing. Preachers preached to the converted; art could be defended only to the artistic; aesthetic arguments lacked edge in the hands of one of the self-confessed Tory wimps. That, no doubt, was why he had been given Art and Culture in the first place. The other, more ornate, more poisonous, poisoned chalice – Northern Ireland – had gone to the other, more important Cabinet wimp, Graham Whitley: on account, no doubt, of his greater importance and his greater wimpdom.

'It won't do us any good to be branded as philistines,' Horace countered pragmatically. 'With the press if not with the public.'

'It will do us even less good to dispose of a chunk of the National Health Service.'

'But Art and Culture is chicken-feed,' he said, taking his other pragmatic tack, although the sailing imagery was inappropriate: pragmatic arguments, from whatever source, weighed leaden, lacking the buoyancy of ideas. He had done his duty but it would be to no avail: he would have to lose a million just to make Kathleen Cheeseman feel alive again in the room. No need even to tremble, the tension had gone. He might as well await his fate with grace, as one might tip an executioner. In this case, only a cool stare was available by way of gratuity.

In his cool stare, something gleamed.

It was evanescent, faint, muted by comparison with the shining lacquer above and behind. Just a dim twinkle from the Prime Minister's ear which, in its half-concealed intricacy, had always seemed to Horace her only feminine feature. As he looked, he realized. Perhaps his senses were heightened by his impending fate. Perhaps, too, he had some quality of a cat himself, because as soon as he realized, he pounced. What good it would do him, the lord only knew: pragmatism wasn't his forte. Wit was his forte. In a lifetime constrained if not by circumstances in a general way, since his background was one of privilege, certainly by the single circumstance of his mother, dressed in his memory, in the eternal photo album, as if she were a cloth-covered dining-table or a three-piece suite in Edwardian upholstery, and seated on some pebbly English beach as though to show Canute how a woman of her generation *could* hold the waves at bay, in such a lifetime wit provided the only means of dealing with the female antagonist, since wit meant breaking out, not breaking in, the latter option to his despair (his hormones, out of gear with his upbringing, obstinately jiggling the heterosexual way) being unavailable to a man of, how ironic the phrase, his breeding. So wit it was, and be hanged to the consequences. At least it might preserve his department's budget for another day, whatever it did to him.

In his most precise, his clearest and most elegantly articulated tones: 'Those are pearls,' he said, 'that were her ears.'

CHAPTER TWENTY-ONE

Horace

She had been crushingly pompous, making remarks about good taste. That had only fed Horace's verve: the notion of Kathleen Cheeseman lecturing *him* about good taste. He nearly said it. But she was already winding up the meeting, laying particular stress on her traditional reminder about secrecy. She wanted to see Horace next Tuesday – that presumably would be the end of the road: he had never been conspicious for travelling in the Right Direction. To be a Cabinet wimp was bad enough; to be an offensive Cabinet wimp was the political equivalent of spontaneous combustion. The spontaneity he had already enjoyed; the combustion awaited him in the early part of next week. He would have been writhing in the flames this very afternoon, no doubt, if the Prime Minister had not had to hurry off to an engagement in Scotland. For that matter he had an appointment of his own: a hunting weekend, for heaven's sake, in darkest Shropshire with some brutal squire who might be persuaded to part with a small, no, a large fortune, to Tory party funds. It was a dismal way to spend one's last weekend in office, particularly as several of his colleagues had laughed out loud when he told them where he was going. 'Our Kath never *did* like you, did she?' remarked Andrew Carstairs.

'What's the matter, then, with this Rutherford fellow?'

'Sorry old lad, on the qui vive for a g and t' And

Andrew, barely able to restrain his purple and mottled glee, hurried off to pickle himself further.

Frankie Rutherford lived in a decaying manor house, originally Tudor but obviously largely rebuilt in the eighteenth century. Horace remembered childhood visits to relatives in such places: wallpaper peeling, draughts under every door, damp rising like sap as though the building had run the gamut of civilization and was now resorting to the organic world once more. There was, indeed, a great deal of woodland nearby; rooks cawed.

Rutherford was not prepossessing: small, with a kind of hard plumpness, wearing a quilted sleeveless anorak and many jumpers. He probably regarded it as a mark of integrity that he didn't dress up for Cabinet Ministers. His face, not at such a late stage of setting as Sir Andrew's, lacked the latter's twilight splendour: it was solid pink. Moreover, a certain parsimoniousness in the region of the cocktail cabinet tended to imply the colour was derived from natural causes: blood pressure or rude health. Certainly he was not a man to suffer from chronic embarrassment. They ate a cold hot dinner together, served by a common, well-rounded, middle-aged housekeeper who profusely apologized for the coldness, blaming it, no doubt justly, on an antiquated Raeburn and long corridors. There were no other guests.

'I thought, seemed a bit silly, with us getting up at the crack of dawn tomorrow. My little syndicate will join us then.'

'I see,' said Horace, somewhat icily. Presumably he would have to thaw a little in the direction of possible money as the weekend evolved, but in the meantime he preferred to keep his defences, so to say, in position. Two men together. Every component of Horace's life – his background, upbringing, his lack of sisters, of a father, the fact of his mother – pointed the same way. His environment, without any choosing on his part, was such that the heterosexual act would have seemed not merely surprising but almost perverse. However not even Kathleen Cheeseman could ask him to yield to the pressure of his circumstances for the sake of Tory Party funds. It was hard to exude a chill that was discernible in this October house, but he succeeded in retiring, unharassed, to bed.

The next day dawned, so literally, bright and sharp, leaves crisping, conkers in prickly scrota, the grass almost crunching underfoot, the first fine edge of autumnal decay. Horace found himself squeezed into Frankie Rutherford's Range Rover along with the three members of his syndicate, provincial fat cats, two farmers and the head of a building firm, and taken across parkland, past fields, into woods. It was like travelling backwards in some spluttering time machine which, as an unfortunate side-effect of its method of propulsion, cancelled the past out as it went, so that no aspect of their journey seemed real. When they disembarked in a woodland glade it was as on to planking; Horace had an appalling hilarious intuition that they would commence to address each other in song. Not that any sylvan maidens would trip out from behind the painted sets: his fantasy could not, alas, stretch that far. Nor would Kathleen Cheeseman, Valkyrie-helmeted, begarlanded, appear from a riven oak and sing of reconciliation in rich mezzo tones, ears twinkling. No, it was now impossible to cope with her via absurdity; on Tuesday she would swallow him and spit him out. The prospect made his stomach go hollow, as it was prone to do in the watches of the morning, breakfast or not: cold cooked breakfast there had been indeed, awaiting him on the sideboard, as appetizing as an urn on a mantelpiece. The housekeeper had apologized as before; no socket, apparently, for a hotplate. Clotted egg, congealing bacon pulled like hunger at his innards as he thought of Kathleen Cheeseman next Tuesday. Perhaps, after all, it was a day for shooting.

A pheasant, ludicrously elaborate in its finery – it ought to sing, how unfortunate that all it could do when flushed was gobble like an athletic turkey – flew across the sky. Horace fired, and its head disappeared, leaving the rest of the creature intact, no longer bird but feathered meat, incongruously up in the air. There was something about the way the head was eradicated that reminded Horace of

cheese in a grater – no, no, of a session at the British Film
Theatre when he presided, in his capacity as Secretary of
State for Art and Culture, over a showing of American
underground movies which featured a film of a demonic
pop singer killing a chicken by inches, by millimetres, as he
beat it against the strings of an open piano. He had walked
out; he was Horace Bentley not Joseph Goebbels; leave
such sights to those who delighted in them. But what was
the difference now? The trajectories of his shot had
stretched like wires across the sky; into which the bird had
flown. As a Cabinet Minister might fly into a hail of hearing
pearls.

The syndicate melted away after whiskies that evening,
leaving Frankie and Horace face to face over a meal which,
contradicting previous apologies, was hot. There were
candles in the candelebra. Frankie had changed: he was
wearing a shirt and a blazer. A fire roared in the grate.
Horace's heart, at this sudden access of cosiness, sank.
Perhaps disloyalty was indeed built into his nature, since a
fat cheque was no doubt browning in the same oven which
had produced this treat. It was patently the Right Direction; but the road, before arriving at its destination, would
take Horace through a long dark tunnel. He had thought
before that there were some things, one thing, which
Kathleen Cheeseman would not expect of him. Now he
realized he had forgotten how you became a Prime Minister; not for nothing did she pride herself on positive
thinking. The question to ask was not: what would she *not*
expect of him? It was: what would she *in fact* expect of him?
And the answer, of course, was the fat cheque.

'I thought, perhaps, we ought to have a word about
financial matters,' suggested Horace, as the meal drew to
an end.

'Oh yes,' agreed Frankie. 'I was wondering if it might be
better to discuss that in my room upstairs.' Leaning over
the table towards him: 'More private, if you see what I
mean.'

The point was, thought Horace, as he followed Frankie
up, not that the cheque would redeem the events of last

111

Friday; nor that the cheque would buy him a future in his position. (What a position!) The point was that the cheque would make it impossible for Kathleen Cheeseman to use the absence of the cheque as an excuse for firing him. She would therefore have to revert, implicitly at least, by appropriate silence no doubt, to the matter of the hearing aids. To the extent that her dignity would be lost, his would be saved.

How ironic to think of dignity, of *face*, at such a moment!

CHAPTER TWENTY-TWO

Horace

He awoke in Frankie's arms, or rather – the distinction was absolute, only that old world of pressing circumstances which turned into pressing embraces enabled a moment of sleepy confusion to arise – he awoke with Frankie in *his* arms. Sunlight streamed through eighteenth-century glass, it was blissfully past dawn. Indeed, there was a knocking on the door.

Of course. Somebody would now come in and spoil it. Now he had found what – who – he had been searching for all his life, it, she, would be taken from him. For Frankie was delightfully, unbelievably, secretly, she. Horace's background had left him such a constricted area in which to operate, excluded as he had always seemed to be from the heterosexual cut-and-thrust, repelled as he was by sterile homosexual encounters, marooned in effect on a tiny island in the turbulent seas of sex; and last night, beyond phallic palms, he had discovered Frankie's sweet lagoon. It was as though those far-reaching but minimal Bentley privileges had qualified Horace exclusively for a third sex, and – who would believe it? – a third sex had indeed shown up, one based on the physical principles of his mother.

For Frankie was undeniably like Horace's mother, with the same squat hardness. Some women give forth a sense of being males encumbered by soft lumps on the chest; but Frankie's toughness invaded such lumps, his aggressiveness and drive gave to the very lack between his legs a tangible substance. Horace remembered the firmness of his mother, a firmness which underlay Edwardian plush and tassles, a firmness which emanated from her soul. Frankie had the same determination and authority; but Frankie had also relaxed finally into Horace's arms and whispered 'Thank you'. Nobody had ever thanked Horace in bed before.

And now somebody was knocking on the bedroom door.

Frankie, sensing Horace stiffen, awoke and stirred enjoyably.

'There's somebody at the door,' Horace whispered.

'Then come in,' replied Frankie ambiguously. The door opened and the housekeeper came in, carrying a tray.

'I've brought you some tea,' she said. 'It's nearly eight.'

'Thank you, Mrs Palmer,' said Frankie, collecting himself a little and pulling himself up in the bed. 'Just put it on the bedside table.' He turned to Horace, looked down at him, ran his hand through his hair. Horace shivered, with pleasure and fear. 'I wouldn't bother with breakfast,' Frankie continued softly, talking to Mrs Palmer but still looking seductively at Horace, 'for an hour or so anyway.'

'It takes that long to get the Raeburn going,' Mrs Palmer replied bitterly, unfazed, and left.

Almost a movement of revulsion. Not at Frankie, not at the prospect of sex, but at the obvious impossibility of maintaining this already threatened equilibrium. Horace pulled himself up, and found himself nose to nose with Frankie, teetering on the verge of his pink face; but he resisted the magnetism of that pinkness, the pinkness of acceptable flesh, of living in the body, one's own and someone else's, and swung his feet over the side of the bed.

'What is it?' Frankie asked.

'Oh please!' Horace replied sharply. 'I'm in public life, don't you remember?' Not after next Tuesday, I won't be, he thought suddenly, in strained joy. No, a chimaera like all the others. He would still be a Member of Parliament, god willing, and in any case how monstrous if some scandal – not some, *this*, it was already a scandal in all sorts of ways, most of them, to the public eye, to the PM's pearls, risible ones – if this scandal should surface in the weeks after his dismissal and cast a retrospective and sexual light on the whole affair, justifying Kathleen Cheeseman's ruthlessness, obscuring her hatred of wimpdom, blotting out the matter of the hearing aids.

'Oh I see!' exclaimed Frankie, patently relieved. Indeed he actually essayed a short laugh. 'You're worried about Mrs Palmer!'

'I have very good reason to be,' replied Horace, feeling almost sulky at Frankie's refusal to appreciate the problem. He remembered Andrew Carstairs' mirth at the prospect of this visit. Frankie obviously already had a reputation; and no doubt had learned to live with it. But you didn't have to offer yourself for public evaluation in order to retain a seat of the manorial kind. 'She could put me in a very difficult position. And anything I do to prevent her from putting me in a very difficult position could put me in a worse one.'

'You don't need to get your knickers in a twist about Mrs Palmer,' Frankie said rumbunctiously. Now he *did* seem the brutal squire. 'She's the soul of discretion.'

'They're always the soul of discretion until they blow the gaff,' said Horace bitterly, remembering housekeepers of his childhood.

'I said,' affirmed Frankie, pulling Horace round to face him, 'that she was the soul of discretion, and I'll prove it to you.'

'Oh yes?' Horace replied sluggishly, his inertia offering itself as a stepping-off stone for an act of recoil. He didn't want to hear what Frankie had to say: it would be cheap, ineffective, at least unconvincing. Certainly unconvincing. There was nothing in the housekeeper line, at least in that line when it traversed the route of a Cabinet Minister's indiscretions, that could reassure him. Nothing, anyway, that he could imagine.

But then again Horace could not imagine what Frankie

was going to say, resourceful as his imagination was. Custodian as *he* was of the public imagination. Indeed Frankie's information lay precisely on the yonder side of the imagination, public or private. It was another great surprise, like the surprise of last night, one which struck with the sort of force that turns worlds upside-down, but which in Horace's case had the extraordinary effect of turning an askew world the right way up. It was another great bonus, a gift out of all proportion to its squat source: a transfiguration.

The gift was wrapped mundanely enough. 'Mrs Palmer,' Frankie said, 'has a brother called Jack. He lives in Battersea, with his wife who is known as Queen. I know them quite well. My son Tom is their lodger. I asked Queen to keep an eye on him. She's a shrewd customer, she is. She runs a vegetable stall on the local market.'

'Oh yes?' Horace asked.

'Do you know why they call Queen Queen? It's not her real name.'

'Why?'

'She's called Queen because she's our beloved leader's sister.'

'Our leader?' asked Horace, grasping even for a disadvantageous sanity in the face of a blessing that had struck with the force of a blow.

'The Prime Minister,' Frankie explained testily. The reductive tone gave a hard and acceptable reality to the statement. Nevertheless it was a statement which changed everything, the appearance of the past and the shape of the future. It changed the nature of time itself. It certainly transformed next Tuesday.

CHAPTER TWENTY-THREE

Tom

The green cockroaches enfiladed from the left. Meanwhile the white triangle jiggered nervously in the middle of space. It had no cover.

The trouble was, getting into the mentality of the little bastard. What the hell does a white triangle *think*? What does it *see*?

The cockroaches were more obvious, marching in sequence just like the ones Tom had seen in the kitchen of Lu's takeaway. Disciplined sods, and hard as iron. You scrunched them underfoot and they staggered off on crumpled legs, their carapaces semi-mushed in. Some of Lu's had been so big you could see their sex-organs.

Still, the triangle must have some way of doing them harm. Tom pressed its button. Sure enough, it fired from its apex, *deep deep deep deep pip*! A cockroach disappeared into a small cloud, which faded away leaving nothing behind. The gap marched on, in proper order, disappearing from the screen on the right, returning on the left.

Tom fired his triangle again. This time he missed and the trace went square through the crevice between two of the cockroaches. Immediately the whole squad went wild. They came at the triangle from all angles, jaws snapping.

Tom pulled the joystick to one side and then discovered that instead of going straight from a to b the triangle wibbled from side to side as it went, describing a wavy line, which perhaps made it harder, from the cockroach point of view, to pin it down, but also made it more likely, from the point of view of the triangle controller, that you were going to take a kamikaze dive down some insect's jaws by sheer accident. The sound *wibble* occurred electronically as it travelled, and what with the *deep deep deep deep pip* of the somewhat random firing that Tom continued with as it

116

went, and a sort of dry clicking sound that the cockroaches made during their scatter, one which seemed to be absent when they were enfilading in line, there was a welter of noise-data intended to confuse the controller. Tom cut it out as best he could and kept his triangle on the move but it was only a matter of time, cockroaches were crowding him from all angles, he would soon . . . *deep deep pip*, he'd hit, a cockroach vanished, and suddenly they were all back in line again, going solemnly from left to right of the screen with two gaps in the marching order now.

That was it. While you hit you were on top, and they stayed in order; when you missed all hell broke loose, and stayed loose unless you hit again. Of course, the more you hit, the more gaps appeared in the line, and the more likelihood there was of missing next time. That wasn't exactly realistic, but it would bring the battle to a big climax, if you stayed alive that long.

He fired and hit; another gap joined the procession. Then he wibbled slightly sideways and –

And Queen walked in.

'What are *you* doing?' she asked.

'I've just got this to look after.'

'That thing'll suck in all the electric in the whole house.'

'I've got to practise.'

'What for?'

'I pay you rent. That includes my electricity.'

'What *for*?'

'The Third World War, that's what for.'

'Tom!'

'Well, so what? What do you think we do in the Terrors, at the weekends?'

'I've got a pretty good idea what you Terrors get up to, don't you worry.'

'Come on then.'

'Go to bed with women, I wouldn't be surprised.'

'In the Brecon Beacons? You been there, Queen?'

'It doesn't have to be *done* in bed. All neat and tidy.' Her voice suddenly went husky, a thick voice for such a thin woman. 'On the other hand, there's no reason why not.

Jack won't be back till six. You know he's regular as clockwork.'

Yes, thought Tom. Why not? All neat and tidy. He looked at Queen. Jesus, when you thought about it, she was fifty-five if she was a day. But there was a prettiness in her, if slightly worn, and a tight, orderly body, neat and tidy. It was so far removed from the Brecon Beacons, that barn, the poor girl's moans, his sensation of drowning, the rat. With Queen, there was a clean smooth friction, like planing a plank of wood. And when he came in her it was always a big one, *he* did the moaning.

Afterwards, while they were lying side by side, there was a knock on the front door.

'That's not Jack, I hope,' said Queen.

'It wouldn't come as much of a surprise to him.'

'That'd be even worse. Confirming his suspicions.'

'You said yourself he's regular as clockwork. It's still only half past five. Anyway he'd let himself in.'

'You answer it. I got to get myself organized.'

Tom looked down at the thin organized body. 'All right,' he said, and got up.

His father was at the door, with another man.

'Hello Tom,' Frankie said.

'I wish you'd leave me alone.'

'Not exactly strong in the filial area, are you, my boy?'

'You're not exactly . . .' he let it hang for a minute . . . 'a perfect father yourself.'

'We all have our faults,' said Frankie. 'We've come to see Queen as a matter of fact.'

Tom stepped to one side and Frankie came in, followed by the second man who was wearing an expensive gaberdine mac with the collar turned up. He had distinguished greying hair, a hawk-like nose; the effect was rather spoiled by a receding chin. There was something familiar about him.

'You're not VAT are you?' Tom asked.

'Good god no,' the man replied, shocked.

'Mr Bentley is in the government,' Frankie said.

'Oh yes,' said Tom.

'This is a confidential visit,' Bentley said.

'Queen!' Tom called up the stairs.

'How are the war games getting on?' Frankie asked Tom. He turned to Bentley. 'My boy's in the Territorial Army,' he explained. 'SAS. I don't know why he doesn't do it full-time, instead of scraping a living.' He pointed through the doorway of the front room at the Space Invader. 'Stuff that falls off lorries.'

'I'll mind my own business,' said Tom. 'You mind yours. And if Queen's got any sense, she'll mind hers.'

Queen came down the stairs. She was wearing fluffy slippers and a blue dressing-gown with a big pink cabbage roses on it. Tom felt embarrassed at having gone to bed with her.

'I've been having a lie-down,' she explained. 'You'd better come in here.'

The two men followed her in. 'Hey, Tom,' she called, 'come here and switch this thing off. I'm sorry about that,' she said to Bentley. 'Makes this place look like a pub.'

'It's a very nice house,' Bentley said, sitting down on the settee. He was still wearing his coat. 'But if you don't mind my saying so, it's not exactly the sort of house one might expect the Prime Minister's sister to be living in.'

'It's the sort of house you expect someone who sells veg on a market stall to live in,' Queen said sharply. 'And that's the sort of thing you expect a shopkeeper's daughter to do. It's Kathleen who's the odd one out. Always was.'

Tom switched off the Space Invader and the marching cockroaches disappeared. Suddenly he felt hungry.

'I'm going to the takeaway,' he said, and left.

CHAPTER TWENTY-FOUR

Queen

The blue skies of Irene's childhood were overcast. A cold wind always blew down the street outside the family shop.

School smelled of wee and steadily moved towards incomprehensibility, except for playground games which were sharp and detailed. In the 1930s your clothes prickled and people's faces were grey, although vegetables had brighter colours and when you opened a tin of corned beef its scent filled the room.

Kathleen was tiny, pink-eyed, pale: a white mouse. Irene enjoyed taking her to school, holding her hand while she trotted alongside. She was even slower at learning than Irene was, and the other children didn't seem to like her. But she was stubborn in a quiet way.

And then, one day, Irene's teacher sent her along to Kathleen's class. Kathleen was standing at the front of the room, her hands clasped in front of her, deep in her own thoughts.

'I want you to give this letter to your mother,' Kathleen's teacher told Irene.

'Yes, miss.'

Irene took the letter and began to leave the room.

'What about Kathleen?' the teacher asked.

'Miss?'

'Why aren't you taking Kathleen?'

'I'm going back to my class, miss.'

'Why are you going back to your class, Irene?'

'It's my class, miss.'

'What did I just tell you to do, Irene?'

'Take this letter to my mum.'

'Then why are you going back to your class?'

'Sorry, miss.'

Confused, she began once more to leave.

'Where are you going, Irene?'

'Home, miss.'

'Why aren't you taking Kathleen then?'

On the brink of tears she walked over, took Kathleen's passive hand, and left. There was some rule that hadn't been explained to her, some information that was missing. It was the same when she did her lessons. She and Kathleen walked through the streets of New Mills, their Derbyshire village, hand in hand. The wind blew; the grey hills hunched around the village like the shoulders of school-mistresses. When they reached the shop, their father was upset.

'What are you two doing home at this time? What will your teachers say?'

He put his hand on Irene's shoulder, as he so often did when talking to her, particularly when he was telling her off. Irene handed over the letter and her father read it. His face went white as he did so. He turned at once to Kathleen, who was standing to one side, as usual in her own world. He picked her up, calling 'Mother!' as he did so. Then, with Kathleen in his arms, he turned back to Irene.

'She's deaf,' he said, his voice choked.

Irene was sent back into school, where she got into trouble from her own teacher for going home during the day.

'I had to take a note home about Kathleen,' she explained.

'I'm not talking about Kathleen,' her teacher said angrily. 'I'm talking about *you*.'

When Irene got home that afternoon, everything had changed.

'Kathie's ears were chock-full of wax,' their father told her. 'Poor little devil. Mum's with her at the surgery. Oh Irene,' he said, almost in tears, 'she's having them scraped.'

Her father had never shown any sign of emotion about Kathleen before; nobody had. But that now changed, along with much else, including Kathleen. She was as quiet and self-contained as before but suddenly she was good at school, ploughing through book after book until she had far outdistanced Irene, outdistanced everybody. Irene herself carried on much as previously, except that now she couldn't claim the dubious status of having a dimmer sister.

Home was worse, however. Their mother had always made a point of treating them as equals. Once their Auntie Doris had made the mistake of pronouncing Irene's name as Irenee.

'No dear, it's Irene,' their mother pointed out promptly. 'Irene, to chime with Kathleen. My two little belles.'

Two little belles they might have been but of course Kathleen had never rung a lot. Now suddenly she struck a chord in her mother's heart. She had become a reader, a writer, a sum-doer: perhaps she would master the piano that dominated their back parlour. Perhaps eventually she would become a councillor, as some legendary great-uncle of theirs had once been. Irene found herself taking refuge more and more in the shop, with its scents of cheese, vegetables, even of unopened cans. Father would give her wistful, affectionate looks, although he was caught up in Kathleen's progress also. They both felt that what was going on in the living-room behind the shop was out of their control.

There was a compensation. The shop was all Irene had ever wanted.

She lost it in 1945, when she was eighteen and Kathleen was seventeen. Kathleen had a chance to go to Cambridge, but it would cost a lot of money. Father was beginning to nudge retirement age. So they – they being mother, Kathleen, father – decided to sell up. Irene wasn't even consulted: her agreement was taken for granted. It was only at this point that she understood the nature of the unwritten rule which had been dogging her all her life. It said, simply: Irene doesn't matter.

Irene had been working full-time in the shop for four years already. Let Kathleen have the piano, the back room, mother, the ladies of New Mills. Irene would hear Kathleen offering sandwiches and biscuits at the teas that were held in the parlour, speaking in a strange strangled voice that sounded as if it had never been used before. Irene meanwhile had learned to joke with the old men, swap confidences with the women, tease the children. To her amazement grown-up life had proved so far to be more like the playground than the classroom. Beyond the shop-window the New Mills wind blew as strong and grey as ever; inside she was still, despite wartime's depletions, surrounded by produce. And then suddenly, just as the bell would always end playtime, the unwritten rule was invoked.

It was at this point that she started going out with Jack.

Jack was in the same position as her – working in his family shop in nearby Glossop – except that he was nearly ten years older. As they walked out together on Sundays, over the grey hills, Irene tried to convince herself that she was attracted to him. He had a big head, balanced on his shoulders as a rock might be on a drystone wall.

Her mother was shocked at the news.

'You're not going to marry Jack Colclough!' she said, almost laughing. 'You can do better than *him*, surely. He's old enough to be your father.'

Irene knew what she really meant: he was a shopkeeper. Their own family shop had been forgotten already. But this time Irene was determined to get her own way.

'I've got to marry him,' she said. 'I'm pregnant.' In point of fact she wasn't. She never did become pregnant.

'But your husband's shop was also in the Peak District,' Horace Bentley said.

'Jack's sister got married,' Queen said. 'She was entitled to her share. Jack and me didn't have the cash to buy her out, so we had to sell up. That's when we came down to London. We tried to start a business here, but our capital didn't go far. In the end I got the chance of a market stall and Jack got a job with Polish Bacon.'

'And you've never had anything to do with your family since you came here?' Mr Bentley asked.

'Jack's my family. That's the way I like it. That's the way our Kathie likes it too, you can be sure of that.'

'I'm quite sure you're right.'

'I'd thank you to make sure it doesn't get to the papers. What I do. Where we live. It's *my* life.'

'I'll be the soul of discretion,' Mr Bentley assured her.

CHAPTER TWENTY-FIVE

Tom

'Here, meat pie and chips,' said Lu. He handed over the packet and looked at Tom with symmetrical willow pattern eyes.

'Ta,' said Tom.

'Some day you ha chow mein or somefin like at,' he suggested. He talked the way Chinese do, like someone imitating the way they talk. 'These pie are jus fro factory.'

'How I like them, son,' said Tom. 'Talking of cock-roaches, how about having a Space Invader in here?'

'Ay? No.'

'Look, I'm not talking about one belonging to the mafia. Your *own*. I can let you have one for a song. Cockroaches from a galaxy far far away. You waste the little sods with a triangle.'

'Ah yis. And then the police come. Yes sir, I got it fom back of lolly. I don't unnarstand, boy like you, why you don work. Come roun, selling rubbish. What your dad say?'

'A good question,' said Tom.

In many ways, Tom thought, I'm a chip off the old block, only not so much marble as potato. Just what you might call, a change of key. Frankie was a parasite on his Shrop-shire estate, good for nothing except potting small birds; Tom was a parasite in Battersea, purveying discarded objects. Like father like son.

No. God forbid. Not like father. Different in one crucial respect. In one small feature. Let's hope the journey from Shropshire to Battersea was long enough to make that point. Like the journey to the barn. It was a point you had to make over and over. And sometimes it seemed the more you made it, the more you felt as if you *weren't* making it. The more you proved the opposite.

Actually his original destination had been the Tottenham Court Road, not Battersea. Not that the place mattered. He'd begun with a certain past: public school, 'A' levels, the Shropshire upper crust. And then one day he'd discovered that his father was his mother, or rather vice versa, and a corresponding shift in his own circumstances was necessary as a result. *His* transformation though was into a wide boy: living on his wits and working a fiddle in the waste disposal business.

Of course Frankie, with his extensive hunting experience, hadn't taken long to track him down the Tottenham Court Road. Tom stood by his new identity, however, and Frankie was hardly in a position to argue. He did insist, though, that Tom should move to Battersea, and stay with Mrs Palmer's brother and his wife.

'You're not too young for a bit of mothering,' he'd told Tom.

'Plis not eat pie hee-ar,' said Lu politely. 'This is take-away.'

'No need to be a stickler, old son,' said Tom.

'But you drop crumbs, then the insects come. Then all herr break out.'

'I'm a tidy eater. And you got insects already.'

'We all got insects. It get verr hot in kitchen. They bleed.'

'You wouldn't send me out on the street, an orphan.'

'Orphang?'

'No mum or dad.'

'Ah, so.'

'That too.'

Lu gave up and went into the kitchen. A few minutes later Porter came in.

'Jes*us*, I thought it was you,' Porter said.

'Have a pie,' said Tom. 'This is an eat-in takeaway.'

'Listen,' said Porter. 'Renwick's been outbid.'

'You what?'

'No kidding.'

'But I mean, what you talking about, outbid? I didn't know anything was up for bidding.'

'Everything's always up for bidding, you know that.'

'Fuck me,' said Tom, and put his remaining crescent of pie down on the formica counter, which was done in swirls. 'Who?' he asked.

'Some bastard called the Fat Man.'

'Bloody hell.'

Lu came to the kitchen doorway.

'Yes?' he asked.

'Not you, Lu,' Tom said.

'Tell the yellow peril to piss off,' said Porter.

'Is verr bad eating in takeaway,' said Lu. 'But not eating in takeaway verr verr bad.'

'Why don't you go into that kitchen of yours, Lu, and boil up some prawns or something,' Tom said soothingly.

Lu gave them, in turn, a bright dead stare, like a bird's, and went.

'We been supplying him prawns from Seabags, the frozen fish place,' Porter said. 'Renwick's had their garbage contract.'

'Had?'

'Had. Had. This fat shit runs this operation called Northern Industrial Disposal. He just went round to each of Renwick's clients in turn and underbid fifty percent.'

'Fifty percent?'

'Fifty fucking percent.'

'Good god. Easy as that,' said Tom. He picked his pie up and with one of its prongs outlined 50 on the counter. 'Easy as that,' said Tom. 'And then I suppose he just goes along in a couple of weeks, and doubles up, and the little sods are in his pocket so they pay, and they're back where they started from and we're down the plughole.'

'His terms are guaranteed for a year. And then he says he'll only go up by the rate of inflation.'

'Who's he trying to kid?'

'That's the deal,' said Porter, shaking his head.

'Nobody can run a business like that.'

There was a pause. Tom stared at a line of Vimto bottles on a shelf behind the counter. 'Oh shit,' he said softly. He put the final piece of pie in his mouth and chewed it with care. 'The bastard's plugging into the game,' he said.

126

'Hole in one,' Porter said. 'He knows about it for sure. Every company he approached, that's every company Renwick's had a contract *with*, he makes sure he nobbles some individual that's getting nothing whatsoever from us. It's too much of a coincidence. He doesn't make a contract with a single one of our people, it's only characters who are sucking from a different tit altogether. Or they're clean as a whistle. It's against the law of averages. It means he must have known who our stooges are. The kind of organization he must have.'

'Talk about taking the goose that lays the golden eggs,' Tom said.

'Yeah. Or wringing its fucking neck. That's the other possibility.'

'Don't say it. That would put the clampers on poor old Jack that would, for sure.'

'Bugger Jack. Jack's not here or there. It's us. We could have policemen right and left.'

'Dear god.'

'If the Fat Man really *is* in the clean-up business.'

'It's not possible.'

'You could say that's what waste-disposal's all about,' Porter said grimly. 'See you later.'

Porter left the shop. Tom pressed his finger on the crumbs that lay on the counter, as if pressing so many tiny buttons. Suddenly a Bulge roared over the tannoy, Lu's contribution:

> She leaned over the bed
> Took my earhole in hand
> Pressed her lips right up close
> In a whisper she said:
>
> You'll always remember me
> Yeah, you'll always remember me
> You little freak
> Whenever you need to pee
>
> I think you'll think of me
> Each time you take a leak
> In a whisper she said, leaning over my bed

You'll think of me, each time you take a leak
When she was gone
I turned my head on the pillow
And watched the morning sun
Rise over Shit's Creek

And I watched the sun
I watched the morning sun
I watched the sun rise
Over Shit's Creek.

'Thanks very much, Lu,' Tom said, and left.

CHAPTER TWENTY-SIX

Jack

Dogs with the bloke whose face bulged out to one side, as if it had been stood too near the fire and had begun to melt, but that was Thursdays. Ted. Jack was beginning to forget names, but not faces. Never faces. Certainly not whosit's face. You could say it was a face that was beginning to forget itself, forgetting how to *be* a face. Jack had that experience himself sometimes, not with his face, but his heart, it would miss a beat, there would be a long black pause, just as if his heart was forgetting what to do next, like you might try to remember a word or a name and stand there snapping your fingers, saying the bloke with the face but not getting . . . not getting the flicking name . . . but in the heart's case it was the beat, what the eff do you do to get a beat, I've beaten so many millions of times I've bloody forgotten how you do it . . . and then suddenly it comes back, like whosit comes back into your brain. The little man inside you bongs his little gong once more.

Face-ache Thursday. For whosit's sake, let it not ache. He never said it did, but then maybe he wouldn't. He never said it didn't ache either. He never said anything about it.

Thursday dogs. Ted, that was it. They only met, bumped

into each other, between races, discussed fancies.

Wednesday, a drink with George. Always two pints. Two pints for Jack, that was. George always had six, being there before Jack came in, and staying long after Jack left. George would talk regularly as clockwork about the Razor's Edge, a topless bar he always went to on Tuesdays, always saying, Bugger me if she didn't nearly drop one in me pint, I would have said to her, that's my beer you got on your plumpy, I paid for it and by god I'm going to drink it. Plumpy, Jack would think disgustedly, where did the poor old sod learn parts of the body. There had been a boy in Jack's class at school who'd learned to call the contents of his trousers his twig and berries. Poor George was a life-long bachelor, scratching at the wall. Jack could talk, *he*'d been a life-long bachelor for nearly four years.

Wednesdays and Thursdays broke the back of the week. It was nice to stay in Fridays because there was often something on the telly and anyway the weekend was on its way. Mondays were grim but that was how Mondays were supposed to be. Tuesdays he could remember Wednesdays were coming up. On Mondays, Tuesdays and Fridays, the world beyond his armchair was no-man's land. Anything could happen outside on a Monday evening, perhaps people went about dressed as white rabbits, all he could say for sure about Monday evenings was that they had steak and kidney pie, mashed potatoes, and peas, followed by ice-cream. Then Queen had a sit while he did the washing-up, listening to the Archers on the radio which he propped up on a shelf above the sink while he did so. Then he went into the front room, and read the paper for half-an-hour. Then he made a cup of tea and they watched telly for an hour. Then he had a bit of a read of his library book and they went up to bed at about ten. For all he knew they could be eating each other on the streets meanwhile.

But now it *was* Monday evening, and instead of being at home here he was sitting in Polish Bacon's big yellow building, nobody else, just him, with the purring freezers full of frozen meat, and the building getting colder and colder. Queen would be at home waiting; the Archers would be on. The uncurtained windows of the warehouse went black.

At last a car drew up, the fire door opened, and in walked Mr Andrews. Mr Andrews was in charge of the London region of Polish Bacon. He was known as the Cigar, because he was always puffing one.

'Sorry to keep you waiting, Jack,' the Cigar said. He always seemed to know everyone's name. 'We're all comrades together,' was one of his favourite sayings.

'No trouble, Mr Andrews,' Jack said. 'Cup of tea?'

'Not just now, Jack, I've got a lot on my plate.'

'You're working late, anyway.'

'You wouldn't believe the hours I work sometimes. Our friends don't realize they don't own you body and soul like they do in the motherland.' He puffed his cigar thoughtfully. 'You're getting on a bit now, aren't you, Jack?'

'Sixty-three,' Jack said.

'Not far off retiring age.'

'No.'

'Let me put it this way. I got some bad news on the rubbish front this morning.'

'On the rubbish front, Mr Andrews?'

'That's right. Renwicks. The industrial waste people.'

'But I don't do rubbish, Mr Andrews, that's Charley's job. I do orders.'

'Oh, I know that Jack, I know that. But if you remember, we took out the Renwick's contract after we were approached by a young man, a relative of yours. A nephew, wasn't it? His terms seemed reasonable at the time. Better than the corporation's anyway.'

'A lodger.'

'A lodger, that's it. I thought it was a lodger.'

'That was nothing to do with me, Mr Andrews.'

'Don't get me wrong, Jack, nothing wrong with keeping things in the family. We're all brothers together in this organization. But that nephew of yours been a bit naughty, that's the only problem.'

'Look, Mr Andrews, that's all Charley's –'

'If you can't be loyal to me, Jack,' the Cigar said harshly, 'you might refrain from dropping Charley in the shit. You know, everybody here knows, our turnover rota. Six months for frozen meat, one year for canned goods. If they aren't sent out in that time, they're chucked. It's public health regulations, there's notices about it all over the walls. So you quietly put the odd side of beef on one side, the occasional box of beans in a corner somewhere, and wait for the deliver-by date to expire. Then you heave the stuff in the direction of your pals in Renwick's and they unload it through the channels they got at their disposal. It's fool-proof. At least it made a fool out of me. You convert good food into rubbish and get the rubbish man to take it away. But then you got such a margin to play with, being that the public health people don't know their arse from their elbow, you can convert the rubbish back into good food again, and flog it through the back-of-a-lorry market. It's very neat, Jack.'

'Mr Andrews, stock's nothing to do with me. I do orders. Bert Chandler's on stock. You ought to speak to him.'

'Nothing's nothing to do with you, is it, Jack? It's all Charley or Bert. The simple fact remains that Renwick's was *your* family connection. I wasn't born yesterday, Jack. You weren't, neither, and it's time you thought about retirement. Early retirement. Very early. Dating from a couple of hours ago. Piss off, Jack.'

The Cigar glowed. Jack walked off through the cold building, out the fire door. It was raining on the street. Now at least he knew what took place in the outside world on a Monday evening.

CHAPTER TWENTY-SEVEN

Tom

Queen was sitting in the back room, with the telly on. She had a shrunken meal on a plate on her knees and was eating unhappy little forkfuls. She was still in her dressing-gown. Frankie and Horace Bentley had left.

'Where's Jack?' Tom asked.

Queen didn't look up at him but carried on eating. She answered faintly, with her mouth full: 'I don't know.'

Determinedly positive, since she was determined to be cowed: 'Not like him. Perhaps he's found a bit on the side.'

Now Queen did look up. 'Thank you very much,' she said, and clonked her knife and fork down on the plate. She put the plate on the arm of her chair.

'Not to worry,' said Tom, his heart sinking at the thought of Jack in the hands of the police. 'He's a big boy now. He can look after himself.'

The front door opened and shut. Queen clutched what there was of her left breast. What have I been doing, going to bed with her? Tom wondered. It's like having sex with a piece of string. It's like going to bed with a bloke. Oh god, he thought, thinking of his father.

In came Jack. His big head was damp. Tom remembered Queen's story about her early life, the everlasting wind, the greyness, the man running the shop in the next godawful little town. Glossop. Jack had blue eyes, grey with misery or fatigue.

'Been on the town?' Tom asked cheerily.

'You shouldn't have done it, Tom,' Jack replied.

It was true then, what Porter said, this Fat Man was cleaning up the rubbish business, for whatever reasons of his own. God knew where it would end, the garbage could fly in every direction forever.

So unexpectedly it was as if a ventriloquist was in the room, Queen spoke: 'It wasn't *his* fault, Jack.'

What the shit? How did *she* know or not know whose fault it was? How did she know whose fault *what* was?

Then she went on: 'It was *my* fault.'

She continued, a stick woman in an armchair, her shrivelled food on the arm beside her: 'It was *my* fault. What do you expect, at your age? I've still got some life in me, I can't help it. What do you expect, Jack?'

Jack was just standing, looking at her. He looked empty but not hollow, he was too big and square even at his age to

132

look hollow. He looked as if he'd been filled up with sawdust or stone.

'It's about something at work, Queen,' Tom said quietly. Queen continued to look at Jack, she had no choice, there would be Glossop so clear that you could probably make out the individual dreariness of the houses and shops of the village, and the big sad moorlands all around, and the grey wind blowing across everything. Poor poor Queen, thought Tom, how I've fucked her. Poor Queen, poor Jack, how I've fucked both of them. How I fuck generally. Then the wind was blowing round a pub in the Beacons, and over the little rutted Welsh lane outside, and along the lane the Terrors were staggering: Tom, Porter, the Professor, a girl. Porter had picked the girl up and he and the Prof had an arm each round her. The men had been kipping in a barn, 'on survival' as it was called in the Terrors, and the barn was just ahead. They climbed the stone wall and staggered in.

'Where the shit are we?' the girl asked suddenly.

'In a bleeding barn,' said Porter.

'You what?' said the girl.

'An edifice for the storing of hay,' explained the Professor.

'I thought you were taking me home,' said the girl. Now she was frightened her voice suddenly sounded very Welsh, lilting.

'Take your clothes off,' said Porter.

'You what?' she said.

'Off.'

'You?'

'Naked,' the Professor said.

The girl looked at Tom. It was dark, except for a torch Porter was flashing. It caught her face, eyes. She looked like a rat in a trap.

'Naked, the man said,' said Tom.

As she undressed Porter's torchlight ran over her, physical as licking. When she was naked, Porter put his torch on the ground, still lit. You could hear him unzip himself in the dark.

'Me first,' Porter said. 'I caught the fish.'

'By all means,' said the Professor. 'You can dip the old elbow in the bathwater.'

'Lie down,' Porter told the girl.

'Piss off,' she said, trying to be brave, but the piss off sounded very Welsh and songlike.

'Lie down,' Porter said more roughly. She didn't realize what a pathetic creep he was, putting on an act. Anyway, what difference did it make? It might be an act but he would do it.

'You are being invited to recline,' explained the Professor. Porter had picked up the torch again and was shining it at the girl. Naked, she looked white as a ghost in the darkness of the barn. She sat stumblingly down, obviously hoping to compromise.

'I think you were told to lie,' said Tom. She gave him a look, as much as to say, you too, and lay back. Her legs were clamped tightly together. There were little moans amongst her breathing, even those were Welsh. Tom thought: if you have any sense you wouldn't do that, it makes matters worse.

Porter stepped round to the feet end, carrying his torch. Its beam caught his prick, which lolloped out of his trousers, only half-mast. He bent down and placed the torch on the ground so that it shone on the soles of the girl's feet.

'Take a leg each,' Porter said. It took Tom a moment to realize that he was talking to him and the Professor, not the girl. Tom picked up a leg by the calf and ankle; the Professor did the same; the girl didn't resist. The torch drastically illuminated her crotch. Then Porter went down on her. He put one hand over her mouth. The other was down below, working him in, which took a long time, for obvious reasons. Finally he was in, and began. That took a long time too, not because he was a man but because he wasn't. Tom got bored, standing there holding the girl's limp jumping leg.

Then it was the turn of the Professor. Porter, prick still out, now held the other leg. When the Professor reached his climax, he said: 'Ah. Excellent.'

134

Then Tom.

'Please,' the girl whispered, as he lay on top of her.

'Certainly,' he said. But he knew she was meaning please not as she looked up at him. Some torchlight had skirted her crotch and slipped between their two bodies while he was lowering his: it streaked upwards over her face like when you put a torch under your chin at Halloween, making her eyes dark and deep. The light disappeared as he rested his weight on her. Her cunt was gummy, awash, sucking at him like a sea anemone, while her eyes, just below his, retreated from him in the darkness. He pulled himself out, but was aware of the Professor and Porter on each side of him, holding her legs like stone lions guarding a gate. He couldn't go back into her, not the way her cunt horribly pulled at him despite the girl's wishes, like a greedy animal. He felt it would pull him in completely, as a porthole pulls when the glass breaks on a pressurized aircraft.

'Turn her over,' he said.

'What?' said Porter.

'That,' he said, pointing down at the girl. 'Turn it *over*. I'm not going to follow in other men's footsteps.'

'There you are,' the Professor told Porter, 'a public schoolboy to the core.'

The important thing was, her eyes were no longer looking up at him. Or not looking up at him. But when he was deeply in, and beginning to throb, he turned his face to one side, and there, on the floor a few inches away, just looking at him, was a small form, tapering, wedge-shaped; a rat. It was albino in the faint white torchlight, it looked naked.

'Shit!' shouted Tom, and the rat scrabbled off.

Porter giggled. 'What you expect,' he said, 'in a haybarn? Big bloke like you. In the Terrors. Diddums do it attums?'

'It wasn't,' said Tom. 'It wasn't.'

'It wasn't,' Tom said.

Queen continued to look at Jack, but her attention switched to Tom.

135

'It wasn't,' he said. 'You know. It was at work. At Polish Bacon.'

'You what?' Queen said, still looking at Jack.

'I've lost my job,' Jack said.

'Oh god,' said Queen. 'Oh bloody god.' She picked up her dinner and dropped it on the floor. The plate landed the right way up and didn't break. The congealed food stayed in place. Queen put her hands over her eyes. Jack turned to face Tom.

'You little bastard,' he said.

'It was nothing to do with you,' Tom said. 'The rubbish business, I mean. You should have told them.'

'I did tell them.'

'I suppose you did.'

Jack turned back towards Queen. 'Well, that's the end of that, I suppose,' he said.

Queen took her hands away from her face. She hadn't been crying. She was too dry a woman to cry. She picked her plate up and rose to her feet.

'Your food's in the oven,' she said. 'You ought to have something to eat.'

She went out to the kitchen. Jack walked over to his place at the small dining-table over against the wall. The evening paper was there, waiting for him. He picked it up and began to read.

Tom left. It was pissing down on the street, and he didn't have a coat. He ran down to the offie at the bottom. Little Gerald jumped when he saw him.

'Blimey,' Gerald said, 'I thought for a moment you was going to rob the bleeding till.'

'What made you think that?'

'The way you rushed in.'

'I just want a bottle of scotch.'

'You got a good way of running into a room, though. I suppose that's what they teach you in the Terrors.'

'That's right.'

'All those weekends,' said Gerald, wrapping up the bottle. 'On manoeuvres.'

'Yes.'

'Unless it's all kiddology.'

'What do you mean?'

'Like having a lady friend tucked away somewhere. Dirty weekends. We've got no proof.'

'You been to the Brecon Beacons?' Tom asked, and left.

He took the bottle back through the rain. Queen was watching the television. Jack was still at his place at the table, eating his meal and reading the paper. His food was one stage further on – or back – from Queen's: it looked as if, by some process of reverse cookery, it had returned to its original minerals. Sawdust, or stone.

'Anyone want a tot?' Tom asked.

Queen took no notice. Jack looked up from his paper.

'I don't think so, Tom,' he said. 'Wednesday's my night for the booze.'

'Suit yourself,' said Tom.

'I just been reading this article about the copper, didn't have a care in the world, going to get married to a nice girl, the lot, who topped himself, just like that. Hanged himself from the trap door to the loft.'

'I haven't read the paper yet,' Tom said.

'Funny what people do,' Jack said musingly. He turned back to the table.

Tom carried his bottle out of the room. As he left, Queen called after him.

'If you going to use that Space Invader, and our electric goes through the roof, you better make it good, do you hear, Tom?'

It was as if nothing had happened. Jack was just sitting there as usual, reading the sad bits out of the paper, eating his dinner, as if it was any other Monday night, except two hours later. Did he think that's how it would continue to be from now on, the same as usual only two hours later? Perhaps he did. He was a man who had always been regular in his habits, but at the same time, in some sense deeper than punctuality, he'd always been late.

137

CHAPTER TWENTY-EIGHT

Tom

roach   roach roach roach roach roach roach roach
ch roach roach   roach roach roach roach roach roa
oach roach roach roach   roach roach ro -p- roach r

```
                                    i
                                    p
                                    p
                                    e
                                    e
                                    d
                                    p
                                    e
                                    e
                                    d
                                    p
                                    e
               i                 b  le
            w  b b  le   wi   b
```

roach roach roach roach   roach roach moan roach roac
ch roach roach roach roach   roach roach   roach r
ach roach roach roach roach roach   roach roach roac
     roach roach roach roach roach   roach roach r
roach   -p- ach roach roach roach   roach ro

```
              i
              p
              p
              e
              e
              d
              p
              e
              e
              d
              p
              e
         i        l  e
       w   b  b   l e
```

roach roach   roach roach   moan roach roach roac
ach roach roach   roach roach   roach roach roach r
roach roach roach   roach   roach roach roach
oach   roach roach ro - p - h roach   roach r

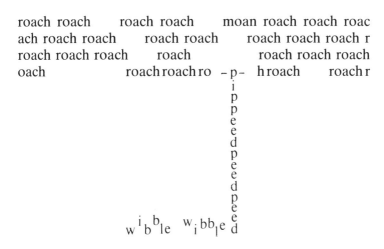

moan moan moan moan moan moan moan moan moan m
  roach roach   roach roach   roach roach roach roa
ch   roach roach   roach roach   roach roach roac
roach   roach roach   roach roach   roac

click

c l i b bl e

click

click

click

Shit's creek wibble eeurk click wibble bottle deep sh
it wibble deep deep shit thank God for bottle bottle PING

139

The white triangle had gone, swallowed in a gulp by a gree
n cockroach. Blank screen.
Then:

roach roach roach roach roach roach roach roach roach ro

They were back. Wibble. Bottle. Mother's milk. Wibble cl
ick. Deep deep deep pip fuck me got one straightaway boo
ze must improve the aim ought to try it in the terrors deep
deep bottle fucking missed fucking missed fucking cockro
aches crawling all over PING

Blank screen. Then:

roach roach roach roach roach roach roach roach roach ro

Gerald said: you got a good way of running into a room S
AS ossifer thump thump wibble no not wibble get into posi
tion first before the fuckers get ready to move before the fu
ckers that's it stand on tiptoes ready to run forward on you
r angle ready to wibble just in case the fucking clicks can se
e you who knows what they see and head straight for wher
e you were gap not the only ones who can fuck about with
gaps deep deep wibble deep pip got the sod anyway bottle
on your angle again set go deep wibble deep deep wibble m
issed here come the little green men peril yellow peril Lu P
ING arse hole

bottle roach roach roach roach roach roach roach roach ro
angle wibble deep shit missed straight off wibble fuck here
come the bastards wherever you look click click hot as hell
in the effing kitchen hot as her deep bottle deep pip got a f
ucker but but but moan

One cockroach, jaws clamped, in retreat, bumps into tri
angle which happens to be blocking its way back to the line.
What happens now? Triangle survives of course, it's alread
y scored, the other cockroaches are returning to line, but t
his poor fucker can't make it, it's on the wrong side of the
triangle, wibble fuck pressed wrong button deep pressed d
eep button instead deep deep deep pip shit shot another o

f the cockroaches in line

Arse hole. Accidental circuit. Yellow peril said mess tidy e
ater said tidy but pressed but but moan pressed deep insid
e of wibble bottle better shit what happens not in circuit sh
ot a cockroach while one still trying to get back to line line
enfilading with new gap wibble the triangle to one side wib
ble it round and make room bottle shit bloody cockroach a
lso moving in that direction following line's motion from le
ft to right of screen forgot not back with its mates shit it's o
verlapping the triangle eating no mounting triangle shit's c
reek they're having sexual intercourse in there that's the so
rt of manoeuvres they wibble but the triangle is still stuck u
nder wibble with wargh moan moan mum mum mum

hot enough to see their sex organs naked the man said

Blank screen. Then

roach roach roach   roach roach roach roach roach ro
ach roach roach roach rat roach roach roach roach roach r

Oh mum green cockroach plus white triangle equals small
form tapering wedge-shaped: an albino rat. Shit's creek sh
it deep

roach roach roach roach roach rat roach roach roach roa
ch roach roach roach roach roach rat roach rat roach ro

oh mum bottle arse hole peril ah so mum mum

Queen: Turn that bloody thing off!

What what she bottle

Queen: playing that thing for hours turn it off sucking up
         the electric

Queen through wall turn it off yes bottle turn the bleeder
off unplug the rats

Blank screen. Then:

Blank screen

Ah so heart soul

scrinch scrinch

Naked the arse scrinch

The invaders off no fire bottle

Scrinch scrinch

Deep shit eff scrinch

My god fuckers inside hatching cockroach eggs hatching b
ottle white triangles with feelers hatching rats

My god bottle empty deep deep shit arse hole

Scrinch

not in here hot in her scrinch

naked

scrinch scrinch

CHAPTER TWENTY-NINE

Tom

Tom wrestled with the Space Invader. It was square and
heavy, impossible to lift, but you could walk it by leaning it
from side to side and pushing it forward. It thumped the
living-room floor as it went.

Suddenly Jack was in the room. He was wearing blue
striped pyjamas.

'What the hell you doing, Tom?'

'I'm shifting this Space Invader, what's it look like?'

'But you got no clothes on, lad.' The 'lad' sounded

142

suddenly northern in amongst Jack's London speech, and friendly. Tom felt close to boozy tearfulness.

'I got hot,' he explained.

'You got pissed,' Jack said. 'You put away that whole bottle. You could kill yourself, drinking like that.'

'So what? It might not be a bad idea.'

'There's enough people killing themselves as it is,' said Jack. 'What you want to move this thing for, anyway? Oh, I suppose it's that rubbish business. The lid's blown off that good and proper, with whatsername's being taken over, I suppose. I wish you'd let me know what you was up to earlier. I might have kept my job.'

'Can you hear it?'

'What?'

'The noise this thing's making.'

'Have you got it unplugged?'

'Of course I've got it unplugged.'

'Thank gawd for that. Queen would do her nut. You been playing it for hours, you know. She's frightened the electric'll go through the roof. The point is, what we don't know is, what it consumes.'

'Listen to it.'

Jack stepped over and put his ear to it. 'Oh yes,' he said, 'it's making a sort of crunching noise.'

'That's what I mean,' said Tom, relieved.

'Well, it's just the insides, cooling down. Probably the circuitry's not up to scratch, and got a bit overheated. You're not the only one who can pull a fast one, you know. You think about it, my lad, you go around making out you're picking up rubbish and taking away good stuff, one of your suppliers might go one better and make sure you get some rubbish in any case.'

'It's bloody rats.'

'You what?'

'There's rats in there. They've been breeding in it.'

'You better get it out of here in that case, before Queen finds out. She'll lose her rag.'

'That's what I'm bleeding trying to do.'

'You want to put your clothes on first. What do you think

143

people will think, carting a Space Invader down the street in the middle of the night with no clothes on? You'll catch your death.'

'I'm going to have a slash,' Tom said. He went up to the lavatory and was sick. Then he leaned against the lavatory wall and thought about his battle with the Invader. One of the green cockroaches gets stuck on the wrong side of the white triangle. The triangle controller tries to press the wibble button to get the triangle out of the way, but presses the firing-button by mistake, and wastes one of the cockroaches that have returned to line. Then he succeeds in moving the triangle to one side but just at that moment the stray green cockroach, under the impression probably that it had already got back into line with the others, decides to start going from left to right instead of carrying on towards the top of the screen and straightaway bumps into the white triangle. That's what they need in order to reproduce: a cockroach going astray, the triangle firing at another cockroach while the lost cockroach is cheek by jowl with him, the triangle moving to one side and presenting the exact angle for the cockroach to mount him from the rear. It was a form of sex which took three, none of them the right kind. And what you got was a white rat.

He was cold now. He went across the landing and into his bedroom. Shit, his clothes were downstairs, in the front room. He couldn't go down there and put them on in front of Jack. Not after going to bed with his wife. Christ, he'd been naked in front of him already. He must have been drunk out of his mind, and that bottle of scotch had made him unbearably hot. Now he was cold as ice.

His Territorial Army uniform was in the wardrobe. Why not? He'd been fighting with the shitting machine all evening.

'Blow me,' said Jack, when he was down in the front room again. 'You go up naked as nature intended and come down in full combat gear.'

'Is it still making that noise?' Tom asked.

'Not so much. I think it's cooling down. I'm sure it's the circuitry.'

Tom went to listen. Scrinch scrinch. Yes, it did seem fainter. They'd probably eaten just about everything there was to eat in there. God knew what they'd do next.

'Let's get this thing out of here,' he said.

He began once more to walk the Space Invader. Jack helped him to get it through the door into the hall and then through the front door on to the pavement. It had stopped raining.

'Keep an eye on it a minute,' Tom said. 'Porter's lent me a pickup.'

He left Jack grumbling in the doorway, still in his pyjamas, and went round the corner to the little Renwick's pickup Porter had got hold of for him in case, with the Fat Man on the scene, some rubbish disposal was necessary. He drove it round to the house.

'Can you give me a hand getting this thing up on the back?' he asked Jack.

'I've still got my pyjamas on.'

Tom got the tailgate down and began to manhandle the machine towards the back of the pickup.

'I must need my head examined,' Jack said, coming across to help. They slid the Invader upwards and shoved it into place. Tom stepped round to the cab and got in.

'How you going to get it off again?' Jack asked.

'I'll manage.'

'Give me a minute to get my clothes on.'

Tom started the engine.

'What's the bleeding hurry?' Jack asked. He walked round to the other side of the cab and got in. They drove off.

Renwick's had a collection skip by the shopping precinct. By the time they reached it, the rain was coming down again.

'My pyjamas are going to be sopping,' Jack said.

Tom insisted on manhandling the Invader right into the skip. He wanted to wash his hands of it. As they began to drive off the pickup's headlights caught the skip's side.

'Bloody hell, they work fast,' Tom said. It wasn't Renwick's skip after all. Northern Industrial Disposal had put their own in place already.

'But this is the *south*,' Jack said.

'They're expanding,' Tom said, 'from what Porter says. Anyway that's one bit of rubbish they're welcome to.'

The pickup drove off. The Fat Man watched from his dark car across the street. He was doing a tour of the company's inputs, checking that the changeover had been effected. Speed was of the essence. When the pickup appeared he'd turned his lights off out of curiosity, to see what would materialize from it. A soldier, an old man in pyjamas, a Space Invader. Life was full of surprises, he'd sprung a few himself. And of course all sorts of strange beings would come out of the woodwork, now that Renwick's had been squeezed out, and the crooked dealing brought to a stop.

The Fat Man had a motto: keep the rubbish business clean. It could be applied, with varying degrees of ironic emphasis, to many aspects of his activities.

CHAPTER THIRTY
Mrs Cheeseman

The trouble with running the country from a terraced house, however conveniently situated, was that there was such restricted access to the light. Even at ten o'clock in the morning the Cabinet Room neon had to be on. Whether or not it was hissing was a matter she hadn't given herself the opportunity of considering: she'd left the door open. And of course 10 Downing Street was full of noise. Derek would be upstairs, tinkering with his little boat, civil servants would be rushing around with pieces of paper, security staff were patrolling the building, somebody was hoovering somewhere, no doubt too many cooks were preparing her tiny lunch.

She'd made various attempts to economize in the kitchens, but to little effect. No doubt the newly converted Joseph would approve of the notion of too many cooks but she herself would always remain a monetarist at heart. True, she had been forced to set in motion a series of events which would considerably modify the monetarist basis of her policy, but with luck nobody would notice. You didn't notice that the world was spinning, because you span at the same speed. That was an important truth to bear in mind. What she proposed was not to abandon the Right Direction for another one, but to insert a substantial curve in her original route. Poor Joseph would no doubt be racking his brains at this very moment for a viable solution to the impasse, whereas she had already embarked on a course of action that would deal with the problem; and later would take her plan another step further. She was confident of her ability to sell a curve as a straight line; not for nothing, she reflected, was she the product of a corner shop.

'I'm sorry, Prime Minister,' Horace said. 'The door was open.'

'Then come in, Horace. Oh, you have.'

At least Horace had the sense to go straight to his own chair. Raymond would no doubt get into a terrible muddle. What a prospect, dealing with the two smallest men in the Cabinet in quick succession. At least it was the last time she would have to cope with this one.

'Dismal weather,' she went on. She had looked out of the upstairs dining-room earlier, and watched the drizzle fall on Downing Street.

'I suppose it is,' Horace said judiciously. 'But of course one is cossetted. Door to door transport. "A closed car at four", so to say.'

'It is ten o'clock according to my watch. And I have something to say to you, without further ado.'

'I assume,' said Horace, 'that you are about to refer to my rudeness of last week. Could I pre-empt your comments by apologizing? My behaviour was disgraceful.'

Mrs Cheeseman stared at him in surprise. Did he really imagine he could talk his way out of the fix he'd so conveniently talked his way into? Surely not even Horace could be as naive as that.

He was continuing: 'I hope you will be prepared to put it down to the fact that politics is something of a rough game even among colleagues, and that I experienced an access of uncontrollable exuberance when I unexpectedly discovered what I felt to be your Achilles' ears.'

For a moment she thought she'd gone deaf again. But no, she'd heard every word. A ferocious wimp, the world was full of wonders. He'd obviously decided to go out in a blaze of glory. It was like being beaten with soft feathery blows.

'We have reached,' she said, 'the point of no return.'

'Before I forget,' Horace countered, 'I bring familial greetings.'

CHAPTER THIRTY-ONE
Raymond

While Horace Bentley was closetted in the Cabinet Room with Mrs Cheeseman, presumably being sacked, Raymond Durrant, Secretary of State for Defence, waited for his interview in the hallway outside. His spirits were low. His wife, Olivia, had intuited that something was up. 'Watch her,' she'd told him this morning, 'her' being Mrs Cheeseman, 'I just have a feeling.'

As Raymond thought of Olivia now, her image supplanted that of the Prime Minister's. She was naked, significantly enough, except for her inevitable cigarette. She had round, firm breasts, 'tits' she always called them. In the same way she said 'fuck' with a sort of languid drawl which made it sound like having tea at the Dorchester. Coming from an earnest middle-class background himself he'd been fascinated from the beginning by her aristocratic earthiness. Sometimes during his career as a backbencher, and even as a Junior Minister, Raymond had reproached himself for failing to deliver a career equivalent of her position and property. Perhaps their marriage had been the product of two strategic miscalculations. He had seen in her the possibility of access to caste and property, the necessary foundations of political power. She had seen in him the possibility of political power, the necessary affirmation of caste and property. Had they missed a step in the logical sequence somewhere? Had she weakened his upward thrust with her aura of eccentricity and hauteur? And had he failed *her* by lacking the savoir-faire, the manipulative ability, the patrician's familiarity with the sources of power?

Perhaps not. Raymond was well aware of the danger of pessimism. Olivia had all the vicarious ambition a politician could ever hope for in a wife: her frankness and confidence didn't make her in the least complacent. And while he, Raymond, lacked her intuitive qualities, well surely that was the whole point, he could make use of *her* intuitive qualities. And in any case he tried to compensate by dedicating his intelligence almost exclusively to strategic considerations. Not that he would describe himself as a cynical man. Certainly he appreciated Olivia for her own sake. Nevertheless when she finally made him Secretary of State for Defence, Mrs Cheeseman actually said: 'You've got this job because you're happily married.' Then added: 'You *are* happily married, aren't you?'

'Oh yes, Prime Minister. More than happily.'

She gave him a sharp look. 'There's no need to overdo it, Raymond. Happily is enough.'

'Happily, Prime Minister.'

'Sometimes,' she said, 'I get the impression that if my colleagues aren't philanderers, they're . . . the other way entirely. And Defence is of course a very sensitive department. Why people can't be satisfied with straightforward family values is quite beyond me.'

Raymond was perfectly aware, of course, that it wasn't as simple as that. For one thing, Mrs Cheeseman had conjured up a vision of cosy domesticity which her own career abruptly contradicted. Oddly she always under-

149

valued women, seeing them as helpmates, housewives, loyal props. Luckily that was clearly how she saw Olivia, ignoring her ambition and force of character.

In any case, Raymond himself had prepared the ground for his promotion. His initial appointment at the Defence Department had been as Minister for Military Strategy, a cul-de-sac, in times of peace, if ever there was one. But he'd managed to make the best of its limited opportunities. He'd taken a leaf out of Mrs Cheeseman's book and appointed himself a personal adviser, a university lecturer in military history. From him he'd acquired the concept of 'milking the grid', a notion in which Mrs Cheeseman had shown great interest when he'd finally got the chance to bring it to her attention.

Nevertheless, Olivia had *deserved* his elevation, there was a satisfying appropriateness about it. Moreover the post of Secretary of State for Defence had a certain sexual cachet, which brought them round full circle. Joanie Lubbock, for example, his secretary, had become suddenly bra-less, and had taken to leaning forward over her typewriter with her dress gaping open. Raymond had to admit that was pleasing even though he remained impervious. Joanie's invitation was to disaster, sex being the great enemy of security. That's what Mrs Cheeseman had meant about upholding family values. Moreover, Olivia was quite enough for any man, even one in charge of the military.

What Olivia shared with Mrs Cheeseman was intuition. Raymond could never credit himself with such prescience. He simply had to weigh up his chances as best he could. He'd been doing so before he left the house this morning, when Olivia had unnerved him with her warning. She'd gone on to proffer advice: 'Whatever the Prime Minister tells you, you must refuse point-blank to accept any cuts. She'll respect you all the more for it.'

At last the Cabinet Room door opened and Horace Bentley hurried out. He was smiling to himself.

'Good morning, Raymond,' he said.

'Good morning,' Raymond replied. Horace was obviously determined to put a brave face on it.

'She says you're to go in.'

'Thank you.'

Raymond entered.

'Raymond,' Mrs Cheeseman said as soon as she saw him. 'Dismal weather.'

'It's cleared up, as a matter of fact. The sun was shining as I came in.' The Cabinet Room was of course windowless, for a combination of security and architectural reasons. Mrs Cheeseman had recently installed strip lighting, and its bright flat illumination emphasized the enclosed nature of the space and reminded Raymond of certain claustrophobic environments he had to inspect from time to time as part of his duties: submarines, nuclear bunkers, officers' messes that were perpetually curtained and impregnated with booze.

Mrs Cheeseman's expression hardened. Of course, she'd spent the morning in here firing Horace. What an opening move, to cross her straightaway! It would have done no harm at all to agree with her about the dismalness of the weather.

'Really?' Mrs Cheeseman said. 'However, I didn't ask you in here to discuss the weather.'

Raymond could make an intelligent guess as to why she had in fact asked him in, but he paused to ensure he didn't commit another blunder. She had summoned him in immediately after sacking Horace, so it must be to do with that. But Mrs Cheeseman would not relish his putting words into her mouth. If she had something to say, let her have the privilege of saying it.

'I don't know, Prime Minister,' he said.

'I think, Raymond, that without being a complete Machiavel, you might occasionally put your nose to the political wind.'

He felt a frustrated anger bubble up in him, out of the sheer injustice of her remark. She obviously thought he was so much less complicated than he actually was. What was extraordinary about her was that she had managed to rise to the top by taking a simplistic view of things herself. It was as though things actually *became* more simple than they were because she looked at them in that light, just as, in her presence, he felt himself becoming more pedestrian and clumsy than he normally was. The explanation, of course, was that she only saw one surface, one facet, of whatever she looked at; but because of her powers of intuition, it was always the relevant one. He couldn't help wondering how Dr Clifton, his deceased adviser, would have reconciled that talent to his theories about the way events arranged themselves.

'Yes, Prime Minister,' he said.

'I'm referring to our conversation of last week.'

'Yes, Prime Minister,' he said again. 'I thought Horace behaved abysmally. I don't blame you in the least.' He didn't mind if he sounded slightly patronizing. The sheer stress of analysing, calculating odds, deciding on an approach, had dispelled his anger, but his adrenalin still flowed, and under its stimulus his intellectual processes accelerated – and took him suddenly in a direction he didn't want to go. The obvious explanation of why he had been summoned here by Mrs Cheeseman was that he was going to be given Horace's job, Art and Culture. He was going to be demoted.

'I'm not talking about Horace,' Mrs Cheeseman snapped.

'No, thought Raymond grimly, you're talking about *me*.

'I'm talking about cuts.'

For a second the word 'cuts' sounded threateningly personal. Then he realized. Olivia's intuition was right, as usual. Mrs Cheeseman was simply talking about *cuts*. His heart thumped with relief. He was going to survive.

'It was merely a preliminary skirmish last week,' Mrs Cheeseman was continuing. 'The real battle is to come. Art and Culture is neither here nor there, we both know that. Compared to the armed forces, I mean.'

The adrenalin, of which Raymond had possessed so much only a few seconds ago, had now deserted him. It was hard to start raising defences when you had just discovered that you were not going to be a casualty yourself. 'I think we must bear in mind the fact that we stand for strong

152

government,' he said. Even as he spoke he realized how tentative he was sounding.

'We must also bear in mind the fact that we are a monetarist administration, waging a perpetual war on waste. That is the struggle we *must* win. That is the only way we can achieve real strength and develop the sort of leverage we need to conduct a properly vigorous foreign policy. The secret of success, Raymond, and you know it as well as I do, lies in productivity. I want to tighten this country up until it is a coiled spring. How can I do that when I have thousands of men roaring about the country-side in jeeps, or sailing about the oceans in enormous ships, *do*ing absolutely nothing? Military exercises, that is the phrase your department constantly uses. But you have to remember that I am not here to play games.'

'It doesn't seem the right moment in time, if you want my opinion,' he suggested. Once again his remark seemed to lack sufficient dimension to counter Mrs Cheeseman's arguments. Even as he spoke his mind was weighing up, evaluating, criticizing – it was so demoralizing that Mrs Cheeseman only ever saw the tip of the iceberg. This time he was thinking of Olivia's parting remark. He could remember it word for word – his memory was unusually good. 'Whatever the Prime Minister tells you,' she'd said, 'you must refuse point-blank to accept any cuts. She'll respect you all the more for it.'

All very true, no doubt, but like so many things easier said than done. Raymond had never been in a real battle for example, but he'd devoted a great deal of attention in recent years to analysing those of the past and to antici-pating hypothetical ones in the future, and it had struck him forcibly as he did so how different a real battle must look from your plans, even if it was actually *go*ing to plan.

'It is always the right time to –' Mrs Cheeseman began.

Now or never, Raymond told himself. This is for *you*, Olivia, he thought. 'Not to cut back on the armed forces,' he said. He spoke quietly but his remark seemed to accrue force from its quietness.

Mrs Cheeseman looked at him long and hard. Then,

equally quietly, she asked: 'What are you getting at, Raymond?'

What was he getting at? He was getting at a whole series of things, each one slight in itself, but gaining significance when it was juxtaposed with the others.

CHAPTER THIRTY-TWO

Raymond

One day while he was still a Junior Minister Mrs Cheeseman had summoned him to her office at the House of Commons. It was a few weeks after he had finally managed to suggest to her the possibilities for military strategy implicit in the notion of 'milking the grid'.

'I was most interested in what you had to say to me recently, Raymond, on the subject of "milking the grid",' she began.

'I thought you might be,' he replied, with new-found confidence. He could sniff promotion in the air. She had never called him Raymond before.

'I was wondering if you could explain this grid business to me in more detail.'

Therein, of course, lay the rub. Detail was what Raymond was short of. Not through any fault of his own; indeed, not through any fault of anybody. It had to be put down to circumstances. He thought back on his meetings with Dr Clifton.

Clifton had begun his career as an anthropologist. He had had a particular interest in makeshift or temporary communities, the sort that manifested themselves in refugee camps, hospitals, places of work. One of the reasons that he'd switched to military studies was that one day it had occurred to him that a battle too was a community, *one made up*, he pointed out, *of both sides*. 'What you have to bear in mind, Mr Durrant, is that enmity is a form of human relationship.'

His other reasons for switching over to military studies was that he had realized that his principal analytical tool, the grid system, could be used in an active rather than a passive manner, as a strategic instrument.

Grid analysis, on the face of it, was straightforward enough. 'Imagine,' Clifton said, 'that you want to copy a picture. The most efficient way is to place a grid over it, and then to place an exactly corresponding grid over your blank sheet of paper. Then you copy your material one square at a time. By that means you carry over all the details and proportions of the original.' When you look at a picture, Clifton had explained, you tend to order it according to your own priorities, your own notions of the picturesque, or, almost as bad, according to what you assume are the artist's notions of the picturesque. You tend to ignore or undervalue certain elements of the material. The grid approach evens your concentration.

The same problems occurred when one was trying to make a model of a community. In this context the equivalent of the hierarchy of the picturesque was the hierarchy of power. The dangers of applying one's own assumptions about authority and the structure of political power to any given community were obvious; but once again it was almost as bad to take on trust the community's *own* assumptions about the sources of power. Power was on tap everywhere: in that sense the grid was like one of the electrical variety. At any given juxtaposition between people, a power game was played out, and social energy was correspondingly being made available. 'The illusion of central authority is that it has total reach,' Clifton had explained. He was a pale, bulky man, with a threadbare, depressing moustache. 'That is because central authority has a limited notion of totality; and therefore no notion of totality at all.' Raymond was to remember this point in his subsequent dealings with Mrs Cheeseman.

Clifton applied the techniques of transactional analysis to communities at large – and of course, since his shift to military studies, to battles. When you looked at the social intercourse of the battlefield, inch by inch, you developed a very different perspective indeed from that generated by the geographical overview of the generals standing on nearby vantage points, or the historical overview of the same generals writing their memoirs at a subsequent date. The legend of the Christmas Day celebrations during the First World War was an example of the public's intuition that battles involved a set of relationships not normally covered in military history. As a result of grid analysis Clifton had come to a number of original conclusions about the course of various battles of the past, and even, in certain cases, about their outcome.

But of course all this was of merely academic interest. The real crux of the matter, Clifton explained, was that he believed it was possible to 'milk the grid'. Communities on the whole were retrospective arrangements. They just happened, and once they were there you tried to find out where they'd come from, how they'd evolved, what their traditions and customs were. This was true even when you built factories and hospitals, because you didn't *build* the community, merely the function. The community just happened. But a battle was a community pure and simple. Its only outcome was a reordering of human relationships. And yet battles had to be arranged in advance.

Raymond understood that a fundamental inversion was being proposed by Clifton. The grid was to be laid, as it were, over a blank sheet, and then the details were to be allocated. Clifton summed up the proposal. In the case of a battle of the past, one's assumption about the source of power was that it was centralized; grid analysis, however, showed that power interchange occurred at all points, and the whole notion of leadership was little more than a myth. In the case of a battle of the future, however, grid projection should mean that the whole pattern of power exchange was predictable, and thus the central authority would be enhanced.

'I make no apology for applying my methods in this direction,' Clifton concluded. 'It is a very human need to have events brought into sharp focus, however much of the scene is omitted as a result. All I have done is to discover a way of making events focus *themselves*. That is what I mean by milking the grid.'

Clifton agreed to prepare a specimen of grid-milking for their next meeting. 'It will be very small-scale,' he admitted. 'At the moment I can only work with little grids.' But the next meeting never took place. Clifton suffered a massive coronary, and died.

Luckily that wasn't the sort of detail Mrs Cheeseman was interested in. 'I leave the theoretical side to *you*,' she said briskly. 'What *I* want to know is this.' She'd been having some eye trouble and was wearing dark glasses, which made her appearance rather sinister. 'If you could choose what war to fight, and where to fight it, what would you do?'

It was, Raymond had felt at the time, a final test. He was being auditioned for the role of Secretary of State for Defence. He answered cautiously.

'I think it should be small-scale, Prime Minister,' he replied. 'The world being what it is.'

'You mean simply a matter of flexing muscles? What do they say, a stand-off?'

But not too cautious. 'Not exactly. I think the best thing to do with a battle is to win it. That has always been my policy as Minister responsible for Military Strategy, anyway.'

'But you haven't had any battles to fight.'

'It has been necessary for me to have a policy, nonetheless.'

'So what *do* you mean?'

'I mean that the engagement should be on a small scale.'

'With a small country? There are obvious political problems there, Raymond. Can you imagine how it would look if we went to war with, I don't know, Monaco, perhaps?'

'I wasn't referring to a small *country*, Prime Minister. I was referring to small *place*. An island, for example.'

The one thing that had been clear from his discussion with Dr Clifton was that if you were going to milk a grid, you needed to have a grid you could handle.

Nothing more had been said on the subject. The battle,

like all Raymond's battles, had been hypothetical. But a few weeks later he had been shuffled into the post of Secretary of State for Defence. He had passed his test.

However, a couple of months ago, another odd incident had occurred. Once again Mrs Cheeseman summoned him to a confidential meeting. This time she wanted him to act as a go-between. His task was to locate somebody who would be able to undertake a difficult under-cover task for the government. Raymond asked her why she had not employed the official secret agencies and her reply was characteristically contemptuous. The matter was confidential. It was necessary to find a person who could not be identified with government policy at any level, and who would never, in any circumstances, be identifiable as an agent of it. Someone strictly mercenary. Preferably an anarchist.

Raymond had found the Fat Man.

So there was a history behind his present query to Mrs Cheeseman. There was the matter of grid analysis. There was the matter of 'milking the grid'. There was the matter of her question about a hypothetical war. There was, above all, the matter of the Fat Man. He'd had all this in his mind when he'd suggested that the present moment might not be the optimum one for inaugurating a cut in the armed defence of the country. When, in response, Mrs Cheeseman asked him what he was getting at, he was getting at quite a lot.

'Well, the fact that . . . something's up, isn't it, Prime Minister?'

'I think, Raymond, it would do no harm to be a little more explicit. This room *is* soundproof, you know.'

As so often a strategic calculation had to be made. He had just received an instruction from Mrs Cheeseman to be explicit. This had to be balanced against a previous instruction never to mention a certain series of discussions again. Mrs Cheeseman's features, under the bright lights of the Cabinet Room, were simultaneously sharp and obtuse, refusing to pick up what he was getting at, yet probing relentlessly to the heart of his confusion.

In the end, as a political animal, she was most alive in the present. He would obey her most recent order.

'The Fat Man,' he said finally.

He realized as soon as he had spoken that it was a mistake.

CHAPTER THIRTY-THREE

Raymond

There was a long pause.

'What do you know about the Fat Man?' Mrs Cheeseman finally asked in an icy voice.

'If you remember, Prime Minister, *I* was the person who made the arrangements.'

'But you don't know *why* the arrangements were made, do you, Raymond?'

'No,' he replied. He wondered whether to bring their other little interchanges into the arena, grid-milking, the hypothetical war, and thought better of it. The Fat Man had not been a success. 'I simply had an . . . intuition that something important was underway.'

'You are not in the position of Secretary of State for Defence in order to have "intuitions",' Mrs Cheeseman responded harshly. Raymond's adrenalin flowed once more. His great drawback was that he didn't *have* intuitions. And five minutes ago Mrs Cheeseman had been berating him for not keeping his nose to the political wind. 'I must make something quite clear,' she continued. 'I must say, I thought it was clear already. My goodness, it ought to be. You are never, ever, to mention that person again.'

'As you said yourself, this room is sound-proof.'

'You must never mention him *even to me*. Even to *yourself*. As long as you live. Do you understand that, Raymond?'

159

'Yes, Prime Minister.' There was no point in flogging a dead horse. He needed to reserve his adrenalin to fight on another front.

Suddenly Mrs Cheeseman snapped out of her mood and became amiable. 'Don't look so anxious,' she said. 'I don't see that you have anything to worry about.'

Be firm, Olivia had said. He mustn't allow himself to be jollied out of his responsibilities – out of his adrenalin – by Mrs Cheeseman's change of mood.

'I'm afraid I find the prospect of cuts in the defence budget very worrying indeed, Prime Minister,' he said.

'Never mind, Raymond. I'm talking about a long-term process. What I want is for you to initiate a departmental review. I envisage a thorough, well-researched document. I suggest you take nine months over it.'

Nine months! Raymond's spirits leapt. Nine months took the edge off the cuts and no mistake. Anything could happen in nine months. Some international crisis, perhaps, that would make cuts in military spending impossible. And meanwhile he would demonstrate a Machiavellian side to his character, despite Mrs Cheeseman's scepticism. He would go home and put it to Olivia that he had won nine months reprieve as a specific concession from the Prime Minister. And there could well be an element of truth in the claim. Mrs Cheeseman might never have offered it if he had taken a more accommodating line in their negotiation.

Unfortunately, while he was busy analysing the implications of his breathing-space, Mrs Cheeseman was taking a step forward. If Raymond had really possessed that intuition she'd rebuked him for, he would have taken her news dolefully, grudgingly. As it was, he'd shown his relief, so she attacked.

'Don't look too pleased with yourself, Raymond. When they come, the cuts will be severe. Your review will propose savings of fifteen percent in real terms.'

'My god, Prime Minister, that's impossible.'

'Nothing's impossible, Raymond. Nothing in this world. Not if you take a positive attitude.'

'But a cut of that magnitude will weaken the whole –'

'Not if your report explores the possibilities sensitively enough. There's no need for draconian measures. And just in case you get too much of a taste for swinging the axe, I've arranged for the recommendations of your report to be scrutinized by my new Inner Cabinet, who will be responsible for its ultimate implementation.'

Whatever Dr Clifton's reservations about the effectiveness of centralized power, there was no doubt that Mrs Cheeseman knew how to unleash wave after wave of hostile forces to maximum effect. Raymond, still reeling under the ferocity of the proposed cuts, now found himself having to cope with the existence of an Inner Cabinet.

'I didn't know you were proposing to form an Inner Cabinet,' he said, aware that his tone was forlorn.

'I only made my decision over the weekend. So far only the members have been informed.'

So he, Raymond, wasn't a member! To have reached this stage in his career only to become a second-class citizen! He smiled grimly. 'Might I ask who the members are?' This time he achieved a firm, sarcastic note.

'The Home Secretary, the Foreign Secretary and the Chancellor of the Exchequer. Oh yes, and the Secretary for Art and Culture. He was a more recent inspiration.'

'Horace!'

'That's correct, Raymond. Horace.'

'For heaven's sake!'

'I thought a smaller department should have a look-in. Somebody who could take a more disinterested view.'

'But Horace is hardly disinterested. Look how he behaved last week!'

It was the nearest he'd ever come to taking the Prime Minister to task, but he couldn't see that he had anything to lose.

To his amazement, Mrs Cheeseman smiled.

'You're more aware than you sometimes let on, Raymond. It is precisely because he made such a fuss that I *put* him in the Inner Cabinet. Make him defend the government's policies, there's no surer way of defusing a maverick.'

It was absurd. The whole concept of defusing Horace made about as much sense as defusing a Christmas cracker. While Raymond was trying to work it out, Mrs Cheeseman reverted to her original line of attack.

'You have nine months, Raymond.'

'Thank you, Prime Minister.'

'If you want a hint from me,' she went on, 'I'd start with the navy.'

Yet again he was taken aback. The navy was such a visible, quantifiable, finite organization. Every cut would be glaringly apparent. Ships were so *large*.

Needless to say, this was Mrs Cheeseman's very point. 'Those ships are dreadfully expensive,' she said. 'Not to mention the dockyards and the ship-builders. We are keeping a moribund industry alive, which scarcely conforms to the government's general economic policy. It's the survival of the fittest, let's face it. Raymond.'

'But what about public opinion?' He cast about in his mind for a way of emphasizing the special place the navy held in the affections of the British. All he could come up with on the spur of the moment was the picture of a bearded sailor on twenties of Players. Olivia smoked Players. Mrs Cheeseman, on the other hand, loathed cigarettes and forbad smoking in the Cabinet Room.

'I think we should have the courage of our convictions,' Mrs Cheeseman said in a voice that brooked no further discussion.

Raymond thought of all the admirals with whom he would have to argue. The navy was more upper-crust than the other services; Olivia knew a lot of its leading lights socially. Like her they tended to have a formidable follow-through beneath the aristocratic facade.

'I know you're worried about the employment implications of all this, Raymond,' Mrs Cheeseman went on. 'But there is no point in paying people good money for doing very little. By ensuring they do nothing we are giving the real doers of this country the chance to roll up their sleeves and get on with the job.'

'Yes, Prime Minister,' Raymond said tersely. He didn't

need to have monetarist logic spelled out to him. The problem was that from a larger viewpoint the logic didn't seem to hold up. How could a Prime Minister who prided herself on her strength tolerate – indeed, inaugurate – a weakening of the country's defences? What made the problem even more intractable was that Mrs Cheeseman was not a person to succumb to inconsistency. From her perspective the whole issue must make sense. But try as he might, Raymond was unable to achieve her perspective.

At last he took his leave. It was pouring down outside. Even the weather seemed to lend its support to Mrs Cheeseman's point of view.

CHAPTER THIRTY-FOUR

Jack

Yesterday going to the library, waiting at the bus stop, that woman standing there. Making idle conversation. He noticed he could do that nowadays with women, probably now that everybody thought he was old. Queen thought he was old. She blamed him for them not doing it over the last four years. He could swear on the Bible that it was her who'd just shut up shop all of a sudden. Of course, when you looked back on something like that, something that had stopped happening, it was hard to tell. Perhaps when you stopped doing it with your wife you always thought it was your wife who'd stopped, you sort of forgot that you couldn't make it any more. Perhaps being dead was like that. Perhaps you hardly noticed. You just quietly forgot what it was like being alive.

But yesterday, going to the library, talking to that woman at the bus stop, just passing the time of day.

'These buses get worse,' he said.

'I got to go to the hospital,' she said. 'My daughter's had her eye out.'

You can put her on your list. Everything that happened

practically could go on the list. Things happening were just a list, when you thought about it. His whole life had been like a series of daily order forms. One, Polish Bacon, two three etcetera all the things you did there, ringing up people for *their* orders, nineteen, coming home to dinner, steak and kidney pie, mashed potatoes, peas. Already food seemed to have lost its point, now he wasn't in the trade. Twenty, washing up. Twenty and a half, the wireless propped up behind the sink.

You mustn't let yourself get into a depression, Queen said, you've got to eat. It's only young girls let themselves starve to death. But you only had to read the papers. In fact even on that very subject: a top model ate herself to death. She'd eaten a whole cauliflower, two pounds of turnips, two pounds of liver, most of it raw, having cooked a normal amount and then going ape with what was left, three pounds of potatoes, a pound of carrots, a jar of pickled onions, a whole loaf in the form of bread and jam, six eggs beaten up in milk, three pounds of apples, two packets of crisps, a large chocolate bar, a pound of custard creams. The poor little bitch had burst inside before she had a chance to throw up. It was like one of the orders he'd dealt with at Polish Bacon. Slimmer's disease. Who would believe you could have slimmer's disease and die of overeating? The girl hadn't eaten for a whole week before she killed herself. People were killing themselves all the time.

George had cried. After all these years, right in the middle of the pub. It seemed too much of a coincidence, at this moment in time. Perhaps George had always been miserable and Jack had just not noticed, too busy going from a to b, Polish Bacon, washing-up, television, etcetera. But George had always seemed cheerful enough. He seemed cheerful enough on Wednesday, pouring pint after pint down himself. Better have another, to nail the one before, was what he always said. He was talking about drinking in his topless bar as usual.

'She bloody near dropped one of her thingums right in it. I thought to myself – you know what I did, Jack? I took a look at her and I suddenly cried like a baby.' As he said it he did it, wah, wah, just like a baby wanting a feed. Like he was acting what he actually did the night before at the topless bar. People in the pub looked at him, and the landlord came over.

'Taking you the wrong way tonight, George?'

George said nothing, he just carried on crying. The landlord looked at Jack.

'Does sometimes, you know. I seen grown men cry like a baby in this actual pub, I have honest.' He had a kind tone even though he seemed to have forgotten George was crying like a baby. He went off to polish some glasses.

George started talking again. The tears were still coming down his cheeks but his voice was normal. 'I suddenly cried like a bloody baby. I was thinking to myself, in all the years I been alive I never put my hand on one of them things.'

'I don't know what you worrying about, George,' Jack said. 'Queen never had any in the first place.'

'What she's got, you've had, Jack. Some of the girls at the bar got piddling little ones but god almighty it don't make them boys, do it?'

'Queen and me haven't done it for four years,' Jack said.

'I haven't done it *ever*.'

'Four years *is* flicking ever.'

It was the wrong thing to say. You could see George doing the sum in his head. If four years was ever, how many years would be how many times ever. Panic came into George's eyes.

'I didn't get married till I was nearly thirty,' Jack said. 'I just run our shop up north.'

George didn't reply, unless you counted the tears still coming out one at a time, like little round wet words. For a moment Jack thought of bringing Tom into it, saying about Tom and Queen. No, like not having it for four years it would just be an example of what he'd had before he'd lost it. Jack's own sex-life being in the past made it worse for George, because if it was in the present George could think perhaps there's still time but because it was in the past it was all too late. Too late. Jack knew about being too late.

'I just lost my job,' he told George.

165

Sure enough, the lack of a job elbowed the other lack out of the way, George's tears dried, his panic slowly faded. But Jack remembered how he'd looked. He felt the same way himself these days.

CHAPTER THIRTY-FIVE

Jack

Jack just sat there, looking out of the window or reading his newspaper. Sometimes he read out bits about people killing themselves. Sometimes he would talk about what had happened to him, explaining bitterly about Tom and the rubbish business. That always made her cringe, as if the word rubbish really meant her. But even that was better than when his big head went slowly towards the grey window, and he watched hardly anything happen on the street outside for hours at a time. She remembered being in the shop in New Mills in her childhood, watching that cold wind blow outside. Now, funnily enough, she had a market stall out in the open three days a week, and even in bad weather she was glad to get out of the house, Jack was so sad and bored.

Tom had left altogether, which was just as well. He was going to sign up in the army full-time, so he said. Now he wasn't here any more, she kept having the feeling that it was all his fault, that he'd used her for his own purposes, taken advantage of her. She had only been his landlady, but he'd made her into other things, starting with his mother. Of course, that had been Frankie Rutherford's idea.

'Be very grateful if you'd keep an eye on him. Lad's never had a mother, you know. Young beggar needs a woman's touch to keep him on course.'

And, of course, woman's touch had been only too easy to provide.

*

She and Jack had stopped making love before Tom ever arrived in the house. It had been getting more and more drawn out, more and more thin, as time went on.

On the night it happened, or rather didn't happen, it was raining. Queen and her old-faithful Jack heaved in the bed, tick tock went the rain, on and on went Jack, dry pumping, dripping gutter. A cat yowled outside, on the pavement.

And then Jack gasped, and lay still on top of her.

'We're not getting any younger,' she whispered, trying to be nice. He didn't reply.

'You all right?' she asked.

He lay on top of her. She could feel all the separate bits of him, it was like lying under a dry stone wall.

'I thought my heart conked out for a moment,' he said finally.

'Conked out, Jack?' she said. 'It's thumping away like there's no tomorrow.'

It was the wrong thing to say. 'Perhaps there isn't going to be a tomorrow,' he replied sadly.

'You are a fool,' she said. 'Of course there's going to be a tomorrow. You're going to get up, as usual, and go off down to Polish Bacon. And I'm going to get up, put my plastic mac on, and go off through the sodding rain to my stall and sell fruit and veg all day, like every Thursday.'

That did the trick. He rolled off and lay quietly beside her.

'Do you think it'll still be raining?' he asked.

'According to the forecast it'll be raining all day. You know how my bloody awning drips.'

And all the time they talked, she thought to herself, never again. Never ever again. The cat yowled, the gutter dripped, the rain beat steadily down. Never again.

She never turned him down, she wasn't that type of woman. She just made sure that things didn't get to the point where he tried to. She learned to fall asleep very fast, which in its way suited a man of regular habits.

And then Tom moved in, and she was asked to provide a woman's touch.

167

It had begun on a Sunday night. Jack always went to the pub on Wednesday and Sunday evenings, to meet his friend George. Tom had been away all weekend with the Terrors. He came in about nine that evening, still in uniform, very muddy.

'You look a mess,' she said.

'I've been crawling over the Brecon Beacons all weekend.' He was cheerful, excited.

'You've brought most of them back with you.'

'You do love playing mother. I'm a big boy now.'

'I was told to keep an eye on you.'

'Anyway, I scored this weekend.'

'I wondered if that was your game.'

He gave her a long, mischievous look. 'I don't know what you mean, Queen. I've been crawling all over the Beacons. There's only sheep in those parts. I've been on survival. You score if the other lot don't get you.'

'What I've heard about soldiers,' Queen said. And next thing she knew, they were up in her bedroom, making love. There was an hour before Jack came home from the pub. When Tom came he relaxed into her, his face in the crook between her head and shoulder, almost like a child, moaning softly. She thought to herself, if Jack hadn't always been so dry, I'd have been a mother in my time.

Anyway, that was all over now. Jack had lost his job at Polish Bacon; Tom was in the army full time. She watched Jack sitting in his chair and her heart ached. He seemed to be collecting stories from the newspaper about people who'd killed themselves. She waited for Jack to kill himself. Not with aspirins or a polythene bag or anything like that. She couldn't imagine him pulling a plastic bag over his big slow head. He'd become *so* slow, his routine was gone. She expected him soon to stop altogether.

Instead, he made a suggestion.

'Queen,' he said one day, turning his head from the window towards her, 'I think we ought to sell up and buy ourselves a little guest house in Southsea.'

CHAPTER THIRTY-SIX

Premo

I sit in my dressing-room. Outside it is autumn in Aber-ystwyth. Inside, it is Shrewsbury, early summer. I am reading a letter and trying to remember a face. I can remember the rain, of all things. The first night there were lots of tiny fingers, twiddling. The second, just the occasional drop. Like urine down a trouser leg. Like the flash of tears in a bright room. Like a face with a few freckles. I can't remember the face, only the freckles.

A face appears behind mine in the dressing-table mirror. Mine is as usual, the eyes in bags, the bald patch not shining, my hair long and greasy. The other face is bearded, with watering eyes. Steg has come in on his silent legs.

'Steg,' I say.

'Don't give me that shit,' Steg says.

'I only said Steg.'

'I saw yous do a big frown. In your mirror there. You said it like you didn't want to know me, Prem. Like you got nothing to give. We all need give, Premo.'

'What do you want, Steg?' I ask.

'I got to toot, Premo. I got to toot a line. What it is, I don't like Wales, that's the point. I don't like Wales at all. I been standing on Aberystwyth beach, Premo.'

Premo tries to picture it. Steg, beard ruffled by sea breezes, eyes watering with the sting of salt air, standing upon his bendy legs on Aberystwyth beach.

'Getting some fresh air,' I suggest.

'I been standing on the beach and watching the sea come in. I watch the sea come in, and I think, behind me are all those Welshmen. I fear the Welsh, Premo, I always have. They're little bastards. I had a dream about them once. Hundreds of them. Thousands. They all had top hats with mirrors on, and they all had the same face, and they just walked towards me, nearer and nearer. They go so *near*.'

'What do you expect in Aberystwyth, for heaven's sake?'

'I've got to toot, Prem. I've got to.'

'You sound fully tooted as it is,' I reply. 'At the risk of being personal. What do you need further toots for?'

Steg drifts nearer. He lowers his voice. 'It smoothes the edges, Premo. You know that.'

By now of course I've unravelled the ethical system that culminates in Steg's concept of 'give'. He wants me to lend (i.e. *give*) him sufficient to purchase a dollop of snow. He needs to insulate himself from the men in the top hats.

'Look Steg, draw it out on the firm,' I say. 'If you must.'

There is a pause. Steg just looks. That's something Steg can do, just look, one of his stronger points. Except that his eyes tend to flow, as they are doing now.

'You bastard,' Steg says. He turns and begins to leave the room.

'Wait a minute, Steg.'

His legs stop hopefully, just in the middle of feeling their way towards the floor. His body continues forward, under its previous momentum, but he doesn't fall over. He never falls over. It reaches the end of its arc and drifts upright again. Now he leans in my direction. He hasn't turned round of course so it's his back that leans but that doesn't make much difference, except that I can't see his eyes.

'What've you done with it?' I ask.

His blank hairy head says nothing. It stares at me.

'I said, what've you done with it, Steg?'

He speaks from the face on the far side, but I can still read the thin mirror-writing: 'What you saying, Premo?'

'I'm *saying*, the firm. I'm *saying*, the firm's money.'

'The firm's got no money, Premo.'

I try to remain calm. 'Steg. We've been on the road for over four months. We've been to Shrewsbury. Chester. *Man*chester. Newcastle. Glasgow. Edinburgh. God knows where. We're in Wales now, for chrissake!'

'I fear the Welsh, Premo,' the head replies. It'll say anything not to get to the point. 'They got –'

'They do not have top hats, in the name of sanity. You know what Steg, you're beginning to hallucinate. Our concerts have sold. 'Shit's Creek' is fifty-three in the hit parade. Where's the fucking money, Steg?'

Steg's head nods. 'Yeah, fifty-three,' it says. 'Fifty-three. How do you think it gets to number fifty-three?' it asks. 'They won't play it on radio or TV. How do you think we get enough people to buy it to get to number fifty-three, Premo?'

'People buy it because they *know* it's not going to be on radio or TV.'

'They got to know it exists first,' the head points out. 'Think of the advertising. Think of the entertaining I've done, Premo.'

I try to visualize Steg entertaining. Sitting in some cubicle in the gents at the Empress, being served toot by Mr Cool. And all his guests in a line in the other cubicles, being likewise. And then all getting into a huddle afterwards, talking business with numb lips.

'I can just imagine it,' I say. 'Steg's devotion to duty. Getting snowed on the firm.'

'That's right,' Steg's head surprisingly agrees. 'My nostrils been in the ring for you, Prem. I got junk coming out of my ears.' It's funny looking at ears from the back. They have pink rims, with no way in. Blind ears. 'It cost more to get 'Shit's Creek' to number fifty-three than what we get in sales,' Steg's head says, concluding its argument.

Suddenly my body tingles. My wings, are they about to sprout? 'Tell you what, Steg, get yourself a nose-full,' says Premo. 'Us pigs got to stick together.' Steg's head whimpers. I take some notes out of my drawer. Steg's hand materializes, palm upward. Only the elbow is reversed. I place the notes on his hand.

'You got give,' Steg's head whispers hoarsely. He leaves the room with rapid downward movements of his long thin legs, like a stork running into take-off.

Premo is alone with the letter. He remembers his hopper. She is the one he cannot remember. *The* one. She has freckles, he remembers that, but the freckles don't focus into a face, they just fall loosely over her face and body, pale gold. Residual drips. My hopper is beautiful, and true.

CHAPTER THIRTY-SEVEN

Premo

Grand finale.

This hall in Aberystwyth is as far as I'm going. It is full of Welsh people, more guys than parrots which is somewhat unusual. They seem big, I didn't know the Welsh were big, but when they laugh they do so musically, with Welsh accents.

Tonight the popsies are wearing white high-heeled shoes, white tights, white mini-skirts, bright green blouse things. Suddenly I realize what they're up to. The little twats think they look like leeks. I am uncompromising, dressed as usual in my lime green tee-shirt with PISS OFF stamped on it, my model of a pair of jeans, my coffee and pink old-fashioned dress.

I begin on my last song. The audience look up at me appreciatively. They seem to have enjoyed themselves. No doubt it makes a change from chapel.

> I say it's time to toot a line
> I want to toot
> I need to snow inside my head
> Don't care what the weather forecast says.

The popsies clap their small hands. They sing the reprise:

> Don't care what the weather forecast says.

I peer over my shoulder at them. They are swaying to and fro, giving their interpretation of 'weather' I suppose. They don't sway as far as Steg, but they sway enough, like a Welsh wind blowing through a leek-bed. I turn back and resume.

Those Welshmen on the march, they getting so near
Wearing their big hats
Not going to wash them away with beer
Or place my digit in some twat.

The audience shift uneasily. A couple of them laugh. I turn to the popsies again. I feel the need to savour them for the last time.

Place his digit in my twat

they sing in their tinkling voices. On 'twat' they put their hands over their o-ing mouths in cute shock. I turn back and proceed:

Welshmen got mirrors on their heads
See your face in them
Got leeks and marrows in their beds
Complexions green as phlegm.

Feet shift a bit. I resist the temptation to check up on the popsies this time. Some of these Welshmen are *surprisingly* large, steamy with rugby. There are distinctly fewer parrots than you might expect, which is a pity in all sorts of ways. From behind, the popsies:

Complexions green as phlegm.

Premo, my voice unnuanced, rancid, pig, continues:

Toot me a line, catch me on your hook
Don't roll no joint
I read about these Welsh gits in a book
Snow smooths my edges, yeah, that's the point.

The popsies flick their fingers, so that it sounds as if they are snapping off each individual word from a great big word-bar:

Snow smooths our edges, yes, that's the point.

I gird my loins as I approach the climax. Quite a lot of shuffling is going on. Welshmen certainly wear sensible shoes.

Those Welshmen getting near, I need a coke
Those Welshmen getting near, no effing joke.

The popsies snuggle round me, as popsies never do in life. All together now:

Those Welshmen getting near, we need a coke
Those Welshmen getting near, no effing joke.

I grasp each side of my cleavage, and pull, to show the full scope of my PISS OFF. There is silence. Even the shuffling has faded away. Nobody laughs, or cheers. You can hear the after-sound of the music. 'No effing joke' bounces around the hall, fading to a whisper.

Then, at the far end, back right, some movement begins. Not like people moving. Like insects, or a shoal of fish, a flutter, flurry, in the crowd. As if a breeze stirs among Welshmen.

The sudden detail of a fist whacks somebody on the cheek. He cries ow like a schoolboy.

Near the front, a big man in a leather jacket moves to the side of the hall, grabs a heavy gym bench that is stacked there, raises it like a gigantic club, prepares to swing, and then finds the weight too much, and lowers it whimpering to the floor again. He sits on it but is immediately shaken off by a huge youth who picks it up and swings it in a grand arc, knocking a skinny parrot as completely flat as if she's been changed into a bench herself. The leather-jacketed man is just rising from the floor when the bench hits him too and returns him there.

A hopper middle front has a whole wide strip of dress pulled off leaving the remainder hanging in place like a cross-section drawing. MANHOLE COVER is printed across the front of her pants. Pig knickers. Perhaps my PISS OFF has had an influence. How unexpected it is to find a cultural niche. The hopper tries to hide her pants with her hands, blushing from her face right down the long strip as she does so.

The leeks, behind me, have been screeching for some time. Now they flee, although strangely nobody has made

174

any attempt to attack the stage, source of the insults. I stand mid-stage, just watching.

Suddenly, a yabbering noise behind me, and now Steg rushes past on long gangly legs, nose newly red, eyes even redder, and this time, as he reaches the edge of the stage, he does take off, flap flap like a great crow, flying through the air so slowly, like those slow-motion films of athletes where they always seem to jump higher or further than they do at normal speed, Steg flying through the air in graceful slow-motion, one foot coming down and beautifully kicking a face, then continuing on his way down the hall, kicking occasionally to right and left as faces offer, flapping his arms and flying just above the crowd as if at last he's found an atmosphere heavy enough to support his weight.

Premo meanwhile takes Nicola's letter out of his pocket and reads it again.

Dear Mr Bulge
I don't expect you remember me, but we met when you were in Shrewsbury. I'm writing to to inform you that I'm expecting your baby. I've decided to have it. I don't require you to do anything, or anything of that kind, but I thought you had a right to know. It is due in the early part of March next. The two of us will be fine, so you can put your mind at rest.

Yours sincerely,
Nicola Gilmour.

Below and in front of me pig is erupting like a bud in the sun. I can see my face in all those Welsh top hats. I can also see my face inside Nicola. It is a different face. I try to memorize it.

I go to my dressing-room, and take my dress off. When I've changed, I collect a few things, and EXIT by the stage door.

CHAPTER THIRTY-EIGHT

Nicola

Nicola thought of her womb as small and round, like one of those snow-scene shakers you have at Christmas, full of water, with the snow falling down on a plastic deer and Santa Claus. If she shook hers she could feel it sploosh a little, but there was no sign of life, no answering kick. It was a closed circle, which no one could enter or leave.

'It won't kick yet,' her mother said. 'It's early days. I'm surprised you're as big as you are.'

But her mother had been the mother of a dead baby as well as a living one: her advice was unreliable.

As the days wore on Nicola's womb grew; but it also grew colder. Sometimes she felt she was sitting in it herself, in a dark, icy place, under water. She had left work – her father had actually told her to.

'I don't think a secretary with a bun in the oven is much of an advert for an insurance company,' he said bitterly.

So she sat at home, day after day, imagining a dead baby forming inside her. It would have white crinkled skin, like you get on the bulbs of your fingers when you've lain in a cold bath for too long. When she had had sex with Premo Bulge she had thought she was exorcizing a ghost; now her dead sister was closer to her than she had ever been.

One morning in October Nicola woke up to find her mother standing over her. There was the smell of bacon, as if her mother had mysteriously sprayed it on herself as a perfume. She was looking down at her with that perpetually worried naked face she had these days, strangely out of tune with the smart housecoat.

'I thought you might like a bit of breakfast,' she said, nodding towards Nicola's bedside table. Nicola moved her head to look. There was a plate, with a slice of buttered toast on it, and a rasher of bacon upon the toast. To one side was a pool of tomato sauce, red as blood.

'Oh no,' she half-whispered, half-groaned.

'I know you feel a bit queasy in the mornings. But I used to find the best way of dealing with that was to have something to eat.'

Suddenly Nicola's bitterness welled up. Why not? You could blame your mother, who else was there? One day her child would be blaming *her*.

'I don't think you're much of an example to follow.'

Her mother was galvanized for a second, as though struck; then she relaxed into her usual anxiety and sadness. Sunlight was streaming through the window and in its illumination her face shone with a fresh unhealthy whiteness, like that of a maggot.

'I'll take it down then.'

As she picked up the plate Nicola noticed a plaster capping her left thumb.

'What did you do to yourself?' she asked. Now that the bacon was being removed she became aware of her own beddy smell, almost menstrual despite the fact that she was pregnant.

Her mother smiled in relief, gladdened by the enquiry.

'I cut the top, when I was chopping an onion,' she said.

'Oh.'

'I thought I'd make a casserole for tonight. Don't look like that. It's only a teeny bit. But it's a bit sore.'

There was a ring at the front door.

'Oh dear,' her mother continued. 'If that's Mrs Grover wanting to use the phone again, I'll scream. I'll see you in a minute, when you get up.'

She left the room. Nicola remained in bed, thinking about her mother's thumb. It was only a teeny bit. But the teeny bit mixed itself up with all the other teeny bits that together composed the flavour of dead baby: chopped thumbs, casseroles, bacon, bed, menstruation. The smell of dead baby was the intimate smell of her body; after all, the dead baby was now inside her.

Suddenly her mother's voice came up, cheerful, welcoming: 'Come *in*, do.' Whoever was at the door, it obviously wasn't Mrs Grover for the phone.

Some talking took place. Nicola couldn't hear the words; just her mother's bright, welcoming tone, and a gruff man's voice responding. And then in a flurry of steps her mother had climbed the stairs and was back in the bedroom. Her face looked naked as before, but flushed, smiling, insistent.

'Up you get,' she said to Nicola.

'I don't think –'

'You've got a visitor. A young man.'

Premo rose from the depths of a Scandinavian settee. He was wearing a tie, a tweed sports jacket, cord trousers. He looked exactly like someone from her parent's world who for some reason was wearing a Premo Bulge mask, except that the mask had now been shaven, slimmed, cleaned up.

'Hello Nicola,' he said.

'I'll get you both a cup of coffee,' her mother said, backing from the room.

'To tell you the truth, Mrs Gilmour, I was wondering if Nicola would like to come for a walk.'

'That's a splendid idea. It would do her the world of good. In her condition . . .' She trailed off.

Nicola could have laughed out loud. She could see the alternatives flitting across her mother's expression: which would be the best tactic, to pretend it hadn't happened, or to be briskly frank about it? The problem was compounded by the fact that her mother had no idea whether Premo was the man responsible or not. In response to the dilemma, her face closed. She turned to Nicola with a smart house-wifely expression for the first time in months. Nicola didn't mind: she herself had nearly *laughed* for the first time in months.

'Yes, I would like a walk,' Nicola said. 'It's such a lovely day.'

CHAPTER THIRTY-NINE

Nicola

They walked along the towpath of the North Shropshire canal, which passed quite near Nicola's house on the outskirts of Market Hanking. The sky was a clear blue, and the cool air had warm slats in it, as if the sun had played on its invisible surfaces as it played on the slats of the venetian blind in Nicola's bedroom window. There were some tall bushes on the left of the path, festooned with damp spiders' webs. Through the thinning leaves you could make out a series of fields which sloped down towards Market Hanking.

'You're very thin,' Premo said.

'I've got this,' she replied, patting her belly.

'The rest of you.'

She couldn't explain, of course, that to eat in her own right had seemed greedy. That while the baby grew she ought to shrink. That she was not eating for two but starving for one.

'It's just the way it's taking me,' she said lightly.

They stopped to watch a lock fill up, the brown water turning white as it fell. A man on a barge slowly rose towards ground level. He was smartly dressed, wearing a blue blazer and flannels, but he clearly felt at a disadvantage because he kept casting glances up at them with embarrassed eyes.

Suddenly Nicola realized it was Terry Sutton. He was obviously pretending not to notice her, perhaps because of her pregnancy, perhaps because of Premo's presence – perhaps both. It made her want to laugh out loud. And two could play at that game.

'Are you really called Bulge?' Nicola asked Premo.

'Yes.'

'I mean in real life.'

Terry's head surfaced above the edge of the towpath.

'You can bite my ankles if you like,' Premo suggested to it. The head, muttering, its hair carefully swept back and damped down with brylcreem, turned away. 'It's a good job Steg isn't here,' Premo told Nicola. 'He wouldn't be able to resist a head at foot level.'

'Who's Steg?'

'My manager.'

'Oh yes. Him. The one you said was unbalanced.'

'He's unbalanced all right. But the funny thing about Steg is, he never fell over.'

Nicola peered down at the nearly full lock. She tingled all over. 'It's a lovely day, isn't it?' she asked Terry. He pretended not to hear.

'My mother put it on my birth certificate,' Premo went on. 'I was illegitimate. The registrar kept pestering her about my father's name, so that's what she said it was. That's where I'd come from, she said.'

'Like mine,' Nicola said, touching her belly. Her womb felt warmer, as if the sun had finally caught it. Terry had stepped off the barge on to the far side of the canal, and was opening the lock gate.

'Like father like son,' Premo said. 'I found out in the end my dad worked for the Gas Board in Blackpool. He came to London on a course, and had a fling with my mother. His name was Stone. I've never met him.'

Terry had now almost pushed the lock gate arm into the open position, practically parallel with the canal. Suddenly his foot caught a patch of mud. He gave a sudden shout, slid forward under the arm, and slithered into the narrow strip of canal that ran between the lock-side and his barge. For some reason he made hardly a splash but entered the canal with the neatness and rapidity of a water rat. After a few seconds his head bobbed above the surface.

'You all right?' Premo called out. 'I'll rescue you if you want.'

Terry didn't reply but grasped the side of his barge and pulled himself aboard, gasping with the effort and the cold. Then he went straight to the rear of the boat, slipped the motor into gear, and steered it out of the lock, keeping his gaze fixedly ahead while he did so. His hair, clearly water-repellent, remained in place; his dripping clothes looked even smarter than before, as if they'd been varnished.

'Is that why you went pig?' Nicola asked Premo.

'What do you mean?' he replied.

'Not having a father.'

'I went pig,' Premo said, 'so that I would meet you.'

The putter of the barge diminished with distance, and Nicola could hear the stirrings of a faint breeze: the rustle of browning leaves, dry grass, the click of the eddying water.

'Don't be silly,' she said.

'You know what they say. When pigs have wings.'

As they walked on, patches of raw mud, like the one Terry had slipped on, appeared from time to time on the otherwise dry footpath, the result of seepage from the canal. Every now and then the sun struck these damp surfaces, and turned them into gold.

'Premo and Mrs Bulge,' Premo said. 'We can buy a little house somewhere. I've got enough to put down. I never trusted Steg.'

'But what shall we *do*?'

'You'll have the baby, that's what you'll do. What I'll do, who knows? I'll find something. It won't be pig, that's for sure.'

CHAPTER FORTY

David

It was a bright October day, the landscape dense with available detail if only David had had the lenses to perceive it. But at least he caught glimpses in the general blur – a curling lip of water on the canal as the breeze lifted the surface, a sudden, webby tuft of grass, the wrinkling effect of almost bare twigs and branches against the intensely blue sky. He had had a pre-lunch sherry at the manor-house with Frankie Rutherford and a number of his shooting cronies. Actually, David must have misread the invitation because he had been under the impression that lunch was included too. The amount of reading he'd been doing recently for his book had exacerbated the condition of his eyes, and it really was absurd that he still couldn't bring himself to go to an optician. Disappointment was automatic, despite the fact that it was hardly his sort of occasion. He sensed that as soon as he and the other outsiders – the village doctor, chemist, a pair of local school teachers – made their exit, Frankie and his pals would sit down to some sort of boozy feast: game pie, no doubt. There was a man from the government there so no doubt Frankie would kill the fatted calf. David had never been a particularly hungry man; it was the booze that he regretted. There had been an atmosphere of celebration in Frankie's manor-house.

'Just celebrating a piece of good news,' Frankie had said, pouring David an inevitable sherry.

'Oh yes?'

'My boy Tom seems to have settled down at last.'

'Really?'

'He's been scratching a living in Battersea, silly arse.'

'And what's he doing now?'

'Joined the army. I always thought he was cut out for it. Never met him, did you, padre?'

'No.' As far as David knew Tom hadn't been home during the three and a half years of his ministry in the parish. He wasn't easy to picture either: with Frankie for a parent you could hardly talk about someone being a chip off the old block.

'Little fathead wouldn't do it properly. Insisted on going straight in as a noncom. In the SAS, at least. He was a sergeant in the Terrors, you know.'

David nearly dropped his drink. The already blurred surroundings shifted and swam. Frankie's features developed the suppleness and animality of a nightmare, as in a Francis Bacon painting. It was difficult for David to hold on to his drink because his hand felt like the hand of another person.

'The Terrors?' he asked, almost in a whisper.

'The Territorial Army,' said Frankie. 'Boy scouts for grownups.'

Frankie's face settled back into banality. David's relief was so great that he felt a sudden irrelevant surge of warmth towards the whole company, and he was correspondingly sorry when Frankie shortly made it clear it was time for him to leave.

Now, as he walked, his fear returned. Not with its previous intensity, but seeping back into his system by inches, until he could no longer imagine how he had managed to exorcize it so readily before. He must have deluded himself that the supernatural lacked the capacity to pun or explore the realms of *double entendre*. On the contrary: it was precisely by such methods that the past would invade the present. The secret language of generations would be a dubious muttering, a speaking with forked tongues, an opening of semantic chasms in the most ordinary words, just as a vision of the persistent past would eschew the claptrap of Hammer horror and might choose to appear as a projection of your aching tooth. The dead didn't have materials of their own to work with; they had to use what they could find in the present.

He was now walking along the towpath of the canal. Despite the bright dry conditions it was puddly in places, presumably where water from the canal had seeped into the bank, and he had to be careful where he put his feet. As a result, after some minutes he almost bumped into a young couple coming the other way. He apologized and walked on. The girl had been pregnant. How lucky, he thought, to be moving through time *that* way.

He looked at his watch. It was only one-thirty, the Cricketers would be open for another hour and a half. Why not? He made his way over the fields in the direction of the pub.

The Cricketers was busy and fuggy at two-fifteen, when

he finally arrived. He pushed his way through the crush of people to the bar and caught Jean's eye.

'Hello, vicar,' she said. She was a woman who registered your presence warmly – even to an extent sexually – but not today. She poured him a pint and leaned confidentially towards him across the bar. 'I'm glad you've come, David. Have you seen over there?'

David turned to look but all he could see was the press of talking men.

'What?' he asked.

'At the table in the corner. Terry.'

'Oh yes? What about him?'

'He came in about twenty minutes ago. He was soaking wet from head to foot. I said to him, "Terry, what's the matter with you? You fallen in the duck pond?" He didn't say anything in reply, he just ordered a drink. And then, when I was serving it to him, he just burst into tears. He began crying like a baby.'

'Good heavens!'

'I asked him what was up but he wouldn't say anything. He carried his drink over to the table in the corner. He's still bawling his eyes out now. I've never had anybody do that in my pub before, not even when they've had too much to drink. I'd be glad if you could have a word with him, vicar.'

'Of course I will,' said David, his heart sinking. Terry was the last person he felt like talking to at the moment. He was so coarse-grained, simple-minded, hapless and cynical. When he thought he was cock of the walk he had been tiresome enough; what he would be like in a fit of depression, David dreaded to think.

Nevertheless he picked up his drink and left the bar. Jean was already busy with another customer.

Sure enough Terry was sitting at a table in the corner, making no attempt to staunch or disguise his tears, but crying nakedly and loudly. Moreover instead of being his usual impeccable self he was soaked to the skin, and there were even bits of waterweed on the shoulders of his jacket. All his clothes, beneath their film of water, were in order however, so he'd taken the trouble to dress to his usual standard before disaster struck, which was possibly a good sign. It rather depended on what the disaster was. Despite the crowding in the room there was a space around Terry's table, and the regulars were making a point of not noticing his state. David took a leaf out of their book and approached him as if nothing untoward were happening.

'I'm glad I spotted you, Terry,' he said breezily. 'I wanted to have a word.' He sat down at the table. Terry made no sign of recognition but continued to weep. His eyes were virtually closed, but every few seconds tears popped out, rather obscenely, from between the lids and rolled down his cheeks.

'Yes,' David went on regardless, 'I wanted to thank you for your good offices regarding Lorna's insurance. Settlement was made the other day, and the company only deducated a nominal penalty, which they said they had to do *pour encourager les autres*. I'm sure that without your legwork it would have taken longer, and cost me more.'

As if bringing a cumbersome vehicle – a train, or an aeroplane – to a halt, Terry began to stop weeping. The sobs gradually lessened, the tears started to stop coming from between his lids, he wiped his eyes with the backs of his hands, each in turn, and took a sip of his beer. When he spoke, his voice quavered slightly but his tone was normal.

'Nothing to do with me,' he said.

'Oh, come on,' David argued, 'I know you put in a good word.'

'A good word from me's the kiss of death. I got the sack months ago.'

'What!' David thought back rapidly. Yes, he'd seen Terry several times in the last few months; no, Terry had never mentioned losing his job. In point of fact David could swear he'd talked about work in the usual way.

'I'm sorry, I didn't realize that,' he said.

'It's not the sort of thing you shout from the rooftops.'

That was obviously it. He'd bottled the information up until he could cope with the pressure no longer, and had to release it perforce.

185

'It's obviously upset you a great deal.' It suddenly occurred to David that Terry's wet state could be the result of a suicide attempt. 'A very great deal,' he reiterated.

'I'm pissed off,' Terry agreed. 'But it's not that. Not just that anyway.' He looked up at David and his features began to swim and coalesce almost as Frankie's had done an hour or two previously. This time however, it was no optical illusion or subjective impression: Terry was crying again. 'I fell into the bloody canal,' he said between sobs.'

'Why don't you come back to the vicarage,' David suggested, 'and tell me all about it?'

At least it provided an opportunity to become legitimately tiddly. While Terry went home to change into dry clothes, David went into the village shop and bought four four-packs of beer. Donald Blanchard, the shopkeeper, had no means of knowing what the occasion was, and yet for some reason David felt able to look him in the eye while they completed their small transaction. Then he walked on home with both arms triumphantly loaded.

Terry arrived a few minutes later, suddenly well-groomed, although his face was a little bloated from weeping. They drank the afternoon away.

Terry's troubles were predictable enough. He hadn't really got over the break-up of his marriage when he lost his job; the two events combined had left him, underneath the rather blustering manner, alone and forlorn. His pride had led him to play down the first of his catastrophes, and to conceal the second altogether, so he had been living what was virtually a double life. To take his mind off his woes he'd decided to book a barge for a weekend, despite a shortage of cash, and have a mini-holiday. He also set himself the target of finding a girl-friend, by the time he sailed, who would go with him. In this respect he'd unexpectedly succeeded; at least, he thought he had. Unfortunately the girl backed out of the trip at the last moment.

'I realized I was on a hiding to nothing,' Terry said. 'And then to top it all I fell into the bloody canal. I decided to moor the bloody thing and hare off to the Cricketers.'

'I know it sounds corny, Terry, but what you've got to do is make a new start.'

'Thank you very much.'

'You'll get another job.'

'Not in insurance I won't. They'll have put me on the black list.'

'But didn't you have another line before?'

'Catering. I was in catering.'

'Well then. Get a job in catering. You'll feel different when you've got some money in your pocket. It won't be long before some young lady appears over the horizon, you mark my words.'

Terry looked sceptical, but David could sense his underlying interest in the proposal. They finished the beer. Then Terry mentioned he had some chops in the deep freeze, and they walked back to his cottage. They drank together for much of the evening.

When he finally got to his spinning bed, David dreamed shallowly, sweating and uneasy. He awoke in the early hours with the thought in his mind that the thermometer outside his church had dwindled to zero. A shape loomed against the window. But it was black, not white, only his clothes on a chair. Nevertheless he lay still a long while, thinking about the way the Fat Man had pursued Tom Hartley across England, across the centuries, right up to the present, perhaps beyond.

The next morning, over breakfast, David looked at last week's copy of the *Christian World* in order to take his mind off his forthcoming sermon. His eye slid over the situations page, and then stopped, caught by a word:

> Experienced clergyman required for
> C of E ministry in Farquhar Island.

Farquhar Island.

It was only yesterday he'd been telling Terry Sutton about how advisable it was to make a new start. He, David, needed a new start too, although that phrase was hardly appropriate in regard to Farquhar Island, there seemed such an inevitability about the prospect. Farquhar Island was after all the place Tom Hartley had chosen for *his* new start two centuries ago.

CHAPTER FORTY-ONE

Jack

George put his glass down. 'Any luck with your house, Jack?' he asked.

'We've had some enquiries. Queen's seeing a young couple tonight.'

'That's all right then. Sooner the better as far as I'm concerned. I can't wait to get shot of that place in Southsea. It's the responsibility.'

'I would have thought you wanted to hang on to it. For old time's sake.'

'What would I want with a guest house? I had enough of the place when I was a kid. Anyway, you saw for yourself how rundown it's got.'

'Queen and me'll get it into shape.'

'Good luck to you. Mind you, you're getting it for a song.'

'Says you.'

'Yes, I got enough on my plate as it is. I was down the topless last night.'

'Oh yes?'

George chuckled. 'The way them girls handle your pint. What a health inspector would say, gawd only knows. Talking of which, will you have another?'

'No thank you, George. I've had my quota.'

'Why don't you stretch a point? Stretch a pint, I should say. You got nothing to get up for in the morning nowadays.'

'Not till we take on your place in Southsea, I haven't, no. But Queen'll be expecting me. It worries her if I'm late.'

'Suit yourself, Jack.'

The young couple were still with Queen when Jack arrived back home.

'Ah, here you are,' said Queen. 'I was hoping you wouldn't be late. Mr and Mrs Stone hung on to meet you. This is Mr and Mrs Stone.'

'Hello,' said Jack. 'I'm sorry to keep you waiting. I'd have come earlier if I'd known. I was only down the pub.'

'That's all right,' said Mr Stone. 'We were talking to your wife.'

Mr Stone was broad, deep-voiced, solid-looking, bald. His wife was pregnant, but otherwise thin as a rake.

'You ought to eat a bit more,' Jack told her.

'Jack! Just because people are interested in our house, there's no need to get personal.'

'I know what young girls are like,' Jack said. 'You read about them in the papers.'

'You'll have to excuse him,' Queen said. 'He thinks he can talk to the opposite sex how he likes, now he's long in the tooth.'

'I don't mind,' Mrs Stone said. 'It's just the way it's taken me. I've been eating like a horse just lately.'

'Jack can talk, in any case. He's been moping about like a young kid himself.'

'We've been waiting on to make you an offer,' Mr Stone said. 'We need somewhere convenient to Woolwich. This would suit us nicely.'

'Oh yes?' Jack said.

'I've just signed on,' Mr Stone replied. 'In the army.'

'I was saying,' Queen said, 'perhaps he'll meet Tom.'

'The army's a big place,' said Jack. 'And I thought Tom was doing his training at that place in Wales.'

'Oh yes,' Queen agreed, 'he did say Wales.'

'Wales is very nice,' said Mr Stone. 'I was there not long ago myself.'

189

CHAPTER FORTY-TWO

Horace

As Horace entered Number 10 for a meeting of the Inner Cabinet he met Andrew Carstairs, Secretary of State for Health and Social Security, coming out. Even the hallway had strip lighting now and under its probing illumination poor Andrew looked more like a garish sunset than ever, his red nose sinking in clouds of violet. The sunset was articulated by a plump betweeded body which stopped in mid-scuttle at the prospect of its colleague.

'Hellow Andrew,' Horace said amiably. 'What are you doing here?'

'I've been given a thrashing by our Kath,' Andrew replied with doleful frankness.

'Really?'

'I've been opening my mouth too much, that's the trouble.'

'About what?'

Sure enough, having opened his mouth too much, Andrew was quite prepared to open it again.

'Business transactions. Conflict of interest, apparently.'

'That's a bit rich, Andrew. We all dabble.' It wasn't strictly true, since Horace had never had the slightest inclination to play the stock market himself. He'd been left a substantial fortune – another of those Bentley privileges – more than he could ever spend, although spending was one of his stronger points. But solidarity was the name of the game.

'Of course we do, Horace,' Andrew replied. 'But it was this Euro-Garbage business.'

Euro-Garbage! What sort of world did poor Andrew live, move, and make his investments in!

'You've only got to read the papers,' Andrew was continuing, 'to see how Northern Industrial Disposal swallowed Renwick's just like that. Obvious next step for them to go international. You could see it coming a mile off. I mean, between you and me, Horace, Raymond did let something out. But it was there for all to see.'

'Quite right.'

'Kept mum of course. Admitted nothing. But I'll lose a hospital, sure as eggs.'

'Surely not.'

'Anyway, must rush. On the qui vive for a g and t.'

As Andrew stomped through the front door, Horace speculated briefly on what possible connection Raymond Durrant could have with an organization like Euro-Garbage. The question was intensely trivial, as were so many associated with the Secretary of State for Defence.

Mrs Cheeseman was gracious when Horace stepped through the door of the Cabinet Room. No doubt she was digesting her pound of Andrew's ample flesh.

'*Do* come in, Horace dear,' she said. 'It's nice to see *one* member of my inner team has the courtesy to be punctual.'

'To be frank, Prime Minister, I think I'm slightly early.'

'That's what I mean, Horace.'

She no longer wore her dark glasses and her eyes, above her welcoming smile, were sharp as knives. Her meticulous hairdo, the product, Horace fancied, of those skilled artisans who hammer sheet metal into the requisite industrial shapes, now concealed her ears completely, but Horace couldn't avoid being aware of a certain subterranean twinkle, like the glow of a tiny moon behind dappled cloud, on each side of her head. That awareness no longer filled him with seditious exuberance however. Indeed, he now wondered at his incarnation of a few months ago, when he had actually insulted Mrs Cheeseman and then compounded the insult with the threat of family revelations. A different Horace. Or rather, two different Horaces. The first, author of the initial, unexpected, and withering *mauvais mot*, or rather adapter of same from the works of the immortal Bard, was a desperate and consequently perceptive Horace, stripped of his budget, lowly in Cabinet status, above all a wet who had nothing to look forward to but the final and inevitable blotting-up. Five days later, however, with the sort of paradoxical necessity one might spend one's days in Art and Culture dreaming of, Horace had been transmuted into something rich and strange, at least to his own perception. He had experienced his initiation with Frankie Rutherford; and as if that were not enough, Frankie had provided him with an extra bonus, a sort of gratuitous gratuity, in the shape of the goods on Kathleen Cheeseman's sister, Queen. Armed and motivated by these events, with something to fight *with* and something to fight *for*, Horace had strode determinedly into the Cabinet Room for his confrontation. The wimp had made a stand.

Now, of course, the situation was different, and so, correspondingly, was the Horace. The current one had something to lose. He had not merely survived, he'd been rewarded for his defiance. That, indeed, was the whole problem. He had been rewarded almost too well.

His obvious *quid*, continuing reticence on the subject of Queen, didn't seem quite proportionate to the Prime Minister's *quo*. His reticence would have been purchased, in any case, by his mere survival in the Cabinet; it didn't account for and, more importantly, it couldn't by itself sustain, his promotion to a place in the inner circle. But there was a strategic explanation. Perhaps Mrs Cheeseman needed a wimp in her Inner Cabinet for the sake of a balanced appearance, and if that were the case quite probably Graham Whitley, Secretary of State for Northern Ireland and the other candidate, might have seemed to her, to vary the metaphor, too big a fish. But of course to be useful by dint of being a small fish was not, regrettably, the same thing as having a power base.

It had become vitally important to Horace to maintain his position, if for no other reason than that it gave him an edge on Frankie. Frankie, apart from his other exquisite features, had an exquisite four-squareness, a bluff directness of approach which gave their relationship its ballast. Horace, therefore, was left with the task of providing an equally essential tinge of magical elusiveness. And who could be more magical and more elusive than Mrs Cheeseman's only Inner Cabinet wimp, the first Secretary of State for Art and Culture to have political clout since, quite probably, the golden age of some decadent Roman emperor?

The other members of the Inner Cabinet arrived and took their places. Then Mrs Cheeseman announced that Raymond Durrant was to be invited in to present them with a specific proposal relating to the defence budget. In Raymond came, palpably uneasy and conscious of the ambiguity of his position. He hovered on the periphery of the meeting for a while, keeping close to the door as if it were a bolt-hole, until Mrs Cheeseman suggested that he take his usual seat.

It all seemed a sledgehammer to crack a nut. Raymond's full-scale plan wasn't to be unveiled for another three months; this was simply to an interim measure, the scrapping of the Antarctic survey vessel, the *Expedition*. Raymond argued that the saving that would be effected – two million pounds a year – would be a token to the public at large that the government meant business as far as making cuts in the defence budget was concerned. It would be an opening salvo.

A straw in the wind, Horace thought, would be a more appropriate form of words. And the public wouldn't even notice it. The only people who would would be the service chiefs, and surely that would only prepare them for the storm that was to come? In due course they would be giving Raymond a whirlwind to reap. Horace looked sidelong at the slight, anxious, ineffectual form of the nation's Secretary of State for Defence and thought of his awful wife Olivia, who sprinkled her conversation with words like tit and pong in some dunderheaded attempt to show she had flair. You couldn't help feeling a twinge of pity for the man.

He considered what line to take. The proposal to scrap the *Expedition* obviously originated with the Prime Minister, whatever her motive might be. However, the scientific side of the vessel's role seemed to lay claim on his attention as Secretary for Art and Culture. Moreover, as the wimp representative in the Inner Cabinet it was perhaps his responsibility to make the case against cuts, wherever and whenever they were proposed. Finally – and this was the newly-fledged pragmatic Horace thinking, the Horace who enjoyed his elevated status and associated it with other forms of elevation made possible by Frankie – Mrs Cheeseman was likely to respect a colleague who made at least an attempt to put forward an alternative point of view, and demonstrate he had *bottom*.

'I can't help wondering,' he said, 'whether the withdrawal of the *Expedition* might be interpreted as a sign that we have lost interest in the South Atlantic. Given that one of our territories, Farquhar Island, is only a few hundred miles from the mainland of Costanagua, and that there has been a certain amount of ill-feeling –'

'The fact that we have had our difficulties with Costanagua,' Mrs Cheeseman put in sharply, 'makes it all the more imperative that we do not allow that country to dictate to us in matters of naval policy.'

There was muttered agreement from the Inner Cabinet at large. Horace inspected Mrs Cheeseman as narrowly as possible from his somewhat remote position at the lowly end of the table. She was up to something, but what? And what on earth could the Costanaguans possibly have to do with it?

CHAPTER FORTY-THREE

Raymond

'Well, Raymond,' Mrs Cheeseman said. 'Thank you for presenting this proposal to us. I'm sure we all agree you've given us food for thought.'

'Thank you, Prime Minister,' Raymond replied. It was a bit rich being thanked by Mrs Cheeseman for making a proposal which she'd insisted on in the first place. Still, at least it had received a smooth passage, apart from Horace's predictable quibbling. It would be a different story of course when he had to confront the admirals.

'A penny for them, Raymond?' Mrs Cheeseman suddenly asked, in a rather sarcastic tone.

Raymond realized that there had been a slight hiatus. Perhaps he'd been expected to say something more?

'I was just reviewing our discussion about the *Expedition* in my mind,' he said in a calculatedly casual voice, as if he hadn't noticed Mrs Cheeseman's asperity.

'I think, Raymond, that weighing up the pros and cons is now a matter for the Inner Cabinet.'

For some reason she obviously felt the need to remind him of his second-class citizenship. Since, whatever her limitations, she was never a petty person, she must have some good reason for doing so. Raymond tried to work out what it was. Possibly, since his review of cutbacks in military expenditure would effectively spearhead the government's policy of financial retrenchment, she feared that he stood to gain too much of a reputation as the strong man of the administration.

'I quite agree, Prime Minister,' he replied blandly. It was important to be unfazed. Horace was staring at him fixedly, no doubt gloating. Suddenly Horace placed a hand – fleetingly – on his knee. What was *he* up to? A patronizing gesture of comfort? Or something worse?

Meanwhile Mrs Cheeseman was also peering down the table at him.

'*Well*, Raymond?' she suddenly asked, in a kind of bullying wheedle. Perhaps Horace's innuendo, at that fateful meeting last summer when the subject of economies had been introduced, had had some substance after all, however absurd it had seemed at the time. Perhaps Mrs Cheeseman *was* a little deaf.

'I said,' Raymond replied, in a somewhat loud voice, 'that I quite agree.'

'There's no need to shout,' she said in a chilling tone. 'I'm not deaf.' There was another mysterious pause. When she next spoke her voice had become normal, even friendly, again, and it took a few moments for the significance of what she was saying to dawn on Raymond. 'I find it very difficult, Raymond,' she said, 'to comprehend your attitude to your chair.'

'My chair, Prime Minister?'

'The one on which you are sitting at this very moment.'

Baffled, Raymond looked down at his chair. 'I'm sorry?' he asked. He glanced rapidly at his colleagues on the off-chance that they would share his puzzlement at Mrs Cheeseman's eccentricity, but they all avoided his gaze, even Horace. Raymond turned back towards the Prime Minister and gave her a hot smile, hoping to communicate the message that the game didn't amuse him.

'I pride myself on having a certain forcefulness of personality, Raymond,' Mrs Cheeseman said. 'And yet it takes all my willpower to persuade you to sit on your chair when you come into the room, and I have so far found it completely beyond my abilities to get you off it when it is time for you to leave.'

Raymond rose to his feet. He felt like shouting with fury. The trouble was that his adrenalin was flowing from two directions: from his anger at the Prime Minister's embarrassing trap, and from his own failure to see the obvious while he occupied himself with analysing irrelevant nuances. Turbid waters indeed, not usable. 'I'm very sorry, Prime Minister,' he said. 'I thought that since scrapping the *Expedition* was . . .' he deliberately left a significant pause, 'my policy, I ought to be here while –'

'It is your responsibility to present policy *to* the Inner Cabinet. Then we must decide, *as* the Inner Cabinet, whether to accept your proposals or not.'

'I see.'

Her tone had been mellowing. Now it became positively friendly. 'Why don't you go across to the sitting-room? Have a chat with Derek perhaps, while you're waiting?'

Raymond left, without a backward glance.

In the hall, he paused for a moment. From somewhere upstairs came the sound of an electric saw. Derek was obviously at work on his carpentry. He'd sooner be alone anyway. He went on across to the sitting-room.

196

It was cold in here, almost clammy, with no fire in the grate, and the radiator switched off. He almost turned it on but thought better of it. There was no point in alienating Mrs Cheeseman any further. He sat down in an armchair. Never mind, he suddenly thought, perhaps it's all been for the best. The unpleasant scene that had just taken place would at least serve the function of making it clear to the Prime Minister that he felt a sense of injustice at being excluded from the Inner Cabinet.

He'd been on bad terms with Mrs Cheeseman ever since last summer. First of all she had presented him with those daunting cuts; then excluded him from the Inner Cabinet. And then, a few weeks later, by way of putting the tin lid on it, there had been that business of the Fat Man.

The story had reached Raymond through the newspapers. A terrorist bomb had gone off prematurely, somewhere in Manchester. One of several casualties was the terrorist who had planted it. There was his photograph, larger than life. The Fat Man. The Fat Man was dead.

Raymond's mind had gone into overdrive. He could hardly be held responsible for what had happened, even though he had acted as a go-between. It had been Mrs Cheeseman's decision to employ an anarchist. Nevertheless the situation was awkward, to say the least – if for no other reason because somebody else would be needed to take the Fat Man's place. Of course Mrs Cheeseman had warned Raymond in no uncertain terms never to mention the subject again, but she was hardly likely to have been anticipating this particular circumstance. And she would no doubt attach some importance to ministerial initiative. He went round to Number 10 immediately.

She was working at her place at the head of the Cabinet table, alone. She looked round as he came in.

'This is an unexpected pleasure, Raymond,' she said cuttingly.

Raymond got straight to the point. 'I've come about the Fat Man, Prime Minister.'

The Prime Minister, without a muscle moving, a nerve twitching, exploded. She rose to her feet with the powerful slowness of a space rocket lifting off. Her voice was quiet, with the intensity of a shout.

'Only a few weeks ago, Raymond, I received your solemn assurance that you would never mention that name again.'

'I know, Prime Minister.'

'How dare you say you *know*, when you've just done so!'

'But the Fat Man is dead.'

'What has *that* got to do with it?'

'I thought that you would need a . . . a replacement.'

'And why did you think that?'

'For heaven's sake!'

'All this has been allowed for in our original understanding, Raymond. My arrangement with the Fat Man will continue as if nothing had happened.'

'But I don't see how that's possible.'

'Well, you'll have to use your imagination, won't you?'

Dry-mouthed: 'I must say, it seems to be taking delegation of responsibility a bit far.'

'What does?'

'Dying.'

'Raymond, can I suggest you leave the question of delegation to me?'

'Yes, Prime Minister.'

'And I must insist that this subject is never mentioned between us again.'

Unfortunately, it wasn't quite as simple as that. Raymond was still expected to be some kind of go-between, but he was more mystified than ever about what he was supposed to be conveying, and to whom, and for what. Money was involved, that at least was certain: sufficient funds to enable a company called Northern Industrial Disposal to take over a similar London firm called Renwick's; and then an even larger capital sum so that the new company could take over a continental concern, and transform itself into Euro-Garbage. Baffled, Raymond had dropped a few hints in the direction of Andrew Carstairs, who played the market and usually had a fair idea of what was in the wind. He had hoped Andrew would be able to interpret these manoeuvres for him, but instead the mercenary bastard had rushed out and bought a chunk of Euro-Garbage for himself, so that a substantial percentage of the tax-payers' money with which Raymond had been entrusted had ultimately landed up in Andrew's own pockets.

Mrs Cheeseman had been beside herself. Raymond had had a long session with her yesterday afternoon; Andrew had had his this morning.

Still, Raymond had survived. Survival in politics was what mattered. And having survived, it would do no harm to try to strengthen his position. And giving notice to Mrs Cheeseman that he was a little restless at being excluded from the Inner Cabinet might have done just that.

The door of the sitting-room opened. Raymond began to rise to his feet, but it was Horace's head which poked round it, so he rather obviously sat down again.

'We're going our separate ways,' Horace said.

'Oh yes?' Raymond replied uninterestedly.

'Message from our leader. She says she's got to go out for a minute. If you can hang on, she'll communicate the fruits of our discussion to you.'

'I see. Thank you.'

Horace did an odd downward movement of his hands, obviously intended to signify what those fruits were – presumably Mrs Cheeseman was hovering somewhere in the background. Raymond couldn't tell whether he was indicating the sinking of the *Expedition* or the failure of Raymond's proposal to sink her. Surely the former? Of course, you could never be absolutely certain with someone of the political calibre of Mrs Cheeseman.

'Thank you,' Raymond repeated, throwing Horace's ambiguity right back at him.

'You didn't take my hint,' Horace mouthed at him.

'You what?'

'About leaving the meeting.'

'Oh.'

'See you anon,' Horace concluded in a normal voice, and left. There had been smugness in every gesture. It was extraordinary the delusions of grandeur that could be triggered off by membership of the Inner Cabinet.

Raymond consoled himself that nothing could alter the relative status of their two ministries. Being Secretary of State for Defence had a certain cachet that the Secretary for Art and Culture could never even conceive of, however adept he might be at playing power-games round the Cabinet table.

Raymond remembered this morning. That, certainly, had been a scene Horace couldn't conceive of.

CHAPTER FORTY-FOUR

Raymond

He and Joanie Lubbock, his secretary, had been having a working session in a safe room in the Ministry of Defence. He had only recently succeeded in getting top security clearance for Joanie, and she made no secret of her glee in having access to the sealed environment in the basement of the building. They had been going through some data relating to his task of achieving the requisite cut in the navy budget. This had necessitated sitting opposite each other at a table of papers, and of course it was impossible to ignore the fact that her blouse was unbuttoned to the halfway point. Every time she leaned forward over a document it became clear that, as so frequently these days, she wasn't wearing a brassière.

After an hour or so he had had to leave the room for a couple of minutes. When he returned he discovered, to his amazement, that Joanie had removed her blouse completely. She was still in her place at the worktable, naked from the waist up.

'Joanie,' he said, 'isn't that being indiscreet?'

'This *is* a safe room, Raymond,' she replied simply. 'And it's terribly hot.'

'It's a little distracting, that's all.'

Strangely, she gave him a look of sheer puzzlement, as if she had no idea what he was talking about. 'What is?'

'They are.'

She looked down at her bosom as if she had only just remembered it was there. Then she looked back up at him. There was a cool challenge in her eyes. 'Perhaps we could *do* with a little distraction,' she said. 'We've been working very hard.'

Suddenly Raymond found himself answering the challenge. He hadn't forgotten his own obligation to be discreet, but as a man – indeed, as a Secretary of State for Defence – he had other obligations also. One was to maintain his morale, and after the scene with Mrs Cheeseman yesterday afternoon, it was sorely in need of a boost. He stepped round the table, leaned down, and gave Joanie a kiss.

As he straightened up again, she said: 'I didn't mean on the lips.'

'What?'

'I meant . . .' She glanced swiftly down at her breasts.

Raymond thought quickly. He could almost hear Olivia's voice saying: Kiss the poor cow's tits for her, what kind of a man are you? Olivia had a robust, almost horsey attitude towards sex, without any of the average middle-class person's hang-ups. Jealousy, for example, was foreign to her nature. All right, then. The trouble was, the positioning was so difficult. If he'd learnt nothing else during his time as Minister responsible for Military Strategy, he'd learnt that all problems have their topographical dimension. He lowered one knee to the floor, and sank his face in Joanie's breasts. As he did so, he slid a hand up her skirt and began caressing as much of her groin as he was able to reach while she remained seated.

And then the very awkwardness of his stance brought him to his senses. Or perhaps it was the contrast between Joanie's softnesses and the hard surface of the chair on which they were ultimately resting. His position was hedged round with barriers. A sexual peccadillo on his part

201

was a chink in the armour of the nation. There were times, quite simply, when you had to put state above self. Or to put it in a slightly more Machiavellian light, when you had to put one aspect of self-fulfilment above another. He rose to his feet. Joanie, misunderstanding, looked up at him with a face like a torch.

'I'm sorry, Raymond, this chair is a bloody nuisance.' She glanced quickly down towards the somewhat functional Ministry of Defence carpeting. 'Shall we . . . ?'

'We've got work to do,' Raymond said quietly.

She looked back up at him. Once again her puzzlement was genuine. 'What?'

'The cuts.'

Her colour deepened so that fingers of red encroached upon her bosom. 'Well,' she said huskily, 'you know where mine is.'

'I said *cuts*,' he repeated, almost brutally. He wished profoundly that his erection wasn't pressing at the front of his trousers.

As he remembered the scene now, in Mrs Cheeseman's chilly sitting-room, his trousers moved slightly at the thought of that moment, despite its concomitant embarrassment. Obviously the outcome of the situation had been unsatisfactory, in more ways than one. Nevertheless it had proved a point, a point which the likes of Horace would never be able to understand. Which Mrs Cheeseman, in all probability, would never be able to understand. In its own way, it was a scene to savour. The very notion of a woman's naked breasts in the basement of the Ministry of Defence was piquant in its own right. Suddenly Dr Clifton's phrase came back to him: milking the grid. That seemed to sum the experience up, even if, in the end, the grid had inevitably reasserted itself.

'Penny for them,' came a voice, close at hand.

Raymond couldn't restrain himself from starting, somewhat guiltily, with surprise.

'You were miles away,' Derek Cheeseman said. He was standing in front of the fireless grate in his white carpentry overall.

202

'Things on my mind,' Raymond said, clasping his hands in his lap.

'Kathleen's gone out, you know.'

'She told me to wait until she came back.'

'I think she'll be gone quite some time.'

'I'm a patient man.'

'It's a bit nippy in here. Shall I put the radiator on for you?'

'No, don't worry. I'm not one for feeling the cold.'

'I see. Good point. Tell you what, what about a cup of tea? Or something stronger?'

'A cup of tea would do fine,' Raymond said.

'I'll ring down for it. It'll be stewed, like as not, if that isn't an insult to stew. The only thing you can say about the present kitchen staff is that at least they don't poison people like the last lot. Do you remember them, Raymond?'

'I remember them.'

'In the meantime, why don't you watch the box?'

Derek stepped over and switched on the television. It was an old one, black and white. The Cheesemans had possessed it for years, as the Prime Minister had once informed the nation at large. 'Some of you,' she had announced on television, 'who are perhaps unemployed, or on old age pensions, will nevertheless be watching me on up-to-date, colour television sets. Derek and I, meanwhile, are perfectly content with our excellent, but elderly, monochrome receiver. If a product is well made it will give sterling service. It is always worth paying for quality and the bonus is that it costs less in the long run. In the same way, an economic policy that takes a certain human toll will eventually produce a human reward.'

Nevertheless the Cheesemans' television set took an inordinately long time to warm up. Derek went to the far end of the sitting-room to ring for tea while Raymond sat watching the blank humming screen. As he waited he thought of all the unemployed, as he sometimes did these days when he was tired and disillusioned from grappling with his cuts, their empty faces, superannuated valves, and wondered whether they would indeed be switched on again one day, and if so, what flickering monochrome features would be revealed, what weaknesses in the horizontal hold.

A pale but attractive young lady appeared on the screen, reading the news. Instead of the brightly dressed females with chaotic hairdos who appeared on the Durrants' colour set, she was old-fashioned, with hair parted at the side and brushed in long waves to just below her ears, a string of pearls around her neck, and an ornate early 1950s ballgown. Moreover she wasn't sitting at a desk but at a well-polished wooden table on which stood a vase of flowers. Raymond wondered whether her appearance and manner testified to the age of the television set or the dignity of the PM's sitting-room, or both. Her tones were feminine, rounded, rich.

'. . . Several years ago, the tragedy caused by the explosion at a chemical plant, owned by the Hautbois Company, in the town of Sereno, in Italy . . .'

'Oh lord,' said Derek, returning from the phone. 'The bally news again. There's enough news going on in this house already. Why can't they –'

'Hang on a minute,' said Raymond, leaning forward towards the set. The word 'Euro-Garbage' had suddenly surfaced amid Derek's disapproval:

'. . . contract for the disposal of dioxin-polluted soil. In view of public anxiety about the possibility of the barrels arriving in this country, a spokesman for Euro-Garbage announced this afternoon that the material would not, in fact, be brought into Britain but would be disposed of outside Europe altogether. For security reasons he was not prepared to be more specific.'

'Don't tell me,' said Derek, 'that you've got shares in Euro-Garbage as well?'

'No, no.'

'Thank goodness for that. Kathleen gave poor old Andrew a terrible hiding this morning, you know, because he'd bought some. I don't care what they say about the soundproofing in that Cabinet room, I could hear it upstairs in my workshop. Keep clear of Euro-Garbage, that's my advice. For some reason even mentioning that firm drives our Kath up the wall. Why people want to stick their money in rubbish in the first place is beyond my ken. There's plenty of clean companies –'

At that moment there was a knock on the door and a sulky-looking girl carrying a tray of tea came in. Derek poured.

As they drank their tea, Derek talked about his latest project. 'I'm building a ship,' he said.

Raymond, preoccupied with his naval cuts, thought for a moment that Derek was being facetious and winced. But no – not even Derek would know of the proposed cuts at this stage.

'A boat, if the truth be told,' Derek went on. 'But it's a pretty ambitious job by my standards. If you don't mind, I'll get back to it.'

Raymond didn't mind. He welcomed the relative peace of the TV set. He watched it for hours until, finally worn out by the events of the day, the drained quality of the monochrome picture, he fell asleep.

'Raymond,' exclaimed a voice in his dream.

He opened his eyes.

There in the doorway of the sitting-room was Mrs Cheeseman, flickering in the bright tubular light that she'd obviously just switched on. She strode over and switched the television off, then stood in front of it, gazing down at him.

'What on earth are you *doing* here, Raymond?'

'You told me to wait, Prime Minister.'

'Heavens, I didn't mean you to wait as long as this. I assumed you'd use your initiative, and realize I'd been held up. It's rather alarming to think of you dozing here in front of a television set while no one's at the helm in the Ministry of Defence.'

'I hadn't thought of it in those terms, Prime Minister.' The room had become terribly cold, and he tried to stifle a shiver. 'I was anxious to hear the outcome of the Inner Cabinet meeting.'

'Oh yes,' she said, her mood changing at the recollection. 'Yes, that went through quite sweetly, I'm pleased to say, Raymond. Your policy on the *Expedition* met with our approval.'

'That's a relief,' Raymond said without enthusiasm.

'I expressed some misgivings, if you'd like me to be entirely frank. I felt Horace made some very valid points. But on balance we concluded that since this proposal is obviously so important to you, it would undermine your position if we stood in your way. So I think you can regard this afternoon's meeting as a personal triumph, Raymond. Congratulations.'

'Thank you, Prime Minister.'

'So all you've got to do now is sell it to the navy. If you would like my advice, I'd try not to shiver while you do so.'

'No, Prime Minister.'

'Raymond, there's absolutely no need to look so frightened. Dealing with the admirals will be disagreeable but it's no more than a mopping-up operation. As Secretary of State for Defence you've won your first sea-battle. That's how you must look at it. The admirals are a mere detail.'

Raymond's spirits rose, though not as much as Mrs Cheeseman suggested they should. Of course it was gratifying that he'd succeeded in sinking the *Expedition* with all hands. But to think of this outcome in terms of winning a battle seemed somehow inappropriate. Raymond wished he could call on the services of Dr Clifton in this respect. There was no doubt that Clifton's strong point lay in reformulating traditional terminology.

CHAPTER FORTY-FIVE

David

It was a sleety morning in early January. David stood on the platform of Shrewsbury Station watching rain flickering down upon the tracks, which gleamed greyly as they always gleam, whatever the light or darkness. Among the thin lines of rain, dots of snow bounced about, and the combined effect reminded him of something. Suddenly it came back: the pinball machine in the common room at theological college. Rows of little nails had been set in formation, and the ball, like these specks of snow, skittered about amongst them. As he remembered, the atmosphere of that room returned: the smell of tea urns and polish, student earnestness, 1950s austerity, all-male minimalness, and his heart sank in memory of all those occasions on which it had sunk before. He had imagined at the time that his life as a cleric would continue in much the same vein; Lorna had come as such a surprise. She filled the shabby vicarages to which they were assigned with vitality and warmth, they laughed so much, they made love so often. During his student days he'd taken a Pauline view of marriage – its grimness fitted in with the surroundings. Lorna had taught him otherwise, or rather, she had decisively changed the surroundings. He could picture her much more clearly now than he had been able to a year before, perhaps because in going to Farquhar Island he would relinquish her geographically as well as historically. In his mind's eye she appeared in casual shirt and jeans, large and robust. There was such a thing as an aristocracy of nature; her generous femaleness contrasted sharply, roundly, with the delicately-scented, stick-like church ladies. You needed to let go of something in order to see it properly. Even the mere thought of that grey little island at the other end of the world had sharpened his memory, given him a point of focus. There would be nothing there to deflect one's concentration, not even a tree. It was the nearest he could get to going nowhere. Lorna would, in effect, be sitting upon a stark rock, like some being who had surfaced from the sea, real beyond the literal detail of daily life. Often in theology one came across the notion that it was necessary to step outside time in order to see time aright. Nobody quite knew, of course, how time would look from that angle, but one common theory was that it might all be present simultaneously, both the past and future laid out in front of you as on a map. David wasn't interested in the future, all he wanted was to be able to travel back to the past, back to Lorna. Suddenly he found himself crying quietly on the platform, his tears mingling discreetly with the rain.

The train came at last. At least he was able to leave his parish without regrets; and he was no doubt unregretted. He had never experienced any sort of rapport with the farmers, the Frankie Rutherfords, the Terry Suttons. Odd really that he should be, to a degree, following in the footsteps of the latter, although Terry hadn't made a complete break, since he'd hung on to his cottage, at least for the time being. He'd obtained a post on a cruise liner and had been back for a couple of weeks' leave just before Christmas. He was cheerful, cocky, sexually successful (there was a preponderance of lady passengers on the liner and, if they couldn't necessarily find romance, they could at least make the acquaintance of the likes of Terry), comprehensively obnoxious. In other words, he was cured. Whether David would be in his turn was of course another question altogether.

When his train got into London he took the underground to Waterloo, rather enjoying the experience of being swept along in crowds of hurrying people. It was a world protected from the elements, full of sudden meaningless intimacies, very different from his ultimate destination, Swan Creek, which would be a place of acute simplicity.

He was in good time for his train at Waterloo, and sat down at a windowseat. An elderly couple took the two places on the opposite side of his little table. They bustled in in a private hail-storm of suitcases, parcels, shopping-bags, and settled themselves with an anxious fussiness that would have been more appropriate to a Jules Verne expedition than to a train which was going no further than Portsmouth. On the table in front of them the woman arranged a flask, cups, packets of sandwiches, spheres and wedges of foil that obviously contained tomatoes, hard-boiled eggs, slices of cake. She was a thin busy woman, with a face that was lined and hard at the same time, and quick shrewd eyes. Her husband was on a different scale altogether, large, with a bovine, slowly-moving head, and hands that stumbled as he helped his wife arrange their provisions.

'I hope this train's going to be warm enough,' the woman said to her husband. Then she turned towards David, and added by way of explanation: 'They always make them too cold, or too hot, one bally thing or the other.'

David's heart sank. 'Yes,' he replied rather vaguely, and leaned back in his seat, half-closing his eyes.

'You going all the way?' the woman asked.

'Leave the reverend alone, Queen,' said the man. 'Can't you see he's trying to have a nap?'

'Yes, I'm going all the way,' David said.

'We are too. All the way to Portsmouth,' the woman said, with a certain satisfaction. 'Well, Southsea as a matter of fact. That's the seaside bit of Portsmouth. Are you going to Southsea?'

'No. I'm going further south than Southsea.'

'We bought a guest house there. Off a friend.'

'Queen, give him a chance,' the man said. 'He wants a kip, he doesn't want to know all our business.'

'We're getting a bit old to go out to work,' the woman said defiantly, 'so we thought we might as well do some work at home.' Nevertheless, she sounded a little more subdued than previously, and soon began to direct her chatter towards her husband. Possibly out of a distaste for insincerity, David found himself confirming the man's story by falling asleep for real, and he let himself fall. He awoke with a start at Guildford.

'Oh!' he exclaimed.

'You dozed off,' the woman said. 'It's only Guildford.'

'Thank goodness for that. I hope I didn't snore.'

'You slept like a baby. I think I'll try to pour this lot out while the train's stopped.'

She began unstoppering her flask. David glanced out of the window. Two or three people came into focus as they approached the train. Beyond them the details of British Rail faded into indistinctness, but he was aware of other individuals, waiting for a different train, standing solemnly on the platform like penguins on a beach. Several penguins waddled to one side and beyond them, for a moment, he was able to see –

Only for the tiniest part of a second. But with a clarity beyond the capacity of his eyesight. As if that great mass could squeeze itself into a single frame of the long spool of his journey. Subliminal bulk. The very speed of the imprint must have determined its sharpness, because David had taken it all in, the bald head, the unseasonal lightweight suit, the fat body, its back to him but the face angled so he could glimpse a mole upon the cheek, the whole form poised in an eddy of the crowd which immediately surged back to blot it out once more. But David had seen it. At the same time he felt he had not seen anything at all, as though the image had entered his mind without making use of the mechanism of eyesight. Like seeing a ghost.

David could have cried out at the thought of the madness from which he must be suffering. Or the possibility that he wasn't mad after all.

'You all right?' the woman asked anxiously. 'Jack, he's gone as white as a sheet.'

David didn't reply for a moment. He was wondering if Tom Hartley had succeeded in finding a refuge from the Fat Man on Farquhar Island two centuries ago.

'Have a cup of tea,' Queen went on. 'It'll do you good.'

'Leave him a minute,' Jack put in. 'Let him relax. It might be heart.'

'My Jack's got heart,' Queen said. 'Haven't you, Jack?'

'I'm all right,' said David. 'I just had a bit of a shock. I thought I saw someone I couldn't have seen.'

'Oh, I see,' said Queen sagely. 'Someone who's dead, you mean?'

David didn't argue. It wouldn't be easy to explain to total strangers that he meant someone who shouldn't have existed in the first place.

CHAPTER FORTY-SIX

The Fat Man

The Fat Man had to go to Italy on business. He didn't take a plane – you were too noticeable on planes. Instead he took a train down to Southampton and then went as a foot-passenger on the car ferry to Le Havre. He spent much of the evening on deck, to avoid the scrutiny of the people in the lounge. It was a cold clammy January night with patches of fog billowing about on the sea. That had its advantages. He was alone for most of the evening.

At about eleven, however, a woman came out on to the deck. In the light from the doorway the Fat Man observed that she was big, with a sleeveless quilted jerkin, a thick rollneck sweater, jeans, walking boots. She may have just come out for a breath of fresh air, but on the other hand she looked hardy: she might choose to stay. She leaned over the rail a few yards away, taking no apparent notice of him. He waited a while to see what she would do.

After a few minutes, a man came through the door. He was obviously one of the boat's catering staff, since he was still wearing his white tunic, flimsy clothing for such a bitter night, as flimsy as the Fat Man's own. He walked up to the woman and took her in his arms. No doubt he had his love to keep him warm. At least while they were absorbed in each other they wouldn't be bothering themselves with the Fat Man. They talked in low tones; then began to kiss.

And then things went wrong. An element of stridency appeared among their small noises. The girl was pushing the man away. Obviously not wanting to take no for an answer, he lunged at her again. She stepped to one side to escape him, and at that moment the ship rolled on the swell and with a sudden sad cry the man went overboard.

His white jacket caught the dim light from the windows on the ship's side as he fell, and the Fat Man was able to watch him all the way down. Strangely, the interplay of the forces to which he'd succumbed – sexual desire, wave motion, wind, gravity – caused his trajectory to take on all the appearance of a calculated dive. He performed a graceful slow somersault for most of the fall but straightened out just in time to enter the water cleanly, head first, with his arms more or less by his sides.

The Fat Man had to think quickly. The last thing he wanted was to be the hero of the hour; but it would be equally conspicuous to refuse to help. The girl had already looked up from the small splash and was turning towards him.

'Oh god,' she gasped. 'He'll drown.' Unexpectedly she had an American accent.

'No, he won't,' said the Fat Man reassuringly. 'Look, he's surfaced already.'

Fortunately he had. A dark smooth sphere of head, gleaming faintly in the light reflected along the surface of the water, was bobbing over the swell. One arm waved towards the ship.

While the girl stared down at the water, the Fat Man hurried to the lounge door, opened it, and without going inside called out: 'Man overboard!' He then ran along the deck towards the bridge steps, calling as he went. As he reached the steps he fell silent, however, went beyond them, and concealed himself in a small walkway between two of the units of the ship's superstructure. Someone clanged his way down the steps crying out: 'Where, where?' Luckily the girl was shouting by this time, so there was no ambiguity on that point. The Fat Man felt a shuddering as the ship's engines were thrown into reverse.

There was now a great deal of shouting and running going on. He made his way to the far side of the ferry, entered the lounge by that door, walked across and mingled with the crowd that was pressing towards the scene of the accident. Soon they were ushered back to their places by one of the ship's officers. Shortly after that came the announcement that the man was saved. Just as well. The last thing the Fat Man needed would have been an inquiry on the subject. He had gone to a lot of trouble to achieve his present degree of anonymity. It had involved, last summer, the construction of a unique, or at least almost unique, alibi.

He was dead.

CHAPTER FORTY-SEVEN

Laurette

A snatched visit, an *invitation au voyage*, a rite of passage. Since the pool Laurette had vowed not to repudiate any aspect of her past. You had to live through a symphony of your experiences, however goddam loud and discordant.

So. She'd written Joe Harper regularly in the years since they'd parted, and received certain stiffish missives back, with Denise's pouts and frowns in every other word, in the handwriting even, which had stopped being his old scrawl and now caught the delicate curve of her nostrils, the crispness of her clothes and bedlinen. Maybe power had something to do with it also. There was nothing like power for taking the life out of a man, constipating his style.

The snatched visit, Laurette had originally suggested, should be in Scotland. She was in Scotland on a trip, and Scotland seemed so far from England, far enough to do Joe some good. Those Scottish eagles, quick feathery life bucking on the air, a life commensurate with the sweep of landscape, the cragginess, the raw soft snow. Or kestrels, whatever they called those birds.

She called Joe up. Luckily Denise wasn't in. Scotland

isn't England, that was precisely the theme he took up, his voice tiny and tight-assed over the phone. 'You Americans, distance isn't the same in the UK, Scotland isn't England, you know.' That explained so much, distance isn't the same in the UK, you're telling me buster, that explains a certain miniaturization of equipment that proved to have a certain charm to a certain American gal who liked, so to say, to put sex in its place, who saw a chance in short, in short indeed, to become a virgin again by dint of screwing within certain defined limits, like the way she had dived plumb in the center of Joe's cute little breast-stroking circles. Sure, you can stay a virgin, Denise, just keep pruning the flowers in your English cottage garden, chop back the roses, plant your shrinking violet. Keep your house clean and tidy. Your house is the spirit of your body, and a dime to a dollar our Denise makes a sweet little English housewife. Well, not *wife* exactly, even wife is too much of an affirmation, easier to stay a virgin in some pseudo, political, part-time, non-existent, de facto marriage, like 'I, Denise, am Mr Harper's live-in girlfriend, we have an understanding.' Except they don't understand *any*thing.

So Joe couldn't get up to Scotland. In any case he was shortly going to a conference in Paris. International economics. Laurette, it so happened, was going to the Camargue. Horses, bulls, flamingoes. Weigh it up yourself. Anyway they arranged to meet on the car ferry, ships that passed in the night.

Joe seemed a little abstracted. Somewhere behind all his facial gear, the thrusting spectacles and woolly beard, she sensed a sort of tentative worried frown hunched in the undergrowth.

'How's it going, Joe?' she asked.

'Complicatedly,' he replied.

'I thought your economy was a model to the world. I mean, take the medicine, bimbo, and you'll be on your feet before you know it.'

'Not exactly. But don't quote me.'

'For heaven's sake, what's with the paranoia? Like I'm

going to tell the world's press, the adviser to the British Prime Minister says things are going *complicatedly*. Anyway, you're still going straight down the monetarist line, aren't you? I saw in the paper this morning that the government was going to sink one of its ships to save money. Wow, like those admirals sure laid into the Secretary of Defence guy. It looked like civil war was breaking out. I thought to myself, that'll cheer Joe up, saving some bucks.'

'Yes,' he replied, like he wished he could say no.

'You don't mean you –'

'As I said, don't quote me.'

'Jesus H.'

'Let's have something to eat,' he said.

'Sure thing. You want to change the subject, why not?'

They went up to the restaurant. The flunkey who served them looked like he was on the run from the Ritz or somewhere, with a little white ironed jacket, black pants, and well-brushed hair, but long. These English and their hair, they all think they're Samson or something, but he was dapper with it. But the soup!

'Yuk,' said Laurette. 'What *is* this stuff?'

'Tomato soup, madam,' the waiter replied.

'Canned *junk*, that's what this is. This is supposed to be a restaurant, for chrissake. Don't you English ever want to do a hearty crap?'

The waiter didn't reply but retreated, muttering.

'I don't know why you have to come on so strong,' said Joe.

'Gee,' said Laurette, 'I guess the poor guy thought I was insulting him. I meant crap literally, you know?'

'Oh god,' Joe said, 'what is it you're into now, high-fibre feminism?'

'High fibre, yes. Feminism, so so. It depends what you mean. What I'm *not* into is that kinda rampant clitoral feminism, shaping up to sex like you want to compete with men in the very area where you cannot win. The same with buggery. Heterosexual buggery, I'm talking about. I mean it's very earthy no doubt but it's never been my bag because it means the very bit of you that is essentially you isn't being used. I mean, who wants to be an ersatz *male* homosexual? I'm a profoundly vaginal woman, Joe, vaginal to the core. That's what I been given to make my distinctive response to experience *with*. I don't buy this crap about the vaginal orgasm being a red herring. I mean, that's because our orgasmic expectations are male-orientated. I *know* there's such a thing as a vaginal orgasm, because I been there, Joe. Not always, but recently.'

'Congratulations,' he said, perhaps a little bitterly. Perhaps he took the moral.

'Boys will be boys, and girls girls. That's one thing you can say for Bud, he sure was a genuine boy. If that's unliberated, then that's my bundle. But I'm not submissive, you know that, Joe.'

'Yes, I know that.'

'I can't *eat* this gloop.'

'So if you're not into the women's movement, what *are* you into these days? Apart from the bowel movement, that is.'

'Gee, you English are witty, they can't take *that* away from you. I'm into nature study.'

'Oh yes, of course. Your trip to the South of France.'

'That's just the start-off. I'm going a lot further south than that.'

The waiter had reappeared. 'Have you finished, madam?' he asked.

'Oh yes, I don't drink this stuff. But look, about that crap business.'

'Look,' the waiter said, in almost a hiss, 'it's out of my control. This is a boat, remember. Our facilities are limited.'

'Is that so?' Laurette replied, trying to sound conciliatory. 'I just thought maybe you were fixing to *poison* us.'

CHAPTER FORTY-EIGHT

Joseph

Mid-Atlantic man, thought Joe sourly, what a joke. Mid-Channel man was more like it. If Ian Priestley had been the architect of the UK's economic policy, he, Joseph, was at least its civil engineer. And now here he was, not on Concorde but a cross-Channel ferry, sailing rather forlornly to a conference in Paris in the hope of finding new ideas.

A mid-point *must* be possible, though, look at his own private life. Meeting Laurette again was a welcome vindication of his decisions in that field. Laurette insulted waiters, celebrated nature study, pontificated loudly about different aspects of that female anatomy of which she possessed so much; she was sloppy, bad-mannered, arrogant, bursting at the seams in all sorts of directions. Emma by contrast had been icy and silent in her home counties dwelling, with all the flair and vitality of a stuffed animal in a glass case. Denise, however, contrasted impressively with both extremes. She was intellectually curious without being strident or evangelical, sexually vigorous without being obsessive or obscene, reserved but not humourless. She had good manners without being mannered. What Joseph had searched for, ever since that mystical experience on Hampstead Heath, was an equivalent of Denise in the realm of economic theory.

Of course it could be argued that Cheesemanic monetarism represented a kind of unintentional synthesis in itself since, as Joseph had come to believe, it was actually propelled by what in the end was a Keynesian mechanism, but one that operated on reduced power. Sound money had turned out to be empty rhetoric, however much sincerity had gone into its formulation both on his own and Mrs

Cheeseman's part, since when you poured money down a bottomless pit it lost its substantiality and fluttered into the abyss like so much paper, which was indeed what it had become. Unemployment, so dear to the monetarist heart, was that bottomless pit. Unfortunately of course it simply wasn't bottomless enough. The whole ethic behind monetarism prevented the government from giving the unemployed enough paper money to provide them with worthwhile spending power, and their tightly restricted consumerism could do little to help to stimulate productivity again. Even orthodox Keynesianism had run into this difficulty. The TVA project may have cost millions but the millions were drops in the ocean.

It had taken the Second World War to provide a bottomless pit, or an ocean, large enough to get the economies of America and Germany on their feet again. The Depression had been finally terminated by a war. Ever since his talk with Mrs Cheeseman in her hospital Joseph had been terrified that the same thought would strike her. In point of fact she gave every sign of pursuing exactly the opposite course – undertaking a review of defence expenditure in order to make substantial cuts, and inaugurating the whole process by getting poor Raymond to announce the scrapping of the *Expedition* this morning.

Focussing her attention on one unimportant and indeed inexpensive ship was characteristic of Mrs Cheeseman's attention to detail – of her pettiness, as some would have it. Yet the announcement had surprised Joseph and made him feel uneasy. Of course she wouldn't spare a thought for the savaging Raymond had received from the admirals, but nevertheless the *Expedition* announcement had been like firing a warning shot across the bows of the navy. Attention to detail was one thing but not, surely, if it was likely to put at risk a large-scale strategy?

All day long he'd been puzzled at Mrs Cheeseman's apparent readiness to show her hand. And now here he was on a tatty ferryboat in mid-Channel, eating a meal with perhaps the least politically intuitive woman in the whole world, and suddenly the explanation began to dawn.

Indeed it was Laurette's own chance phrase that had suggested it: civil war.

Q. Why did Napoleon tweak his generals' noses?

A. To make them ready and willing to *fight*.

The waiter appeared and began to pick up their soup plates. 'Would you like plaice and chips or steak and kidney pie? And chips,' he asked.

'Aw hell,' said Laurette, 'this is supposed to be a *rest*aurant.'

'That's all we've got.'

'It better be fish, I guess.'

'Sir?'

'The same,' Joseph replied shortly.

The waiter left.

'You English,' said Laurette. 'You sir and madam people half to death and all you got to offer is goddam fish and chips.'

Joseph, preoccupied with his fears, said nothing. After a few moments the waiter reappeared, with crumbed plaice, chips and peas. Laurette looked at her plate incredulously.

'What in hell *is* this?' she asked the waiter.

'It's what I said,' he replied nervously. 'Madam.'

'This is some kinda fish out of a fish machine. You got some kinda fish dispenser back there, turn the handle and some goddam plaice fillet pops out. Listen, waiter, this is pre-prepared *frozen* fish. You didn't say anything about *that*. The point I'm trying to get at is, this is a goddam *boat*. We're at sea. And you've got the nerve to serve me *frozen* plaice.'

'It's not a fishing boat, madam, it's a cross-Channel ferry.'

'You are missing the *point*,' said Laurette, 'I'm not asking you to *fish*, I'm talking about ecology, is all, relating to the environment. Look, think about your digestive tract for a moment. It's got two ends, right? You put stuff in one end, and it comes out the other. That's ecology, all by itself. What you eat, you *crap*.'

'I've got to go,' said the waiter. 'I've got a lot on my plate.' He hurried off.

Suddenly Joseph was furious. 'You Americans make me sick!' he almost shouted. 'Even when you're dieting you're the greediest people on earth.'

'There's nothing wrong with being interested in food. Animals are interested in food. We're animals aren't we?'

'Some of us are more animal than others.'

'Some of us maybe don't get to be predatory enough. Anyway, I'll tell you something for free. The person the most into high fibre I ever met is an *English* girl. I met her in Scotland. A lovely girl, Katie Totness. I never met anybody knew as much about fibre as Katie. I get sick of your goddam crap generalizations.'

'You're the one who generalizes about crap all the time. Do you think that waiter understood what you were talking about? He just thought you were insulting him again.'

Laurette's face fell.

'Do you think so?' she asked.

'You talk about relating to the environment, and you can't even relate to the man who waits on your table.'

'Gee,' said Laurette. 'Poor guy. I guess I better have a word with him. Apologize.'

'You *do* that,' Joseph said. 'I've got to go.' He rose from the table.

'But you didn't eat your meal yet.'

Suddenly Joseph's temper evaporated and he felt almost sorry at the thought of leaving Laurette on her own. It was underhand to take out his worries on her.

'I'm sorry, Laurette, I just don't feel like it, thanks all the same. To tell you the truth, I've got something on my mind.'

'I remember,' she said. 'What you said before. Or nearly said. But let me tell you something, Joe, for free. Whatever the meaning of life is, it isn't *economic*, that's for sure.'

'It is for an economist.'

'There's no such thing as a goddam economist. It's all a matter of *people*, Joe. By which I mean, animals. Beasts of the field.'

'I'm sure you're right. Goodbye, Laurette. Nice to see you again.'

'I'll send you a postcard.'

'That'll be nice. From the Camargue.'

'I wasn't thinking about the Camargue. Everybody goes to the Camargue. I was thinking about where I'm going in March. Farquhar Island. I'll send you a postcard from Farquhar Island.'

'Farquhar Island?'

'I booked on a great nature study package. Penguins and all.'

'I look forward to getting a postcard from there then. If they *have* postcards, that is.'

'Goodbye, Joe. Till we meet again.'

'Goodbye Laurette.'

She was right, he reflected as he walked away, they *were* ships that had passed in the night. And he had other things on his mind. He feared a great shadow was falling over the land.

CHAPTER FORTY-NINE

Terry; Laurette; Terry

It was hardly a cruise liner, as he'd told the vicar. But how could he spell out that he served rubbishy food on a tinpot ferry in the middle of the English Channel? And even worse, that sex didn't seem to happen between the ports of Dover and Calais. Look at this evening, being sworn at by a big American woman in hiking gear. Every time he served her she thought fit to come out with some new obscenity.

What made it all the more sickening was being identified with breaded plaice and tinned soup, as if they were a reflection of his personality. He'd always taken pride in his cooking. Funnily enough Ange had actually mentioned it in her last letter.

He'd read it sitting on his bed in Southampton's Seaman's Hostel. It was hardly a salubrious environment and he intended to move out as soon as he could. He'd kept on his cottage for the time being, but of course it was too far to go except during leave.

Ange had used thick creamy vellum with the letterhead Garsington House in blue, in that sort of gothic script which made each letter look like a coat of arms in itself. She'd begun with a list of the goodies she'd been acquiring, which this time included a mini for her birthday, a holiday in Sri Lanka over Christmas, and an antique desk as a no reason at all present. 'I am scribbling at it at this very moment,' she wrote. At the end of her inventory, however, just before signing off, she'd suddenly said: 'I do miss your lovely cookery. I can still taste that olde English game pie. Alex can't cook for toffee, and of course, you know me. But we go out a lot, and if people come we get a firm in.'

At the time he'd taken it as another dig. To be summed up, as a man, a husband, by the words 'game pie'. But now, smarting under the American woman's invective, he wondered if Ange hadn't meant it nicely after all. Perhaps game pie was more important in the great scheme than he'd been thinking recently. Once upon a time he'd taken the importance of that sort of thing for granted: cookery, keeping his house in order, joining a shooting syndicate. But that had all been destroyed the morning he shared Frankie's bathroom, and now here he was, a waiter on the high seas serving TV dinners to a bad-tempered American; now it wasn't game pie that summed him up, but breaded plaice.

Until, that was, he served the dessert.

The dessert ought to have been the most disastrous course of all: it was pink blancmange-like stuff that you got in dried form from a packet, made up with water, and served with a red glacé cherry on the top. Terry girded his loins for more insults from the American, and carried two bowls of dessert over to her table.

The man had gone.

'What *is* this?' the woman asked.

'Raspberry mousse, madam.'

'Mousse? It looks more like rat to me. No, gee, what a cheap crack. I don't know what's got into me tonight. Look, siddown a minute. Joe's gone.'

222

'I can't, madam.'

'Aw, come on. What do you think, I'm gonna *eat* you?'

'We're not allowed to sit with the customers.'

'Wow, do you *buy* that junk? Gee, that's cute. Well, look, when you can take a short break from propping up all this outmoded kinda class structure, perhaps you and me could have a tête-à-tête?'

Terry stared down at her in astonishment. There was only one explanation for this sudden change of tune. She had been trying to be provocative all along.

As a matter of fact the restaurant was due to close anyway. Terry began to clear the other tables. Soon the place was deserted except for the American.

'I'm sorry,' she said as he approached, 'I couldn't sorta handle the mousse. The mousses, rather.'

'Oh, they're crap,' he said bluntly, picking them up.

'You don't have to *say* it. That's what I want to talk to you about. I'll see you up on the deck in a coupla minutes.'

Terry hurriedly dumped the bowls of mousse in the kitchen. He wondered if he should go to his sleeping quarters and change. No, the woman had gone for him as he was dressed at present, and it was essential to strike while the iron was hot. He hurried on to the deck.

It was like walking into a deep freeze. The cold took his breath away. All the more reason to get close. The woman was waiting for him by the rail.

'Hi!' she said, 'that was quick.'

'Oh. I can be very quick.' Suiting action to word, he moved in on her.

'I wanted to tell you. That crap stuff, I meant it *literally*. It wasn't, you know –'

'Don't worry about it,' Terry said, kissing her. 'I understand.' He kissed her several times, getting little response. He put his hands on her breasts, feeling their shape through the thick jumper. She pulled back a little.

'Look,' she said, 'don't get me wrong. I'm not one of those cock-teasing feminists. Don't think it. Like I'm a deeply vaginal person but this isn't the time or the place.'

Terry, wound up by the events not merely of this evening

but of the last months, screwed tight by an endless series of unconsummated Channel crossings, and by all the disasters and demoralizations that had occurred before he went to sea, caught only the references to vagina and plaice. The plaice was an image he was going to disprove; and the vagina was where he was going to disprove it. She was bound to have a cabin, being an American. His luck had turned at last.

He took a deep breath of icy air, lined up on his target, dived

Into the destructive element. Like, Jesus, what was with that coming *on* so heavy, she only wanted to explain about her diet. Sure, she didn't buy that class-structure garbage, like she could only open her legs for professional men, university professors and such. OK, Joe Harper had been a little over-refined in certain directions, but sexually speaking Bud was a man of the people. In fact he'd shortly vanished in the crowd. All along she was heading towards some centrality: the beginning had been a pubescent pool in North Carolina; the end would be to make that pool *bloom*. The beginning had been her terror of drowning in a medium thick and thickening; the end would be a celebration of what was primal, tumescent, *salt*, in all experience. If that meant promiscuity, so be it. But – watching the waiter's gleaming head bobbing on black water – gee, she wasn't yet *that* promiscuous.

In the meantime that guy would be all right. He could swim like a fish.

Of *course* he could swim like a fish. He was an in*hab*itant of the destructive element when all was said and done. He was the kinda bastard never had a sexo-spiritual problem in his life.

The cross-Channel ferry discharged its passengers in Le Havre the following morning and picked up a fresh contingent. On the way back to Southampton Terry became feverish and was sent to his bunk. There he entered a dream.

There was no fog here. Breaded plaice swam in a tomato sea, while above trailed low clouds of raspberry blancmange. And then, rising from the waves, a naked form, pink as a peeled shrimp. He had women's breasts, each tipped with a glacé cherry, but down below his equipment seemed normal. He was carrying a shotgun and walking towards Terry over the surface of the water.

A crow beat across the scene, skimming over the red water like a small black albatross. Frankie got nearer and nearer.

Terry realized that he, Terry, was carrying a gun too. He lined it up on the crow and fired. He could actually feel the pellets strike home, he *knew* he had scored. But the bird flew on. He turned to face Frankie once more and suddenly realized that the man's body was spattered with red. Oh god, no, surely he couldn't have . . . no, of course, it was all right, he'd just been splashed by the soup.

And then Terry realized that Frankie's genitalia were missing.

Frankie walked right up to him, face to face, smiling, unresentful. 'I'm a deeply vaginal person,' he said, and Terry began to sink, sink into unutterable depths. But strangely he could still hear Frankie's voice. 'I'm a deeply vaginal person,' Frankie repeated, 'and you, Terry, you are a breaded plaice.'

CHAPTER FIFTY

Queen

He lay with his head on the pillow, his hair still neatly arranged in a bushy old-fashioned style, almost Teddy Boy. He'd been asleep a long time. She put a hand on his forehead. Quite cool now.

'Long time no see, Terry,' she said.

'No sea,' he said suddenly, loudly, and sat up. He looked at her as if he was seeing a ghost.

225

'It's only me,' she said. 'Queen.'

Slowly realization dawned, and he sank back on the pillow. 'I thought I was drowning,' he said.

'It was only a dream. You're safe in bed.'

'I thought I was on the boat. I thought I was in the sea.'

'You've been in bed with a fever for nearly a week. Your mates at the hostel were getting a bit worried about you. They found our address in your wallet.'

'Oh yes.'

'Nice to know you thought of us. I often think of that time when you lodged with us and worked at 10 Downing Street. Talk about seeing how the other half lives.'

'I was going to write. Now you're down here. See if you had a room.'

'It's nice and convenient, isn't it, us being here?'

'You've got a nice place here,' said Terry, just his eyes surveying the room while his head stayed weakly on the pillow.

'This room's all right,' Queen said. 'We've done this room. We got some paper cheap from a shop in Portsmouth. You ought to see the rest of the house. It's still a mess. Start with the bedrooms, that's the best policy when you're decorating a guest house. And we've only been here a few days of course. But we've already had a guest. Lovely man. A reverend gentleman. He sailed this morning from Portsmouth Harbour. He's going to Farquhar Island, off South America. Taking up a parish there. That's what I'm going to like about this place, the way people come and go. Not like Battersea. Nothing ever happened in Battersea.'

Suddenly she thought of Tom and felt herself blush. Terry wasn't at all like Tom. He was big, slow-moving – he'd always reminded her of a younger Jack. Even lying here, ill, he reminded her of how Jack had lain with his heart that time, and then more recently how he'd sat in his chair after losing his job, just moving his head to look out of the window or read the paper. Terry's head protruded from the sheets like a stone on the top of a drystone wall.

'Nothing good, anyway,' she concluded.

'Where's Jack?' asked Terry.

'He's gone down to the pub.'

'Oh, it's his day, is it?'

'Every day's his day these days. He hasn't got a routine going yet. That's the best part about moving to a new place, getting a new routine. Jack says he's got to get to know the pubs, so he can pick his local. I said to him, I wouldn't mind you getting to know the wallpaper a bit better as well. But I like him going out for a lunchtime pint, to tell you the truth, Terry. Gives him an appetite. Mind you, he hasn't had much trouble in that department since we came here. He's been eating like a horse. I think it's the sea air. His face has got a bit of colour in it, you'd be amazed. Eyes bright. I said to him, you're one of those people whose eyes change colour when they get near the sea. They look quite blue. I always thought of him having grey eyes. But it's done him a world of good, coming here. Us both.'

'Lucky you,' Terry whispered, shutting his eyes. He sounded bitter.

'I hear you was up to a bit of something on that boat when you fell in, Terry,' she said, trying to cheer him up. 'Bit of horse-play with a young lady, what I've heard.'

Terry said nothing, but lay with his eyes shut. After a few moments a tear trickled out of the corner of one of them.

'You all right, Terry?' Queen asked anxiously.

'Horseplay,' he said in a kind of croaking voice. 'When do I ever get any horseplay?'

Lord, thought Queen, not another one. All these young men to mother. She'd had enough of that nonsense with Tom. It had nearly done for Jack – for her, too, for that matter. There was only one word for how it had made her feel: rubbish.

No, she was done with all that, whether with Tom or Terry or Jack himself. Coming to Portsmouth might mean a new life in all sorts of ways but it didn't mean *that*. Four years ago she'd thought Jack had died on her; all that side of life *had* died on her now. Be content with what you have, like she used to be all those years ago, in her shop, with the cold wind blowing down the street outside. Outside her guest house it was different of course: walks along Southsea front, the bustle of Portsmouth, ships, the sea. She'd come a long way from New Mills; from Battersea even.

'Not to worry,' she said. 'A nice girl'll come along one day.'

'Oh, nice girls keep coming along all right. But they just go straight past,' said Terry.

'Sounds like you go straight past *them*, judging by what happened to you. Look, I'll go and get you some soup. That'll make you feel much better.'

'Oh no,' Terry said, sincerely repelled. 'No. The way I feel I couldn't eat a thing.'

Jack arrived back about twenty minutes later. 'I'll just go up and see him,' he said cheerily. 'Whatsisname.'

'I wouldn't,' said Queen. 'Not at the moment.'

'He's all right, isn't he? Terry.'

'He'll be all right in due course. He's just a bit low and upset, that's all. He's been having a cry.'

'A cry!' exclaimed Jack, his blue eyes startled. 'Well I'm buggered. A cry. I thought I'd seen the last of blokes crying when I got shot of poor old George.'

'Never mind,' Queen said. 'Just give him time. Come and have something to eat, Jack. Your dinner's in the oven.'

CHAPTER FIFTY-ONE

David

The *Expedition* sailed southwards across an Atlantic not vast perhaps as eternity but certainly large enough to provide a substantial caesura in the continuum of time and space; only to culminate, David hoped, in an outcrop, Farquhar Island, which would provide a vantage point from which *his* time and space could be viewed, at last, with clarity, with that sharp immediacy of telescopic sight.

Inevitably the limbo was incomplete, the vacuum imperfect. For one thing he had his responsibilities as acting chaplain of the vessel to carry out. The church and the navy, strapped for resources, had arranged what amounted to a deal: David would provide a ministry to both the military and civilian personnel of the vessel in exchange for free passage to his new parish. There was in fact plenty of available accommodation on the ship as a result of recent government cut-backs; David had been given the VIP suite, which was almost embarrassingly luxurious. His duties, as it happened – and as, perhaps, his cabin implied – were social rather than pastoral. The ordinary sailors gave few hints of requiring the services of a man of God, quite the contrary; the officers and scientific complement on board, however, were at least thirsty for conversation. David did his best to provide his share with good grace, although silence would have been more in keeping with his inner state.

There was another, more serious distraction. Shortly before the *Expedition* sailed, the government announced that they had decided to recall and scrap the ship as soon as it had docked at Farquhar Island, and disband the crew. Gloom and despondency were immediate and widespread, although again an accidie derived from political contingency was not really within David's sphere of influence to mitigate or resolve. He did at least commiserate, although he felt a little hypocritical as he did so. One of the officers vividly complained they were going on a voyage to nowhere; that, David couldn't stop himself from thinking, was precisely the destination he wanted to head for.

As they continued south from the equator the sea and the sky went from blue to grey. The north was now warm, the south cold; winter was now summer, summer winter. It was late February, early autumn. David waited for a larger season to go into reverse. Not literally: Lorna would not rise from these chilly waters. In fact she would have found the very notion of Venus laughable – she was too immediate a woman to want to mythologize her experience. But David was concerned with visualization, not with seeing. Botticelli's pastel virgin, too beautiful even to *be* a body, had risen from impossibly turquoise waters, certainly by the standards of the South Atlantic.

One day, with a deep grey swell and a low ribbed sky that looked like an upward reflection of the sea, David was leaning over the side of the *Expedition* talking to one of the scientists, Benjamin Taylor. Ben was regretting the cancellation of the ship's Antarctic expedition, and recounting trips he had made in the past. He told of coming upon a dry valley once, bare rock, no snow, the driest place on earth because of some fluke in the movement of air, a place dry, clear-skied, and profoundly cold. In the middle of the valley lay a seal, bizarrely far from the sea. Presumably it had got lost, struggled into the valley, and was now sleeping off its exertions. When they approached, however, they realized it was dead. On analysing its tissues, they discovered it had been dead for more than two centuries.

Ben's story gave David a momentary spasm of excitement; which waned however as he reflected that freeze-drying was not the resistance to time that interested him. The sea was rising and it had begun to snow, for the first time on the voyage, an unexpected interchange of white between two grey elements. The flakes seemed to pause before entering the water, like snowdrops flowering briefly on the growling sea.

The ship received a fortnight's stay of execution. An unknown expedition had been sighted on the Luitpold coast of Coatsland, on the main Antarctic continent. They might be lost; they might be up to something which threatened the protected status of the region. David was permitted to join the landing-party – they would go inland for two days on motorized sleds, then come back whether contact had been made or not. Winter was not far off.

Penguins were arrayed upon the rocky coast, each with an egg balanced on his feet, like a silent welcoming party of male nuns. Ben explained that they would wait there throughout the winter while the most ferocious weather howled all round, and miles of ice built up between them and the open sea. Again David had a sense of the awesome futility of slowing the processes of existence – in this case, those of metabolism rather than decay – down to such an extent, becoming a statue rather than a corpse.

The landing-party, on the afternoon of their second day, in driving snow, received a glimpse of their quarry, a bulky figure disappearing in the swirl. To David's eyes the effect was of reverse pointillisme, the form blotted out by the imposed white, distance intensifying the effect of nothing there at all. But the renegade penguin had left behind its eggs. There were a dozen metal barrels, already half buried in snow; on each one a brass plate, neatly engraved: DIOXIN.

'That's his idea of being responsible, the bastard,' Lieutenant Thwaite said. 'Making sure that whoever comes across them knows what's inside.'

'What is it?' David asked.

'It's that poison that polluted a town in Italy. This lot of cowboys must have been hired to dispose of the stuff. I'm amazed they bothered to lug it all the way here. They could have dumped it down some old mineshaft and nobody would have been any the wiser.'

'Are we going to take it away?'

'It's a hot potato, this stuff. We take it on board, *we* have the problem of disposing of it. We would hardly be welcomed with open arms, wherever we went, apart from the fact that our ship's going straight back to the breaker's yard anyway. No, this load of junk is the last thing in the world we want to saddle ourselves with. We'll leave it here, let some other buggers worry about it. Ten to one it'll stay here for ever, by the time the authorities have finished arguing.'

Two days later the landing-party were back on the *Expedition*. They had come upon no further traces of the waste disposal people, but then they had hardly expected to. Antarctica was an enormous continent, there were thousands of miles of emptiness in which to be concealed.

In any case, while distances were long, time was short. The *Expedition* set sail for Farquhar Island, its last port of call before it, too, was transformed into waste, and disposed of.

CHAPTER FIFTY-TWO

Horace

Horace was beginning to become aware of a certain problem intrinsic to the activity of sailing hitherto uncharted seas or, to revert to a previous metaphor, to sounding hitherto (by him) unplumbed lagoons. The lagoon in question, of course, was sweet indeed, a Third Sex without those depressingly bewrinkled dugs of Eliot's Tiresias and, even more importantly, lacking the latter's glum omniscience; possessed, indeed, of a pink robustness that to Horace seemed the exact shade, the exact degree, of the inner pinkness and deep down robustness of life itself, the robustness of the unfolding bloom, the pinkness of the early petal.

The problem was of course that of generating a corresponding quota of pink robustness on his own part, or to put it in political terms, of maintaining his clout. This was a task indeed, for two reasons. The first was that his clout had come to seem to him not pinkly robust, but hollowly mocking. As soon as he'd lost his struggle to save the *Expedition* Horace's position in the Inner Cabinet had begun to pall. He had felt that, as *the* Cabinet wimp, he had been *intended* to struggle; he felt also that he'd been intended to lose. It was hard to affirm clout when you had to jump through hoops; even harder when you had to miss them.

The second reason lay in the problem of marriage. How could he remain in the Inner Cabinet if he announced to the Prime Minister that he was affianced to someone so profoundly incompatible with the Cheesemanic version of reality as Frankie Rutherford? She would be appalled; there was no place for a Third Sex in her world of dog eat dog. No, she wouldn't be appalled, she simply wouldn't hear.

But marriage was in the offing, that was the whole, the increasing trouble, if trouble was the word for an affirmation that Horace profoundly wished to make – as did Frankie. In his gruff and husky way Frankie had – well, if not for obvious reasons actually proposed, at least indicated that his hand was ripe for the taking. Frankie was lonely in that damp manor of his, as Horace was lonely in his elegant London apartment; Frankie was lonely sustaining the role of the Third Sex amongst a cretinous country squirarchy only capable of counting up to two, just as Horace was lonely sustaining the role of the Third Sex's opposite number in a metropolitan environment which believed that the height of sophistication lay in accepting the simple inversions of male and female; Frankie above all was in love with Horace, as Horace was in love with him. But if Horace loved Frankie's pink robustness, Frankie, Horace couldn't help thinking, loved Horace's *clout*.

It was a Gordian knot, if one was entitled to consider clout knotted.

Horace was sitting at an escritoire in his Kensington flat, aware of his position in exactly a roomful of calm while March weather whirled and tossed in the streets outside. Unfortunately the inner man, the Inner Cabinet man, found himself in tune with the outer elements. He was working on Raymond Durrant's interim report on military expenditure – that is to say, on military cutbacks. The final version was going to be presented to the Inner Cabinet the following afternoon but the material would be exactly the same. Only the glaze would be harder, so that the document, rubber stamped as it would certainly be by the Inner Cabinet, could go straight from there to the full Cabinet to be rubber-stamped once more, and immediately thereafter be published as a White Paper. The proposed cuts were savage, fifteen percent overall. The navy's share amounted to nearly twenty-five percent of its strength.

Horace explored every angle of the report, looking for a way out. His dilemma was that as a wimp he was opposed to cuts; but by the same token he was also opposed to heavy military spending and the paranoiac aggressiveness it implied. There *was* no way out. Certainly he couldn't break through the impenetrability of the proposals with his puny clout. He was trapped.

And then there was a knock on the door.

It was almost, Horace couldn't help feeling, an emblematic encounter. He, Horace, in *le smoking* (not that he ever touched the noxious weed, despite a looming necessity to spit out all the butt-ends of his days and ways), while Joseph Harper was in some savage Norwegian sweater, with a bristling weatherproof beard that looked as if it had been knitted from the same coarse wool, and big spectacles that were not an addition to his appearance but an essential, thrusting, component of it.

'Can I get you a drink?' Horace asked wanly.

'Scotch,' Harper replied. He strode over to the escritoire. 'I see you've got Durrant's navy proposals.'

'That document is supposed to be highly confidential.'

'Don't worry. I know what's in it.'

'I imagine you would.' Horace handed him a scotch. He poured himself a glass of claret from a bottle he'd decanted at his solitary lunch. 'I suppose, all things considered, you are its true author. The Bacon, one might say, to its Shakespeare. The ghost in the machine.'

'Wrong,' Harper said. He tossed off his scotch. 'It's Mrs Cheeseman's own handiwork this time.'

'Inspired by you, no doubt.'

'No. Yes. Well, in a back-to-front sort of way I suppose. I need another drink.'

'Perhaps I should slide the bottle along the bar to you,' Horace said stiffly.

'What bar? Oh, I see what you mean. I wouldn't mind drowning my troubles, that's the truth.'

'I suppose when it comes to cutting the armed forces, you monetarists are in a somewhat ambiguous position. You risk alienating the very people who provide your most vigorous support.'

'You've got the same problem from the wimp angle, surely? With the terms reversed.'

Blast, thought Horace, the man is bright enough. A bright monetarist seemed a contradiction in terms, like an artistic Nazi. Monetarism might prevail, as an axe might prevail, but the only sort of brightness involved should be a metallic glitter.

'Anyway,' Harper went on, 'believe it or not, this is not a monetarist document.'

'I beg your pardon?' asked Horace.

'It is very important that you understand exactly what it is I'm saying,' Harper said in brusque, patronizing tones. 'This document is not the product of monetarist economics. Mrs Cheeseman is no longer a monetarist. This is in fact –' he paused to drain his second scotch at a draught, and when he continued something terrible had happened, the silence in the room, the storm outside, had both strangely intensified, so that Horace's head was filled with an interwoven fabric of raw turbulence and numb quietude. Lord save me, he thought, I am being presented with information with which I cannot cope, and, like Mrs Cheeseman, I have become deaf as a result.

And then Harper coughed and the extraneous noise and silence diminished to an acceptable volume. 'Sorry,' Harper continued, 'the scotch went down the wrong way. Took my breath. What I was trying to *say* was, our Mrs Cheeseman has become a post-Keynesian.'

It was Horace's turn to lose his breath. The full complexities of the paradox could not, of course, be unwrapped immediately but Horace was perfectly aware that when they were, the contents of the package would include Horace himself, naked and shivering. His position vis-à-vis Mrs Cheeseman had seemed sufficiently complex already; if it was true that she was a post-Keynesian, where in the name of sanity did that leave *him*?

Harper went on to explain. A miracle upon Hampstead Health! Miracles would never cease, but that manifestly was the point. Harper lay great emphasis on the fact that the experience involved was indeed revelatory, not a matter of conversion. Indeed, it was necessary to correct his opening announcement. Neither Harper himself nor Mrs Cheeseman had *become* post-Keynesian: what Harper had suddenly understood was that they already *were*. The

Keynesian dynamic of excess had evolved into the monetarist principle of efficiency. When Mrs Cheeseman's administration trimmed the fat, what they had really been utilizing, to give the economy such momentum as it had achieved, was the trimmed fat itself. It wasn't the strenuous productivity of those people left in work which was keeping the country going, insofar as it was going at all, but the demand created by that non-functional quantity: the consumerism of the unemployed. But of course their consumerism was inevitably low-level, constricted, strained: thus the economy had limped along.

'I put all this to Mrs Cheeseman a year ago,' Harper said. 'Another scotch.'

'What on earth did she make of it?' Horace asked, pouring him one. Then he realized. 'Oh my god!' *That* of course was the information that had sent her deaf.

'It's what she's been making of it ever since that worries me,' Harper said. The scotch disappeared. 'That's why I've come to see you. Things are heading for a point of no return. The crunch. The point is, Bentley, that one of the truisms of twentieth century economic analysis is that the Great Depression was actually solved by the Second World War. Look at the two major powers involved, Germany and the United States, circa 1930. Both up shit's creek. What they basically did during the next ten or fifteen years was to waste all the money they didn't have on armaments and war. The result? They boomed for decades after the war ended. Mrs Cheeseman's cottoned on to it. We're heading towards a war and it's going to be my fault. It's enough to give you delusions of grandeur. Well, delusions of *some*thing. I think I'll have another scotch. That's the sort of delusion I prefer. What makes it worse is that I've had a pretty good idea of what was in the wind ever since she began thinking along these lines, but I promised to keep my mouth shut for a year. Well, the year's up now. You're the first person I've told.'

Horace poured him another scotch. It was strange to see Harper in this state, even if in the end it was the man's very demons which were delusive. There was nothing like the presence of demons for humanizing a man.

'I think war's the last thing you need to worry about,' Horace told him. 'Remember that Mrs Cheeseman is just about to disband half the navy.'

It was then that Harper dropped his bombshell. The Durrant proposals *proved* that the country was about to go to war. The proposals were to slash the navy: ergo the imminent war would involve a heavy naval commitment. The opening salvo of those proposals had sunk the *Expedition*, an Antarctic survey vessel. Ergo the war was to be fought in the South Atlantic. There was only one important British possession in those regions, Farquhar Island, along with its uninhabited dependency, South Hanover. Ergo the war was to be fought over that.

'The whole strategy,' Harper said, 'is to threaten the navy with disbandment. Then, suddenly, you give them a great chance to prove themselves. Which they grab with both hands. It's perfectly logical, in its way.'

Horace stared at him in horror and astonishment.

'That's why I've come to you,' Harper went on. 'As the Inner Cabinet wimp you're the only person in a position to do anything about it.'

CHAPTER FIFTY-THREE

The Fat Man

The Fat Man walked across the great sunlit plaza of Angelico, shaded intermittently by dusty oleanders with their sudden lavish pink blossoms poking through tired foliage. His journey had been along endlessly puckered and tense meteorological tracks, through London drizzle, the dank cold of mid-Channel, the coastal fog of France, the white swirl of Antarctica, but now his lightweight suit was surrounded by other examples of sunny plumpness and thin clothing in the Costanaguan crowd.

Every now and then he passed a litter bin, buzzing with

flies, bursting at the seams, stinking. What the collection arrangements were, god only knew. A scruffy urchin approached, palm out, but as he drew near the Fat Man he seemed to lose interest and passed on, oblivious, intent on pestering someone else. Ironically the Fat Man was prepared to indulge in precisely that sort of gratuitous transaction, liberating money from the capitalist structure, creating his own micro-climate in some eddy of the prevailing economic system. That was why, as an anarchist with his own designs on history, he had accepted a cash commission from a monetarist Prime Minister in the first place.

Angelico, like everywhere else, was a fabric of fascist concrete and glass, bank architecture. There were some older, Mediterranean-style buildings dotted about however, and the office of the Junta's Military Procurator was situated in one of these, an edifice of golden stone with a carved door-surround and intricate and impractical wrought iron balconies in front of each window. It faced the plaza, which perhaps accounted for its survival. A slovenly glum guard stood on the pavement outside it, smoking. He took the Fat Man's papers, limp-wristed, uninterested, cautious. He spat out his cigarette, shook his head, tutted.

The Fat Man spoke, in Spanish: 'My appointment with the Procurator has been arranged at the highest level.'

It was clearly the Spanish rather than the content of the claim that caught the soldier's attention. 'You speak Spanish, señor?' he asked redundantly.

'Castilian only,' the Fat Man said. 'I apologize.'

'Is very good,' the soldier remarked politely in English, impressed. Suddenly, threateningly, he whistled loudly, as if he had changed his mind about being on good terms. A moment passed while the Fat Man and the soldier calmly regarded each other. And then the large ornate wooden door of the building slowly opened to reveal a cool and cavernous dimness beyond. Without turning to look, the soldier said in Spanish: 'Conduct this gentleman to the office of the Procurator.'

'*Si*,' came a voice from the darkness. The Fat Man was conducted in.

The office of the Military Procurator was predictably lavish: it was his profession to procure things, after all. There was a leather-topped gilded desk, with delicately worked legs, a large display cabinet full of English, German, and Chinese porcelain, an eighteenth-century chaise longue and easy chairs, a Persian carpet on the marble floor. The Procurator himself, sitting in studied absorption at his desk, was somewhat less refined than his room. He was in the full military regalia of a banana republic, his epaulettes, medals, gold braid, splodged about a tailcoat of the exact maroon worn by ushers in English cinemas. He fiddled with papers while the Fat Man calmly stood by the desk, looking down at him.

Finally, as if he'd only then become aware of a presence in the room, the Procurator looked up.

'Sit down,' he said testily in English.

'*Muchas gracias*,' the Fat Man said, and sat down. He continued in Spanish: 'It is very good of you to spare the time.'

'You speak Spanish?' the Procurator asked, also in Spanish.

'Castilian only.'

'Very good.' The man's thin aristocratic features relaxed slightly, revealing a certain sensualism and grossness – not sexual exactly; possibly sadistic. The face of a man who had watched a large number of people disappear. Why not? thought the Fat Man. He had too, although since he'd neither shown nor indeed felt any emotion while he did so, the experience had not left its mark. Their conversation continued in Spanish.

'Forgive me, I do not understand why you are here,' the Procurator said.

'I think you have been informed that I have interests in refuse disposal,' the Fat Man replied.

'World Wide Waste, I have seen your papers.'

'Ah yes, but we have also been incorporated here in Costanagua.'

'Really?'

'The Scrap Metal and Reprocessing Company of Angelico.'

'Congratulations. It is not often that a foreign company receives local incorporation in that fashion.'

'Ah, but much is to be done here. I was looking at the litter bins in the plaza as I strolled to your office this morning. I must make enquiries about a contract. I think we have something to offer in that respect. We have very high standards. Of cleanliness.'

'A clean company in a dirty world.'

'Precisely. You may have heard of that dioxin scandal in Italy. A company called Hautbois had a little difficulty.'

'It was in the newspapers.'

'Precisely. Well, World Wide Waste, or Euro-Garbage as we were known until a couple of weeks ago, handled the problem of disposal for them. Discreetly, of course. Indeed, it was that project which turned my attention to this part of the world. Or should I say, to an adjoining part. The Antarctic wastes, you understand.'

'What I do not understand,' the Procurator said, slightly impatiently, 'is what you want with me. I am the Military Procurator, what have I to do with waste?'

'I would have thought you might have an interest in scrap metal. You must need a great deal of metal to manufacture equipment. It might prove both economical and ecological to utilize the reclamation and reprocessing services I can offer.'

'I really think, at the risk of sounding rude, that this discussion could have been conducted at a lower level in my department. As you can probably tell from my ceremonial dress, I have a function to attend shortly.'

'I think this conversation needs to be conducted at the highest level, if you in turn will excuse my disagreement. A certain amount of, shall we say, tact, is involved. My company can be very tactful, as the little matter of the dioxin will I hope have demonstrated. We have great experience in the removal of the most inconvenient substances.'

'And what inconvenient substance are you interested in now? A moment ago you were talking about scrap metal.'

'I am still. It is not the scrap metal itself that is inconvenient. It is the location of the scrap metal that is inconvenient.'

'I see. And where is this scrap metal located?'

'On the island of South Hanover. There is a disused whaling station there. All sorts of unwanted equipment. Ideal for melting down.'

'But South Hanover is a dependency of Farquhar Island. A British possession.'

'But historically and morally, I believe, a province of Costanuaga. As I said, I run a clean company. We prefer to make our arrangements with the true owners of the territories in which we have an interest, rather than with their unjustified, and if I may say, temporary, rulers. And there are two pieces of information which are relevant here. The first you no doubt know already. The British Antarctic survey vessel *Expedition* will shortly be returning home from Farquhar Island. When it arrives in Britain it will go to the breaker's yard. Naturally this is a subject which concerns me. Indeed, I am considering submitting a tender for the contract.'

'I see. And what is the other item of information in which I might be interested?'

'Tomorrow the British authorities will be considering an important proposal by the Secretary of State for Defence. The proposal in question involves cutting the size of the armed forces. In particular, the intention is to cut the size of the British navy by twenty-five percent. The proposal will be accepted and made public within days. The point hardly needs underlining, I presume, that islands like South Hanover and Farquhar are accessible to Britain only by sea. If one places these two developments side by side – the scrapping of the only UK ship that is permanently based in the South Atlantic, and the savaging of the British navy at large – one is forced, I think, to only one conclusion. What we can discern is a waning of interest on the part of the British in their more distant and inconspicuous possessions.'

'This possibility deeply interests me,' said the Military Procurator. 'Like the British I too have a concern for economy. Not to mention ecology also, of course. The recycling of scrap metal, as you suggest, might be an important new departure for my department.'

'Perhaps even for Costanagua as a whole?' the Fat Man suggested.

'Yes, yes, indeed. Perhaps even for Costanagua as a whole,' the Procurator agreed.

CHAPTER FIFTY-FOUR

Horace

A dusty street, a jumble of mean lowering ticky-tacky buildings along each side. Silence. Even the clocks have stopped working. The baked atmosphere seems inimical to the processes of life, but *principles* can operate here. Principles trudge along the centre of the road, towards a confrontation. How high is noon?

That was the title Horace had suggested to the British Film Institute for their current season. To no avail, of course. Shoot-outs in the Sun: The Treatment of the Duel in Western Movies. Sometimes Horace wondered how to account for his own interest in the cinema, given the pedestrianism and lack of poetry in the souls, if indeed they had souls in the first place, of most of the aficionados. Just because their concern was with a technological art, they clearly felt that the necessary concomitant was an industrialization of vocabulary, whether in terms of the tired clichés aforementioned, or the even more dreadful manifestations of structuralism, post-structuralism, deconstruction, feminist structuralism, heaven knew what, handicapped structuralism possibly, whereby semantic fissure and collapse are taken as an enactment of a tendency towards arthritic paralysis or abrupt amputation in the biological field. We articulate *ourselves* into the narrative weave, an Indian film critic had explained to him at the conclusion of *Gunfight at the O.K. Corral*, via the interpenetration of our vulnerabilities, the director's and my own. Thus, she continued, smoking a cigarette toughly and in abrupt contradiction of the implication of her sari, jewellery, forehead spot, my vulnerability as a woman, functioning within the woman's givens as of our society, circa 1982, responds to the vulnerability implicit in the experience of being shot, which is the fear established – and, when I say fear, she had said, I mean it in the Aristotelean sense, pity and fear, that is to say, *mounting* vulnerability – throughout the movie, and endorsed by the fictional reality of certain individuals' actually *being* shot at the climax. Indeed, the very phrase *being shot*, with its jostling and urgent contradictions, its capacity indeed to shoot itself down . . .

Horace developed the hazy notion that the woman was arguing that to be a woman felt something like being a dead man, but he confined himself to saying, as cuttingly as possible, 'There's no *circa* about it, it *is* 1982. I have one of those useful watches which inform one of the date and the year,' he'd gone on to explain, and then in contradiction of the very spirit of the western movie, had hurried off to safety, pondering as he did so on the powerful identity of his mother, and the fact that she hadn't seemed much like a dead man. Or then again, perhaps on second thoughts she had. It all depended on what you meant by *dead*, of course, not to mention *man*.

Nevertheless, whatever the toing and froing in the *salon*, at a certain point in your existence you did, as it were, mount the stairs, necktie in place and so forth, and head towards your destiny; the time came, Horace reflected, as he trudged down the dirt track of Number 10's hallway, observing the nervous eyes of the citizenry behind their unpainted shutters, the symbolically déraciné tumbleweed bouncing on towards infinity, the merciless light, the time came when a man's gotta do what a man's gotta do. The merciless light in particular emphasized the point, illuminating the analogy, picking your bones, bleaching you white, the remorseless probing noontide neon which Mrs Cheeseman had characteristically had installed at Number

10 over the last year or so. In point of fact it was gone noon; it was almost two in the afternoon. It wasn't gone neon, however, and never would be during her tenure of office. The Inner Cabinet was due to meet at half-past.

He knocked at the door of the Cabinet Room, and entered. If the neon in the hallway was merciless, that in the Cabinet Room was sadistic. Mrs Cheeseman's hair glowed with such intensity you could actually make out reflections of the strip-lighting upon its hammered surfaces. The room was filled with a low hum as streams of light proceeded along their filament tubes. Only principles could survive in this parched landscape and Horace wondered whether his principles were, *as* it were, fully loaded and capable of coping with what they were going to encounter.

'How nice to see you, Horace!' Mrs Cheeseman exclaimed, putting her pen down. She behaved for all the world as if this were an unexpected treat, blandly ignoring the fact that he had spent the morning in frantic negotiations with various of her minions in order to be granted the audience.

'And, as always, to see you too,' Horace replied in his most charming tones.

'What is the weather doing outside?'

'Tempestuous, Prime Minister. I was quite buffeted during my short sprint from the closed car to this sanctuary.'

'Oh dear, poor Horace!'

'Oh, I enjoy such brief interludes *en plein air*. One dips a toe, as it were, into the nitty gritty and then retires abruptly to a womb-like interior. No offence, of course.'

She replied with a short silence and a steely smile. 'At least your little excursion –' she surveyed his whole person for a few moments with surgical intensity – 'didn't ruffle your plumes. Not a hair out of place. But talking of hair, Horace, I see you're becoming a little thin on top. I never noticed it before.'

'It happens to us all, Prime Minister. At least, begging your pardon, it happens to us men.'

'As long,' she replied rather menacingly, 'as it is not the result of the cares of office. We couldn't permit that.'

That was placing her cards on the table. There was nothing for it but for Horace to do likewise.

'I was worried about a certain implication behind the Durrant Report,' he said. 'There was something I thought it would be better to broach in privacy before the meeting began.'

'Oh yes?'

'I was struck by the possibility that the proposed naval cuts were a straw in the wind. That they indicated the imminent prospect of a conflict which could heavily involve *er* the navy.'

There was silence. Horace noticed that the hum of the neon had intensified, just as at a bleak crossroads the flap of a bird's wing, the trudge of feet in compacted dust, the beating of the sun, intensify. Mrs Cheeseman's eyes glittered appraisingly at him.

'Horace,' she said at length, 'I must say I'm very impressed by the extent of your political development since you've been a member of the Inner Cabinet.'

Suddenly Horace felt panic. The prospect of a shoot-out in the sun had been bad enough, but what, but what, if the confrontation *itself* should prove to be impossible? What if, having as it were squeezed the universe into a ball, he discovered that she was merely going to toss it back to him?

Horace reviewed Joseph Harper's claim that everything that had happened, and was going to happen, participated in a remorseless dialectic. One arranged to withdraw a South Atlantic patrol vessel in order to commit oneself to South Atlantic interests; one threatened to cut the navy in order to launch possibly the biggest fleet of modern times; one placed a wimp in the Inner Cabinet so that the Cabinet could administer a war. If this was so, poor Horace was not a gunfighter confronting his destiny but a leaf tossed in the wind. If this was the case, moreover, Mrs Cheeseman was the cat that lay in wait. But the fact of his leafiness, the fact of her cattiness, these facts were not determined by either of them as individuals but by the fundamental arrangements of the universe at large, a universe that could not be squeezed into a ball but obstinately resolved itself into *two* balls, between which thought, experience, history, shuttled with frantic futility. In short, Mrs Cheeseman's apparent toughness was in reality a coloration from the intractable procedure of events themselves, the after-image of the nitty-gritty. Essentially she was quite different from what she seemed, she was the soft medium in which history, for the moment, was embedded. That Indian woman's talk of an interpenetration of vulnerabilities suddenly came back to him. Heavens, perhaps her structuralist jargon had been correct after all. As he'd listened to it he'd felt as if he were witnessing the very birth of clichés, a form of words so dull that even though you'd never come across it before it nevertheless struck you as tired, trite, above all without life. But on the other hand what were clichés but inert truths? For a second the dark face of the Indian structuralist superimposed itself on Mrs Cheeseman's brilliant one, and entered Horace's imagination, via a deft sideways skip along the gamut of oriental religions, as a gaunt female version of that platitudinous Buddha who could make even *one* hand clap.

Nevertheless, as out of the strong comes forth sweetness, so out of dialectic, synthesis. That was Joseph's word of course, or one of them, but it struck a chord in Horace. What was the Third Sex, but synthesis? His own experience should have told him that one didn't have to accept duelling as the answer. Joseph used other words too: pantheism, at-one-ness, ecology. Service.

Joseph had been working for months on the problem of introducing Keynesianism into the economy without a) anybody noticing and b) resorting to war. The task had been made all the more nightmarish because he was not of course an economist at all, but simply an applier of other people's economic theories. Nevertheless he had hammered out some sort of solution: service industry. The point, of course, was that one couldn't construct TVA-style dams indefinitely and in any case there was a contradiction built in to projects of that kind: they had an end-product. But to convert the economic infrastructure of the UK into a vast system of service industries avoided, or at least minimized, that difficulty. Insurance, tourism, banking, entertainment, above all high tech, all produced the most intangible of end-products; moreover they could lead to a cultural shift in which large-scale unemployment became the sine qua non in a new celebration of leisure values, a kind of catholicism of self-expression to replace the old puritan work-ethic. No, Joseph corrected himself, that was swinging the pendulum *too* far. To *complement* the old puritan work ethic. Because one had to *work* at leisure. Synthesis. The phrase was service *industry*.

Now Horace thought about it, that phrase had its points of similarity with *being dead*. Service: abstract; Industry: grimy. Service: generous; Industry: cruel. Service: human; Industry: mechanical. Yes indeed, the contradictions were urgent enough to satisfy one's every need in that direction.

Joseph had put his proposals to Mrs Cheeseman on a number of occasions over the last few weeks, but each time she had turned a deaf ear. She was polite, but uninterested. Or, to use her own word, she was resolute.

'The point is, Bentley, she's hypnotized by that slogan, the "Right Direction". She's proud of never changing course.'

'But surely,' Horace had replied, 'she already has, if you're right about this war business?'

'Of course she has. Everybody always does. History is an endless series of zigzags. But obviously if you're always going in the *last* direction, and ignoring the one that's currently being mapped out on your behalf, you give the impression of obstinately maintaining your bearings despite what everybody throws at you. It must have cost her a bundle, switching to a post-Keynesian strategy of fostering a war. But as soon as I come along and offer an alternative, the war solution becomes out-of-date, and therefore begins to feel to her like the "Right Direction" after all. It's a bloody mess, Horace. The more I talk to her about service industries, the more inevitable it becomes that people are going to die out there on Farquhar Island.' He had gone as white as a sheet.

The long and short of it was that Horace agreed to do what he could. The question that then remained outstanding was, of course, what exactly was that? The philosophy of contrarities would suggest that he should *oppose* the military cuts, or at least the naval ones. His grounds, implicit but unarticulated, would be that keeping the armed forces intact would preserve the peace. Unfortunately, however, that same philosophy of contrarities also suggested that Mrs Cheeseman would promptly oppose *him*. Indeed, it was undoubtedly his function as Cabinet wimp to *be* opposed, and thereby to contribute to a public effect of hard-won accord when he was overruled. This being the case, and with time too short to work out a more sophisticated strategy, Harper felt that Horace should march straight in to Mrs Cheeseman, try to dissuade her from war, and endeavour in the most direct way possible to sell her the doctrine of service industry. The fact that Horace was a different source from Harper himself might, just might, give Mrs Cheeseman pause.

'The point is,' Horace now said, 'if there is any question of bloodshed, I would like to put on offer a more civilized alternative.'

'I'm as interested in civilization as you are, Horace,' Mrs Cheeseman said. 'In my own way. That's why I believe that the values of civilization must be defended. I'm sure you would agree with that. There are some unscrupulous powers in this world, Horace. Powers without our standards of behaviour. Powers that might take it upon themselves to challenge the fabric of our civilization. If by proposing to cut the size of our navy, with all that that implies, we can minimize the danger, I think our duty is clear.'

The interpenetration of vulnerabilities. On the one hand, a state lacking in our standards of behaviour. On the other, a navy under threat. Horace felt at a loss for words.

Mrs Cheeseman wasn't.

'Imagine, Horace, imagine an island of ours, thousands of miles away from us across the sea. Imagine we had to go to its aid. Protect it militarily. Support it economically. Preserve its institutions. I'm talking of a limited engagement of course, what our friend Raymond Durrant, with his original turn of phrase, would call a "little grid", but

248

even so, the cost would be huge. Nevertheless, Horace, I think it would be a cost this country would happily bear. It would be the noblest form of service. That's how I for one would regard it. As a form of service. In fact, between ourselves, this is a new principle I intend to formulate, a key to the recovery of this country, both in economic and moral terms. Service industry. It's a phrase to conjure with, don't you think?'

The possibility hadn't even occurred to Harper, nor to Horace himself. War as the ultimate service industry. Was there *any* idea this woman couldn't convert to her own ends?

It had become vital, imperative, for Horace to establish *some* sort of opposition. Even if that meant political suicide. Indeed, possibly the only way one could differentiate onself from Mrs Cheeseman, with her remorseless capacity for survival, was to burn out with a bright flame. But what would Frankie think?

Suddenly Horace had an inspiration – no, more than that, a revelation. His own little Hampstead Heath. This was where he had been heading all along, *this* was what he could offer Frankie. He would burn himself out, politically speaking, on Frankie's behalf. He would take clout into a new dimension altogether. What could be more decisive, forceful, *principled*, than throwing one's own career on the funeral pyre? Clout would flame out, tumescent; clout would be apotheosized.

The logic of his position was now clear. He would have to attack Mrs Cheeseman by exposing his own vulnerability.

'I wonder,' she was saying, 'if you would mind leaving me for a few moments to collect my thoughts? Our meeting will be commencing shortly. Unless you have anything else you'd like to broach with me, that is?'

'There is just one thing,' Horace said boldly. 'Of a rather personal nature.'

'Oh yes?'

'I'm proposing to get married, Prime Minister.'

Mrs Cheeseman's eyes lit up.

'Horace!' she said. 'That's wonderful news! I've been

249

thinking to myself lately that the only thing that stands between Horace Bentley and further political advancement is his bachelor status. This is *exactly* what's required. Do I know the lucky person?'

'You may do,' Horace said. 'He's quite a heavy contributor to party funds. His name is Frankie Rutherford.'

The humming in the neon tubes had intensified to a severe degree. Mrs Cheeseman's smiling, glittering surfaces remained untroubled. The noise had obviously prevented her from taking in the full gist of what he had to say.

'I'm sorry about that row,' she said. 'Do you know, I used to think it was the fluorescent lights that were faulty. Then of course I realized it's dear Derek's electric drill. This room is not quite as soundproof as we've been led to believe. I've known all along that Derek was building a boat of course, but I thought it was one of those little ones in a bottle. However, it turns out to be a full-size one. I went up to his den this morning and saw for myself. I could hardly believe my eyes. I said: Derek, how on earth are we going to launch it? Did you say Frances Rutherford?'

'Yes,' Horace replied.

'Wasn't her maiden name Hartley? How splendid! I was up at Cambridge with her. Always an outdoor type, I remember.' She rose to her feet and took Horace's hand. 'Horace, I'm so pleased.'

As Horace left that piercing room he thought to himself, however much you try to be your own man, this woman would fling out her arms to embrace you, as far as Farquhar Island, if necessary. No shoot-out awaited you in the OK Corral, just a brightly-illuminated, deafening room, no principles, just the interpenetration of vulnerabilities. So on you trudged, in the relentless, icy light, on and on, faster and faster, one two one two, no Third Sex only one two one two the interpenetration of vulnerabilities one two no funeral pyre no transcending clout one two one two Horace and Frances one two the rhythm of the forced march over difficult terrain – what had Raymond Durrant said it was called these days? yomping – no music of the spheres but songs for yomping.

PART TWO

Songs for Yomping

'Far on the ringing plains of
windy Troy.'

CHAPTER FIFTY-FIVE

David

Farquhar Island was an anti-climax in the centre of a surprise, a lump of dun grey rock that rose like an old tooth from a jewelled blue sea. Where the blue sea had come from, goodness knew: it was extraordinary to see its calmness, clarity, radiance, after days upon the turbid waters of the Antarctic region. Presumably some eddy in the currents of the ocean or the bearing of the winds or the passage of the seasons – whatever the cause the effect was of icy dazzle, as bright, uncomplicated, inhuman, as a medieval book of rich hours. Icy certainly; there were no sentimental overtones to its beauty. Even from the deck of the approaching *Expedition* David had sensed a coldness rising from it, just as you can sense heat emanating from a radiator.

The island, though surrounded by this intensity, was monochrome, featureless: a restatement of the facts of ordinariness in the surprising context of its waters. David felt disappointed. He had been hoping for a lessening of the pressure of reality, not a leaden insistence.

His parish was a cluster of white, clean-cut houses, rather surprisingly wooden since the island was treeless, which were positioned between a low hill and a long, narrow, curved inlet of the sea. The church however was local stone, which made it blend in with the scree and tired grass against which it was set to such an extent that the building was hardly visible, particularly with habitual grey cloud hanging above it.

His first Sunday service was attended by what was apparently the maximum congregation, about forty in all. When the service was over he stood by the door shaking hands with his new parishioners and introducing himself to them in turn. Both men and women were dressed in heavy quilted coats or parkas, boots, woollen bobble hats, and the children were miniature versions of their parents.

Greetings and welcomes were offered. The local accent was strange, a little like west country perhaps, or even Australian, but the generosity of broad vowels was mitigated by hard Yorkshirish consonants, as if a northern dourness maintained its control however far south the people might be in other respects. Outside the church porch snow was falling. Rather to David's surprise, however, the congregation didn't disperse after their handshakes, but hung in an uneasy clump on the church path, near a strange construction made, apparently, from a whale's jawbone. Even after David had spoken to the last parishioner to leave, the phalanx still remained, with the snow swirling round it. Beyond was the church wall, and then the ground sloped down past a group of houses, and on to the creek. The details, to David's poor sight, were blurred, but the sea remained strangely blue, although even while he watched its colour began to fade under the onslaught of the weather, like the colour of a dead eye.

'Bit of a bruiser, this,' one of the parishioners called out to him from the throng.

'A bruiser?' David asked, puzzled.

'The weather. You got to get used to the way it takes a corner like this.'

'It's gone very dark,' David agreed. 'And this snow.' He glanced down at his own white surplice, and back up. 'I feel like a snowman myself.'

The people looked back at him, grave-faced. David suddenly realized that in the few days he'd been here he'd not seen anyone laugh. Perhaps not even smile – it wasn't the sort of thing you kept an inventory of. The solemness of the people, the way they huddled together on the path and yet moved restlessly about each other, never quite touching, made him think of penned animals. Nobody seemed to know what to say or do next.

'Oh well,' David said, in as final a tone as possible.

'We were wondering,' one of the men said, 'if you would

come along for some eats and drinks. To get acquainted. Pre-lunch.'

It had been done with the cumbersome false casualness of adolescent courtship, and touched David correspondingly – despite the inconvenience. He wanted to get back to his white wooden rectory and be alone. But nevertheless drinks were a thought. He'd – warily – drunk his share on the *Expedition*, but had had none since he arrived on the island. Of course it would be tantalizing as usual, downing a sherry or two when he wanted beer, but it would plug him into the quid pro quo circuit, mean that he could order some booze in return, from wherever you ordered it, without eyebrows being raised.

The man was a farm manager called Douglas Grant. He and his wife Jennifer led the way up a stony track towards their house which was positioned further up the hill than the rest of the settlement. The whole congregation, plus David, struggled in their wake, all leaning forward at the same angle against the wind and snow, miming the slope of the ground.

The Grant household contradicted its bleak surroundings, being stuffed full of fancy bric-à-brac. There were imitation horse brasses, china women in milkmaid outfits, book club books in leatherette binding, an electronic organ which worked, Duggie proudly explained, from the farm generator. You could press a button and it played various sorts of dance rhythm all by itself. Duggie demonstrated.

'Sometimes it goes a bit slow,' he told David, 'when the juice isn't coming through full force.'

'I see,' David replied, puzzled. Sure enough, whatever rhythm it was sounded flaccid and demoralized, a foxtrot Farquhar-style.

'Eats and drinks!' called Jennifer, coming in from the kitchen pushing a trolley. It was obviously a set phrase in these parts. On the trolley were crisps, peanuts, cups and saucers, an enormous bone china teapot. David's spirits plummetted. A teapot! Was this the idea of celebration on Farquhar Island? A teapot, decorated, floral, almost translucent, but built on the scale of a canteen urn. Of course it would be, the logic was clear. At this distance from the trammels of civilization the insecurities of sub-Antarctica expressed themselves in orgies of cosiness, in expensive teapots modelled with priapic exaggeration. More English than the English, these people would not even offer their man of God a glass of sherry. David watched as Duggie went the rounds, pouring a slug of whisky in the men's cups. He, David, was excluded. His religious role would make him an honorary woman. He had already discovered they were great respecters of women down here, they had to be. Only one man in two was married, and there were, apparently, only two unattached women on the whole island.

Needless to say the crisps were stale.

Jennifer stepped over to talk to him. She was about forty, well-rounded, pretty. Her features seemed to insist on approaching a smile, despite the prevailing solemness.

'I thought I'd take a break in my hostessing for a minute,' she said. 'Are you enjoying your tea?'

'It's very nice,' David replied.

'We make a good cuppa down here. It's the water, you know. Peaty. So it's a good cup of tea if you like peaty tea.'

David looked at her as intently as he dared, to see if she was joking or not. Certainly her expression was hovering on the brink of amusement, like a solution that was near saturation point. He had a strong and immediate sense that she, out of all the people he'd so far met here, took an independent line. How did you show it in a place where geographical constraints were matched by social claustrophobia? By being the same as everyone else of course, but with a faint, dry exaggeration. Good heavens, thought David, her teapot is ironic! He had a sense of the tension, frustration, discipline, involved in maintaining her stance, in living a lifetime of suppressed laughter.

'You meet us at an exciting point in our history,' Jennifer said.

'Do I?'

'Yes. It's catty time. Only happens twice a year.'

David had a sudden mental picture of a Farquhar festival

256

of misrule, in which the decorum and reserve of the islanders gave way to flyting, bitchiness, abuse. It was suggestive, he reflected, that every time he had tried to explain people's behaviour to himself during his brief experience of the social life here he resorted to imagery of Bacchic excess, of repression giving way to anarchy.

'Catty time,' he said thoughtfully.

'The catalogues come through. You know. Jonathan Edwards. Great Universal Stores. Mail order.'

'Oh, I see.'

'It's our chance to get ourselves fixed up. Buy our Princess Di frocks and suchlike. Of course it's always the wrong season. The spring ones are just coming through now that winter's on us. But that doesn't matter a lot because by the time our orders arrive it'll be practically the right time of the year after all. At the moment we're all mulling over the new stuff on offer. Catty time's a great event on Farquhar Island.'

'I suppose it would be.'

'You're not married then, reverend?'

'Was. I'm a widower.'

'Oh, I'm very sorry.' She spoke not exactly insincerely but without surprise. She was obviously just confirming what she already knew, testing the ground.

'Yes. Thank you,' he replied.

'Recent?'

'A couple of years ago.'

'Oh dear. That's a great pity. Would you like another cuppa? There's more tea in the pot.' She looked at him again with that odd infectious imminence in her face, as if daring him to laugh. 'There's always more in the pot.'

'That's very kind,' David replied, handing her his cup. She carried it over to the trolley, and filled it. Then she brought it back. Just before she gave it to him however she obviously thought of something.

'Hang on,' she said, and squeezed through the relative bustle of the room to Duggie. David watched her speak to her husband, who looked puzzled, glanced rapidly back towards David, shrugged his shoulders, and poured a tot of whisky in the cup. Then Jennifer carried it back.

'Thought you might like to warm your cockles,' she explained.

'That's very kind. My cockles could just do with it.'

'Mind you, the snow's stopped.'

'Has it?' David stepped over to a window and looked out over his small clustered parish, and the sea beyond. There was a skin of snow over everything, but the sky was a paler grey than before, and the iris of the sea had reverted to its piercing blue.

Jennifer's whisper at his side came through, soft and intense.

'I'll come over to your place later. Something's up. I've got to have a word.'

CHAPTER FIFTY-SIX

David

At least there were no ghosts in David's vicarage: everything was new. The three-piece suite, the light oak sideboard, the pine table and dining chairs, the fitted kitchen. That was rather odd really, considering there had been a vicar here until a few months ago. Possibly things had deteriorated during his ministry. Domestic things. Perhaps the contents of the vicarage had been in a shocking state. Who was it, somebody famous had – oh yes, Beethoven. When Beethoven sat on a chair it had to be thrown away afterwards. So they said, anyway. It was probably a legend, even a sort of allegory. All that music coming out of his mind, so something grisly, by a process of compensation, must be extruded from the other end.

Talking of laws of compensation, what was David doing now, sitting in a pristine, ghost-free residence, and building a past presence for it, something fecal, rotting, pervasive? There was a painting, *American Gothic*, which depicted spare, New World, wooden architecture, blank simplicity, showing no accretions of age, no fingermarks, footprints, bloodstains, no shadows of human commitment, no past. And yet, of course, you could be haunted by a blank.

The vicarage was full of the oily warmth of central heating but David was cold. There was so much wind and weather outside, it was bound to seep in. In England it was cosy sitting on the inside, looking out. On Farquhar Island the sheer pressure of the outside brought it within your walls, however soundly clinkered, and once here it insinuated itself among the paraphernalia of cosiness, like an unexpected shiver, a goose walking over your grave.

David was wearing a sports jacket, corduroy trousers, dog-collar. He had debated whether to put on a polo-necked jersey also but decided against it. If Jennifer Grant wanted spiritual sustenance the visible collar would be a resource for her; if some other sustenance was required it would be a safeguard for him.

No, that was a callous, pompous, above all, a selfish way of looking at it. Protection for her. It was her equilibrium that mattered, not his. Nevertheless, he felt restless waiting for her. He ought to settle down to something. The village history, his old recourse, now seemed irrelevant, quite apart from the fact that his source materials were on the other side of the world.

He ended up irritably rummaging through one of his packing chests of books, finally picking out a volume of Cézanne reproductions. He stopped leafing through it at one of the *Grandes Baigneuses* series, remembering a TV sketch about the painting at the time when there was a public campaign to prevent it from being exported from Britain. Two dirty old men in mackintoshes had shuffled past it, one expounding its finer points to the other: in particular, how the bums followed you round the room as you walked. Lorna had laughed until she nearly wept. At the time he'd felt her reaction was partly a rebuke directed at what she called his 'po-faced' attitude to art. The human countenance as a bottom, the ultimate blank look. Beethoven. Of course he'd taken her point, it was a point he clutched at eagerly during all their time together. He'd laughed too. And yet the point had missed its mark. Cézanne himself was the po-faced one, and he was po-faced because he established no hierarchy between po and face, and therefore could see nothing amusing in juxtaposing the two or substituting one for the other. His bathers' arses were simply part of the scenery. He had painted a picture, not performed an exercise in the picturesque.

There was a soft knock at the front door. David put his book down and walked, with deliberate casualness, although no one could see him, to answer it. There was just the dark outside. The light from his small vestibule disappeared into it immediately and abruptly. Then, suddenly, there was a movement from one side, from along the house wall, and a small oval form, in quilted coat and bobble hat, pushed past him and into the house. David shut the door, his heart simultaneously sinking and pounding. So it *was* to be furtive and difficult. He could imagine Lorna's glee at his discomfiture.

'You took me by surprise,' he said.

'Well, you heard my knock.'

'Yes.'

'I'm so sorry. But people easily get the wrong end of the stick down here.'

'I see. In that case, what about your husband? Duggie.'

'No problem. He knows I'm here.' She was pulling off her hat and coat. 'I said I'd come to see you about the altar. We can't put flower arrangements on it as a rule. Too few and far between. Do you mind if I take my boots off, it's mucky on the track. That snow's turned into goo, wait until the winter comes proper.'

'Of course not.'

'I should have brought me little furry slippers with me, but I didn't think of it.'

She was wearing a blue woollen dress that was clearly thick and warm, yet showed her contours at the same time. One stockinged foot gently, almost shyly, toed the other one. David felt a slight tremor run through his body.

'Go on in, Mrs Grant,' he said.

'Thank you,' she replied, and headed into his living-room. He followed. She sat down in an armchair opposite the one where he'd been looking at his book. 'Don't call me Mrs Grant,' she said. 'It's Jennie.'

'Ah yes.'

'Duggie. Jennie. Everybody on this island ends in "ee". That's because we're all very friendly, I suppose. That ends in "ee" too. We're so friendly that we all know each other's business, which makes it much easier to gossip and stab each other in the back. You'll probably end in "ee" soon enough. Although being a parson you might be immune. The last one was called Twitch.'

'Was he?'

'He used to make involuntary movements during his sermons.' She looked up at him with that plump, so nearly amused face. 'Only of his arms, I may add.'

'Call me David,' David said.

'It's a bit frosty in here, David.'

'I thought so too. I've got the central heating full on.'

'What you want is a peat fire in the stove. I'll show you how to light one some time.'

'Thank you.'

'We're a peaty lot, us Farquhars, with our peat fires and our peaty tea.'

'Talking of which,' David said, 'can I make you a cup of tea?'

'There's no need. I've got a bottle in my handbag. It's a nice big bag, all the necessities of life in it.'

She opened her bag and pulled out a half bottle of whisky. 'See!' she said, with something of the air of a conjuror pulling a rabbit out of a hat. Then her expression faded, went dull, as if she had suddenly thought of something melancholy. She wasn't looking at him but slightly to one side.

'I'll get some glasses,' he said.

'Do,' she replied, perking up again.

He went into his smart kitchen and brought two glasses back.

'Those tumblers, I'm afraid. They must think vicars only drink lemonade.'

'All the better,' she said, and poured out a large measure for each of them. He resumed his original chair and looked across his glass at her. She took a quick drink from her glass, with that self-consciousness of a woman drinking, as if it's really a private matter made public through some social accident. She lowered her glass and swept a hand briskly over her bosom, not provocatively – to David's relief and disappointment – but rather by way of checking if it was still there.

'You were saying,' David said, 'that something had cropped up.'

'I was lying,' she replied baldly.

'I see.'

'Not exactly lying. But what I meant was, nothing's cropped up. Nothing ever crops up.' She was speaking perfectly calmly, without intensity. In fact she had her not quite amused look on her face, as if she were coolly inspecting herself as she spoke and was not quite amused at what she saw. 'You've only been here a week,' she continued, 'but I imagine it's struck you. Nothing ever crops up here. I'll tell you what, David,' she said, at last turning her eyes to him, 'the most exciting thing that ever happens to me is whisky.'

'Of course it's always a bit of a lonely existence, being in farming,' David said.

She had obviously been over this ground before. 'You know what they say,' she said, 'you die alone. Well, if that were true, it shouldn't make any difference whether you die on some faraway planet or at home surrounded by all your bawling friends and relatives. But it does. It sure as eggs does.'

'Surely we're talking about living, not dying?'

'What's the difference?' Even now, there was no edge to her voice; her feelings might be strong, but they followed well-worn grooves.

But of course, in his own way, he'd been over some of this ground also.

'I suppose, when they look at a place like this,' he said, 'people might think, good heavens, nothing's going on, there's no cinema or theatre. But how many people who live in London, say, actually go regularly to the cinema or the theatre? In the end it's all a matter of other people. Just people. And there are people here like everywhere else.'

'I've been on this island for nearly ten years,' she said quietly. 'If you tell me there's nothing different anywhere else it gives me nothing even to hope for or imagine.'

She drained her whisky and poured herself some more. She waved the bottle at David. He got up, a little shakily, and went over with his glass. He was excited by her and what was worse he had a sense of Lorna's shade thoroughly endorsing his response, of welcoming the fact that he'd come alive again, even though these new stirrings were taking place in a complete cul-de-sac, both geographically and ethically. Surely, surely, he thought, as he watched the brown pour of the drink, the myth of Venus rising from the waves must amount to more than this. Did it refer solely to the mindless readiness of the phallus to stand itself erect, whatever the circumstances? Was it simply a narrative method of making the point that the erotic can appear out of the blue? He took his drink and hurriedly sat down again.

'But there's your husband, Duggie,' he said, almost in desperation. '*You*'re not alone.'

'Oh Duggie,' she replied. 'Playing his electric organ. Oompah oompah. Stick it up your jumper.'

Suddenly she laughed. Her laugh crackled from her chair to his, probably via the thought of Duggie's organ, like a leap of electricity. She laughed! It was as if a new layer of her face altogether had been exposed, as if somewhere among her features something had been unzipped. David recoiled in fear. She was laughing at her husband! He, David, represented the zipper-up of the marital relation, and here she was laughing about it to his face, inviting him to join in. And he could feel the bubbles of laughter rise, the analogy in experience was so seductive, all that laughing between himself and Lorna. But that had been within wedlock of course, the analogy didn't hold. Jennie's was an outburst of long-repressed Farquhar laughter.

Farquhar laughter.

David was suddenly tipsy. The charged atmosphere must have added to the whisky's potency. He had a vision of this island, so long so low on the human horizon, suddenly rising from its blue waters and proving to be the hump of some enormous sea-monster. There was that whale's jaw-bone in his churchyard, so much scaffolding, so little articulation; he sensed its massive presence lurking behind Jennie's small, pretty face. His damped down laughter came out as a sympathetic murmur.

Her laughter faded away but its sexuality remained in the room. The whale in the rectory. It seemed so pagan to have an animal's bones in a churchyard; on the other hand what about that wooden device at Saxton to which the dreadful Frankie Rutherford had objected so vehemently? An economic indicator in the Lord's garden, set for so long at 1766, like a jammed altimeter in a time machine. Churches *were* time machines after all, with their offer to take you back to the source of your yearnings.

'You'll have to excuse me a moment,' David said. He rose to his feet, left the room, and went upstairs to his lavatory, where he rapidly masturbated. Better to masturbate than to burn. However contemptible it might seem, it was a way to crank yourself back towards parsonical objectivity. He thought of his predecessor with his involuntary movements. Twitch. The unpleasant part of it all was that if there *were* a God you could never be private. Although David felt he had no choice in doing what he did he also had a disagreeable sense of the possibility of being observed while he did it. A God who was prurient, disapproving, relentless, that Pauline figure from whom Lorna had, for her lifetime at least, emancipated him.

Suddenly David realized that he was thinking of God as the Fat Man.

CHAPTER FIFTY-SEVEN

David

It all happened very quickly. News came through that a party of Costanaguan scrap merchants had landed on the nearby uninhabited dependency of South Hanover and begun to dismantle a disused whaling station there. Costanagua had not, of course, asked permission, either of the British authorities or the Farquhar council. A small party of marines, the total force stationed on Farquhar, was shipped over to South Hanover to evict the trespassers. Then Costanaguan troops landed on Hanover and captured the marines. The Union Jack was lowered down the flagpole of the empty, unwanted, unecological whaling station; the Costanaguan one was raised. Four days later occupying forces arrived at Port Livingstone, capital of Farquhar Island, which was now, of course, completely undefended. Within hours the island had capitulated. The *Expedition* was recalled from its voyage to the UK, but of course it was too lightly armed to do anything but cruise impotently at a safe distance.

A few days later troops covered the slopes around Swan Creek like a green winter. It was perfectly silent. About an hour afterwards there was a single loud bang as a cannon on a Costanaguan frigate fired a warning shot at the shore. Half an hour later another report, somewhat softer; half an hour later still, a distant dull thud. The Costanaguans were marking out their new boundaries.

The troops melted away, leaving twenty-odd men camping on the hill overlooking the Swan Creek inlet. Duggie and David were summoned to see the area commander, who explained in graceful English that nobody was to have any fear, the residents must continue with their ordinary life, the only restriction on freedom would be a dusk to dawn curfew for the time being, hopefully nobody would do anything foolish, no supplies would be appropriated by the troops except where necessary, perhaps a few sheep, you understand. Plenty of them here. Plis, not worry the head. We are not your enemy, we are your fren. An impish smile. Perhaps, soon, your countrymen.

David went the rounds, but really the people were very calm. Mainly they felt a bitter resentment against Britain. But of course within a couple of days came the announcement that Mrs Cheeseman was sending an enormous fleet. Resentment passed through jubilation and became fear. The local commander, whom David had to see every two or three days, lost his urbanity. At least, thought David selfishly, Jennie Grant couldn't continue to complain that nothing ever cropped up. Sometimes, succumbing to the anxiety and paranoia that was developing throughout the community, David began to feel that the whole situation was some sort of monstrous punishment for his attempt to escape from the loneliness of his life in Saxton into some limbo where he could search out his past.

The world was reaching out large hands to grasp his sanctuary.

CHAPTER FIFTY-EIGHT

Terry

It wasn't an aristocratic menu, it wasn't even on Downing Street level. Train smash. Pig turds. Thread worm. Cow pats. Eyeballs on toast. It wasn't in fact up to the standard of the food that he'd served between Southampton and Le Havre. But still, Terry found himself taking a pride in it.

For one thing, he was actually doing the cooking. Not that much real cookery was involved. Poached eggs. Tinned spaghetti. Tinned soup. Sausages. Instant potato, beefburgers, tinned vegetables. Freeze dried curry. Tinned fruit salad. But that was nobody's fault, supplies and space were limited, and Terry made a point of serving everything

266

as appealingly as possible. And the men were hungry, ravenous. The combination of sea air, the boredom of an 8000-mile journey on a cramped ship, and their nervousness about what would happen to them when they arrived on Farquhar Island, had made them obsessed with food. They gobbled down what they were given, they came back for more, they were full of compliments. Terry would stand in the galley passing trays through the hatch to the counter staff, and exchange banter with the men as they queued for grub, and for the first time since he had worked as a barman in a pub, years before, he felt that he belonged. He had a niche.

He didn't mind the long, slow journey. At least they were *going* somewhere. The eternal shuttling between Southampton and Le Havre could drive you crazy if you thought about it. It wasn't just that you had no ultimate destination; you began to think that there *was* no destination for anybody, anywhere in the world. Sexual frustration only emphasized the point. Of course there were no women at all on this journey, but that made things better. You couldn't feel sexually frustrated in the same way on a ship where there *was* no sex. And the sheer length of the voyage seemed to imply that it would have an outcome. You didn't go to the end of the world for nothing.

The ship bellied slowly, in a long diagonal, across the whole of the Atlantic Ocean, part of a huge extended convoy. She was loaded with jeeps, armoured cars, diggers, tracked supply vehicles, and on what used to be the passenger decks part of an infantry battalion was quartered. In the short period between being requisitioned and sailing, the car ferry had received two small anti-aircraft cannon on her upper deck, one fore and one aft. Otherwise she was very much as usual, and therefore strangely out of place in the middle of the sea and in the company of warships. All the more reason to feel pride in her, and in oneself.

Terry slept where he worked, in the galley. At least this meant he had access to running water, and could keep shaved and clean, which was more than most of the soldiers could do. He kept his few possessions neat and tidy and, as always, took care over his appearance. During his short periods of free time he exercised diligently on the upper deck. He felt he'd been born for a war, even if his contribution would have to be measured in terms of meat pie and chips. There was more sheer masculinity involved in doing one's duty in that respect than in toting a shotgun in Frankie's pathetic syndicate, lumbering through the undergrowth in pursuit of crows. This was grownups' business. Sometimes Terry remembered the area insurance office in Market Hanking, and Flowers sitting at his desk looking out of the window, scrutinizing the fine print of the rain. Another world. Or, more accurately, not the world at all. The world was here, in his galley.

Nevertheless it was a relief to get beyond the equator, towards cooler waters. One day the temperature had reached 124 F in the kitchen, and hadn't dropped below 100 all the following night. Terry knew because he had lain awake watching the thermometer as an insomniac might watch his alarm clock. But almost imperceptibly, day by day, the climate changed. Eventually the sea and sky had dulled nearly to the battleship grey of the frigate that cruised about a quarter of a mile astern of them.

But as the temperature sank, tension mounted. The men made fewer jokes about sex, more about war, some of them very sick. Of course they took the approaching climax in different ways. Some were blustering, some quiet, a few were pasty-faced and obviously scared. But all of them ate and ate and ate. Terry once leaned out of his galley hatch and called across the servery: 'All you lot will have to do is sit on the Costies and squash them to death.'

'It won't be the *weight* that does for them,' one of the men replied. He was a Welshman, Gareth Evans, and spoke melodiously. 'They'll be gassed to death by these shirt-lifters you've given us.' He pointed to the green dollop of mushy peas on his plate.

Terry was silent.

Two days before Terry had sailed, while he was still staying at Queen's house in Portsmouth, Jack had come back in the late afternoon from a stroll around the harbour. He'd been watching the Task Force's preparations, and was cheerful, excited. Queen was quite right about his eyes turning blue – certainly he'd never been bright-eyed in Battersea. He talked to Terry about the loading he'd been watching. Terry's boat was going to depart from its usual port, Southampton, and Jack and Queen were going to come along and wave him off.

'It makes me feel I've got a stake in it,' Jack said. 'Best thing we ever did, come down here.' He turned and called out to Queen, who was in the kitchen: 'Is dinner ready yet?'

'What you on about?' Queen called back. 'It's not time for another hour yet.'

'It's the sea air,' said Jack. 'Gives me an appetite.'

'Loafing about bone idle, more like,' Queen said, coming in from the kitchen. 'You haven't got into a routine, that's your trouble.'

'Not interested in it,' Jack said. 'A routine's just a way of filling in time. Down here it's not necessary, there's so much going on.'

'Not where you stand, there isn't,' Queen said. 'There's all that decorating to be done.'

'There's plenty of time, that's what I've been saying.'

'There's plenty of time for your dinner too,' said Queen. 'If you're not going to scrape off the walls you might as well have a sit and read the evening paper.'

'Bugger the paper,' Jack replied. 'Nothing but doom and gloom.'

Terry went up to his room to get on with some packing. Half an hour later Queen called up that dinner was ready.

'That was quick,' Terry said, as he came into the dining-room.

'Look at Jack, talk about quick,' Queen said. 'He's tucking in already.'

Terry took his place.

'I was wondering,' he said to Jack, 'I thought you and me could go out for a pint after dinner. Goodness knows when I'm next going to have the chance.'

Jack turned to face him. 'I don't know,' Jack said. He put another forkful in his mouth, and chewed it thoughtfully. He stopped chewing to say, 'People are always bawling their heads off in pubs.'

'What did you say?' asked Terry. He could feel himself blush.

'I can't remember,' Jack replied. The bright blue eyes slowly closed. With careful, clumsy movements Jack pushed his plate out of the way and, leaving his arms outstretched, he brought his head slowly down to rest on them.

'Would you believe it,' said Terry, 'he's gone to sleep.'

'Sleep, hell!' cried Queen. 'For god's sake, his mouth's full! Empty it, Terry!'

Terry forced Jack's mouth open. Inside, it was green, full of peas. They were a little hard, as Queen hadn't had time to cook them properly, and when he winkled them out they ran about on the table.

'No offence boy-o,' Gareth Evans said.

'You what?' asked Terry.

'Your peas are done to a turn, man. Sheer perfection.'

'Thank you very much,' Terry said. All the men were generous with compliments, the biggest one of all being sheer appetite.

Gareth Evans appeared at the servery first thing the following lunch-time.

'You're in a hurry,' Terry said.

'I've come for a quick pea, isn't it?' Gareth replied. 'No, to tell the truth, the CO wants to see Premo Stone. He wants me to fetch him. I thought to myself, he's sure to roll up here, sooner or later.'

'Premo Stone,' Terry said. 'That's an odd name.'

'They say he used to be Premo Bulge. A pop singer. He sang very nasty stuff, one of them pig singers. It's difficult to be sure, because he was never on "Top of the Pops", like.'

'Oh yes,' said Terry. 'A girl I knew used to be one of his fans.'

270

'Really, now? That is a surprise. From what I remember of the sort of things he sang, I wouldn't have thought he 'ad any fans.' He gave Terry a long, intense look. He wasn't much more than twenty, stocky, dark, with a pale clear face. 'I suppose everybody's got a fan,' he went on. 'Don't you think so?'

'I suppose.'

'Look at you now. The whole blooming ship's company are your fans. The chef. We all have to keep in with you. You're life and death to us, you are.'

'Quite right too,' said Terry blandly, and turned back to his work.

A little later Premo Stone appeared at the servery, and Gareth was able to give him the message. Premo looked anxious.

'I hope you haven't been a naughty boy,' Gareth said.

'Thank you,' Premo said absently, and hurried off.

'There, that's over,' Gareth said to Terry. 'Now I can turn my mind to other things.'

'Would you like your lunch?' Terry asked.

'I wasn't thinking of lunch, to be quite honest,' Gareth said. 'I was wondering what time you came off duty.'

CHAPTER FIFTY-NINE

Premo

The CO's cabin was just below the bridge, and to reach it Premo had to walk across part of the upper deck. He felt himself slowing as he went, although he was in a hurry. The wind blew strong and grey across the grey breakers, and suddenly he didn't have the energy to push himself through it. He leaned against the rail and watched the sea. Dots of white foam flew up from the crests of the waves, cold as snow. He tried to remember Nicola's face, but he couldn't. She wouldn't come into focus. Wherever he looked there was nothing but sea and sky, and the white dots. It was an unfocussed scene. Nicola had freckles, he remembered that. Something strange began to happen.

At the horizon the sea was calming and turning blue. It was an unexpectedly happy colour, as if it wasn't simply another sort of sea but another sort of place altogether, although no land was visible. Premo felt a kind of impatience at being pestered by the CO when he would like to stay here at the rail and watch the blueness spreading. He walked over to the CO's door.

'There you are,' said the CO. He was a plump man, pink-faced, jowly. He was wearing an army sweater with no insignia. He wasn't wearing his regulation tie and his shirt collar was open. Premo got the impression that he'd deliberately dressed casually to see him.

'Yes,' Premo said.

The CO got up from his desk, came round, and sat on it. He motioned to a chair.

'Sit down, Stone.'

Premo sat down.

'I don't believe in beating about the bush, Stone.'

'No, sir.'

'I have to break some very bad news to you, I'm afraid.'

Premo felt a peculiar desire to be thoughtful and understanding towards the CO, as if, because he had the bad news and Premo didn't, the bad news belonged to the CO.

'I'm very sorry, sir,' he said.

'It's about your wife.'

'Yes, sir.'

'As you know, she was expecting a baby.'

Suddenly a wild hope arose in Premo. Perhaps it was just the baby. Perhaps the baby had died.

'Thank you, sir,' he said stupidly.

'I don't think you follow me, Stone,' the CO said with a touch of asperity. Then his voice softened. 'She's very ill, I'm afraid.'

'The baby?'

'Your wife.'

'I see,' said Premo. Again he felt a desire to make things easier for him. 'Oh well,' he said resignedly.

272

'Yes, *very* ill,' the CO said. He raised his eyebrows a little at Premo, as much as to say, do you follow my drift?

'How ill, sir?'

'She's dead, I'm afraid, Stone. Died in childbirth.'

All Stone thought was: now I've *got* to remember her face. He tried, quickly, but couldn't. It was almost the same with the conversation. He could of course remember what they were talking about but he couldn't think how to talk about it.

'Oh dear, sir. I'm sorry, sir,' he stumbled out.

'Of course you are, Stone,' the CO said comfortingly. 'And so am I.'

'I didn't know people died in childbirth these days,' Premo said, as if he were interested in the medical side of the problem.

'She was a frail girl, I understand.'

'She ate a lot, sir. After we got married.'

'I'm very pleased to hear it, Stone,' the CO said, as if they were talking about a death-bed conversion. There was a long silence.

'And what about the baby?' Premo asked eventually.

The CO slid off the desk and walked over to him. He rested an arm on his shoulder, and looked down at him with small intent eyes. He cleared his throat, grunted. 'The baby is alive,' he said. 'But.'

The sea is all blue now. The breakers have gone, to be replaced by choppy, faceted waves. The sea is sharp and bright blue; the air is still and icy. I stand at the rail, looking at the bright blue sea. The sky is grey, and is outshone by the sea. I look at the hard blue waves so hard that they form into Nicola's face. I can see her face, so I know she is dead. It is a blue face, with no freckles.

A speck appears over the horizon. It is a white dot, set against the dark brownish grey of the sky. It is approaching very fast. Pigs have wings. It is a fighter plane. As it nears it drops something. I don't know what it is. Like dropping a baby. But.

The white dot curves off, fades. Its offspring continues to approach. It is getting so near, no effing joke.

CHAPTER SIXTY

Terry

Gareth Evans was waiting outside the servery when Terry finished his lunch shift.

'So here you are then. Finished. Do you fancy a chat?' he asked as Terry pulled the hatch-blind down.

'Why not?' said Terry. 'But I like to have a wash after I've done the lunches. Get rid of the smell of food.'

'Of course, of course,' said Gareth. 'I'll just wait out here.'

Terry went back into his kitchen. His counter staff had already gone off-duty, so he had the place to himself. He gave himself a good strip-wash at the sink, and then put some cream on his athlete's foot, which had got even worse since he'd taken up a life at sea. Hardly surprising, really: swimming pools were what gave you athlete's foot, and being on a ship was like being on the edge of a swimming pool all the time, except that the water was on the outside.

Instead of dressing in a new set of whites, he put his civilian clothes on for some reason. He was quite entitled to do so of course, not being a member of the armed forces, but normally he didn't bother; in fact if he wasn't doing exercises he took a sort of pride in going about in his chef's kit, which he kept white and well pressed. It was, after all, the uniform in which he was going to fight the Farquhar war. Now, though, he had a sense of occasion, the first for a long time. He put on a shirt, a pair of grey flannels, a sports jacket.

'Good gracious, man,' Gareth said. 'I 'ardly recognized you. I thought to myself, here's some big tycoon, come to buy up the whole bloody ship. Why don't you buy Farquhar Island while you're about it, I thought, only cost you a few bob. Then you could give it away to charity and write it off as a tax loss. I hear these Farquhars are nothing but a lot of sheep-shaggers when all's said and done. Save us all a lot of bother. Only kidding, Terry. But you do look, what they call it, the bee's knees.'

'Thank you very much,' said Terry. 'Do you mind if we just go up on deck a minute? I wouldn't mind a breath of fresh air.'

'It's bloody cold up there, knock the breath out of your body, man.'

'At least the ship's behaving,' Terry said. 'So there's not a storm.'

In fact, when they went up on deck they saw that the sea was blue and still. For nearly a week the ship had been tossed about by grey breakers, and the calm seemed almost unnatural. There was no wind but if anything it felt even colder than recently; the flat enveloping chill reminded Terry of his deep freeze. Further along the deck Premo Stone was leaning over the rail, watching the sea.

'Bloody hell,' said Gareth. 'It wasn't like this earlier on.'

'It's funny, the sea being so blue while the sky's grey,' Terry said.

'You know what this means, don't you?'

'No? What?'

'It means we're getting there, boy-o, that's what.'

'My god,' said Terry.

'That bloody Farquhar Island must be just below the horizon,' Gareth said glumly.

They both looked in silence at the flat horizon. Terry had all the sensations of arrival, and they filled him with fear. The empty horizon looked like nowhere at all.

'Tell you what, let's go down to the vehicle deck,' Gareth said. 'There's something I want to show you. It's cold as charity up here.'

They clanged their way down the iron steps until they reached the vehicle deck. It was very dark here, with just a couple of low wattage bulbs going in the whole area, and it took a few moments for Terry to make out the looming forms of the chained vehicles in their three rows.

'Come down this way,' Gareth said, squeezing into a narrow passageway between two jeeps. Terry followed. There was the smell of grease and metal, and through your feet the grinding of the ship's engines, only a deck below. Terry bumped himself several times on flanges protruding from the muffled vehicles. After a few moments Gareth stopped beside an armoured personnel carrier with caterpillar tracks.

'Now, this is the clever part,' he told Terry. 'You watch.' He hoisted himself up on to the top of the track and then scrambled up to the roof of the vehicle. 'The silly bastards left the lid unlocked.' he said, raising what looked like a hinged manhole cover. 'Come and join me.'

Terry climbed up and lowered himself, after Gareth, through the circular entrance to the vehicle. It was pitch black inside, and he trod on Gareth on the way down.

'Hang on a minute,' Gareth said, pushing back past him and standing with his head in the aperture again. He stretched out, caught hold of the lid, and closed it on them. Now it was blacker than pitch. After the thin blue of the sea the darkness felt thick and almost comforting. Suddenly there was a burst of light. 'See here now,' Gareth said. 'I 'ad the sense to bring a torch.' He placed it on the floor in front of the canvas seats for driver and passenger, and then sat down in the passenger seat. 'Make yourself at home,' he said, pointing to the other one. Terry eased his way into it, and they sat side by side in the darkness with the light of the torch playing upwards on them. 'Think about it,' Gareth said. 'Here we are, on an over-crowded ship, with men kipping on all the floor space, and no privacy whatsoever, and you and me can have a chat in a quiet little room of our own, with no one knowing we're here.'

'How did you find it?' Terry asked.

'Easy,' Gareth replied, 'I looked for it.'

They settled down to their 'chat'. Gareth talked about his childhood in Wales, his first girlfriend; his soft, lilting voice became sad and homesick. Then Terry talked about himself, about his days as a barman at the Castle, then about his career at 10 Downing Street, and the way it came to an end.

'But I did all right out of it,' he said. 'I pinched some of their headed notepaper and forged myself a reference. Got a good job in the insurance business. At least I did until the bloody area manager went through my files and rang up Downing Street to check. Then I got the push, of course.' He didn't say anything about Frankie Rutherford and the shooting syndicate.

'You're a rogue, you are,' Gareth said admiringly.

'Oh, I don't mind living dangerously,' Terry said. 'I suppose I wouldn't be here if I did.'

'Tell you what,' said Gareth,' it's getting very hot in here. I think I'll take my clothes off, if you have no objections.'

Terry didn't reply. Gareth wriggled out of his uniform – all of it. Terry watched him in the torchlight, unsurprised. In fact, it was a relief to see his penis – at least he had one. Oh well, Terry thought, perhaps this *is* where I've been heading, all along. He felt resigned, but deep down he was disappointed. He would have liked the oppositeness of the opposite sex. But this was *some*thing.

The armoured personnel carrier jumped sideways, at least a foot. There was the sound of metal tearing. Gareth shouted something in Welsh. Terry's head and shoulders crashed against the steel wall. Then all was still and silent again, but strangely angled.

Terry, one side of his head singing, scrambled to his feet and pushed up the lid of the vehicle; he inserted his head and shoulders into the aperture. A klaxon became audible. The cardeck was already billowing with smoke.

'Come on,' Terry told Gareth, 'we've got to get out of here.'

'You go on,' Gareth's voice came from below. 'I've got to get dressed first.'

'For God's sake, this place is on fire.'

'I can't come rushing out like this, man. Not the two of us together. Think how it would look.'

'Who's looking?'

'You go on ahead. I won't be a minute.'

'If you insist,' said Terry, and scrambled out.

On the companionways and on the middle deck, men were milling about in every direction. Strangely though they didn't seem to be heading for the steps to the upper deck. It wasn't clear whether they were panicking or trying to be useful. Terry pushed his way through them and climbed the stairs.

Sirens, klaxons were blaring, smoke was streaming up from the side of the ship, but the upper deck was deserted except for the body of Premo Stone. Several planes were heading towards the fleet; the frigate, four or five hundred yards off, was firing towards the sky. Terry looked towards the car ferry guns. No one was manning them!

He pulled himself up the steps of the improvised fore-cannon mounting. Everyone had received instructions on how to handle the guns just in case of such an emergency, although of course at the time Terry had taken it about as seriously as the interminable life-boat drills. He sat himself on the firing-seat. God, so long as he could remember.

One of the Costie jets had peeled off, and was heading for him. All you could make out was a straight white line drawing itself through the sky, as though a second horizon was going to end with *you*. There was the firing button. But how the hell did you operate the power-elevation? Terry couldn't remember for the life of him. He began to crank the manual winder, and the gun slowly rose towards the plane.

For a moment his heart pounded with joy. *This* was what he was born to do. It was another world from Gareth and the personnel carrier, Frankie in his bathroom. The gun and the plane: proper opposites. Terry was born to shoot.

But he couldn't wind it up fast enough, he would never catch the plane, it was all too late. Fire, fire anyway, even if it *was* too late. He remembered how the last crow had risen from the branch at the very moment he squeezed the trigger of the shotgun. Now he was going to die for being exactly as not too bad at all as Frankie had expected him to be; for being a near miss, which is what Frankie had all along wanted. But fire anyway. Better a near miss than nothing at all.

At the second he pressed the firing-button, his turret was hit by a shell from the Costie plane. The gun lurched. He had an immediate sense of his own shells rising up the barrel, striking off through space, bursting against the aircraft; then he span off into the air himself, and all was sea.

A helicopter picked him up within moments. It was hard to struggle into the harness, he was aware of the icy blue all over him. But he didn't care. Beyond his own crippled, smoking ship the Costie plane was still in the act of crashing into the sea.

Terry was the first Farquhar hero.

CHAPTER SIXTY-ONE
David

There had been a battle out to sea, a re-invasion was obviously imminent. The Costanaguans who had been encamped around Swan Creek had left. One day David had struggled up the slope at the head of the inlet to report as usual to the commander and had found a group of soldiers at the top, bent almost double and backing away from him, flinging small plastic discs on the ground as they went, like so many sowers of seed. David realized at once they were laying a minefield. They were obviously being withdrawn in order to regroup elsewhere, perhaps up north, towards the Sound, where everyone expected the British landing to be made. The soldiers were uninterested in David's presence. A minefield was just as effective when it was known about as when it took you by surprise. Nevertheless if he got the chance it would be his duty to inform the British. He cast about for some landmark so that his information would be unambiguous.

There was a large group of stones nearby, exactly on the

crown of the slope overlooking Swan Creek. Now that he inspected it he realized it was the ruin of what once must have been a gigantic cairn. The fallen stones had weathered and crumbled in their present places, so it was old indeed, certainly predating the settlement. In fact it must have marked the site where settlement was possible. It had obviously been built by the early explorers.

David's heart missed a beat as it occurred to him that Tom Hartley himself might have handled these rocks. He felt his cheek glow a little – no doubt by a process of association, since the broken cairn slightly resembled a decaying tooth in a dank green gum. He bent down and touched the stones which long-dead hands had touched.

The minelayers had finished their work and gone. There would be no way in which David could take the initiative in warning the invading forces about the danger here. Radio and telephone links were inoperable; and the minefield that kept the liberating forces out would keep the inhabitants of Swan Creek in. The only hope was that some scout would land by sea, or have the luck to struggle overland unscathed; and David would be able to tell him to pass the message on.

There was a strange lull after the departure of the Costanaguan troops. Life in Swan Creek actually became rather dull again. The settlement decided to keep to the curfew since they hadn't been told to stop, and since no one knew if or when the Costies would return. During the day people conducted their business as well as they could, within the confines the minefield had set. David found the evenings the worst. They were long, dark, unvisited. He would sit by his sputtering peat, reading and looking at reproductions of paintings. He often found himself thinking of Thomas Hartley and his long-ago one-way journey to this very island, with the Fat Man behind him and . . . no one would ever know *what*, in front.

One evening his thoughts took a rather different turn. He was drinking scotch, having managed to lay in several crates of it on the respectable grounds that one needed to accumulate supplies in the face of a siege. As he drank his mind went back to the unparsonical glimpse he'd had, in this very room six weeks ago, of a sexual opportunity. Then suddenly he found himself remembering a similar experience that had taken place long ago, in the late 1940s in fact, when he'd been in his mid-teens.

He had gone to an open-air swimming pool with a friend of his. They'd been taken by the friend's mother, a widowed lady who owned her own car. She was of course middle-aged – probably, David now reflected, about thirty-five – and big-breasted but rather boxy in her no-nonsense 1940s bathing costume. He had lazed alongside her on the edge of the pool while the hot afternoon wore on and his friend diligently swam his quota of lengths.

Suddenly David began to lust after her. Completely out of the blue. The blue indeed. Blue sky, blue pool. That was why he'd thought of it, of course – the waters round Farquhar had the sharp translucent blue of a Hockney pool, a blue not of innocence but of explicitness. Discreetly he had inspected her ample bosom, its shape distorted but not diminished by the seamed and bony structure designed to accommodate it at the front of her bathing costume. Cautiously his gaze wandered downwards to the fascinating spot where the female body curves inward to the groin. She was wide-hipped and in her case this recession had all the abrupt definiteness of a small shelf.

Then David became aware of being looked at and glanced upwards to find that her eyes were watching his watching. For a split second he had felt severe shame: the gross male, reducing everything to its lowest common denominator, the cheeky schoolboy poking his nose into grownups' business, the gawky adolescent showing his naivety. And then suddenly he realized that her eyes were becoming hot, and that the pinkness on her cheeks was not that of anger. He began to experience an erection; he watched her notice it interestedly. His excitement was stimulated by the fact that she was essentially unattractive to him, and too old. This meant that the only common ground between them was sex itself, and he was able to succumb to lust without any romantic modifications.

281

Of course the situation could not be sustained. The swimming baths were crowded and it was very awkward having an erection within one's bathing trunks. After a few moments he slipped into the pool so that the water could have its usual shrinking effect. But since then, somewhere deep in his consciousness, he had had an intuition of pure sexuality that was somehow bound up with the smell of chlorine and the blueness of blue water. Of course, at the time the experience had shocked him – he'd been such a prude during his teens: indeed until Lorna came to his rescue. But the shock had been part and parcel of the excitement.

Now that he was surrounded, if not by the smell of chlorine, at least by blue waters, a middle-aged, parsonical version of that long-ago adolescent excitement suddenly overtook him. There were, after all, Farquhar equivalents. The whisky in the cuppa. The stockinged feet in the rectory. The sexual overture from the married parishioner. There was something extreme about a swimming pool, a sense of being in a specialized compressed environment, with more body about than in the normal world, and those bodies sharply juxtaposed. He remembered his feelings in the tube as he made his way from Shrewsbury to Portsmouth. The press of people, the unintimate intimacies. At the time he'd imagined that he was meanwhile heading towards isolation, a pure, disinterested perspective. How naive he'd been. On Farquhar one was aware of pressure from the sheer tonnage and mileage of ocean, from geographical and social claustrophobia, from conformism. Underneath the homely decorum of the islanders one sensed sexual possibilities just as one sensed the presence of naked bodies under clothing.

He had drunk a lot of whisky, always the tendency of a natural beer-drinker. The usual inhibition as to bulk had prevented him from adequately stocking up on the local brew, horribly known as Seal Bitter, when he was getting his supplies in. A couple of boxes of scotch didn't seem unduly decadent and could be stacked in Duggie's pickup without people giving them a second thought. People.

Who? Duggie? Duggie hadn't even given them a first thought, he was too busy explaining away his own large order, telling David how he and the lads liked to hit the bottle now and then, covering up for Jennie no doubt. But if David had ordered a correspondingly alcoholic amount of Seal Bitter it would have filled the truck and jerked Duggie from defence to silent accusation. So whisky it was, and now David's stomach, throat, mouth, glowed with its warmth. Especially his old cheek, adjacent to the tooth where the ache had been.

As he sat and thought about it, the warmth pulsed. You couldn't call it pain, but his cheek was glowing *very* warmly, in its own cellular rhythm, like some primitive organism that expanded and contracted as informed by its metabolic cycles. And with the perverseness of the somewhat drunk, David kept drinking in the hope that whisky would eventually wash away the sensation that whisky had brought on.

The room began to seem overbright and he turned his paraffin lamp off. The vicarage had no generator of its own, and the rather shaky electrical supply from the Farquhar grid had been cut down to six hours a day since the invasion. The glow of his peat stove was pleasant, however. Duggie and Jennie Grant, brisk, neighbourly, had come round one day to show him how to light it and keep it going. He sat and watched it and fell into an uneasy trance in which he felt that the fire had entered his mouth, and was licking dangerously round his dead tooth. He would snort and gasp occasionally when these moments occurred.

And then he was dreaming. He dreamed he was beside the swimming pool with his friend's mother. Everything was pale, as though his dream had been overexposed. He was sitting on the white concrete while she approached him bulkily. The water in the pool was off-white, with only the faintest wash of blue. The paleness of everything gave David a sense of great heat; his cheek was burning. The woman came nearer. As he looked up at her she seemed very large. She almost waddled. She reminded him of someone. Lorna? His heart thumped. No, not Lorna.

Surely not. He knew what Lorna looked like, he must know. Lorna was generously built, but this person was *fat*.

Of course, that was it. Fat. The pale bulk approaching along the side of the pool wasn't a woman at all, but a man, a fat man. The Fat Man.

In panic David turned away. There was a skinny, toothy adolescent perched on the perimeter of the pool, looking up in alarm. Again David almost recognized him, as one recognizes oneself in an unexpected mirror, without knowing who it is. By the time he realized he was looking at his own, younger self, that self had already become somebody else, a well-built, good-looking youth whose fear seemed strangely out of place on a strong rugged countenance.

The pool had become rugged also; its edge was now irregular, rocky, jutted. The Fat Man continued to approach along it, you could hear his footfalls, thump thump, although David couldn't now see him since he was looking down at the young man instead. His cheek throbbed. The young man's eyes were still raised. David could make out the terror in them.

David woke, heart pounding. The peat glowed; the room was dark; everything was peaceful. The pounding began to fade.

And then he noticed a dancing bauble of light on the opposite wall. For a moment its paleness and incongruity gave him the strange impression that the small sphere contained his dream, like one of those snow-shakers which enclose a miniature scene. No, no, the dream had gone. He was awake. No matter how much whisky you drank, you had to keep the two states separate. The disc of light had the evanescent, intrusive quality of sunlight on a lens, though it was night-time and when he took his glasses off it was still there. He put them on again. Its movements were jerky, erratic. It *must* come from somewhere. He rose to his feet, turned, and looked.

Of course. He had opened the curtains when he put his lamp out. He'd always loved to sense the interaction of indoors and out, even at the risk of Farquhar draughts. On the window, corresponding to the amoeba of light on the opposite wall, was a moving dot. And outside, over his little garden, beyond the window of his church, was the corresponding source: someone was in there, carrying a candle.

His first thought was: the enemy. Defiling the place. Taking out some grudge on it, expressing some fear, demonstrating contempt. No, surely not. They were religious people, the Costanaguans, they wouldn't desecrate a sister church. And they hadn't been in evidence for days. But if not them, some local coming to say his prayers? That seemed equally unlikely. David was aware of the pressure of religious conformism in the sparse community, but not of the sort of enthusiasm which would lead someone to break curfew and risk his life.

His, David's, responsibility was clear. Despite the curfew he was the minister, and it was his duty to investigate.

He opened the door into his hallway, and almost gasped at the cold. The central heating pump didn't work during the time the electricity supply was switched off, of course; and David still wasn't used to the depths of temperature that sub-Antarctica could plumb. What it was like outside, goodness knew. Already he was wearing a thick rollneck sweater and a heavy jacket. Now he put over them a coarse, locally made wool overcoat which he'd bought from the supply store in Port Livingstone. Finally he pulled on his surplice. It would bolster his confidence and act as protection on the off-chance that some returning Costanaguans should challenge him in the act of curfew-breaking. It was all very constricting, and he must look a fool, but it was cold out there.

He opened his front door. Yes, it was cold. The freezing air took his breath away and made the muscles in his back tighten to the point of cramp. His tooth began to ache sharply.

He walked silently down the rectory garden.

CHAPTER SIXTY-TWO

David

Pre-Raphaelite, not Botticelli. A figure in a dark church, floating in a bubble of pale light. But Venus, if Venus it was, was plumpish, sardonic, within the shimmer of her candle.

'Hello,' Venus said.

Light being what it was, so different from water, it had no skin, and you could enter the bubble by gradations, so that in a few moments David found himself within it with her, and the dark church receded to the margins. Jennie was wearing not a parka but a fur coat.

'What are you doing here?' David asked.

'I was coming to see you. I heard noises on my way down the path. I thought it might be a Costie patrol, so I decided it would be safer to come in here. I was going to say I'd come to do the altar. Thank god I found a candle. I'd forgotten that the church doesn't have a generator. You ought to have seen me groping in the dark.'

'I see,' said David. 'You gave me a shock.'

'I hope,' Jennie replied, undoing her coat, 'I'm still giving you one.'

Suddenly David's arms were within her warm and animal coat and he was kissing her. The last lips he had kissed were Lorna's, dead two years; Jennie's were both cool and warm, so that he lost the distinction between hers and his, inside and out. And then her lips reformed themselves for a moment.

'Good grief,' she whispered, 'you're well padded, aren't you?'

He began to shake, inside his layers, with laughter.

'It's like kissing Father Christmas,' she continued, and he nearly laughed out loud with relief that sacrilege could be so good-humoured and sympathetic. When they kissed

286

again he was aware of laughter still ticking over inside, so that his jaw gently vibrated and his tooth pinked into pain occasionally as the vibrations caught it.

And then he became aware of a movement behind him, somewhere in the darkness of the church.

Jennie noticed it at the same time, and they broke their kiss.

'Bloody hell,' she whispered, 'that better not be Duggie.'

'Oh no,' David whispered back.

'Don't worry,' she said. 'He was playing foxtrots on his organ when last heard of.' Then her voice shrank even lower, with fear. 'Perhaps it's a Costie.'

They waited. Whoever it was had left the door open, and the candlelight blew and swayed. Slowly a man's shape grew less dark against the darkness; they could hear quiet panting, and stumbling footsteps.

And then, fleetingly, the light caught the man's face, and David recognized it as a face in his dream. Rugged and handsome beneath the grime, but the features unexpectedly twisted into fear, the eyes wide, alarmed.

Tom Hartley.

The eyes appeared again in the flickering light and this time David was able to make out the shape of the terror in them. Tom's eyes reflected a pale, wide, tapering form, unnaturally. swollen, illuminated in the white ambiguous light. The form of David himself. David was the Fat Man.

CHAPTER SIXTY-THREE

David

The church smelled of sex, of whisky. Why not? There was nothing more materialistic than the process of resurrection. It brought everything down to earth, that was the whole point. The candle had gone out but it didn't matter.

He'd seen what he had come to Farquhar Island to see. Tom Hartley. He understood now that he'd been Tom's pursuer all along, galloping over half the world like some picaresque hero in search of what he'd lost, intuiting that Tom would lead him to Lorna. Tom and Lorna were two of a kind, after all, fellow-denizens of the past. It suddenly seemed to David that the division between the living and the dead was as significant as that between the sexes: half the members of the human race lived, mysteriously, on the other side.

Tom had now returned to the darkness which had hidden him for so long; Jennie had vanished also. But at last David was not alone, having achieved whatever strange adulterous alchemy converted the present into the past which underlay it. The living past. For he hadn't merely seen Tom Hartley: he'd seen what Tom's dead eyes had seen.

Two centuries ago Tom had arrived here as a member of an exploratory, and colonizing, expedition. No doubt he'd been sent off to lay claim to some section of the island, perhaps to find a site suitable for settlement. Yes, of course. And to identify the chosen place in this anonymous, repetitive, desolate land he would build a cairn.

David stood in his dark, cold church, imagining that distant journey. There were no trees to break the gales into manageable portions, but a bare, rocky landscape with naught but the most intractable and determined grasses and mosses growing upon it; and over that wilderness the bitter southern wind blew without ceasing, and in the crevices and outcrops it rubbed its massive bulk and stretched its sharp claws, and over all the dismal breadth of country it raised a lupine muzzle and – in short, it howled. And across the howling wilderness Tom walked all alone, his back bent under the weight of salt beef, biscuits, and a portion of sail with which to erect a rude shelter during Farquhar Island's bitter nights. But as he trudged through this emptiness he could console himself with one all-important thought: if there was *no* one here, apart from some other members of the ship's company scattered over the island, then by the principles of light and reason and geography, and all sanity, the Fat Man was not here either. If he were it would testify to a casuistry at the very heart of things, the commissioning of a vessel, the arranging of an expedition, the prosecution of a process of bullying innuendo and fright that went beyond all bounds, and must surely lack sufficient cause. And such behaviour would defy the very precepts of Mother Nature herself; unless of course the Fat Man were mad.

So Tom travelled on, through cold wind and whipping rain, with a pinch of snow mixed in here and there for good measure. No doubt from time to time, as days went by, and the uniform greyness and bitter weather continued, he must have wondered if he were not tramping around in ever diminishing circles of the sort that, at the conclusion of their spiral, produce on the part of the unwary geometer a most unfortunate denouement, involving a small and privy circle of his own. And then at last he saw, sitting on some promontory, with the blue sea beyond, he saw a –!

Of course, the place was strange, remote and ambiguous. The light was dim. Our traveller was sorely fatigued, and no doubt by now in the grip of an ague that would shake his whole frame and heat his brow in proportion as it chilled his lower part. And thus Tom espied a – a mermaid!

She was sitting upon a rock, her hair flowing loosely to the wind, the sea behind her, in proper mermaid fashion. Her upper half was indeed womanly, featuring those tender appendages in such ample scale as that the silhouette could be clearly discerned through her clothing even at a distance, and in bad light, and with astonished eyes. Moreover, her lower half narrowed down towards her feet, with none of that outward flurry of a lady's skirts, and was coloured, if not silver like a fish's scales, then blue, like the sea, only darker. But when our hero approached more closely, he observed that her legs were divided in the manner of man- and womankind, however much the latter sex usually endeavour modestly to conceal the fact, and clothed in a sort of coarse blue breeches, as a man might wear for hunting, only more loose-fitting.

The discovery that the figure on the rock was a lady was

no less astonishing to our Tom than if it had been in accord with his initial apprehension; indeed a mermaid, he thought, would have been a more fitting inhabitant for this place. Moreover, during his long voyage across the sea, and his long and lonely march across the island, he had been much troubled by the recollection of certain pranks and escapades in which he had engaged with his companions in the Terrors and in particular with thoughts of a certain night in a barn in Wales; and to come upon a representative of the fair sex in this unlikely spot was as much a reproach to him as if she had been the Fat Man instead. But tho' not a mermaid, she seemed to him more like an *Angel* than a woman, albeit larger and more substantial than that species of being are reputed to be; however, said he to himself, that filmy and aery sort are all very well, and most suitable for the effusions of poets and the like, but how often do they come to the aid of mortals in distress? The rarified kind are a high conception indeed, but too invisible for practical effect; this Angel had a comforting bulk and immediate presence such as to inspire him to confide his woe to her without more ado.

'O G-,' quoth she at the conclusion of his narrative. 'That is a sorry tale indeed.'

Her manner of speech was strange, and, with her clothes and bearing, enforced the notion that she was a visitor from other realms than the mundane and quotidian.

'Are you an Angel?' asks our Tom at last.

At this innocent suggestion she burst into a peal of laughter. 'I am no more Angel than you are,' she says at the conclusion. 'I am but a mere Mortal, like the rest of womankind. My name is L—, but no, let us not barter with mere appellations, but deal with each other as we truly are. Or,' she says, her eyes becoming large and sad, 'as we truly were. Once upon a time, long long ago, in a distant land, I was a Princess. May I return the compliment, and tell you my tale?'

'I am agog,' says Tom, 'to hear it.'

CHAPTER SIXTY-FOUR

The Narrative
of the Lady on Farquhar Island,
or, the Princess and the Frog.

There was once a young Maiden, not rich but fair as the morning, and a real Princess to boot. The Princess was dwelling with her Father, who was the King of a small country, in a summer palace near a lake. The lake was smooth as glass and so deep that the nearby villagers called it bottomless. To one side of it there were dark woods, full of wild animals, from which, in the dead of night, strange cries and howlings were to be heard, so that, if the Princess awoke, they would fill her with dread; on the other side was a pleasant meadow, adorned with every sort of wild flowers. The palace in which the Princess sojourned with her father the King was situate between the woods and the meadow, with one door opening into the dimness of the former, through which door the King would frequently canter on his horse, his dogs running beside him, and his huntsmen following behind; the other door opened on to the sunny meadow, and this was the one the Princess used in order to pick flowers, or play upon the grassy bank with her lady-in-waiting, or with the children from the village.

One fine morning the Princess went out to sport upon the meadow as usual. On this day, however, there was no one to accompany her; the lady-in-waiting was confined to bed with the head-ach, the village children were at their dame school, or helping their fathers in the fields, or their mothers with their household tasks in their cottages, and so the Princess was all alone. But still she was merry and light-hearted, because the sky was so blue, and the sun shone so brightly, and the meadow was so pleasingly dappled with flowers.

291

At first she sate down upon the grass, and picking herself a goodly supply of daisies, she made a chain of them, and adorned her neck with it; for truely, said she to herself, these flowers are more beautiful than the jewels that richer Princesses than I keep in their treasure chests, and durst never wear for fear of bandits or thieving servants, or hypocriticall lovers; these flowers are well named, since for sure they are the eyes of the day.

When this pleasant task was completed, the Princess took a golden ball, which was her favourite plaything and most precious possession, being given to her at her christening by a strange hook'd-nosed old lady who had took upon herself to visit the court, whom nobody knew, and who disappeared as soon as she came, as tho' by magicke; this ball our Princess carried with her everywhere, safely fastened in a sort of pleat in her skirts; which she now removed, and began to amuse herself with tossing it into the air and catching it again as it fell. She continued in this manner for some while, laughing merrily each time she caught the ball, and throwing it higher and higher; until at last she threw it so high that she was not able to reach for it, and it landed in the lake, where it rapidly sank from sight into the depths of the water. Then the Princess began to lament her loss, and said, 'Alas! if I could only get my ball again, I would give all my fine clothes and everything I possess.'

At this, a large frog which happened to be sunning itself on a nearby lilly pad opened its mouth and asked; 'Princess, why do you weep so bitterly?' 'Alas!' said she. 'What can you do for me, you nasty frog? My golden ball has fallen into the lake.' 'Fear not, Princess,' croaks the frog, 'you will have your ball again, if you do as I say.' Thinks the Princess, what nonsense this frog is talking. However, there is no harm in discovering what he proposes. 'So, Sir Frog,' says she, 'how may that be?'

'Why,' the frog replies, 'the answer is simple. All you must do, is, lift up your skirts, and come to me in this lake.' At this, she looks closely at the frog, to see if he is making merry with her. Surely, she thinks to herself, he is a young and handsome frog, as frogs go; green and shiny upon his lilly leaf, with his throat puffing in and out, in the manner of frogs, and a grave countenance with no smile upon his lips. 'O Frog,' says she, 'you must be aware, this lake is bottomless, and, not being a frog myself, but only a Princess –' thinks she, no harm can come from a little flattery – 'I dare not swim in its chilly waters.'

'Princess,' says the frog, 'you have naught to fear. Do but wade to my lilly pad, and I will hold your hand, and we will dive together for your golden ball. No harm will come of it, I assure you.' At this, the Princess was sore tempted and wrestled with the prospect in her mind; for, thinks she, this is no ordinary frog, since he speaks to me so like a man. Mayhap he is some Prince, turned into a frog by a bad fairy and awaiting the day when a Princess will take him by the hand and allow him to retrieve her golden ball, so that he can return to his true form. And if he be but a frog, well, at the least he may help me to swim. With these thoughts she raised her skirts, and entering the warm waters of the lake, began to wade towards the lilly pad, her feet squidging down into whatever goddam goo, dark yet transparent the water, her tapering legs wobbling in the ripples like they had turned to goo themselves, the water licking inexorably up her thighs, the hanging lips of her skirts brushing the surface, frog's lazy drawl coming at her through the warm air, buttery sunshine on her upper half, while down below the primordial slime was clamping on to her deepening extremities. 'Shit!' she cries. 'Princess!' says the frog. 'Hold me for chrissake,' she says. 'Sure,' says the frog, and gee, *was* he a frog, now she was close up, glossy pulsing and green, a frog in every feature, a kinda cross between handsome and repulsive, so that when you hoped he would be like a *not*-frog, he looked like a confirmation of your worst fears, a figure that hovers in your dreams and waits for you round corners and down dark alleyways, the Hyde in the human Jekyll, the troll beneath the bridge, the sex maniac in Prince's clothing, the maggot in the apple, and then when you sorta glimpsed him as frog *qua* frog, he looked suddenly appealing, plump and shiny, his skin stretched over his bulging flesh so it achieved a high patina, and a hard authority in those ancient reptile eyes, a creature of air and water floating on its flower between two worlds, a bonus in the scheme of things, late manifestation of that basic impulse towards the amphibious, the extra dimension. And as she squelched towards him across the sucking bottom, through the thick water, beneath the heavy sun, this second impression of quintessential frogginess, of frog beauty, became more and more dominant, like what you might call, a second impression of the *third* thing, until when she had reached him, and was in his embrace, her feet floating free from the bottom, the bottom having declined from her feet, she thought, gee, it's not that a frog can change into a Prince, it's that when you break through all that playing doctors shit and hit the heavy area, when you are at last *making* it with a frog, the frog itself *is* a goddam Prince, and as she thought that, at the very moment she thought that, made the commitment, affirming the whole Prince and Princess bit, at that very moment when she let herself relax in the watery element, at the exact second of crescendo, the fucking frog exploded. Laurette floundered in its spawn, then splashed shorewards through all the gunk.

CHAPTER SIXTY-FIVE

Laurette

The one thing you could say about the English male was, like despite a certain question mark over his capacity to *come*, he sure as hell merited a gold star for his ability to *go*. An exclamation mark plus. Wow. This storm trooper or whatever he was bolted over Farquhar terrain with practically the velocity of that cross-Channel purveyor of rectum cancer taking a header over the side of his ship. There was no need to write home about the sort of equipment the English carried up front, at least if Joe Harper was a fair example, but they could sure run like there was a rocket up their backside. So much, thought Laurette glumly, about my bit of rough.

That's what it had been, an odyssey towards the rough. The Princess had set sail, consequent upon pubescent trauma, on a long voyage towards the animal dimension, and had ended up on one of the roughest places on earth, studying amphibious specimens like seals and penguins. If that wasn't paying your goddam dues, what in hell was?

She had studied penguins most. It was something in their humanoid waddle that caught her interest: they made footpaths down the cliffs where they'd waddled the same route for centuries. But just when you thought to yourself, these penguins are little tubby *people*, like they've been created by Walt Disney or somebody, something would upset them and they'd bray like a bunch of donkeys, a weird animal noise, a salt noise.

Laurette watched them through her binoculars for hours. Here they were on some icy rock in the middle of the ocean and they waddled about like they were *talk*ing to each other, passing the time of day.

And then one morning the penguin she was looking at exploded.

One minute he was just standing there scratching his goddam chin with his flipper or wing or whatever it was, and the next he'd disintegrated. It was so abrupt, silent, like *de*finite, for a while she thought, would you believe it, I've discovered a new aspect of penguin behaviour, like I'm Henry David Thoreau or some such big-deal exponent of nature study, like when a penguin starts getting the hots or some damn thing, splat, he flies into a million pieces.

And then there was the roar of an explosion, and a few seconds later a crump from a ship out on the horizon, and then Laurette was spattered with pebbles and bits of penguin, and the Farquhar invasion had begun. She'd paid her dues all right, sleeping for the duration in a goddam barn with the rest of the tour, middle-western, middle-aged, middle-executive American men with short hair and heads so cubic they practically had corners, with square glasses and straight mouths, and all the rest of it, like you could stack them without leaving a gap between, and their thin sharp wives who looked like they were spiritually intended to be bitches but didn't have the guts, so were nice as pie instead, so the whole effect was, you may think, deluded little cow, that you're on the fringes of Antarctica in the middle of an invasion, but in reality this is downtown Indianapolis on Labour Day weekend, just *looks* like a freezing barn in the middle of nowhere, is all.

Luckily her colleagues stayed in the barn. Rumour had it the Costies had laid mines round the place, so the courier suggested they better stay put, keeping an inventory of their fingers and toes. Laurette didn't hack that: what was good enough for the penguins, she informed the tight-assed little shit, was good enough for her. There were times when you had to make your act of commitment to the totality of the eco-system, including the human junk that had been inserted into it, and boldly say, this is the world, and I am part of it. And if Nature Expeditions didn't like it, for insurance reasons naturally enough, then fuck Nature Expeditions, go on a Nature Expedition to some other planet. Half the clientèle had no doubt got the wrong end of the stick about it anyway, expecting nude romps and spouse swapping on some remote beach, hoping to bare their razor-sharp tits and rectangular pricks to the grey Antarctic skies. Penguins are what we've come to view ladies and gents, war or no war. Yes, Laurette paid her dues.

And then, one day, bingo! one of the penguins had crept out of the prairie, and waved his little rifle. Tufts of grass poked out of his helmet; he was wearing filthy battle fatigues, big boots, the whole works. My penguin, Laurette thought, my penguin has turned into a soldier, the cycle is complete. Sure enough, from whatever angle you looked, he was the cutest bit of soi-disant rough any normally hungry, high-fibre, marginally screwed up American girl could cast her hot little eyes upon, and she thought, eat your heart out frog, this is the *big* one.

Then ensued a somewhat intricate conversation. Naturally soldier boy is taken aback at seeing American female on Farquhar Island rock. Indeed, he goes straight over the top. Gibbers. Haunted. Some girl he once screwed. In a barn, for chrissakes. She could tell him a thing or two about barns. Barns are places where you endeavour to maintain the formal integrity of American anatomy. But of course that was the whole point, there were all sorts of things they could tell each other. OK, OK, so he'd floundered through a pool of gunk in his time, like so had she, gunk was what the amniotic, seminal, saline fluid *was*, when all was said and done, gunk was the constructive medium, in which we flopped, half in half out, like the seals or penguins or frogs that we were. She gave him his gunk back, let's be *mu*tual about this thing, mutuality being the name of the whole ballgame. She told him her tale.

And the little jerk-off cut and run.

What can you expect, she thought. I've come all this way to be in mid-ocean, and here I am sitting on a goddam island, while the real estate brokers haggle over ownership. Nobody, frog or penguin, economist or soldier boy, is ever going to produce the golden ball a Princess like me requires. She remembered the long-ago, when she was thirteen and her father rented a summer place in the south, between the wood and the meadow, near the lake: I musta taken the wrong door out of that crummy palace, is all, she thought.

CHAPTER SIXTY-SIX

Tom

Tom ran. Not very SAS but he had a long way to go, not much time, military business. And the 'Princess' had held him up. Jesus. Held him up in more ways than one.

What he was here *for* was to suggest a landing site for the second stage of the invasion. The bulk of the force would disembark in Livingstone Sound. Some would yomp south across the island, others would sail round in coastal vessels and land directly on the south shore. Swan Creek looked the most suitable place on the map, but it was his job to survey along the coast and make sure it was the best bet. He was going to start at the eastern tip of the south coast and work back towards the Creek. But when he got to the furthest point, he'd seen a woman sitting on a rock.

She was beautiful, rounded, anomalous. The last place he'd seen a woman in such rough country was the Brecon Beacons. A local, he thought, she'll know the terrain.

'Hello,' he said. 'You *are* a local?'

Stupid question, but she could have been a Costie hanger-on. She gave a stupid answer.

'No.'

'You what?'

'I'm not a local.'

'Oh. Nor me.'

'You're one of the good guys,' she said. She was American. 'Jeez, am I glad to see you. My name's Laurette.'

Tom remembered the introductions to Marie, in that pub in the Beacons. Porter said, 'What's your name?' 'My name's Marie,' Marie said. 'Prof,' Porter said, 'this is Marie.' 'Delighted to meet you, Marie,' the Professor said. 'This is Marie,' Porter said to Tom. 'Hello, Marie,' Tom said. It was as if they were *booking* her, in turn, and she didn't know it. As if by saying her name they were buying tickets to a fuck. They didn't give their own names, in the SAS you weren't supposed to.

'Sit down,' Laurette said.

'I've got a lot to do,' Tom said. No time to do anything but take a chance. 'But I got time for a short hard struggle on the grass.' Worth a try, he was a member of the liberating forces after all.

'Why do you look so sad?' she asked.

Suddenly he wanted to cry. Great. An SAS officer on active duty behind enemy lines, wants to cry. And then it all came out. It went through his mind first, like a film being

298

rewound: the girl hobbling out of the barn, the white rat, the tight shafting, the loose wet cunt. When he had got to the beginning he told it to Laurette. It was the sort of story you could tell in the middle of nowhere, even if you could tell it nowhere else.

When he had finished, Laurette said: 'That sure is an ugly story. Wow.'

'Yes,' said Tom.

'You gotta face it. You did wrong.'

'Yes.'

'That was like an outrage against that Welsh girl's girlhood. Not just her girlhood. Her human-ness.'

'For God's sake,' said Tom. 'I don't need to come all this far to be told that.'

'Well, you sure as hell have come this far for *some*thing,' said Laurette. 'And maybe I know what it is.'

'I sometimes think I'm losing my mind,' said Tom.

'You're screwed up, that's for sure,' Laurette said. 'Holy shit. You remind me of *me*.'

'Talking of you,' Tom said, 'what *are* you doing here?'

'Doing's not a word I like,' Laurette said. 'Doing's what you soldier-boys do. What we need is less doing and more *being*. That's what I'm doing here, being. You gotta learn to take like an aristocratic point of view, a natural aristocracy you might say. I'm just being *me* on Farquhar Island, like the penguins are penguins. You got that Princess back in England, just got married to Prince Charles. You don't go up to her and say, what are you *doing*, Princess. Think of me as a Princess.'

'All right, Princess.'

'Listen fella,' the Princess said, 'you and me can do each other a good turn.'

'Why not?' Tom said hopefully.

'Listen,' she said.

God, he thought, listening's not what I want to do.

'What you got to do,' she said, 'is accept the wild side of yourself. I don't mean like complacency. That Welsh incident was a bad scene. Man, that was *horr*ible. But what it came out of, the bit of *you* it came out of, that's what you got to accept. If you do accept it, it won't come out all back-to-front and screwed up like it did before. What you got to do, my friend, is shake hands with the animal *inside* yourself. Is all.'

That's a start, thought Tom. It could only be a short step from there to shaking hands with the animal inside *her*.

'It's cold,' he said, stepping towards her. 'We ought to huddle together for warmth.'

'Listen,' she said. 'You told me what's bugging you. You been frank. Now I'll tell you what's bugged *me*. If *that* isn't huddling together for warmth, I don't know what is.'

CHAPTER SIXTY-SEVEN

Tom

Two days later Tom reached Swan Creek. The inlet was well named – it came in, twisted in a slow loop, and ended in a sharp point, like a swan's neck, the body being the sea. It looked like an estuary except that there was no river. On its loop the township was situated: a huddle of houses, a church. Overlooking the whole set-up from inland was a low hill, which sealed the harbour and its surrounding development like a lip. On the further side of the hill were signs of a Costanaguan encampment, but it appeared to have been abandoned. On the summit, where Tom lay flat surveying the possibilities, was a large ramshackle mass of stones, the ruins of an old wall or even a cairn: they'd be easy to reassemble into a marker for the coastal fleet. First, though, Tom needed to get down into the township to make contact with the locals and find out a) whether, as far as they knew, the Costies really had moved on and b) if so, whether they had mined the surrounding countryside before they went.

Tom waited until mid-evening, long after the early Antarctic night had fallen. There ought to be a curfew but in the (probable) absence of Costies it was impossible to guess whether it would be observed, and the last thing he wanted was to bump into passersby. He'd been ordered to make contact with the local vicar in the hopes that, being a responsible personage, he was reasonably likely to be discreet. Also his house was next to the church, and therefore easy to identify.

About halfway down the slope he skirted a farm building, and as he did so there came, from the darkness, a sudden blast of organ music. Shit. He dropped flat. Somebody closed a door and the music diminished a little. He heard footsteps going down the track, towards the settlement. Jesus, what was with these people, stuck out in the howling wilderness, playing their organs. He rose cautiously and carried on down the slope.

All was silent in Swan Creek. He crept along the potholey road. It was a dark night but his eyesight was good and he could make out the dim shapes of houses, fences, a parked vehicle. Flurries of snow, like tiny flak, came out of the air. Ahead of him on the left was the black form of the church. He decided to take cover in the churchyard for a few minutes and survey the vicarage. He climbed over a low stone wall and began to walk, bowed, across the bumpy surface, colliding once with a gravestone. There was some sort of large structure, triangular, an archway, in the middle of the churchyard. When he reached it and had rubbed his hand over the surface he realized it was bone, with teeth: a whale's jaw. He stood within it, to lose his own silhouette. It glimmered whitely around and over him.

It glimmered.

There was a light, a faint light. He turned towards the church.

A huge black barn. A window which flickered and glowed. Murmurs, movements, rustling, from inside.

Diddums do it attums. Big bloke like you. In the SAS. He picked his way towards the door and went in.

In a glow at the far end a woman was locked in an embrace. As Tom watched, the other figure released her and turned

towards him. It was huge, tapering, wedge-shaped, albino.
Tom turned, ran.

CHAPTER SIXTY-EIGHT

Tom
Stone upon stone upon stone. Blacker than the darkness.
Piling them up, stopping betweentimes to drink patrol-
issue emergency-only scotch. Something had to be done
and everything said; this is the place. A broken $\triangle$ of
stones. When the late dawn came the stones went from
black to white. The top was still flat. Swig. He kept on
working, no Costies here everything said. Down below
Swan Creek was quiet. Smoke rose from the chimney pots.
The sea was blue. Swig. It was cold but he was hot. Naked,
the man. Ah so. He stripped to the waist. Still hot. Swig.
The stones were hot hot stone upon cold stone heavy the
stones were heavy hot work. He took off his swig bottoms.
If Costies saw not SAS but just a man. Put his boots back on
swig, the stones were heavy on the feet. The top of the cairn
was still flat

time   to

triangle

eyes

Above the cairn a white triangle, with eyes. Peering over
the top, a wedge, a white roach, no, rat, no swig sheep
thank god a sheep

Ah   so

The sheep remained, looking. Tom drank, and looked
back. He was cooling on the outside, but hot hot inside, the
heat rising to the surface . . . The sheep had alien, oriental
eyes, it looked at him without looking at him, it looked as
the animal inside you looks. Ah so. The Princess said: we
all swim in a pool of gunk. Shake hands with the swig

animal *inside* yourself is all. What do you do when you have come all this way? You sure as hell have come this far for *some*thing. Animal inside yourself. Everyone knows swig Farquhars are sheep shaggers.

Even now Tom tried to find something human to respond to in the white woolly face, as you can sometimes see a human emotion flit across the face of a dog. But the sheep was a sheep. Sheep upon sheep. You could imagine a person looking a bit like *it* – soft surface to the face, hardness underneath, deep deep *bland*ness of the eyes, small ruminating teeth that gently grind, but that was not the same as it looking like somebody. But then he understood he was missing the Princess's whole point. Shake hands with the animal *inside* yourself. Swig. It was the alienness of the sheep to which he must react, the fact that it *was* a sheep, sheep upon sheep, just as it is the alienness in the opposite sex which turns you on, the oppositeness.

Tom took the belt off his discarded trousers and hobbled the front legs of the sheep. The sheep bucked a little, the wild life bucking, the animal in *you*. Swig. Then he propped the front legs of the sheep back against the side of the cairn, to get the angle. Swig. We all flounder about in the primeval soup, the Princess said. Swig.

As Tom entered the sheep, the sheep and the world went bang.

CHAPTER SIXTY-NINE

Swansong

Neither the man nor the sheep had legs.
 'Bloody hell, look at that,' said Cartwright.
 'That's why that SAS guy didn't come back,' Sturgess

said. 'Poor fucker. But if he hadn't built that cairn, we wouldn't –'

'We wouldn't be in a fucking minefield,' said Cartwright.

'Oh fuck,' said Sturgess.

'Look at that sheep on the top of it,' said Cartwright. 'It must have been blown there. Probably the sheep which trod on the mine and killed this poor bastard.'

'Blew his bloody clothes off too,' said Sturgess. 'Naked as the day he was born.'

'Not even wearing legs,' Wozzer said.

'Must have been dead over a week,' Cartwright said. 'Of course, you keep in this climate.'

'I wonder why those fucking bastards in Swan Creek didn't come up and bury him,' Sturgess said.

'Because they got too much sense,' Wozzer said. 'We're in a minefield, remember.'

'Fuck,' said Sturgess.

'We haven't got time to sweep before dark. We'll have to stay put,' Cartwright said.

'Oh god,' said Sturgess. 'All night?'

'Of course all night,' Cartwright said.

'Can we put our packs down?' asked Sturgess.

'Oh yes,' said Wozzer. 'Put your packs down and get blown to bits like that fucking sheep and that poor sod.'

'All fucking night,' Sturgess said.

They stood there like statues, until they vanished in the dark.

'What the fuck's that?' asked Sturgess.

'Must be the coastal fleet,' Cartwright said. 'But it's not due to rendezvous till tomorrow p.m.'

'The coastal fleet's not going to be playing fucking music,' said Wozzer.

It was faint organ music, a military two-step, very slow.

'It's a pity old Premo bought it,' said Sturgess. 'He could have done us some numbers. Songs for yomping.'

'We're not fucking yomping,' said Wozzer. 'We're standing still.'

Richard Francis was born in Shawford, Hampshire, England, was graduated from Magdalene College, Cambridge, and obtained his Ph.D. from Exeter University. Since 1972, he has been a lecturer in American Literature at Manchester University, and while on leave from Manchester he taught at the University of Tripoli in Libya from 1976 to 1977. He is the author of four previous novels: *The Whispering Gallery,* *The Enormous Dwarf,* *Daggerman,* and *Blackpool Vanishes.* He lives in Stockport, Cheshire, England.